LADY ORACLE
by
Margaret Atwood

New York Times Book Review
1976 Noteworthy Title

"Brilliant and funny. I can't tell you how exhila-
rating it was to read it—everything works. An
extraordinary book."

—Joan Didion

"Read it for its gracefulness, for its good story,
for its help in your fantasy life."

—Toronto Globe and Mail

"Wholly readable and engrossing. Sex and
sexual passion have not been captured so well
and so humorously since Mary McCarthy's
early novels."

—Saturday Review

"Marvelously funny."

—MacLeans

LADY ORACLE

Margaret Atwood

SEAL BOOKS

McClelland and Stewart-Bantam Limited

Toronto

*This low-priced Seal Book
has been completely reset in a type face
designed for easy reading, and was printed
from new plates. It contains the complete
text of the original hard-cover edition.*
NOT ONE WORD HAS BEEN OMITTED.

LADY ORACLE
*A Seal Book | published by arrangement with
McClelland and Stewart Limited*

PRINTING HISTORY
*McClelland and Stewart edition published September 1976
2nd printing .... June 1977*
Seal edition | August 1977
2nd printing .. September 1977   4th printing .... February 1980
3rd printing .... April 1979   5th printing .... April 1981

ISBN 0-7704-1704-3

*Seal Books are published by McClelland and Stewart-Bantam
Limited. Its trademark, consisting of the words "Seal Books"
and the portrayal of a seal, is the property of McClelland and
Stewart-Bantam Limited, 25 Hollinger Road, Toronto, Ontario
M4B 3G2. This trademark has been duly registered in the Trade-
marks Office of Canada. The trademark, consisting of the word
"Bantam" and the portrayal of a bantam, is the property of and
is used with the consent of Bantam Books, Inc., 666 Fifth Avenue, New York, New York 10103. This trademark has been duly
registered in the Trademark office of Canada and elsewhere.*

PRINTED IN U.S.A.

14 13 12 11 10 9 8 7 6 5

PART ONE

Chapter One

I planned my death carefully; unlike my life, which meandered along from one thing to another, despite my feeble attempts to control it. My life had a tendency to spread, to get flabby, to scroll and festoon like the frame of a baroque mirror, which came from following the line of least resistance. I wanted my death, by contrast, to be neat and simple, understated, even a little severe, like a Quaker church or the basic black dress with a single strand of pearls much praised by fashion magazines when I was fifteen. No trumpets, no megaphones, no spangles, no loose ends, this time. The trick was to disappear without a trace, leaving behind me the shadow of a corpse, a shadow everyone would mistake for solid reality. At first I thought I'd managed it.

The day after I arrived in Terremoto I was sitting outside on the balcony. I'd been intending to sunbathe, I had visions of myself as a Mediterranean splendor, golden brown, striding with laughing teeth into an aqua sea, carefree at last, the past discarded; but then I remembered I had no suntan lotion (Maximum Protection: without it I'd burn and freckle), so I'd covered my shoulders and thighs with several of the landlord's skimpy bath towels. I hadn't brought a bathing suit; bra and underpants would do, I thought, since the balcony was invisible from the road.

I'd always been fond of balconies. I felt that if I could only manage to stand on one long enough, the right one, wearing a long white trailing gown, preferably during the first quarter of the moon, something would happen: music would sound, a shape would appear below, sinuous and dark, and climb towards me, while I leaned fearfully, hopefully, gracefully,

3

against the wrought-iron railing and quivered. But this wasn't a very romantic balcony. It had a geometric railing like those on middle-income apartment buildings of the fifties, and the floor was poured concrete, already beginning to erode. It wasn't the kind of balcony a man would stand under playing a lute and yearning or clamber up bearing a rose in his teeth or a stiletto in his sleeve. Besides, it was only five feet off the ground. Any mysterious visitor I might have would be more likely to approach by the rough path leading down to the house from the street above, feet crunching on the cinders, roses or knives in his head only.

That at any rate would be Arthur's style, I thought; he'd rather crunch than climb. If only we could go back to the way it had once been, before he had changed. . . . I pictured him coming to retrieve me, winding up the hill in a rented Fiat which would have something wrong with it; he would tell me about this defect later, after we'd thrown ourselves into each other's arms. He would park, as close to the wall as possible. Before getting out he would check his face in the rearview mirror, adjusting the expression: he never liked to make a fool of himself, and he wouldn't be sure whether or not he was about to. He would unfold himself from the car, lock it so his scanty luggage could not be stolen, place the keys in an inside jacket pocket, peer left and right, and then with that curious ducking motion of the head, as if he were dodging a thrown stone or a low doorway, he'd sneak past the rusty gate and start cautiously down the path. He was usually stopped at international borders. It was because he looked so furtive; furtive but correct, like a spy.

At the sight of lanky Arthur descending towards me, uncertain, stony-faced, rescue-minded, in his uncomfortable shoes and well-aged cotton underwear, not knowing whether I would really be there or not, I began to cry. I closed my eyes: there in front of me, across an immense stretch of blue which I recognized as the Atlantic Ocean, was everyone I had left on the other side. On a beach, of course; I'd seen a lot of Fellini movies. The wind rippled their hair, they smiled and waved and called to me, though of course I couldn't hear the words. Arthur was the nearest; behind him was the Royal Porcupine, otherwise known as Chuck Brewer, in his long pretentious cape; then Sam and Marlene and the others. Leda Sprott fluttered like a bedsheet off to one side, and I could see Fraser Buchanan's leather-patched elbow sticking out from where he lurked behind a seaside bush. Further back, my mother, wearing a navy-blue suit and a white hat, my father indistinct by her side; and my Aunt Lou. Aunt Lou was the only one who wasn't looking at me. She was marching along the beach, taking deep breaths and admiring the waves and stopping every now and then to empty the sand out of her shoes. Finally she took them off, and continued, in fox fur, feathered hat and stocking feet, towards a distant hot-dog and orangeade stand that beckoned to her from the horizon like a tacky mirage.

But I was wrong about the rest of them. They were smiling and waving at each other, not at me. Could it be that the Spiritualists were wrong and the dead weren't interested in the living after all? Though some of them were still alive, and I was the one who was supposed to be dead; they should have been mourning but instead they seemed quite cheerful. It wasn't fair. I tried to will something ominous onto their beach—a colossal stone head, a collapsing horse—but with no result. In fact it was less like a Fellini movie than that Walt Disney film I saw when I was eight, about a whale who wanted to sing at the Metropolitan Opera. He approached a ship and sang arias, but the sailors harpooned him, and each of his voices left his body in a different-colored soul and floated up towards the sun, still singing. *The Whale Who Wanted to Sing at the Met*, I think it was called. At the time I cried ferociously.

It was this memory that really set me off. I never learned to cry with style, silently, the pearl-shaped tears rolling down my cheeks from wide luminous

eyes, as on the covers of *True Love* comics, leaving
no smears or streaks. I wished I had; then I could
have done it in front of people, instead of in bathrooms, darkened movie theaters, shrubberies and empty bedrooms, among the party coats on the bed. If
you could cry silently people felt sorry for you. As it
was I snorted, my eyes turned the color and shape of
cooked tomatoes, my nose ran, I clenched my fists, I
moaned, I was embarrassing, finally I was amusing, a
figure of fun. The grief was always real but it came
out as a burlesque of grief, an overblown imitation
like the neon rose on White Rose Gasoline stations,
gone forever now. . . . Decorous weeping was another
of those arts I never mastered, like putting on false
eyelashes. I should've had a governess, I should have
gone to finishing school and had a board strapped to
my back and learned water-color painting and self-
control.

You can't change the past, Aunt Lou used to say.
Oh, but I wanted to; that was the one thing I really
wanted to do. Nostalgia convulsed me. The sky was
blue, the sun was shining, to the left a puddle of
glass fragments shimmered like water; a small green
lizard with iridescent blue eyes warmed its cool blood
on the railing; from the valley came a tinkling sound,
a soothing moo, the lull of alien voices. I was safe, I
could begin again, but instead I sat on my balcony,
beside the remains of a kitchen window broken before my time, in a chair made of aluminum tubes and
yellow plastic strips, and made choking noises.

The chair belonged to Mr. Vitroni, the landlord,
who was fond of felt-tipped pens with different colors
of ink, red, pink, purple, orange, a taste I shared. He
used his to show the other people in the town that he
could write. I used mine for lists and love letters,
sometimes both at once: *Have gone to pick up some
coffee, XXX.* The thought of these abandoned shopping trips intensified my sorrow . . . no more grapefruits, cut in half for two, with a red maraschino
cherry like a navel boss, which Arthur habitually
rolled to the side of the plate; no more oatmeal por-

ridge, loathed by me, extolled by Arthur, lumping and burning because I hadn't taken his advice and done it in a double boiler. . . . Years of breakfasts, inept, forsaken, never to be recovered. . . . Years of murdered breakfasts, why had I done it?

I realized I'd come to the worst place in the entire world. I should have gone somewhere fresh and clean, somewhere I'd never been before. Instead I'd returned to the same town, the same house even, where we'd spent the summer the year before. And nothing had changed: I'd have to cook on the same two-burner stove with the gas cylinder, *bombola*, that ran out always in the middle of a half-done meal; eat at the same table, which still had the white rings on the varnish from my former carelessness with hot cups; sleep in the same bed, its mattress furrowed with age and the anxieties of many tenants. The wraith of Arthur would pursue me; already I could hear faint gargling noises from the bathroom, the crunch of glass as he scraped back his chair on the balcony, waiting for me to pass his cup of coffee out to him through the kitchen window. If I opened my eyes and turned my head, surely he would be there, newspaper held six inches from his face, pocket dictionary on one knee, left index finger inserted (perhaps) in his ear, an unconscious gesture he denied performing.

It was my own stupidity, my own fault. I should have gone to Tunisia or the Canary Islands or even Miami Beach, on the Greyhound Bus, hotel included, but I didn't have the willpower; I needed something more familiar. A place with no handholds, no landmarks, no past at all; that would have been too much like dying.

By this time I was weeping spasmodically into one of the landlord's bath towels and I'd thrown another one over my head, an old habit: I used to cry under pillows so as not to be found out. But through the towel I could now hear an odd clicking sound. It must've been going on for a while. I listened, and it stopped. I raised the towel. There, at the level of my ankles and only three feet away, floated a head, an old man's head, topped by a ravelling straw hat. The whitish eyes stared at me with either alarm or disapproval; the mouth, caved in over the gums, was open at one side. He must've heard me. Perhaps he thought I was having an attack of some kind, in my underwear, towel-covered on a balcony. Perhaps he thought I was drunk.

I smiled damply, to reassure him, clutched my towels around me and tried to get out of the aluminum chair, remembering too late its trick of folding up if you struggled. I lost several of the towels before I was able to back in through the door.

I'd recognized the old man. It was the same old man who used to come one or two afternoons a week to tend the artichokes on the arid terrace below the house, cutting the larger weeds with a pair of rusty shears and snipping off the leathery artichoke heads when they were ready. Unlike the other people in the town, he never said anything to me or returned a word of greeting. He gave me the creeps. I put on my dress (out of sight of the picture window, behind the door) and went into the bathroom to swab my face with a dampened washcloth and blow my nose on some of Mr. Vitroni's scratchy toilet paper; then to the kitchen to make a cup of tea.

For the first time since arriving, I began to feel afraid. It was more than depressing to have returned to this town, it was dangerous. It's no good thinking you're invisible if you aren't, and the problem was: if I had recognized the old man, perhaps he had recognized me.

Chapter Two

I sat down at the table to drink my tea. Tea was consoling and it would help me think; though this tea wasn't very good, it came in bags and smelled of Band-aids. I'd bought it at the main grocery store, along with a package of Peek Frean biscuits, imported from England. The store had laid in a large supply of these, anticipating a wave of English tourists which so far hadn't arrived. *By Appointment to Her Majesty the Queen, Biscuit Manufacturers*, it said on the box, which I found morale-building. The Queen would not snivel: regret is gauche. *Pull yourself together*, said a stern royal voice. I sat straighter in my chair and considered what I should do.

I'd taken precautions, of course. I was using my other name, and when I'd gone to see if Mr. Vitroni's flat was available I'd worn my sunglasses and covered my head with the scarf I'd bought at the Toronto airport, printed with pink Mounted Policemen performing a musical ride against a background of purple Rocky Mountains, made in Japan. I shrouded my body in one of the sacklike print dresses, also pink, with baby-blue flowers, that I'd bought off a street rack in Rome. I would've preferred the big red roses or the orange dahlias; this dress made me look like an expanse of wallpaper. But I wanted something inconspicuous. Mr. Vitroni hadn't remembered me, I was sure of that. However, the old man had caught me without my disguise, and, worse still, with my hair showing. Waist-length red hair was very noticeable in that part of the country.

The biscuits were hard as plaster and tasted of shelf. I ate the last one, dipping it into the tea and chewing it up mechanically before I realized I'd finished the package. That was a bad sign, I'd have to watch that.

I decided I'd have to do something about my hair. It was evidence, its length and color had been a sort of trademark. Every newspaper clipping, friendly or hostile, had mentioned it, in fact a lot of space had been devoted to it: hair in the female was regarded as more important than either talent or the lack of it. *Joan Foster, celebrated author of* Lady Oracle, *looking like a lush Rossetti portrait, radiating*

*intensity, hypnotized the audience with her unearthly
. . .* (The Toronto Star). *Prose-poetess Joan Foster
looked impressively Junoesque in her flowing red hair
and green robe; unfortunately she was largely inaudible . . .* (The Globe and Mail). They could trace
my hair much more easily than they could ever trace
me. I would have to cut it off and dye the rest, though
I wasn't sure where I'd be able to get the hair
dye. Certainly not in this town. I might have to go
back to Rome for it. I should've bought a wig, I
thought; that was an oversight.

I went into the bathroom and dug the nail scissors
out of my zippered makeup bag. They were too small,
but it was a choice between that and one of Mr. Vitroni's dull paring knives. It took me quite a while to saw
the hair off, strand by strand. I tried shaping what remained, but it got shorter and shorter, though no less
uneven, until I saw that I'd cropped my head like a
concentration camp inmate's. My face looked quite
different, though: I could pass for a secretary on vacation.

The hair lay in mounds and coils in the bathroom
sink. I wanted to save it; I thought briefly of stowing
it in a bureau drawer. But how could I explain if it
were found? They'd start looking for the arms and
legs and the rest of the body. I'd have to get rid of it.
I considered flushing it down the toilet, but there
was too much of it, and the septic tank had already
begun to act up, burping swamp gas and shreds of de-
composing toilet paper.

I took it into the kitchen and lit one of the gas
burners. Then, strand by strand, I began to sacrifice
my hair. It shrivelled, blackened, writhed like a hand-
ful of pinworms, melted and finally burned, sputter-
ing like a fuse. The smell of singed turkey was
overpowering.

Tears ran down my cheeks; I was a sentimental-
ist without doubt, of the sloppiest kind. The thing
was: Arthur used to like brushing my hair for me,
and that small image dissolved me; though he never

learned not to pull at the tangles and it hurt like hell. Too late, too late. . . . I could never manage the right emotions at the right times, anger when I should have been angry, tears when I should have cried; everything was mismatched.

When I was halfway through the pile of hair I heard footsteps coming down the gravel path. My heart clumped together, I stood frozen: the path led to nowhere but the house, there was no one in the house but me, the other two flats were empty. How could Arthur have found me so soon? Perhaps I had been right about him after all. Or it wasn't Arthur, it was one of the others. . . . The panic I hadn't allowed myself to feel for the past week rolled in an ice-gray wave back over my head, carrying with it the shapes of my fear, a dead animal, the telephone breathing menace, killer's notes cut from the Yellow Pages, a revolver, anger. . . . Faces formed and disintegrated in my head, I didn't know who to expect, what did they want? The question I could never answer. I felt like screaming, rushing into the bathroom, there was a high square window I might be able to squeeze through; then I could run up the hill and drive away in my car. Another fast getaway. I tried to remember where I'd put the keys.

There was a knock at the door, a stolid confident knock. A voice called, "Hello? You are within?"

I could breathe again. It was only Mr. Vitroni, Signor Vitroni, Reno Vitroni of the broad smile, inspecting his property. It was his sole piece of property, as far as I knew; nevertheless he was supposed to be one of the richest men in the town. What if he wanted to check the kitchen, what would he think of the sacrificial hair? I turned off the burner and stuffed the hair into the paper bag I used for garbage.

"Coming," I called, "just a minute." I didn't want him walking in: my bed was unmade, my clothes and underwear were draped over chairbacks and strewn on the floor, there were dirty dishes on the table and in the sink. I hooded myself with one of the towels and snatched my dark glasses from the table as I went past.

"I was just washing my hair," I said to him when I'd opened the door.

He was puzzled by the dark glasses: a little, but not much. Foreign ladies, for all he knew, had strange beauty rituals. He beamed and held out his hand. I held out my own hand, he lifted it as though to kiss it, then shook it instead.

"I am most pleasant to see you," he said, bringing his heels together in a curiously military bow. The colored felt pens were lined up across his chest like medals. He'd made his fortune in the war, somehow; no one questioned these things now that they were all over. At the same time he'd learned a bit of English, and scraps of several other languages as well. Why had he come to my flat in the early evening, surely not the right time for him to visit a young foreign woman, this respectable middle-aged man with the right kind of barrel-shaped wife and numerous grandchildren? He was carrying something under his arm. He looked past my shoulder as if he wanted to go in.

"You are possibly cooking your meal?" he said. He'd picked up the smell of burning hair. God knew what these people ate, I could hear him thinking. "I wish I do not disturb?"

"No, not at all," I said heartily. I stood squarely in the doorway.

"Everything with you is fine? The light is going on again?"

"Yes, yes," I said, nodding more than was necessary. There was no electricity when I moved in, as the last tenant hadn't paid the bill. But Mr. Vitroni had pulled strings.

"There is much of the sunshine, no?"

"Very much," I said, trying not to show impatience. He was standing too close.

"This is good." Now he got to the point. "I have something here for you. So you will find yourself more"—he lifted his free arm, palm up, expansive, welcoming, ushering me in—"so you will be at home with us."

How embarrassing, I thought, he was giving me a housewarming present. Was this customary, what should I say? "That's terribly kind of you," I said, "but. . . ."

Mr. Vitroni dismissed my gratitude with a wave of the hand. From under his arm he produced his square bundle, set it on the plastic chair, and began to untie the strings. He paused at the last knot, for suspense, like a magician. Then the brown wrapping paper fell open, revealing five or six pictures, paintings, done—O lord!—on black velvet, with gilded plaster frames. He lifted them out and displayed them to me one by one. They were all of historical sites in Rome, each done in an overall color tone. The Colosseum was a feverish red, the Pantheon mauve, the Arch of Constantine a vaporous yellow, St. Peter's pink as a cake. I frowned at them like an adjudicator.

"You like?" he asked commandingly. I was a foreigner, this was the sort of thing I was supposed to like and he'd brought them as a gift, to please me. Dutifully I was pleased; I couldn't bear to hurt his feelings.

"Very nice," I said. I didn't mean the paintings but the gesture.

"My, how you say," he said. "The son of my brother, he has a genius."

We both looked silently at the pictures, lined up now on the window ledge and glowing like highway signs in the light of the low golden sun. As I stared at them they began to take on, or give off, a certain horrible energy, like the closed doors of furnaces or tombs.

It wasn't going fast enough for him. "Who you like?" he said. "This one?"

How could I choose without knowing what the choice would mean? The language was only one problem; there was also that other language, what is done and what isn't done. If I accepted a picture, would I have to become his mistress? Was the choice of picture significant, was it a test?

"Well," I said tentatively, pointing to the neon Colosseum. . . .

"Two hundred fifty thousand lire," he said promptly. I was immediately relieved: simple cash transactions weren't mysterious, they were easy to handle. Of course the paintings hadn't been done by his nephew at all, I thought; he must've bought them in Rome, from a street vendor, and was reselling them at a profit.

"Fine," I said. I couldn't afford it at all, but I'd never learned to haggle, and anyway I was afraid of insulting him. I didn't want my electricity to go off. I went to get my purse.

When he'd folded and pocketed the money he began to gather up the paintings. "You have two, maybe? To send your family?"

"No thank you," I said. "This one is just lovely."

"Your husband will come soon also?"

I smiled and nodded vaguely. This was the impression I'd given him when I rented the flat. I wanted it known in the town that I had a husband, I didn't want any trouble.

"He will like these picture," he said, as if he knew.

I began to wonder. Did he recognize me after all, despite the dark glasses, the towel and the different name? He was fairly rich; surely he didn't need to go around peddling cheap tourist pictures. The whole thing might have been an excuse, but for what? I had the feeling that much more had happened in the conversation than I'd been able to understand, which wouldn't have been unusual. Arthur used to tell me I was obtuse.

When Mr. Vitroni was safely off the balcony I took the picture inside and looked around for a place to hang it up. It had to be the right place: for years I'd needed to have the main objects in my room arranged in the proper relationship to each other, be-

cause of my mother, and whether I liked it or not this
was going to be a main object. It was very red. I
hung it finally on a nail to the left of the door; that
way I could sit with my back to it. My habit of
rearranging the furniture, suddenly and without warning, used to annoy Arthur. He never understood why
I did it; he said you shouldn't care about your sur-
roundings.

But Mr. Vitroni was wrong: Arthur wouldn't
have liked the picture. It wasn't the sort of thing he
liked, though it was the sort of thing he believed I
liked. Appropriate, he'd say, the Colosseum in blood-
red on vulgar black velvet, with a gilt frame, noise
and tumult, cheering crowds, death on the sands,
wild animals growling, snarling, screams, and martyrs
weeping in the wings, getting ready to be sacrificed;
above all, emotion, fear, anger, laughter and tears,
a performance on which the crowd feeds. This, I
suspected, was his view of my inner life, though he
never quite said so. And where was he in the midst
of all the uproar? Sitting in the front row center,
not moving, barely smiling, it took a lot to satisfy
him; and, from time to time, making a slight gesture
that would preserve or destroy: thumbs up or thumbs
down. You'll have to run your own show now, I
thought, have your own emotions. I'm through acting
it out, the blood got too real.

By now I was furious with him and there was
nothing to throw except the plates, which were Mr.
Vitroni's, and no one to throw them at except Mr.
Vitroni himself, now plodding doubtlessly up the hill,
puffing a little because of his short legs and pillowy
belly. What would he think if I came raging up behind him, hurling plates? He'd call a policeman,
they'd arrest me, they'd search the flat, they'd find a
paper bag full of red hair, my suitcase. . . .

I was quickly practical again. The suitcase was
under a big fake-baroque chest of drawers with peel-
ing veneer and an inlaid seashell design. I pulled it
out and opened it; inside were my wet clothes, in a
green plastic Glad Bag. They smelled of my death,

of Lake Ontario, spilled oil, dead gulls, tiny silver fish cast up on the beach and rotting. Jeans and a navy-blue T-shirt, my funerary costume, my former self, damp and collapsed, from which the many-colored souls had flown. I could never wear such clothes in Terremoto, even if they weren't evidence. I thought of putting them in the garbage, but I knew from before that the children went through the garbage cans, especially those of foreigners. There had been no place to discard them on the well-traveled road to Terremoto. I should have thrown them away at the Toronto airport or the one in Rome; however, clothes discarded in airports were suspicious.

Though it was dusk, there was still enough light to see by. I decided to bury them. I scrunched the Glad Bag up and shoved it under my arm. The clothes were my own, I hadn't done anything wrong, but I still felt as though I was getting rid of a body, the corpse of someone I'd killed. I scrambled down the path beside the house, my leather-soled sandals skidding on the stones, till I was among the artichokes at the bottom. The ground was like flint and I had no shovel; there was no hope of digging a hole. Also the old man would notice if I disturbed his garden.

I examined the foundation of the house. Luckily it was shoddily built and the cement was cracking in several places. I found a loose chunk and pried it out, using a flat rock. Behind the cement there was plain dirt: the house was built right into the hillside. I scraped out a cavity, wadded the Glad Bag up as small as I could, and shoved it in, wedging the piece of cement back on top of it. Perhaps, hundreds of years from now, someone would dig up my jeans and T-shirt and deduce a forgotten rite, a child murder or a protective burial. The idea pleased me. I scuffed the fallen earth around with my foot so it wouldn't be noticeable.

I climbed back up to the balcony, feeling relieved. Once I'd dyed my hair, all the obvious evidence would be taken care of and I could start being another person, a different person entirely.

I went into the kitchen and finished burning the hair. Then I got out the bottle of Cinzano which I'd hidden in the cupboard, behind the plates. I didn't want it known here that I was a secret drinker, and I wasn't, really, there just wasn't any place where I could do it in public. Here, women were not supposed to drink alone in bars. I poured myself a small glassful and toasted myself. "To life," I said. After that it began to bother me that I'd spoken out loud. I didn't want to begin talking to myself.

The ants were into the spinach I'd bought the day before. They lived in the outside wall, spinach and meat were the only things they'd actively hunt, everything else they'd ignore as long as you put out a saucer of sugar and water for them. I'd already done this and they'd found it, they were marching back and forth between the saucer and their nest, thin on the way there, fat on the way back, filling themselves like miniature tankers. There was a circle of them around the edge of the water and a few had gone in too far and drowned.

I poured myself another drink, then dipped my finger into the saucer and wrote my initials in sugar-water on the windowsill. I waited to see my name spelled out for me in ants: a living legend.

Chapter Three

When I woke up the next morning my euphoria was gone. I didn't exactly have a hangover, but I didn't feel like getting up too suddenly. The Cinzano bottle was standing on the table, empty; what I found ominous about this was that I couldn't remember finishing it. Arthur used to tell me not to drink so much. He wasn't a great drinker himself, but he had a habit of bringing a bottle home from time to time and leaving it out where I would see it. I suppose I was

like a kid's chemistry set for him: secretly he liked
mixing me up, he knew something exciting would
happen. Though he was never sure what, or what he
wanted; if I'd known that it would've been easier.

Outside it was drizzling, and I had no raincoat.
I could've bought one in Rome, but I'd remembered
the climate as unbroken sunshine and warm nights.
I hadn't brought my own raincoat or my umbrella
or many of my own things at all, since I hadn't
wanted to leave any obvious signs of packing. Now
I began to regret my closet, my red-and-gold sari,
my embroidered caftan, my apricot velvet gown with
the ripped hem. Though where could I have worn
them, here? Nevertheless I lay in bed, longing for my
fan made out of peacock feathers, only one feather
missing, my evening bag with gas-blue beads, a real
antique.

Arthur had a strange relationship with my
clothes. He didn't like me spending money on them
because he thought we couldn't afford it, so at first
he said they clashed with my hair or they made me
look too fat. Later, when he took up Women's Lib-
eration for flagellation purposes, he tried to tell me
I shouldn't want to have clothes like that, I was playing into the hands of the exploiters. But it went beyond that; he found these clothes an affront of some
kind, a personal insult. At the same time he was
fascinated by them, as he was by all the things about
me he disapproved of. I suspect he found them arous-
ing and was irritated with himself because of it.

At last he made me so self-conscious that I found
it hard to wear my long dresses in public. Instead I
would close the bedroom door, drape myself in silk or
velvet, and get out all the dangly gold earrings and
chains and bracelets I could find. I would dab myself
with perfume, take off my shoes, and dance in front
of the mirror, twirling slowly around, waltzing with
an invisible partner. A tall man in evening dress,
with an opera cloak and smoldering eyes. As he swept
me in circles (bumping occasionally into the dressing
table or the end of the bed) he would whisper, "Let

me take you away. We will dance together, always."
It was a great temptation, despite the fact that he
wasn't real. . . .

Arthur would never dance with me, even in private. He said he had never learned.

I lay in bed, watching it rain. From somewhere
in the town I could hear a plaintive mooing sound,
hoarse and metallic, like an iron cow. I felt sad, and
there was nothing in the flat to cheer me up. *Flat*
was a good word for it. An advertisement in the back
of a British newspaper would have called it a *villa*,
but it was only two rooms and a cramped kitchen.
The walls were covered with unpainted plaster,
splotched and mottled from water seepage. Across
the ceiling ran beams of naked wood—Mr. Vitroni
must have thought they'd be rustic and picturesque
—and these harbored centipedes, which dropped
from them sometimes, usually at night. In the cracks
between the walls and the floor and occasionally in
the tiny bathtub there were medium-sized brown
scorpions, which were not supposed to be deadly.
Because of the rain outside it was dark and cold, it
was dripping somewhere, and it seemed to echo like a
cave, perhaps because the two flats above were still
empty. Before, there had been a family of South
Americans above us who played their guitars late into
the evening, wailing and stamping their feet so that
chips of plaster fell like hail. I wanted to go up and
wail and stamp my feet too, but Arthur thought it
would be pushy to introduce ourselves. He grew up in
Fredericton, New Brunswick.

I rolled over, and the mattress got me in the
spine. There was one prong that stuck up, right in
the middle; but I knew that if I turned the mattress
over there would be four prongs. It was the same
mattress, with its chasms and pinnacles and treach-
ery, unchanged by a year of others. We'd made love
on it with an urgency reminiscent of motel rooms.
Arthur was stimulated by the centipedes, which lent
an aura of danger (a well-known aphrodisiac, witness
the Black Death). Also he liked living out of suit-

cases. It must've made him feel like a political refugee, which was probably one of his fantasies, though he never said so.

In addition he could think we were going somewhere, somewhere better; and in fact whenever we moved he did perceive the new place as better, for a while. After that he would perceive it as merely different, and after that as merely the same. But he valued the illusion of transience more highly than the illusion of permanence, and our entire marriage took place in a kind of spiritual train station. Perhaps it had to do with the way we met. Because we started out by saying goodbye, we became accustomed to it. Even when he was just going to the corner for a package of cigarettes, I would gaze at him as if I would never see him again. And now I would never see him again.

I burst into tears and shoved my head under the pillow. Then I decided this would have to stop. I couldn't let Arthur go on controlling my life, especially at such a distance. I was someone else now, I was almost someone else. People used to say to me, "You don't look at all like your photographs," and it was true; so with a few adjustments I'd be able to pass him on the street one day and he wouldn't even recognize me. I untangled myself from the sheets—Mr. Vitroni's sheets, thin and carefully mended—went into the bathroom, and ran cold water over a washcloth to deflate my face, noticing just in time the small brown scorpion concealed in the folds. It was hard to get used to these ambushes. If Arthur had been there I would have screamed. As it was I dropped the washcloth on the floor and crushed the scorpion with the tin bottom of a can of cleansing powder, also supplied by Mr. Vitroni. He'd stocked the flat well with products for keeping it clean—soap, toilet disinfectant, scrub brushes—but for cooking there was only a single frying pan and two pots, one minus the handle.

I shambled out to the kitchen and turned on the

burner. I was never any good in the mornings before coffee. I needed something warm in my mouth to make me feel safe; here it was filter coffee and milk from the triangular cardboard container on the windowsill. There was no refrigerator, but the milk wasn't sour yet. I had to boil it anyway, everything had to be boiled.

I sat at the table with my hot cup, adding another white ring to the varnish, eating a package of rusks and trying to organize my life. One step at a time, I told myself. Luckily I'd brought some felt pens; I would make a list. *Hair dye*, I wrote at the top in apple green. I would go to Tivoli or perhaps Rome for it, the sooner the better. With my hair dyed there would be nothing linking me to the other side, except my fingerprints. And no one would bother about the fingerprints of a woman pronounced officially dead.

I wrote *Money*, and underlined it twice. Money was important. I had enough for about a month, if I was frugal. Realistically I had enough for about two weeks. The black velvet Colosseum had set me back. I hadn't been able to take much out of my bank account, since a large withdrawal the day before my death would've looked funny. If I'd had more time I could have arranged it through my other bank account, the professional one. If there had been anything in the other bank account. Unfortunately I usually transferred most of it to my own as soon as it came in. I wondered who would get the money; Arthur, probably.

Postcard to Sam, I wrote. I'd bought the postcard already, at the Rome airport. It had a picture of the Leaning Tower of Pisa. I printed the agreed-upon message in green block letters:

HAVING A SUPER TIME. ST. PETER'S IS WONDER-
FUL. SEE YOU SOON, LOVE, MITZI AND FRED.

That would tell him I'd arrived safely. If there had been complications, I would have written: WEATHER

COOL AND FRED HAS DYSENTERY. THANK GOD FOR EN-
TEROVIOFORM! LOVE, MITZI AND FRED.

I decided to mail the postcard first and worry
about the money and the hair dye later. I finished
my coffee, ate the last rusk, and changed into the
second of my new baggy dresses, a white one with
gray and mauve lozenges on it. I noticed that my
nightgown had a rip halfway down the seam, at thigh
level. With no one looking at me, watching for these
transgressions, would I become sluttish? Why don't
you take better care of yourself, a voice said, don't
you want to make something of yourself? *Needles
and thread,* I wrote on my list.

I wrapped my head up in the scarf with the pink
Mounties and put on my dark glasses. It was no longer raining but it was still gray; the glasses would look
odd, but I couldn't help it. I walked up the winding
cobbled street towards the market square, running
the gauntlet of old women who sat every day on
the doorsteps of their aggressively historical stone
houses, their huge obsolete torsos crammed into black
dresses as if in mourning, their legs like bloated saus-
ages encased in wool. They were the same old wom-
en that had looked me over on the previous afternoon,
the same ones that had been there a year ago and
two thousand years ago. They did not vary.

Bongiorno, each one said as I went past, and I
nodded at them, smiling and repeating the word.
They didn't seem very curious about me. They already knew where I lived, what my car looked like,
that I was foreign, and every time I bought something in the square they would know about that also.
What else was there to know about a foreigner? The
only thing that might bother them was that I lived
alone: it wouldn't seem natural to them. But it didn't
seem natural to me, either.

The post office was in the front part of one of
the damp historical houses. It contained only a bench,
a counter and a bulletin board, with some pictures
tacked to it that looked like WANTED posters: surly
men, front and side. A couple of policemen, or were

they soldiers, were lounging on the bench in their leftover Mussolini uniforms: high stiff boots, leg stripes, sheaves of wheat on the pocket flaps. The back of my neck prickled as I stood at the counter, trying to make the woman understand that I wanted an airmail stamp. All I could think of was *Par Avion*, wrong language. I flapped my arms like wings, feeling idiotic, but she caught on. Behind me the policemen laughed. Surely they would sniff out my passport, which was glowing through the leather sides of my bag like molten iron, like a siren, surely they would ask to see it, question me, notify the authorities. . . . And what would the authorities do?

The woman behind the counter took the card in through her slotted window. As soon as Sam got it he could let me know how well we'd succeeded. I went out, followed by the shiny beetle eyes of the policemen.

It was a good plan, I thought; I was pleased with myself for having arranged it. And suddenly I wanted Arthur to know how clever I'd been. He always thought I was too disorganized to plot my way across the floor and out the door, much less out of the country. I was the one who would charge off to do the shopping with a carefully drawn-up list, many of the items suggested by him, and forget my handbag, come back for it, forget the car keys, drive away, forget the list; or return with two tins of caviar and a box of fancy crackers and a half bottle of champagne, then try to justify these treasures by telling him they were on sale, a lie every time but the first. I would love him to know I'd done something complicated and dangerous without making a single mistake. I'd always wanted to do something he would admire.

Remembering the caviar made me hungry. I crossed the market square to the main grocery store, where you could get tins and packages, and bought another box of Peek Freans and some cheese and pasta. Outside, near the café, there was an ancient vegetable truck; that must have been the horn I'd heard earlier. It was surrounded by plump housewives, in their morning cotton dresses and bare legs, calling their orders and waving their bundles of paper money. The vegetable man was young, with an oiled mane of hair; he stood in the back of the truck, filling baskets and joking with the women. When I walked over he grinned at me and shouted something that made the women laugh and shriek. He offered me a bunch of grapes, wiggling it suggestively, but I wasn't up to it, my vocabulary was too limited; so I went instead to the regular vegetable stand. The produce wasn't as fresh but the man was old and kindly and I could get away with pointing.

At the butcher's I bought two expensive, paper-thin slices of beef, which I knew would have a pallid taste. It was from yearlings, because no one could afford to pasture a cow for longer than that, and I never did learn to cook it properly, it always came out like vinyl.

I walked back down the hill, carrying my packages. My red Hertz Rent-A-Car was parked opposite the wrought-iron gate that led to the path. I'd got it at the airport and there was already a scratch on it, from a street in Rome that turned out to be one-way, *senso unico*. Some of the town's children were clustered around it, drawing pictures in the film of dust that covered it, peeping through the windows almost fearfully, running their hands along the fenders. When they saw me they drew back from the car and huddled, whispering.

I smiled at them, thinking how charming they looked, with their round brown eyes, alert as a squirrel's; several had blond hair, startling against their olive skin, and I remembered having been told that the barbarians used to come this way, ten or fifteen centuries ago. That was why all the towns were built on hills.

"*Bongiorno*," I said to them. They giggled shyly. I turned in at the gate and crunched down the path. Two dwarfish hens, the color of shredded cardboard, scuttled out of my way. Halfway down I stopped: I

was trying to remember whether or not I'd locked the
door. Despite my apparent safety, I couldn't afford
to get careless or lazy. It was irrational, but I had the
feeling that there was someone inside the flat, sitting
in the chair by the window, waiting for me.

Chapter Four

But there was nobody in the flat. If anything, it was
emptier than ever. I cooked lunch without mishap,
nothing exploded or boiled over, and ate it at the table. Soon, I thought, I'd be eating in the kitchen,
standing up, out of the pots and pans. That was how
people got when they lived alone. I felt I should try
to establish some sort of routine.

After lunch I counted my money, some in cash,
some in traveler's checks. There was less than I'd
thought, as always; I'd have to get down to business
and earn some more. I went over to the bureau,
pulled open the underwear drawer, and dug among
the contents, wondering what had inspired me to
buy a pair of red bikini briefs with *Sunday* embroidered on them in black. It was the Royal Porcupine, of course; among other things, he was an underwear freak. It had been part of a Weekend Set; I had
Friday and *Saturday* too, all bilingual. I took them
out of the cellophane package and the Royal Porcupine said, "Put on *Sunday/Dimanche*"; he liked cre-
ating images of virtue violated. I did. "Dynamite,"
said the Royal Porcupine. "Now turn around." He
prowled towards me and we ended up in a lustful
tangle on his mattress. There was a flesh-colored brassiere too, with a front closing. *For lovers only*, the ad
said, so I bought it to go with my lover. I was a sucker
for ads, especially those that promised happiness.

I'd brought this incriminating underwear with

me because I was afraid Arthur would discover it after my death and realize he'd never seen it before. During my life he never would have looked into that particular drawer; he shied away from underwear, he liked to think his mind was on higher things, which, to give him credit, it was, most of the time. So I used my underwear drawer as a hiding place, and from force of habit I was still doing this.

I took out Fraser Buchanan's black notebook. Under it, at the bottom, wrapped in a slip, was the manuscript I'd been working on at the time of my death.

Charlotte stood in the room where he had left her, her hands still unconsciously clasping the casket of jewels. A fire was crackling in the spacious fireplace, its reflections gleaming warmly on the marble family crests that adorned the richly carved mantel, yet she felt quite cold. At the same time, her cheeks were burning. She could still see the curl of his lip, the tilt of the cynical eyebrows in that dark but compelling face, his hard mouth, thin-lipped and rapacious. . . . She remembered the way his eyes had moved over her, appraising the curves of her firm young body, which were only partially concealed by her cheap, badly fitting black crepe dress. She had sufficient experience with the nobility to know how they looked upon women like herself, who through no fault of their own were forced to earn their own livings. He would be no different from the rest. Her breasts moved tumultuously beneath the black crepe as she thought of the humiliations she had suffered. Liars and hypocrites, all of them! Already she had begun to hate him.

She would finish resetting the emeralds and leave Redmond Grange as quickly as possible. There was menace lurking somewhere in the vast house, she could almost smell it. She remembered the puzzling words of the coachman, Tom, as he handed her none too graciously out of the coach. "Don't go near the maze, Miss, is my advice to you," he had said. He was a sinister, ratlike man with bad teeth and a furtive manner.

"What maze?" Charlotte had asked.

"You'll find out soon enough," he had replied with a snigger. "Many a young girl afore you has come to grief in the maze." But he had refused to explain further.

From outside the French windows came a trail of silvery laughter, a woman's voice. . . . At this hour, and in November, who could be walking on the terrace? Charlotte shivered, remembering those other footsteps she had heard in the same place the night before; but when she had looked down onto the terrace from her bedroom window, she could see nothing but moonlight and the shadows of the shrubberies moving in the wind.

She went towards the door, intending to mount the stairs to her own small room, which was on the same floor as the maids' quarters. That was how highly Redmond valued her, she thought with scorn. She might as well have been a governess, one step above a parlor maid or a cook but definitely not a lady. Yet she was as well-bred as he was, if the truth were known.

Outside the drawing-room door Charlotte paused in amazement. At the foot of the stairs, blocking her way, stood a tall woman in a sable traveling cloak. The hood was thrown back, revealing flame-red hair; the bodice of her scarlet dress was cut low, displaying the swell of her white breasts. It was evident that the skill of Bond Street's most fashionable and expensive dressmakers had been lavished on her costume; yet beneath this veneer of civilized sophistication, her body moved with the sensuousness of a predatory animal. She was ravishingly beautiful.

She glared at Charlotte, her green eyes gleaming in the light from the silver candelabrum, decorated with cupids and festoons of grapes, which she was holding in her left hand. "Who are you and what are you doing in this house?" she demanded in an imperious voice. Before Charlotte could answer, the

*woman's glance fell upon the casket she was carry-
ing. "My jewels!" she cried. She struck Charlotte
across the face with her gloved hand.*

*"Softly, Felicia," said Redmond's voice. He
emerged from the shadows. "I had intended the res-
toration of your jewels as a surprise, to welcome you
home. But it is I who am surprised, as you have
come before expected." He laughed, a dry, mocking
laugh.*

*The woman called Felicia turned to him, her
smoldering eyes possessive, her provocative smile revealing small white teeth of a perfect uniformity.
Redmond lifted her gloved hand gallantly to his lips.*

Eight pages were missing, the first eight pages.
For a moment I thought I'd left them behind, in the
apartment, where Arthur would be sure to find them.
But I couldn't have done that, I couldn't have been
that sloppy. Fraser Buchanan must've taken them,
slipped them up his jacket sleeve, folded them and
stuffed them into a pocket when he was in the bedroom, before I could get to him. I had his black notebook though, and my hostage was better.

It wouldn't be too difficult to reconstruct the
opening pages. Charlotte would round the curve of
the spacious lime-tree-bordered driveway in the Redmond carriage, the second-best one, which had been
sent to the station to fetch her. She'd be clutching
her inadequate shawl around her, worrying about the
shabbiness of her clothes and her battered trunk in
the boot: would the servants sneer? Then she would
glimpse the Grange itself, with its feminine bulk and
its masculine turrets and its air of pervasive evil.
She'd be ushered by a contemptuous butler into the
Library, where, after keeping her waiting in an inconsiderate manner, the master of the house would
interview her. He would express surprise that the jew-
el restorers had sent a woman, and would imply that
she wasn't up to the job. She would answer him firmly, even a little defiantly. He would notice the challenge in her lustrous blue eyes, and remark that she

was perhaps a little too independent for her own good.

"In my position, Sir," she would reply with a tinge of bitterness, "one is forced to be independent." Charlotte of course was an orphan. Her father had been the younger son of a noble house, disowned by his family for marrying her mother, a sweet-natured woman who had danced in an Opera-house. Charlotte's parents had died in a smallpox epidemic. She herself had escaped with only a few pockmarks, which lent piquancy to her expression. She was brought up by her uncle, her mother's brother, who was rich but a miser, and who'd forced her to learn her present trade before he'd perished of yellow fever. He'd left her nothing, he'd always hated her, and her father's noble family would have nothing to do with her. She wished Redmond to know that she was not in his house, in his power, by choice but from necessity. Everyone had to eat.

I'd need a working title. *The Lord of Redmond Grange*, I thought, or, better still, *Terror at Redmond Grange*. Terror was one of my specialties; that and historical detail. Or perhaps something with the word *Love* in it: love was a big seller. For years I'd been trying to get love and terror into the same title, but it was difficult. *Love and Terror at Redmond Grange* would be far too long, and it sounded too much like *The Bobbsey Twins at Sunset Beach. My Love Was Terror* . . . too Mickey Spillane. *Stalked by Love*, that would do in a pinch.

I'd also need a typewriter. I touch-typed everything; it was faster, and in my business speed was important. I was a good typist; at my high school typing was regarded as a female secondary sex characteristic, like breasts. Perhaps I could buy a second-hand typewriter in Rome. Then I could fill in the opening pages, write another eight or nine chapters, and send them to Hermes Books with a covering letter explaining that I'd moved to Italy on account of my health. They'd never seen me, they knew me only by my other name. They thought I was a middle-aged ex-librarian, overweight and shy. Practically a recluse, in fact, and allergic to dust, wool, fish, cigarette smoke and alcohol, as I'd explained to them when declining lunches. I'd always tried to keep my two names and identities as separate as possible.

Arthur never found out that I wrote Costume Gothics. At first I worked on them only when he was out. Later I would go into the bedroom, close the door, and tell him I was studying for some university extension course or other: Chinese Pottery, Comparative Religion, courses I never managed to complete for the simple reason that I never really took them.

Why did I never tell him? It was fear, mostly. When I first met him he talked a lot about wanting a woman whose mind he could respect, and I knew that if he found out I'd written *The Secret of Morgrave Manor* he wouldn't respect mine. I wanted very much to have a respectable mind. Arthur's friends and the books he read, which always had footnotes, and the causes he took up made me feel deficient and somehow absurd, a sort of intellectual village idiot, and revealing my profession would certainly have made it worse. These books, with their covers featuring gloomy, foreboding castles and apprehensive maidens in modified nightgowns, hair streaming in the wind, eyes bulging like those of a goiter victim, toes poised for flight, would be considered trash of the lowest order. Worse than trash, for didn't they exploit the masses, corrupt by distracting, and perpetuate degrading stereotypes of women as helpless and persecuted? They did and I knew it, but I couldn't stop.

"You're an intelligent woman," Arthur would have said. He always said this before an exposition of some failing of mine, but also he really believed it. His exasperation with me was like that of a father with smart kids who got bad report cards.

He wouldn't have understood. He wouldn't have been able to understand in the least the desire, the pure quintessential need of my readers for escape, a thing I myself understood only too well. Life had been hard on them and they had not fought back, they'd collapsed like soufflés in a high wind. Escape wasn't a luxury for them, it was a necessity. They had to get it somehow. And when they were too tired to invent escapes of their own, mine were available for them at the corner drugstore, neatly packaged like the other painkillers. They could be taken in capsule form, quickly and discreetly, during those moments when the hair-dryer was stiffening the curls around their plastic rollers or the bath oil in the bath was turning their skins to pink velvet, leaving a ring in the tub to be removed later with Ajax Cleanser, which would make their hands smell like a hospital and cause their husbands to remark that they were about as sexy as a dishcloth. Then they would mourn their lack of beauty, their departing youth. . . . I knew all about escape, I was brought up on it.

The heroines of my books were mere stand-ins: their features were never clearly defined, their faces were putty which each reader could reshape into her own, adding a little beauty. In hundreds of thousands of houses these hidden selves rose at night from the mundane beds of their owners to go forth on adventures so complicated and enticing that they couldn't be confessed to anyone, least of all to the husbands who lay snoring their enchanted snores and dabbling with nothing more recondite than a Playboy Bunny. I knew my readers well, I went to school with them, I was the good sport, I volunteered for committees, I decorated the high-school gym with signs that read HOWDY HOP and SNOWBALL STOMP and then went home and ate peanut butter sandwiches and read paperback novels while everyone else was dancing. I was Miss Personality, confidante and true friend. They told me all.

Now I could play fairy godmother to them, despite their obvious defects, their calves which were too skinny, those disfiguring hairs on their upper lips, much deplored in cramped ads at the backs of movie magazines, their elbows knobby as chickens' knees. I had the power to turn them from pumpkins to pure gold. War, politics and explorations up the Amazon, those other great escapes, were by and large denied them, and they weren't much interested in hockey or football, games they couldn't play. Why refuse them their castles, their persecutors and their princes, and come to think of it, who the hell was Arthur to talk about social relevance? Sometimes his god-damned theories and ideologies made me puke. The truth was that I dealt in hope, I offered a vision of a better world, however preposterous. Was that so ter-rible? I couldn't see that it was much different from the visions Arthur and his friends offered, and it was just as realistic. So you're interested in the people, the workers, I would say to him during my solitary midnight justifications. Well, that's what the people and the workers read, the female ones anyway, when they have time to read at all and they can't face the social realism of *True Confessions*. They read my books. Figure that out.

But that would have been going too far, that would have been treading on Arthur's most sensitive and sacred toe. It would be better to approach it from a materialist-determinist angle: "Arthur, this happens to be something I'm good at and suited for. I discovered it by accident but then I became hooked, I turned professional and now it's the only way I know of earning a living. As the whores say, why the hell should I be a waitress? You're always telling me women should become whole people through meaningful work and you've been nagging at me to get some. Well, this is my work and I find it mean-ingful. And I'm hardly an idle drone, I've written fif-teen of these things."

Arthur wouldn't have bought this, however. Mar-lene the paragon had worked as a typesetter for three months ("You can't really understand the workers until you've been on the inside with them"), and for Arthur, the snob, nothing less would do.

Poor Arthur. I thought about him, all alone in our apartment, surrounded by the rubble of our marriage. What was he doing at that instant? Was he stuffing my red and orange gowns into a Crippled Civilians bag, emptying my makeup drawer into the garbage? Was he leafing through the scrapbook I'd started to keep in those first weeks of childish excitement after *Lady Oracle* had appeared? How naive to have thought they would all finally respect me. . . . The scrapbook would go into the trash, along with all the other scraps of me that were left on the other side. What would he keep, a glove, a shoe?

Perhaps he was regretting. This was a new thought: he was feeling melancholy, bereaved even, as I was. It struck me that I might have misjudged him. Suppose he no longer hated me, suppose he had given up revenge. Perhaps I'd done something terrible to him, something final. Should I send him an anonymous postcard from Rome—*Joan is not dead, signed, A Friend*—to cheer him up?

I should have trusted him more. I should have been honest from the beginning, expressed my feelings, told him everything. (But if he'd known what I was really like, would he still have loved me?) The trouble was that I wanted to maintain his illusions for him intact, and it was easy to do, all it needed was a little restraint: I simply never told him anything important.

But it wasn't more honesty that would have saved me, I thought; it was more dishonesty. In my experience, honesty and expressing your feelings could lead to only one thing. Disaster.

PART TWO

Chapter Five

If you let one worm out of a can of worms, all the other worms will follow. Aunt Lou used to say that; she had many useful maxims, some traditional, some invented by her. For instance, I've heard "The tongue is the enemy of the neck" elsewhere, but never "There's more than one cat in any bag" or "Don't count on your rabbits before they're out of the hat." Aunt Lou believed in discretion, though only in important matters.

That was one reason I never told Arthur much about my mother. If I'd started on her, he would've found out about me soon enough. I invented a mother for his benefit, a kind, placid woman who died of a rare disease—lupus, I think it was—shortly after I met him.

Luckily he was never very curious about my past: he was too busy telling me about his. I heard all about his own mother: how she'd claimed to have known the very instant Arthur was conceived and had dedicated him to the ministry (Anglican) right then and there in her womb, how she'd threatened to cut his thumbs off when she caught him playing with himself at the age of four. I knew about his contempt for her and for her belief in hard work and achievement, so curiously like his own, and about his fear of her orderliness, symbolized by her flower borders which he was forced to weed. I heard about her dislike of drinking and also about his father's bar in the recreation room in that Fredericton judge's mansion he claimed to have left so far behind, with the miniature gold Scotsmen's heads on the bottle-tops, perversely like nipples, or so I imagined them. I knew about the various hysterical letters his mother had written, disowning him for this or that, politics, religion, sex. One came when she learned we were living together, and she never did forgive me.

To all these monstrosities and injustices I listened faithfully, partly out of a hope that I would gradually come to understand him, but mostly from habit. At one stage of my life I was a good listener, I cultivated listening, I figured I'd better be good at it because I wasn't very good at anything else. I would listen to anyone about anything, murmuring at appropriate moments, reassuring, noncommittal, sympathetic as a pillow. I even took up eavesdropping behind doors and in buses and restaurants, but this was hardly the same, since it was unilateral. So it was easy to listen to Arthur, and I ended up knowing a lot more about his mother than he did about mine, not that it did me much good. Knowledge isn't necessarily power.

I did tell him one thing though, which should've made more of an impression on him than it did: my mother named me after Joan Crawford. This is one of the things that always puzzled me about her. Did she name me after Joan Crawford because she wanted me to be like the screen characters she played—beautiful, ambitious, ruthless, destructive to men—or because she wanted me to be successful? Joan Crawford worked hard, she had willpower, she built herself up from nothing, according to my mother. Did she give me someone else's name because she wanted me never to have a name of my own? Come to think of it, Joan Crawford didn't have a name of her own either. Her real name was Lucille LeSueur, which would have suited me much better. Lucy the Sweat. When I was eight or nine and my mother would look at me and say musingly, "To think that I named you after Joan Crawford," my stomach would contract and plummet and I would be overcome with shame; I knew I was being reproached, but I'm still not sure what for. There's more than one side to Joan Crawford, though. In fact there was something tragic about Joan Crawford, she had big serious eyes, an unhappy mouth and high cheekbones, unfortunate things happened to her. Perhaps that was it. Or, and this is important: Joan Crawford was thin.

I was not, and this is one of the many things for which my mother never quite forgave me. At first I was merely plump; in the earliest snapshots in my mother's album I was a healthy baby, not much heftier than most, and the only peculiar thing is that I was never looking at the camera; instead I was trying to get something into my mouth: a toy, a hand, a bottle. The photos went on in an orderly series; though I didn't exactly become rounder, I failed to lose what is usually referred to as baby fat. When I reached the age of six the pictures stopped abruptly. This must have been when my mother gave up on me, for it was she who used to take them; perhaps she no longer wanted my growth recorded. She had decided I would not do.

I became aware of this fairly soon. My mother had enrolled me in a dancing school, where a woman called Miss Flegg, who was almost as slender and disapproving as my mother, taught tap dancing and ballet. The classes were held in a long room over a butcher shop, and I could always remember the way the smell of sawdust and raw meat gave way to the muggy scent of exhausted feet, mingled with Miss Flegg's Yardley cologne, as I trudged up the dusty stairs. My mother took this step partly because it was fashionable to enroll seven-year-old girls in dancing schools—Hollywood musicals were still popular—and partly because she hoped it would make me less chubby. She didn't say this to me, she said it to Miss Flegg; she was not yet calling me fat.

I loved dancing school. I was even quite good at the actual dancing, although Miss Flegg sometimes rapped her classroom pointer sharply on the floor and said, "Joan dear, I wish you would stop thumping." Like most little girls of that time I idealized ballet dancers, it was something girls could do, and I used to press my short piggy nose up against jewelry store windows and goggle at the china music-box figurines of shiny ladies in brittle pink skirts, with roses on their hard ceramic heads, and imagine myself leaping through the air, lifted by a thin man in black tights, light as a kite and wearing a modified doily, my hair full of rhinestones and glittering like hope. I worked hard at the classes, I concentrated, and I even used to practice at home, wrapping myself in a discarded lace bathroom curtain I had begged from my mother as she was about to stuff it into the garbage can. She washed it first though; she didn't like dirt. I longed for a pair of satin toe shoes, but we were too young, Miss Flegg explained, the bones in our feet had not hardened. So I had to settle for black slippers with an unromantic elastic over the instep.

Miss Flegg was an inventive woman; I suppose these days she would be called creative. She didn't have much scope for her inventiveness in the teaching of elementary steps to young children, which was largely a matter of drill, but she let herself go on the annual spring recital. The recital was mostly to impress the parents, but it was also to impress the little girls themselves so they would ask to be allowed to take lessons the next year.

Miss Flegg choreographed the entire program. She also constructed the sets and props, and she designed the costumes and handed out patterns and instructions to the mothers, who were supposed to sew them. My mother disliked sewing but for this event she buckled down and cut and pinned just like all the other mothers. Maybe she hadn't given up on me after all, maybe she was still making an effort.

Miss Flegg organized the recital into age groups, which corresponded to her dancing classes. There were five of them: Teenies, Tallers, Tensies, Tweeners and Teeners. Underneath her spiny exterior, the long bony hands, the hair wrenched into a bun, and the spidery eyebrows, done, I realized later, with a pencil, she had a layer of sentimentality, which set the tone for her inventions.

I was a Teenie, which was in itself a contradiction in terms, for as well as being heavier than everyone else in the class I had begun to be taller. But I didn't mind, I didn't even notice, for I was becoming more wildly excited about the recital every day. I practiced for hours in the basement, the only place I was allowed to do it after I had accidentally knocked over and broken my mother's white-and-gold living-room lamp in the shape of a pineapple, one of a set. I twirled beside the washing machine, humming the dance music in my head, I curtseyed to the furnace (which in those days still burned coal), I swayed in and out between the sheets drying double-folded on the line, and when I was exhausted I climbed the cellar stairs, out of breath and covered with coal dust, to be confronted by my mother with her mouth full of pins. After I'd been scrubbed I would be stood on a chair and told to turn around slowly. I could barely hold still even to have my costumes tried on.

My mother's impatience was almost equal to my own, though it was of another sort. She may have started to regret sending me to dancing school. For one thing, I wasn't getting any slimmer; for another, I now made twice as much noise as I had at first, especially when I rehearsed my tap number in my patent leather shoes with metal tips toe and heel, on the hardwood of the hall floor, which I had been ordered not to do; and for another, she was having trouble with the costumes. She'd followed the instructions, but she couldn't get them to look right.

There were three of them, for the Teenies were doing three numbers: "Tulip Time," a Dutch ballet routine for which we had to line up with partners and move our arms up and down to simulate windmills; "Anchors Aweigh," a tap dance with quick turns and salutes (this was soon after the end of the war and military motifs were still in vogue); and "The Butterfly Frolic," a graceful number whose delicate flittings were more like my idea of what dancing should be. It was my favorite, and it had my favorite costume too. This featured a gauzy skirt, short, like a real ballerina's, a tight bodice with shoulder straps, a headpiece with spangled insect antennae, and a pair of colored cellophane wings with coathanger frames, supplied by Miss Flegg. The wings were what I really longed for but we weren't allowed to put them on until the day itself, for fear of breakage.

But it was this costume that was bothering my mother. The others were easier: the Dutch outfit was a long full skirt with a black bodice and white sleeves, and I was the rear partner anyway. The "Anchors Aweigh" number had middy dresses with naval braid trim, and this was all right too since they were high-necked, long-sleeved and loose around the waist. I was in the back row because of my height; I hadn't been picked as one of the three stars, all with Shirley Temple curls, who were doing solos on drums made out of cheese crates. But I didn't mind that much: I had my eye on the chief butterfly spot. There was a duet with the only boy in the class; his name was Roger. I was slightly in love with him. I hoped the girl who was supposed to do it would get sick and they would have to call me in. I'd memorized her part as well as my own, more or less.

I stood on the chair and my mother stuck pins into me and sighed; then she told me to turn around slowly, and she frowned and stuck in more pins. The problem was fairly simple: in the short pink skirt, with my waist, arms and legs exposed, I was grotesque. I am reconstructing this from the point of view of an adult, an anxious, prudish adult like my mother or Miss Flegg; but with my jiggly thighs and the bulges of fat where breasts would later be and my plump upper arms and floppy waist, I must have looked obscene, senile almost, indecent; it must have been like watching a decaying stripper. I was the kind of child, they would have thought back then in the early months of 1949, who should not be seen in public with so little clothing on. No wonder I fell in love with the nineteenth century: back then, according to the dirty postcards of the time, flesh was a virtue.

My mother struggled with the costume, lengthening it, adding another layer of gauze to conceal the outlines, padding the bodice; but it was no use. Even I was a little taken aback when she finally allowed me to inspect myself in the three-sided mirror over her vanity table. Although I was too young to be much bothered by my size, it wasn't quite the effect I wanted. I did not look like a butterfly. But I knew the addition of the wings would make all the difference. I was hoping for magic transformations, even then.

The dress rehearsal was in the afternoon, the recital the same evening. They were so close together because the recital was to be held, not in the room over the butcher shop, which would have been too cramped, but in a public school auditorium, rented for a single Saturday. My mother went with me, carrying my costumes in a cardboard dress box. The stage was cramped and hollow-sounding but was redeemed by velvet curtains, soft purple ones; I felt them at the first opportunity. The space behind it was vibrating with excitement. A lot of the mothers were there. Some of them had volunteered to do makeup and were painting the faces of theirs and other people's daughters, the mouths with dark-red lipstick, the eyelashes with black mascara which stiffened them into spikes. The finished and costumed girls were standing against the wall so as not to damage themselves, inert as temple sacrifices. The bigger pupils were strolling about and chatting; it wasn't as important to them, they had done it before, and their numbers were to be rehearsed later.

"Tulip Time" and "Anchors Aweigh" went off without a hitch. We changed costumes backstage, in a tangle of arms and legs, giggling nervously and doing up each other's hooks and zippers. There was a crowd around the single mirror. The Tallers, who were alternating with us, did their number, "Kitty Kat Kapers," while Miss Flegg stood in the wings, evaluating, waving time with her pointer, and occasionally shouting. She was wrought up. As I was putting on my butterfly costume, I saw my mother standing beside her.

She was supposed to be out in the front row where I'd left her, sitting on a folding chair, her gloves in her lap, smoking and jiggling one of her feet in its high-heeled open-toed shoe, but now she was talking with Miss Flegg. Miss Flegg looked over at me; then she walked over, followed by my mother. She stood gazing down at me, her lips pressed together.

"I see what you mean," she said to my mother. When resenting this scene later on, I always felt that if my mother hadn't interfered Miss Flegg would have noticed nothing, but this is probably not true. What she was seeing, what they were both seeing, was her gay, her artistic, her *spiritual* "Butterfly Frolic" being reduced to something laughable and unseemly by the presence of a fat little girl who was more like a giant caterpillar than a butterfly, more like a white grub if you were really going to be accurate.

Miss Flegg could not have stood this. For her, the final effect was everything. She wished to be complimented on it, and wholeheartedly, not with pity or suppressed smiles. I sympathize with her now, although I couldn't then. Anyway, her inventiveness didn't desert her. She leaned down, placed her hand on my round bare shoulder, and drew me over to a corner. There she knelt down and gazed with her forceful black eyes into mine. Her blurred eyebrows rose and fell.

"Joan, dear," she said, "how would you like to be something special?"

I smiled at her uncertainly.

"Would you do something for me, dear?" she said, warmly.

I nodded. I liked to help.

"I've decided to change the dance a little," she said. "I've decided to add a new part to it; and because you're the brightest girl in the class, I've chosen you to be the special, new person. Do you think you can do that, dear?"

I had seen enough of her to know that this kindness was suspect, but I fell for it anyway. I nodded emphatically, thrilled to have been selected. Maybe I'd been picked to do the butterfly duet with Roger, maybe I would get bigger, more important wings. I was eager.

"Good," said Miss Flegg, clamping her hand on my arm. "Now come and hop into your new costume."

"What am I going to be?" I asked as she led me away.

"A mothball, dear," she answered serenely, as if this were the most natural thing in the world.

Her inventive mind, and possibly earlier experiences, had given her a fundamental rule for dealing with situations like this: if you're going to be made to look ridiculous and there's no way out of it, you may as well pretend you meant to. I didn't learn this rule till much later, not consciously. I was wounded, desolated in fact, when it turned out that Miss Flegg wanted me to remove my cloudy skirt and spangles and put on one of the white teddy-bear costumes the Tensies were using for their number, "Teddy Bears' Picnic." She also wanted me to hang around my neck a large sign that said MOTHBALL, "So they'll all understand, dear, what you're supposed to be." She herself would make the sign for me, in the interval between the rehearsal and the performance.

"Can I wear my wings?" I asked. It was beginning to seep through to me, the monstrousness of the renunciation she was asking me to make.

"Now, who ever heard of a mothball with wings?" she said in what was supposed to be a jocular but practical manner.

Her idea was that once the butterflies had finished their cavorting, I would lumber in among them in the white suit and the sign, and the butterflies would be coached to scatter. It would be cute, she told me.

"I liked the dance the way it was," I said tentatively. "I want it to be the way it was." I was on the verge of crying; probably I had already begun.

Miss Flegg's manner changed. She put her face down close to mine so I could see the wrinkles around her eyes up close and smell the sour toothpaste smell of her mouth, and said, slowly and distinctly, "You'll do as I say or you won't be in the dance at all. Do you understand?"

Being left out altogether was too much for me. I capitulated, but I paid for it. I had to stand in the mothball suit with Miss Flegg's hand on my shoulder while she explained to the other Teenies, sylphlike in their wispy skirts and shining wings, about the change in plans and my new, starring role. They looked at me, scorn on their painted lips; they were not taken in.

I went home with my mother, refusing to speak to her because she had betrayed me. It was snowing lightly, though it was April, and I was glad because she had on her white open-toed shoes and her feet would get wet. I went into the bathroom and locked the door so she couldn't get at me; then I wept uncontrollably, lying on the floor with my face against the fluffy pink bath mat. Afterwards I pulled the laundry hamper over so I could stand on it and look into the bathroom mirror. My made-up face had run, there were black streaks down my cheeks like sooty tears and my purple mouth was smudged and swollen. What was the matter with me? It wasn't that I couldn't dance.

My mother pleaded briefly with me through the locked bathroom door, then she threatened. I came out, but I wouldn't eat any dinner: someone besides me would have to suffer. My mother wiped the makeup off my face with Pond's Cold Cream, scolding me because it would have to be done over, and we set out again for the auditorium. (Where was my father? He wasn't there.)

I had to stand enviously in the wings, red-faced and steaming in the hated suit, listening to the preliminary coughs and the scraping of folding chairs, then watching while the butterflies tinkled through the movements I myself had memorized, I was sure, better than any of them. The worst thing was that I still didn't understand quite why this was being done to me, this humiliation disguised as a privilege.

At the right moment Miss Flegg gave me a shove and I lurched onto the stage, trying to look, as she had instructed me, as much like a mothball as possible. Then I danced. There were no steps to my dance, as I hadn't been taught any, so I made it up as I went along. I swung my arms, I bumped into the butterflies, I spun in circles and stamped my feet as hard as I could on the boards of the flimsy stage, until it shook. I threw myself into the part, it was a dance of rage and destruction, tears rolled down my cheeks behind the fur, the butterflies would die; my feet hurt for days afterwards. "This isn't me," I kept saying to myself, "they're making me do it"; yet even though I was concealed in the teddy-bear suit, which flopped about me and made me sweat, I felt naked and exposed, as if this ridiculous dance was the truth about me and everyone could see it.

The butterflies scampered away on cue and much to my surprise I was left in the center of the stage, facing an audience that was not only laughing but applauding vigorously. Even when the beauties, the tiny thin ones, trooped back for their curtsey, the laughter and clapping went on, and several people, who must have been fathers rather than mothers, shouted "Bravo mothball!" It puzzled me that some of them seemed to like my ugly, bulky suit better than the pretty ones of the others.

After the recital Miss Flegg was congratulated on her priceless touch with the mothball. Even my mother appeared pleased. "You did fine," she said, but I still cried that night over my thwarted wings. I would never get a chance to use them now, since I had decided already that much as I loved dancing school I was not going back to it in the fall. It's true I had received more individual attention than the others, but I wasn't sure it was a kind I liked. Besides, who would think of marrying a mothball? A question my mother put to me often, later, in other forms.

Chapter Six

At first, every time I repeated this story to myself, underneath my pillow or inside the refuge of the locked bathroom, it filled me with the same rage, helplessness and sense of betrayal I'd felt at the time. But gradually I came to see it as preposterous, especially when I thought about telling it to anyone else. Instead of denouncing my mother's injustice, they would probably laugh at me. It's hard to feel undiluted sympathy for an overweight seven-year-old stuffed into a mothball suit and forced to dance; the image is simply too ludicrous. But if I described myself as charming and skinny, they would find the whole thing pathetic and grossly unfair. I knew this even when I was ten. If Desdemona was fat who would care whether or not Othello strangled her? Why is it that the girls Nazis torture on the covers of the sleazier men's magazines are always good-looking? The effect would be quite different if they were overweight. The men would find it hilarious instead of immoral or sexually titillating. However, plump unattractive women are just as likely to be tortured as thin ones. More so, in fact.

The year after the dancing school fiasco, when I was eight, we moved from the cramped duplex where we had been living to a slightly bigger house, a bungaloid box near a Loblaws supermarket. It wasn't at all the sort of house my mother pictured as the proper dwelling place for her, but it was better than the fugitive quarters, the rundown apartments and the top floors of old houses she'd had to put up with earlier. This meant a new school and a new neighborhood, and my mother felt that the best way to get me adjusted, as she put it, was to enroll me in Brownies. It was characteristic of her that she didn't choose the nearest Brownies, the one most of the girls in my class actually went to. Instead she picked one farther away, in a better neighborhood, attended by children from different schools entirely. Thus her ploy served none of her purposes. It didn't help to acquaint me with the girls in my own school, the reverse in fact as I had to leave school early on Brownie Tuesdays in order to get there in time; and at the Brownies itself I was an alien from beyond the borders.

To get to this Brownies I had to take the street-car, and to reach the streetcar stop I had to cross one of the many ravines that wound through the city. My mother was terrified of this ravine: it crawled with vines and weedy undergrowth, it was dense with willow trees and bushes, behind every one of which she pictured a lurking pervert, an old derelict rendered insane by rubbing alcohol, a child molester or worse. (Sometimes she called them "exhibitionists," which always caused me to have second thoughts about the Canadian National Exhibition.) Every Tuesday she would give me a lecture about them before I set out for school, wearing, even that early in the morning, my brown uniform and the shoes which I had laboriously polished the evening before. "Don't talk to any bad men," she would say. "If one comes up to you in that ravine, run away as fast as you can." She would deliver this warning during breakfast, in a voice that suggested that no matter how fast I ran I would never be able to get away, I was doomed, and my oatmeal porridge would twist itself into a lump and sink to the bottom of my stomach. She never suggested what these men would look like or what they would do if they caught me, which left the field wide open to my imagination. And the way she put it made me somehow responsible, as if

I myself had planted the bushes in the ravine and concealed the bad men behind them, as if, should I be caught, it would be my own doing.

To cross the ravine you had to walk down a long gravelled hill, then across a wooden bridge, which was quite old. It slanted, and some of the planks had rotted away completely so you could see the ground a long way beneath. Then you had to go up a path on the other side, with the leaves and branches almost touching you, like evil vegetable fingers. I would run down the hill and across the bridge, heavily as a trundled barrel, but by the time I got to the upward climb I would be so out of breath I would have to walk. This was the worst part.

After I had gone a number of times by myself, my mother hit on a solution. Like most of her solutions, it was worse than the problem. She discovered that several other mothers on our side of the bridge had aspirations like her own; or at any rate they'd enrolled their own daughters in the same Brownies. I'd known this for some time but hadn't told her, because these girls were older than I was, they were in higher grades, and they seemed formidable to me. Though we followed the same route to Brownies, I made sure that I walked either a safe distance ahead of them or a safe distance behind, and on the streetcar I kept at least four seats between us. But my mother was a great arranger at that period of her life, and she phoned up the other mothers, who knew about the bad men too, and simply arranged that I was to walk to Brownies with these girls. They made me nervous, but I did feel a little safer crossing the ravine with them.

The trouble was that despite the terrors involved in getting there, I worshiped Brownies, even more than I had worshiped dancing classes. At Miss Flegg's you were supposed to try to be better than everyone else, but at Brownies you were supposed to try to be the same, and I was beginning to find this idea quite attractive. So I liked wearing the same baggy uniform with its odd military beret and tie, learning the same ritual rhymes, handshakes and salutes, and chanting in unison with the others,

> A Brownie gives in to the *older* folk;
> A Brownie does NOT give in to her*self!*

There was even some dancing involved. At the beginning of every session, when the slightly dilapidated papier-mâché toadstool which was the group fetish had been set in place on its grassy-green felt mat, and the gray-haired woman in the blue Guide uniform had said, with a twinkle in her eye, "Hoot! Hoot!" the Brownies would hurtle from the four corners of the room, six at a time, and perform a whirling, frenzied dance, screeching out the words to their group songs as loud as they could. Mine was:

> Here you see the laughing Gnomes,
> Helping mothers in our homes.

This was not strictly true: I didn't help my mother. I wasn't allowed to. On the few occasions I'd attempted it, the results had not pleased her. The only way I could have helped her to her satisfaction would have been to change into someone else, but I didn't know this yet. My mother didn't approve of my tree-form style of making beds, nor of the crashes and fragments when I dried the dishes. She didn't like scraping charcoal off the bottoms of pots when I tried to cook ("a cooked dessert" was one Brownie test requirement), or having to reset the table after I'd done it backwards. At first I tried to surprise her with sudden Good Turns, as suggested in the Brownie handbook. One Sunday I brought her breakfast in bed on a tray, tripped, and covered her with wet cornflakes. I polished her good navy-blue suede shoes with black boot polish. And once I carried out the garbage can, which was too heavy for me, and tipped it down the back steps. She wasn't a very patient woman; she told me quite soon that she would rather do things right herself the first time than have to do them over again for me. She used the word "clumsy," which made me cry; but I was excused from household chores, which I saw as an advantage only much later. I sang out the words unflinchingly though, as I stomped around the toadstool in clouds of church-basement dust, with a damp Gnome hand clutched in each of mine.

The lady who ran the pack was known as Brown Owl; owls, we were told, meant wisdom. I always remembered what she looked like: the dried-apple face, the silvery gray hair, the snapping blue eyes, quick to spot a patch of tarnish on the brass fairy pin or a dirty fingernail or a poorly tied shoelace. Unlike my mother, she was impartial and kind, and she gave points for good intentions. I was entranced by her. It was hard to believe that an adult, older than my mother even, would actually squat on the floor and say things like "Tu-whit, Tu-whoo" and "When Brownies make their fairy ring, They can magic everything!" Brown Owl acted as though she believed all this, and thought that we did too. This was the novelty: someone even more gullible than I was. Occasionally I felt sorry for her, because I knew how much pinching, shoving and nudging went on during Thinking Time and who made faces behind Brown Owl's back when we were saying, "I promise to do my duty to God and the King and to help others every day, especially those at home." Brown Owl had a younger sidekick known as Tawny Owl. Like vice-principals everywhere, she was less deceivable and less beloved.

The three girls with whom I crossed the ravine each Brownie day were called Elizabeth, Marlene and Lynne. They were ten, and almost ready to join the Girl Guides; "flying up," it was called if you had obtained your Golden Wings. Otherwise you had to walk up. Elizabeth was going to fly, no doubt about it: she was plastered with badges like a diplomat's suitcase. Marlene probably would, and Lynne probably wouldn't. Elizabeth was a Sixer and had two stripes on her arm to prove it. Marlene was a Pixie and I can't remember what Lynne was. I admired Elizabeth and feared the other two, who competed for her attention in more or less sinister ways.

At first they tolerated me, on those long perilous walks to the streetcar stop. I had to walk a little behind, but that was a small enough price to pay for protection from the invisible bad men. That went on through September and October, while the leaves turned yellow and fell and were burned in the sidewalk fires that were not yet illegal, during roller skating and skipping, past knee socks and into long stockings and winter coats. The days became shorter, we walked home in the dark across the bridge, which was lit only by one feeble bulb at either end. When it began to snow we had to go into leggings, heavy lined pants that were pulled on over our skirts, causing them to bunch into the crotch, and held up by elastic shoulder straps. In those days girls were not allowed to wear slacks to school.

The memory of this darkness, this winter, the leggings, and the soft snow weighing down the branches of the willow trees in the ravine so that they made a bluish arch over the bridge, the white vista from its edge that should have been so beautiful, I associate with misery. Because by that time Elizabeth and her troop had discovered my secret: they had discovered how easy it was to make me cry. At our school young girls weren't supposed to hit each other or fight or rub snow in each other's faces, and they didn't. During recess they stayed in the Girls' Yard, where everything was whispering and conspiracy. Words were not a prelude to war but the war itself, a devious, subterranean war that was unending because there were no decisive acts, no knockdown blows that could be delivered, no point at which you could say *I give in.* She who cried first was lost.

Elizabeth, Marlene and Lynne were in other grades or they would have found out about me sooner. I was a public sniveller still, at the age of eight; my feelings were easily hurt, despite my mother, who by this time was telling me sharply to act my age. She herself was flint-eyed, distinct, never wavery or moist; it was not until later that I was able to reduce her to tears, a triumph when I finally managed it.

Elizabeth was the leader of the Gnomes, and I was one of her five followers during those dusty Tuesdays of rituals and badges and the sewing on of buttons. It was over knots that I came to grief. We had mastered the reef, and Tawny Owl, who was the knot specialist, had decided we were ready for the clove hitch; so with her lanyard—from the end of which hung a splendid and enviable silver whistle —looped over a chairback, she was demonstrating. I was cross-eyed with concentration, I was watching so hard I didn't see a thing, and when it came my turn to duplicate the magic feat the rope slipped through my fingers like spaghetti and I was left with nothing but a snarl. Tawny Owl did it again, for my benefit, but with no better results.

"Joan, you weren't paying attention," Tawny Owl said.

"But I *was*," I said earnestly.

Tawny Owl huffed up. Unlike Brown Owl, she knew about the things that went on behind her back, which made her suspicious. She took my protest for lippiness. "If you won't cooperate, Gnomes, I'll just have to go over and work with the Pixies. I'm sure they are more interested in learning." And she marched off, taking her whistle with her. Of course I started oozing right away. I hated being falsely accused. I hated being accused accurately too, but injustice was worse.

Elizabeth narrowed her eyes. She was about to say something, but Brown Owl, ever alert, came trotting over and said brightly, "Now, now, Joan, we don't like to see unhappy faces at Brownies; we like to see cheerfulness. Remember, 'Frowns and scowls make ugly things, Smiling gives them fairy wings.'" This only made me cry harder, and I had to be secluded in the cloakroom so as not to embarrass ev-

eryone until I had, as Brown Owl put it, got my
Brownie smile back again. "You must learn to control
yourself," she said kindly, patting me on the beret
as I heaved and choked. She didn't know what a lot
of territory this covered.

That blue-black evening, as we crunched our
way home over the snow, Elizabeth paused under
the last streetlight before the bridge and looked at
the others. Then, without warning, they all took off
down the hill in a flurry of hilarious giggles and disappeared into the darkness of the ravine before I
knew what was happening, shouting back, "The bad
man's gonna getcha!"—abandoning me at the top of
the hill to make the crossing by myself. First I called,
then I ran after them, but they were too far ahead.
I sniffled over the bridge, wiping my mucous nose on
the backs of my mittens and glancing fearfully behind me, though of course no child molester or ex-
posure artist in his right mind would have been
abroad in near-zero weather. They would all have
been lurking in railroad stations or the backs of
churches, but I didn't know this. I heaved my way
up the final hill; they were waiting in ambush at the
top.

"Are you ever a crybaby," Elizabeth said with
scorn and delight, and that set the pattern for the
rest of the year.

The game for the three of them was to think up
ingenious variations. Sometimes they would just run
off; other times they would threaten to run off. Sometimes they would claim that their running off was a
punishment, deserved by me, for something I had
done or hadn't done that day: I had skipped too
heavily in the fairy ring, I hadn't stood straight
enough, my tie was rumpled, I had dirty fingernails,
I was fat. Sometimes they would say they wouldn't
run off, or would swear to come back and get me, if
I would only perform certain acts: I had to crawl
around in the snow, barking like a dog, or throw a
snowball at a passing old lady, whereupon they
would point at me and jeer, "*She* did it! *She* did

it!" Sometimes they would ask me, "What would the bad man do to you if he caught you?" It wasn't enough for me to say I didn't know; they would merely take flight, giggling behind their hands: "She doesn't know, she doesn't know!" I spent half an hour one night standing at the top of the hill, singing over and over in a quavering voice, a hundred times exactly, "We're the Brownies, here's our aim, Lend a hand and play the game," before I realized they weren't going to keep their promise and retrieve me. Once they told me to stick my tongue onto an iron fence on the way down to the ravine, but it wasn't cold enough and my tongue didn't freeze to the fence as they'd hoped.

The funny thing was that though the conditions, directions and demands were issued by Elizabeth, I knew it was the other two who thought them up. Lynne was especially inventive: her position was precarious, she didn't have strength of character, she could so easily turn into me. I couldn't tell my mother about any of this because I felt that whatever she would say, underneath it her sympathies would lie with them. "Stand up for yourself," she would exhort. How could a daughter of hers have turned out to be such a limp balloon?

Sometimes, when they'd left me alone in the darkness and cold, I would stand there almost hoping that the bad man would really come up out of the ravine and do whatever he was fated to do. That way, after I'd been stolen or killed, they would be punished, and they would be forced to repent at last for what they'd done. I imagined him as a tall man, very tall, in a black suit, heaving up out of the snow like an avalanche in reverse, blue-faced and covered with ice, red-eyed, hairy-headed, with long sharp teeth like icicles. He would be frightening but at least he would be an end to this misery that went on and seemed as if it would go on forever. I would be taken away by him, no trace of me would ever be found. Even my mother would be sorry. Once I actually waited for him, counting under my breath—he would come after a hundred, he would come after two hundred—for so long that I was half an hour late for dinner and my mother was furious.

"What have you been doing?" she said.

"Playing," I said, and she told me I was selfish and inconsiderate.

The snow finally changed to slush and then to water, which trickled down the hill of the bridge in two rivulets, one on either side of the path; the path itself turned to mud. The bridge was damp, it smelled rotten, the willow branches turned yellow, the skipping ropes came out. It was light again in the afternoons, and on one of them, when for a change Elizabeth hadn't run off but was merely discussing the possibilities with the others, a real man actually appeared.

He was standing at the far side of the bridge, a little off the path, holding a bunch of daffodils in front of him. He was a nice-looking man, neither old nor young, wearing a good tweed coat, not at all shabby or disreputable. He didn't have a hat on, his taffy-colored hair was receding and the sunlight gleamed on his high forehead. I was walking ahead, as ordered (they liked to keep an eye on me from behind), and the others were deep in their plans, so I saw him first. He smiled at me, I smiled back, and he lifted his daffodils up to reveal his open fly and the strange, ordinary piece of flesh that was nudging flaccidly out of it.

"Look," I said to the others, as if I had just discovered something of interest. They did look, and immediately began to scream and run up the hill. I was so startled—by them, not by him—that I didn't move.

The man looked slightly dismayed. His pleasant smile faded and he turned away, pulling his coat together, and began to walk in the other direction, across the bridge. Then he turned back, made a little bow to me, and handed me the daffodils.

The others were waiting above, clustered a safe

way along the street. "What did he say? What did he do?" they asked. "Don't you know that was a bad man? You sure had the nerve," Elizabeth said grudgingly. For once I had impressed them, though I wasn't sure why; there hadn't been anything frightening about the man, he had smiled. I liked the daffodils too, though I threw them into a ditch before I reached our house. I was astute enough to know that I wouldn't be able to explain where I'd got them in a way my mother would approve of.

On the walk home from the next Brownie meeting the girls were especially nice to me, and I thought that now, after my long probation, I was going to become their friend. That seemed to be true, because Elizabeth said, "Would you like to be in our club? We have a club, you know." This was the first I'd heard of it, though clubs were popular at school, but yes, of course I wanted to be in it. "You have to go through the ceremony first," Marlene said. "It isn't hard."

We knew all about ceremonies, Brownies was full of them, and I think they got some of the details of what followed from the joining-up ritual, in which you were led across cardboard stepping stones that read CHEERFULNESS, OBEDIENCE, GOOD TURNS and SMILES. You then had to close your eyes and be turned around three times, while the pack chanted,

> Twist me and turn me and show me the elf,
> I looked in the water and there saw . . .

Here you were supposed to open your eyes, look into the enchanted pool, which was a hand-mirror surrounded by plastic flowers and ceramic bunnies, and say, "Myself." The magic word.

So when Elizabeth said, "Close your eyes," I closed them. Marlene and Lynne each took one of my hands, and I felt something soft being tied across my eyes. Then they took me downhill, warning me when there was a hole or a rock. I felt the bridge under my feet and they turned me around several times, then back, so I no longer knew which way I was facing. I started to be frightened.

"I don't want to join the club," I said, but Elizabeth said reassuringly, "Sure you do, you'll like it," and they led me farther on. "Stand over here," Elizabeth said, and a hard surface came up against my back. "Now put your hands at your sides." I felt something being passed around each of my arms, then around my body, and pulled tight.

"Now," said Elizabeth, still in the same soothing voice, "we're going to leave you here for the bad man." The other two started to giggle uncontrollably, and I could hear them running off. Now I knew where I was: they had tied me with Elizabeth's skipping rope to the post at the end of the bridge, right where we had seen the man the week before. I started to whimper.

Then I stopped. I knew they were probably watching to see what I would do, so I decided for a change to do nothing. Surreptitiously I wriggled my arms to find out if I could get free. They had pulled the rope quite tight enough, so I would simply wait until they got bored with it and came to untie me. I knew they couldn't just leave me there: that would be going too far. When I didn't show up my mother would phone their mothers and they would get hell.

At first I could hear them faintly, tittering among themselves at the top of the hill, and once they called down, "How do ya like the club?" I didn't answer; at last I was tired of them. But after a while I could hear nothing but the repetitive singing of the birds from the ravine below, and then it started to get colder. They must have gone away, intending to come back later, and forgotten about me.

I was snivelling to myself and struggling in the ropes with rising desperation, trying to get one hand across to the other so I could slip the loop down and off, when I heard footsteps coming towards me across the bridge. I froze: maybe it was one of the bad kind, maybe something horrible would finally happen, though I can't have been a very exciting sex-

ual object, a fat, snotty-nosed eight-year-old in a
Brownie outfit. But a voice said, "What's this?" and
the blindfold was lifted off my eyes. (It was Marlene's Brownie tie.)

The man was neither old nor young; he was
wearing a tweed coat and carrying a newspaper under his arm. He smiled at me, and I couldn't tell at
all whether or not it was the man from the week
before, because he had a hat on. I had looked most
at the balding head and the daffodils. This man, unlike the other, was smoking a pipe. "Got all tied up,
did you?" he asked as I looked up at him with dubious, swollen eyes. He knelt and undid the knots.

"Those are good knots," he said. He asked me
where I lived and I told him. "I'll take you home,"
he said. I said it was all right, I knew where I lived,
but he said it was getting dark and little girls should
not be running around by themselves after dark. He
took my hand and we started to walk up the hill
together.

But suddenly my mother was hurrying down towards us. Her hair was flying, she did not have gloves
on, and when she came closer I could see that she
was enraged. I dodged behind the man's tweed coat
but she wrenched me out and slapped me across
the face. She had never done this before.

"What have you been up to?" she said. I said
nothing; I stood and glared at her, I didn't cry, and
this impressed her as even more unnatural. I'd decided I was through crying in public, though of
course I wasn't.

At this point the man interceded. He explained
how he had found me tied up and how he had untied
me and offered to see me home. My mother then became overly gracious, as she usually was with adults.
They shook hands and she led me off. She phoned up
the other mothers, full of moral indignation, and
that was it for Brownies. It was too bad, because I
really did like it. Brown Owl was one of the most
pleasant women I had encountered so far, besides
Aunt Lou, and I missed her.

My mother used this incident as an example of my own fecklessness and general lack of wisdom. "You were stupid to let the other girls fool you like that," she said.

"I thought they were my friends," I said.

"Friends wouldn't tie you up like that, would they? And in that ravine. Who knows what might have happened to you. You could've been killed. You were just lucky that nice man came along and untied you when he did, that's all."

"Mother," I said solemnly, eager to redeem myself in some way but unsure how to do it—perhaps by demonstrating that she was wrong?—"I think that was a bad man."

"Don't be an idiot," she said. "That nice man?"

"I think he was the same one. The daffodil man."

"What daffodil man?" she asked. "What have you been doing?"

"Nothing," I said, backpedaling frantically; but it was too late, the first worm was out of the can and the rest had to follow. My mother was not pleased. In addition to everything else, I was now accused of sneaking around behind her back: I should have told her immediately.

I still wasn't sure, though: was it the daffodil man or not? Was the man who untied me a rescuer or a villain? Or, an even more baffling thought: was it possible for a man to be both at once?

I turned this puzzle over in my mind time after time, trying to remember and piece together the exact features of the daffodil man. But he was elusive, he melted and changed his shape like butterscotch or warm gum, dissolving into a tweedy mist, sending out menacing tentacles of flesh and knotted rope, forming again as a joyful sunburst of yellow flowers.

Chapter Seven

One of the bad dreams I used to have about my mother was this. I would be walking across the bridge and she would be standing in the sunlight on the other side of it, talking to someone else, a man whose face I couldn't see. When I was halfway across, the bridge would start to collapse, as I'd always feared it would. Its rotten planks buckled and split, it tilted over sideways and began to topple slowly into the ravine. I would try to run but it would be too late, I would throw myself down and grab onto the far edge as it rose up, trying to slide me off. I called out to my mother, who could still have saved me, she could have run across quickly and reached out her hand, she could have pulled me back with her to firm ground— But she didn't do this, she went on with her conversation, she didn't notice that anything unusual was happening. She didn't even hear me.

In the other dream I would be sitting in a corner of my mother's bedroom, watching her put on her makeup. I did this often as a small child: it was considered a treat, a privilege, by both my mother and myself, and refusing to let me watch was one of my mother's ways of punishing me. She knew I was fascinated by her collection of cosmetics and implements: lipsticks, rouges, perfume in dainty bottles which I longed to have, bright red nail polish (sometimes, as an exceptional bribe, I was allowed to have some brushed on my toes, but never on my fingers: "You're not old enough," she'd say), little tweezers, nail files and emery boards. I was forbidden to touch any of these things. Of course I did, when she was out, but they were arranged in such rigid rows both on the dressertop and in the drawers that I had to be very careful to put them back exactly where I'd found them. My mother had a hawk's eye for anything out of place. I later extended this habit of snooping through her drawers and cupboards until I knew everything that each of them contained; finally I would do it not to satisfy my curiosity—I already knew everything—but for the sense of danger. I only got caught twice, early on: once when I ate a lipstick (even then, at the age of four, I was wise enough to replace the cover on the tube and the tube in the drawer, and to wash my mouth carefully; how did she know it was me?), and once when I couldn't resist covering my entire face with blue eye shadow, to see how I would look blue. That got me exiled for weeks. I almost gave the whole game away the day I found a curious object, like a rubber clamshell, packed away neatly in a box. I was dying to ask her what it was, but I didn't dare.

"Sit there quietly, Joan, and watch Mother put on her face," she'd say on the good days. Then she would tuck a towel around her neck and go to work. Some of the things she did seemed to be painful; for instance, she would cover the space between her eyebrows with what looked like brown glue, which she heated in a little pot, then tear it off, leaving a red patch; and sometimes she'd smear herself with pink mud which would harden and crack. She often frowned at herself, shaking her head as if she was dissatisfied; and occasionally she'd talk to herself as if she'd forgotten I was there. Instead of making her happier, these sessions appeared to make her sadder, as if she saw behind or within the mirror some fleeting image she was unable to capture or duplicate; and when she was finished she was always a little cross.

I would stare at the proceedings, fascinated and mute. I thought my mother was very beautiful, even more beautiful when she was colored in. And this was what I did in the dream: I sat and stared. Although her vanity tables became more grandiose as my father got richer, my mother always had a triple mirror, so she could see both sides as well as the front of her head. In the dream, as I watched, I suddenly

realized that instead of three reflections she had three
actual heads, which rose from her toweled shoulders
on three separate necks. This didn't frighten me, as
it seemed merely a confirmation of something I'd always known; but outside the door there was a man,
a man who was about to open the door and come in.
If he saw, if he found out the truth about my mother,
something terrible would happen, not only to my
mother but to me. I wanted to jump up, run to the
door, and stop him, but I couldn't move and the
door would swing slowly inward. . . .

As I grew older, this dream changed. Instead of
wanting to stop the mysterious man, I would sit there
wishing for him to enter. I wanted him to find out
her secret, the secret that I alone knew: my mother
was a monster.

I can never remember calling her anything but
Mother, never one of those childish diminutives; I
must have, but she must have discouraged it. Our
relationship was professionalized early. She was to be
the manager, the creator, the agent; I was to be the
product. I suppose one of the most important things
she wanted from me was gratitude. She wanted me to
do well, but she wanted to be responsible for it.

Her plans for me weren't specific. They were
vague but large, so that whatever I did accomplish
was never the right thing. But she didn't push all the
time; for days and even weeks she would seem to
forget me altogether. She would become involved in
some other project of hers, like redecorating her bedroom or throwing a party. She even took a couple of
jobs: she was a travel agent, for instance, and she
once worked for an interior decorator, searching out
lamps and carpets that would match living-room col-
or designs. But none of these jobs lasted long, she
would get discouraged, they weren't enough for her
and she would quit.

It wasn't that she was aggressive and ambitious,
although she was both these things. Perhaps she wasn't
aggressive or ambitious enough. If she'd ever decided
what she really wanted to do and had gone out and

done it, she wouldn't have seen me as a reproach to her, the embodiment of her own failure and depression, a huge edgeless cloud of inchoate matter which refused to be shaped into anything for which she could get a prize.

In the image of her that I carried for years, hanging from my neck like an iron locket, she was sitting in front of her vanity table, painting her fingernails a murderous red and sighing. Her lips were thin but she made a larger mouth with lipstick over and around them, like Bette Davis, which gave her a curious double mouth, the real one showing through the false one like a shadow. She was an attractive woman, even into her late thirties, she had kept her figure, she had been popular in her youth. In her photograph album there were snapshots of her in party dresses and bathing suits, with various young men, her looking at the camera, the young men looking at her. One young man recurred often, in white flannels, with a big motor car. She said she'd been engaged to him, more or less.

There were no pictures of her as a girl though, none of her parents, none of the two brothers and the sister I later found out she had. She almost never talked about her family or her early life, though I was able to piece a little of it together. Her parents had both been very strict, very religious. They hadn't been rich; her father had been a stationmaster for the CPR. She'd done something that offended them— what it was I never learned—and she'd run away from home at the age of sixteen and never gone back. She'd worked at various jobs, clerking in Kresge's, waitressing. When she was eighteen she'd been a waitress at a resort in Muskoka, which was where she later met my father. The young men in the pictures were guests at the resort. She could only wear the party dresses and the bathing suits on her day off.

My father hadn't been staying at the resort; it wasn't the kind of thing he would do. He met my mother by accident, when he'd dropped by to visit a

friend. There were a couple of pictures of them before the wedding, in which my father looked embarrassed. My mother held his arm as if it were a leash.
Then the wedding portrait. After that some photos
of my mother alone, which my father must have
taken. Then nothing but me, drooling on rugs, eating
stuffed animals or fists; my father had gone off to the
war, leaving her pregnant, with nobody to take pictures of her.

My father didn't come back until I was five, and
before that he was only a name, a story which my
mother would tell me and which varied considerably.
Sometimes he was a nice man who was coming home
soon, bringing with him all kinds of improvements
and delightful surprises: we would live in a bigger
house, eat better, have more clothes, and the landlord
would be put in his place once and for all. At other
times, when I was getting out of hand, he was retri-
bution personified, the judgment day that would catch
up with me at last; or (and I think this was closest
to her true feelings) he was a heartless wretch who
had abandoned her, leaving her to cope with everything all by herself. The day he finally returned I
was almost beside myself, torn between hope and
fear: what would he bring me, what would he do to
me? Was he a bad man or a nice man? (My mother's
two categories: nice men did things for you, bad men
did things to you.) But when the time came, a stranger walked through the door, kissed my mother and
then me, and sat down at the table. He seemed very
tired and said little. He brought nothing and did nothing, and that remained his pattern.

Most of the time he was simply an absence. Occasionally, though, he would stroll back into reality
from wherever he had been, and he even had his moments of modest drama. I was thirteen, it must have
been 1955, it was a Sunday. I was sitting in the
kitchenette, eating half of an orange layer cake, for
which I would later be scolded. But I'd already eaten
one piece and I knew the number of words for that
one piece would be as great as for half a cake, so I

ate on, speedily, trying to get it all down before being discovered.

By this time I was eating steadily, doggedly, stubbornly, anything I could get. The war between myself and my mother was on in earnest; the disputed territory was my body. I didn't quite know this though I sensed it in a hazy way; but I reacted to the diet booklets she left on my pillow, to the bribes of dresses she would give me if I would reduce to fit them—formal gowns with layers of tulle and wired busts, perky little frocks, skirts with slim waists and frothy crinolines—to her cutting remarks about my size, to her pleas about my health (I would die of a heart attack, I would get high blood pressure), to the specialists she sent me to and the pills they prescribed, to all of these things, with another Mars Bar or a double helping of french fries. I swelled visibly, relentlessly, before her very eyes, I rose like dough, my body advanced inch by inch towards her across the dining-room table, in this at least I was undefeated. I was five feet four and still growing, and I weighed a hundred and eighty-two pounds.

Anyway: I was sitting in the kitchenette, eating half of an orange layer cake. It was a Sunday in 1955. My father was in the living room, sitting in an easy chair reading a murder mystery, his favorite way of relaxing. My mother was on the chesterfield, pretending to read a book on child psychology—she put in a certain amount of time demonstrating that, God knew, she was doing her best—but actually reading *The Fox*, an historical novel about the Borgias. I had already finished it, in secret. The chesterfield had a diminutive purple satin cushion at either end, and these two cushions were sacrosanct, ritual objects which were not to be moved. The chesterfield itself was dull pink, a nubby material shot through with silver threads. It had a covering of transparent plastic, which was removed for entertaining. The rug, which picked up the purple of the cushions, was also covered with a sheet of plastic, heavier in texture. The lampshades were protected with cellophane. On each of my father's feet was a slipper of maroon leather. My mother's feet and my own were similarly encased, as by this time my mother had made it a rule that no shoes were to be allowed inside the house. It was a new house and she had just finished getting it into shape; now that it was finally right she didn't want anything touched, she wanted it static and dustless and final, until that moment when she would see what a mistake she had made and the painters or movers would arrive once more, trailing disruption.

(My mother didn't want her living rooms to be different from everyone else's, or even very much better. She wanted them to be acceptable, the same as everybody else's, although her idea of everybody else changed as my father's salary increased. Perhaps this was why they looked like museum displays or, more accurately, like the show windows of Eaton's and Simpson's, those magic downtown palaces I would approach, with Aunt Lou, every December along a vista of streetcar tracks. We didn't go to see the furniture though, we were heading for the other windows, where animals, fairies and red-cheeked dwarfs twirled mechanically to the sound of tinkle bells. When I was old enough to go Christmas shopping it was Aunt Lou who took me. One year I announced I wasn't going to get my mother a Christmas present. "But, dear," Aunt Lou said, "you'll hurt her feelings." I didn't think she had any, but I gave in and bought her some bubble bath, enclosed in a lovely pink squeezable swan. She never used it, but I knew in advance she wouldn't. I ended up using it myself.)

I finished the slab of leftover cake and rose to my feet, my stomach bumping the table. My slippers were large and furry; they made my feet look twice as big. I clomped in them sullenly through the dining room, into the living room and past my parents and their books, without saying anything. I had developed the habit of clomping silently but very visibly through rooms in which my mother was sitting; it was a sort of fashion show in reverse, it was a display, I wanted her to see and recognize what little effect her nagging and pleas were having.

I intended to go into the hall, then up the stairs with a sasquatch-like, banister-shaking tread, and along the hall to my room, where I was going to put on an Elvis Presley record and turn the volume up just loud enough so she would repress the desire to complain. She was beginning to worry about her ability to communicate with me. I didn't have any intentional plans, I was merely acting according to a dimly felt, sluggish instinct. I was aware only of a wish to hear "Heartbreak Hotel" at the maximum volume possible without reprisals.

But when I was halfway across the room there was a sudden pounding at the front door. Someone was hammering on it with balled fists; then there was the thud of a hurled body and a hoarse voice, a man's voice, screaming, "I'll kill you! You bastard, I'll kill you!"

I froze. My father leapt from his chair and doubled over in a kind of wrestler's crouch. My mother put a bookmark between the pages of her book and closed it; then she removed her reading glasses, which she wore on a silver chain around her neck, and looked at my father with irritation. It was obviously his fault: who would call her a bastard? My father straightened up and went to the door.

"Oh, it's you, Mr. Currie," he said. "I'm glad to see you're up and about again."

"I'll sue you," the voice shouted. "I'll sue you within an inch of your life! Why couldn't you just leave me alone? You've ruined everything!" The voice broke into long, raucous sobs.

"You're a little upset right now," my father's voice said.

The other voice wept, "You messed it up! I did it right this time and you messed it up! I don't want to live. . . ."

"Life is a gift," my father said with quiet dignity but a slight edge of reprimand, like the kindly dentist who demonstrated about cavities on the television set we'd acquired two years before. "You should be grateful for it. You should respect it."

"What do you know?" the voice roared. Then there was a scuffling sound and the voice receded into the distance, trailing muffled words behind it like a string of bubbles underwater. My father shut the door quietly and came back to the living room.

"I don't know why you do it," my mother said. "They're never grateful."

"Do what?" I said, bulgy-eyed, breaking my vow of silence in my eagerness to know. I had never heard a man cry before and the knowledge that they sometimes did was electrifying.

"When people try to kill themselves," my mother said, "your father brings them to life again."

"Not always, Frances," my father said sadly.

"Often enough," my mother said, opening her book. "I'm tired of getting abusive phone calls in the middle of the night. I really wish you would stop."

My father was an anesthetist at the Toronto General Hospital. He had studied to be one at my mother's urging, as she felt specialization was the coming thing, everyone said that specialists did better than family doctors. She had even been willing to make the necessary financial sacrifices while he was training. But I thought all my father did was put people to sleep before operations. I didn't know about this resurrectionist side of his personality.

"Why do people try to kill themselves?" I asked. "How do you bring them to life again?"

My father ignored the first part of this question, it was far too complicated for him. "I'm testing experimental methods," he said. "They don't always work. But they only give me the hopeless cases, when they've tried everything else." Then he said, to my mother rather than to me, "You'd be surprised how many of them are glad. That they've been able to . . . come back, have another chance."

"Well," said my mother, "I only wish the ones

who aren't so glad would keep it to themselves. It's a waste of time, if you ask me. They'll simply try all over again. If they were serious they'd just stick a gun in their mouth and pull the trigger. That takes the chance out of it."

"Not everyone," said my father, "has your determination."

Two years later, I learned something else about my father. We were in another house, with a bigger dining room, wood-paneled and impressive. My mother was having a dinner party, entertaining two couples whom she claimed privately to dislike. According to her, it was necessary to have them to dinner because they were my father's colleagues, important men at the hospital, and she was trying to help him with his career. She paid no attention when he said that it didn't matter one iota to his career whether she had these people to dinner or not; she went ahead and did it anyway. When she finally realized he'd been telling the truth, she stopped giving dinner parties and began drinking a little more heavily. But she must have already started by this evening, for which I can remember the menu: chicken breasts in cream sauce with wild rice and mushrooms, individual jellied salads with cranberries and celery, topped with mayonnaise, Duchess potatoes, and a complex dessert with mandarin oranges, ginger sauce and some kind of sherbet.

I was in the kitchen. I was fifteen, and I'd reached my maximum growth: I was five feet eight and I weighed two hundred and forty-five, give or take a few pounds. I no longer attended my mother's dinner parties; she was tired of having a teenaged daughter who looked like a beluga whale and never opened her mouth except to put something into it. I cluttered up her gracious-hostess act. On my side, much as I would have welcomed the chance to embarrass her, strangers were different, they saw my obesity as an unfortunate handicap, like a hump or a club foot, rather than the refutation, the victory it was, and watching myself reflected in their eyes shook my confidence. It was only in relation to my mother that I derived a morose pleasure from my weight; in relation to everyone else, including my father, it made me miserable. But I couldn't stop.

I was in the kitchen then, eavesdropping through the passageway and devouring spare parts and leftovers. They had reached the dessert, so I was making away with the extra chicken and cranberry salads and Duchess potatoes, and listening to the conversation in the other room halfheartedly, as if to a tepid radio drama. One of the visiting doctors had been in the war, mostly in Italy as it turned out; the other one had enlisted but had never made it farther than England. Then of course there was my father, who apart from acknowledging that he had been over there too, never said much about it. I'd listened in on conversations like this before and they didn't interest me. From the war movies I'd seen, there was nothing much for women to do in wars except the things they did anyway.

The man who had served in Italy finished recounting one of his exploits, and after a chorus of ruminative murmurs, asked, "Where were you stationed, Phil?"

"Oh, um," said my father.

"In France," my mother said.

"Oh, you mean after the invasion," said the other man.

"No," said my mother, and giggled; a danger sign. She had taken to giggling during dinner parties lately. The giggle, which had a bleary, uncontrolled quality, had replaced the high, gay company laugh she used to wield as purposefully as a baseball bat.

"Oh," said the Italy man politely, "what were you doing?"

"Killing people," said my mother promptly and with relish, as if she were enjoying a private joke.

"Fran," said my father. It was a warning, but the tone was also imploring; something new and rare. I was gnawing the last shreds off the carcass of a breast, but I stopped in order to listen more closely.

"Well, everyone kills a few people in a war, I guess," said the second man.

"Up close?" said my mother. "I bet you didn't kill them up close."

There was a silence, of the kind that comes into a room when everyone knows that something exciting and probably unpleasant is going to happen. I could picture my mother looking around at the attentive faces, avoiding my father's eyes.

"He was in Intelligence," she said importantly. "You wouldn't think it to look at him, would you? They dropped him in behind the lines and he worked with the French underground. You wouldn't ever hear it from him, but he can speak French like a native; he gets it from his last name."

"My," said one of the women, "I've always wanted to go to Paris. Is it as beautiful as they say?"

"His job was to kill the people they thought were fakes," my mother continued. "He had to just take them out and shoot them. In cold blood. Sometimes he wouldn't even know if he'd shot the right one. Isn't that something?" Her voice was thrilled and admiring. "The funny thing is, he doesn't like me to mention it . . . the funny thing is, he told me once that the frightening thing about it was, he started to *enjoy* it."

One of the men laughed nervously. I got up and retreated on my furry slippered feet to the stairs (I could walk quietly enough when I wanted to) and lowered myself down halfway up. Sure enough, a moment later my father marched through the swinging door into the kitchen, followed by my mother. She must have realized she had pushed it too far.

"There's nothing *wrong* with it," she said. "It was in a good cause. You never make the most of yourself."

"I asked you not to talk about it," my father said. He sounded very angry, enraged. It was the first time I realized he could feel rage; he was usually very calm. "You have no idea what it was like."

"I think it's great," said my mother, earnestly.

"It took real courage, I don't see what's wrong
with. . . ."

"Shut up," said my father.

Those are stories from later; earlier he wasn't
there, which is probably why I remember him as
nicer than my mother. And after that he was busy
studying, he was someone who was not to be disturbed, and then he was at the hospital a lot. He
didn't know quite what to make of me, ever; though I
never felt he was hostile, only bemused.

The few things we did together were wordless
things. Such as: he took to growing house plants—
vines and spider plants and ferns and begonias. He
liked to tinker with them, snipping off cuttings and
repotting and planting, on Saturday afternoons if he
had the free time, listening to the Texaco Company
Metropolitan Opera broadcasts on the radio, and he
would let me help him with the plants. As he never
said much of anything, I would pretend his voice was
the voice of Milton Cross, kindly and informed, describing the singers' costumes and the passionate,
tragic and preposterous events in which they were
involved. There he would be, puffing away on the
pipe he took up after he quit cigarettes, poking at his
house plants and conversing to me about lovers being
stabbed or abandoned or betrayed, about jealousy
and madness, about unending love triumphing over
the grave; and then those chilling voices would drift
into the room, raising the hair on the back of my neck,
as if he had evoked them. He was a conjuror of spirits, a shaman with the voice of a dry, detached old
opera commentator in a tuxedo. Or that's how I
imagined him sounding, when I thought up the conversations I would have liked to have had with him
but never did. I wanted him to tell me the truth
about life, which my mother would not tell me and
which he must have known something about, as he
was a doctor and had been in the war, he'd killed people and raised the dead. I kept waiting for him to give
me some advice, warn me, instruct me, but he never

did any of these things. Perhaps he felt as if I weren't really his daughter; he'd seen me for the first time five years after I was born, and he treated me more like a colleague than a daughter, more like an accomplice. But what was our conspiracy? Why hadn't he come back on leave during those five years? A question my mother asked also. Why did they both act as though he owed my mother something?

Then there were those other conversations I overheard. I used to go into the upstairs bathroom, lock the door, and turn on the tap so they would think I was brushing my teeth. Then I would arrange the bath mat on the floor so my knees wouldn't get cold, put my head into the toilet, and listen to them through the pipes. It was almost a direct line to the kitchen, where they had most of their fights, or rather my mother had them. She was a lot easier to hear than my father.

"Why don't you try doing something with her for a change, she's your daughter, too. I'm really at the end of my rope."

My father: silence.

"You don't know what it was like, all alone with her to bring up while you were over there enjoying yourself."

My father: "I didn't enjoy myself."

And once: "It's not as though I wanted to have her. It's not as though I wanted to marry you. I had to make the best of a bad job if you ask me."

My father: "I'm sorry it hasn't worked out for you."

And once, when she was very angry: "You're a doctor, don't tell me you couldn't have done something."

My father: (inaudible).

"Don't give me that crap, you killed a lot of people. Sacred my foot."

At first I was shocked, mainly by my mother's use of the word *crap*. She tried so hard to be a lady in front of other people, even me. Later I tried to figure out what she'd meant, and when she'd say, "If it wasn't for me you wouldn't be here," I didn't believe her.

I ate to defy her, but I also ate from panic. Sometimes I was afraid I wasn't really there, I was an accident; I'd heard her call me an accident. Did I want to become solid, solid as a stone so she wouldn't be able to get rid of me? What had I done? Had I trapped my father, if he really was my father, had I ruined my mother's life? I didn't dare to ask.

For a while I wanted to be an opera singer. Even though they were fat they could wear extravagant costumes, nobody laughed at them, they were loved and praised. Unfortunately I couldn't sing. But it always appealed to me: to be able to stand up there in front of everyone and shriek as loud as you could, about hatred and love and rage and despair, scream at the top of your lungs and have it come out music. That would be something.

Chapter Eight

"Sometimes I think you haven't got a brain in your head," my mother used to say. When I was crying, for some invalid reason or other. To her mind, tears were an evidence of stupidity. I'll give you something to cry about. That's nothing to cry about. Don't cry over spilled milk.

"I'm lonely," I told her. "I don't have anyone to play with."

"Play with your dolls," she said, outlining her mouth.

I did play with them, those crotchless frizzy-haired plastic goddesses, with their infantile eyes and their breasts that emerged and receded gently as knees, unalarming, devoid of nipples. I dressed them up for social events they never attended, undressed them again and stared at them, wishing they would come alive. They were chaste, unloved, widowed: in those days there were no male dolls. They danced by themselves or stood against the wall, catatonic.

When I was nine I tried for a dog. I knew I wouldn't get one but I was softening her up for a kitten; I'd been offered one by a girl at school whose cat had six, one with seven toes on each foot. This was the one I wanted. What I really wanted was a baby sister but this was out of the question, and even I knew it. I'd heard her say over the phone that one was more than enough. (Why wasn't she happier? Why could I never make her laugh?)

"Who would feed it?" my mother asked. "Three times a day."

"I would," I said.

"You wouldn't," my mother said, "you don't come home for lunch." Which was true, I took my lunch to school in a lunch box.

With the kitten it was house-training and scratching the furniture. Next I tried a turtle; there didn't seem much that could go wrong with a turtle, but my mother said it would be smelly.

"No it wouldn't," I said, "they've got one at school and it doesn't smell."

"It would get lost behind the furniture," my mother said, "and starve to death."

She wouldn't hear of a guinea pig or a hamster or even a bird. Finally after nearly a year of failures I backed her into a corner. I asked for a fish. It would be noiseless, odorless, germ-free and clean; after all, it lived in water. I wanted it to have a bowl with colored pebbles and a miniature castle.

She couldn't think of any good reason why not, so she gave in and I bought a goldfish at Kresge's. "It will only die," my mother said. "Those cheap goldfish all have diseases." But when I'd had it a week she did give in enough to ask me its name. I was sitting with my eye against the glass, watching it as it swam up to the top and back down again, burping out pieces of its food.

"Susan Hayward," I said. I had just seen *With a Song in My Heart*, in which Susan Hayward made a comeback from a wheelchair. The odds were stacked against this goldfish and I wanted it to have a courageous name. It died anyway; my mother said it was my fault, I overfed it. Then she flushed it down the toilet before I had a chance to weep over it and bury it properly. I wanted to replace it but my mother said that surely I had learned my lesson. I was always supposed to be learning some lesson or other.

My mother said movies were vulgar, though I suspected she'd once gone to a lot of them; otherwise how would she know about Joan Crawford? So it was my Aunt Lou who took me to see Susan Hayward. "There, you see?" she said to me afterwards. "Red hair can be very glamorous."

Aunt Lou was tall and heavy and built like an Eaton's Catalog corset ad for the mature figure, but she didn't seem to mind. She piled her graying yellowish hair onto the top of her head and stuck extravagant hats with feathers and bows onto the mound with pearl hatpins and wore bulky fur coats and heavy tweeds, which made her look even taller and fatter. In one of my earliest memories of her I'm sitting on her wide, woolly lap—hers was the only lap I remember sitting on, and my mother would say, "Get down, Joan, don't bother your Aunt Louisa"—and stroking the fur of the fox she wore around her neck. This was a real fox, it was brown, it wasn't as mangy as it later became; it had a tail and four paws, black beady eyes and a cool plastic nose, though underneath its nose, instead of a lower jaw, it had a clamp by which it held its tail in place. Aunt Lou would open and shut the clamp and pretend that the fox was talking. It often revealed secrets, such as where Aunt Lou had hidden the gumdrops she had brought me, and it asked important questions also, like what I wanted for Christmas. When I grew older this game was dropped, but Aunt Lou still kept the fox in her closet, although it had gone out of style.

Aunt Lou took me to the movies a lot. She loved

them, especially the ones that made you cry; she didn't think a movie was much good unless it made you cry. She rated pictures as two-Kleenex, three-Kleenex or four-Kleenex ones, like the stars in restaurant guides. I wept also, and these binges of approved sniveling were among the happiest moments of my childhood.

First there was the delightful feeling of sneaking out on my mother; for although she claimed to give her consent when I asked permission, I knew she didn't really. Then we would take the streetcar or a bus to the theater. In the lobby we would stock up on pocket-packs of Kleenex, popcorn and candy bars; then we would settle down in the furry, soothing darkness for several hours of guzzling and sniffling, as the inflated heroines floating before us on the screen were put through the wringer.

I suffered along with sweet, patient June Allyson as she lived through the death of Glenn Miller; I ate three boxes of popcorn while Judy Garland tried to cope with an alcoholic husband, and five Mars Bars while Eleanor Parker, playing a crippled opera singer, groped her mournful way through *Interrupted Melody*. But the one I liked best was *The Red Shoes*, with Moira Shearer as a ballet dancer torn between her career and her husband. I adored her: not only did she have red hair and an entrancing pair of red satin slippers to match, she also had beautiful costumes, and she suffered more than anyone. I munched faster and faster as she became more and more entangled in her dilemma—I wanted those things too, I wanted to dance and be married to a handsome orchestra conductor, both at once—and when she finally threw herself in front of a train I let out a bellowing snort that made people three rows ahead turn around indignantly. Aunt Lou took me to see it four times.

I saw a number of *Adult* pictures long before I was an adult, but no one ever questioned my age. I was quite fat by this time and all fat women look the same, they all look forty-two. Also, fat women are not more noticeable than thin women; they're less noticeable, because people find them distressing and look away. To the ushers and the ticket sellers I must've appeared as a huge featureless blur. If I'd ever robbed a bank no witness would have been able to describe me accurately.

We would come out of the movie red-eyed, our shoulders still heaving, but with a warm feeling of accomplishment. Then we would go for a soda or two or for a snack at Aunt Lou's apartment—grilled crab-meat sandwiches with mayonnaise, cold chicken salad. She kept a number of these things in her refrigerator or in cans on her cupboard shelves. Her apartment building was an older one, with dark wood trim and large rooms. The furniture was dark and large, too, frequently dusty and always cluttered: newspapers on the chesterfield, afghan shawls on the floor, odd shoes or stockings under the chairs, dishes in the sink. To me this disorder meant you could do what you liked. I imitated it in my own bedroom, scattering clothes and books and chocolate-bar wrappers over the surfaces so carefully planned by my mother, the dressing table with the sprigged muslin flounce, bedspread to match, rug in harmony. This was the only form of interior decoration I ever did, and the drawback was that sooner or later it had to be cleaned up.

When we'd had our snack Aunt Lou would pour herself a drink, slip off her shoes, settle into one of her podgy chairs, and ask me questions in her rasping voice. She actually seemed interested in what I had to say, and she didn't laugh when I told her I wanted to be an opera singer.

One of my mother's ways of dismissing Aunt Lou was to say that she was bitter and frustrated because she didn't have a husband, but if this was true Aunt Lou kept it well hidden. To me she seemed a lot less bitter and frustrated than my mother, who, now that she'd achieved and furnished her ultimate house, was concentrating more and more of her energy on forcing me to reduce. She really did try everything. When I refused to take the pills or stick to the diets—

neatly drawn up by her, with menus for every day of
the week listing the number of calories—she sent me
to a psychiatrist.

"I like being fat," I told him, and burst into
tears. He sat looking at me with the tips of his fingers
together, smiling benevolently but with a trace of disgust as I gasped and puffed.

"Don't you want to get married?" he asked when
I had subsided. This started me off afresh, but the
next time I saw Aunt Lou I asked her, "Didn't you
want to get married?"

She gave one of her raucous laughs. She was sitting in her overstuffed easy chair, drinking a martini.
"Oh, I was married, dear," she said. "Didn't I ever
tell you?"

I'd always assumed Aunt Lou was an old maid
because her last name was the same as my father's,
Delacourt, pronounced *Delacore*. "French nobility, no
doubt," said Aunt Lou. Her great-grandfather had
been a farmer, before he decided to improve himself.
He got into the railroad, she said, on the ground floor,
sold the farm to do it; that was how the family made
its money. "They were all crooks, of course," Aunt Lou
said, sipping at her drink, "but nobody called it that."

It turned out Aunt Lou had been married at nineteen, to a man eight years her senior, of good social
standing and approved by the family. Unfortunately
he was a compulsive gambler. "In one pocket and
out the other," she wheezed, "but what did I know? I
was madly in love with him, dear, he was tall, dark
and handsome." I began to see why she liked the
kind of movies she did: they were a lot like her own
life. "I tried, dear, I really did, but it was no use.
He would be gone for days on end, and it wasn't as
though I knew anything about running a house or
managing money. I'd never shopped for food in my
life; all I knew was you picked up the phone and
someone brought it to your house in a box. The first
week I was married I ordered a pound of everything:
one pound of flour, one pound of salt, one pound of
pepper, one pound of sugar. I thought that was what

you were supposed to do. The pepper lasted years."
Aunt Lou's laugh sounded like an enraged walrus.
She liked telling jokes on herself, but sometimes it
made her choke. "Then he'd come back and if he'd
lost he'd tell me how much he loved me, if he'd won
he'd complain about being tied down. It was very sad,
really. One day he just never came back. Maybe they
shot him for not paying. I wonder if he's still alive;
if he is, I suppose I'm still married to him."

I found out even later that Aunt Lou had a boy-
friend of sorts. His name was Robert, he was an accountant, he had a wife and children, and he came to
her apartment on Sunday evenings for dinner. "Don't
tell your mother, dear," Aunt Lou said. "I'm not sure
she'd understand."

"Wouldn't you like to marry him?" I asked her
when she told me about him.

"Once bitten, twice shy," said Aunt Lou. "Besides, I never got a divorce, what was the point? I just
took back my own name, that way I don't have to answer so many questions. Take my advice and don't get
married until you're at least twenty-five."

She assumed there would be suitors clamoring at
my heels; she didn't even acknowledge the possibility
that no one would ask me. My mother's version was
that nobody who looked like me could ever accomplish anything, but Aunt Lou was all for dismissing
handicaps or treating them as obstacles to be overcome. Crippled opera singers could do it if they
would only try. Gross as I was, something might be
expected of me after all. I wasn't sure I was up to it.

After her bad experience with the gambler Aunt
Lou had gone out and gotten herself a job. "I couldn't
type, dear," she said, "I couldn't do anything, the
way I was brought up; but it was the Depression,
you know. The family didn't have money any more.
So I had to, didn't I? I worked my way up."

When I was younger my father and mother were
vague about Aunt Lou's job, and so was she. All they
would say was that she worked in an office for a com-

pany and she was head of a department. I found out what she actually did when I was thirteen.

"Here," said my mother, "I suppose it's time you read this," and she put into my hands a pink booklet with a wreath of flowers festooning the front. *You're Growing Up*, the cover said. On the inside page was a letter, which began, "Growing up can be fun. But there are also some things about it which can be puzzling. One of them is menstruation. . . ." At the bottom of this page was a picture of Aunt Lou, smiling maternally but professionally, taken before her jowls were quite so large. Around her neck was a single strand of pearls. Although she did wear pearls in real life, it was never just one strand. Underneath the letter was her signature: "Sincerely yours, Louisa K. Delacourt." I studied the diagrams in the pink booklet with interest; I read the etiquette hints for tennis games and high-school proms, the wardrobe suggestions, the advice on washing your hair; but I was even more impressed by Aunt Lou's picture and signature—like a movie star, sort of. My Aunt Lou was famous, in a way.

I asked her about it the next time I saw her. "I'm head of Public Relations, dear," she said. "Just for Canada. But I didn't really write that booklet, you know. That was written by Advertising."

"Then what do you do?" I asked.

"Well," she said, "I go to a lot of meetings, and I advise on the ads. And I answer the letters. My secretary helps me, of course."

"What kind of letters?" I asked.

"Oh, you know," she said. "Complaints about the product, requests for advice, that sort of thing. You'd think they'd all be from young girls, and a lot of them are. Girls wanting to know where their vagina is and things like that. We have a form letter for those. But some of them are from people who really need help, and those are the ones I answer personally. When they're afraid to go to the doctor or something, they write me. Half the time I don't know what

to say." Aunt Lou finished her martini and went to
pour herself another one. "I got one just the other day
from a woman who thought she'd been impregnated
by an incubus."

"An incubus?" I asked. It sounded like some sort
of medical appliance. "What's that?"

"I looked it up in the dictionary," said Aunt Lou.
"It's a sort of demon."

"What did you tell her?" I asked, horrified. What
if the woman was right?

"I told her," said Aunt Lou reflectively, "to get a
pregnancy test, and if it came out positive it wouldn't
be an incubus. If it's negative, then she won't have to
worry, will she?"

"Louisa is beyond the pale," my mother said
when she was explaining to my father why she didn't
have Aunt Lou to dinner more often. "People are
sure to ask her what she does, and she always tells
them. I can't have her using those words at the dinner
table. I know she's good-hearted but she just doesn't
care what kind of an impression she makes."

"Count your blessings," Aunt Lou said to me
with a chuckle. "They pay well and it's a friendly
office. I've got nothing to complain about."

The psychiatrist gave up on me after three sessions of tears and silence. I resented the implication
that there were yet more things wrong with me in
addition to being fat, and he resented my resentment. He told my mother it was a family problem
which couldn't be resolved by treating me alone, and
she was indignant. "He has his nerve," she said to my
father. "He just wants to get more money out of me.
They're all quacks, if you ask me."

After that she entered her laxative phase. I think
by this time she was frantic; certainly she was ob-
sessed with my bulk. Like most people she probably
thought in images, and her image of me then must
have been a one-holed object, like an inner tube, that
took things in at one end but didn't let them out at
the other: if she could somehow uncork me I would
deflate, all at once, like a dirigible. She started to buy

patent medicines, disguising her attempts to get me to take them—"It'll be good for your complexion"— and occasionally slipping them into the food. Once she even iced a chocolate cake with melted Ex-Lax, leaving it on the kitchen counter where I found and devoured it. It made me wretched but it didn't make me thin.

By this time I was in high school. I resisted my mother's plan to send me to a private girls' school, where the pupils wore kilts and little plaid ties. Ever since Brownies I'd been wary of any group composed entirely of women, especially women in uniforms. So instead I went to the nearest high school, which was second-best in my mother's opinion but not as bad as it might have been, since by now we were living in a respectable neighborhood. The catch was that the children of the families my mother viewed as her peers and models were sent to the kind of private school she wanted to send me to, so the high school got mostly the leftovers, from the smaller houses around the fringes of the area, the brash new apartment building which had been opposed by the established residents, and even worse, the flats above the stores on the commercial streets. Some of my classmates were not at all what she had in mind, though I didn't tell her this as I didn't want to be forced into uniform.

At this time my mother gave me a clothing allowance, as an incentive to reduce. She thought I should buy clothes that would make me less conspicuous, the dark dresses with tiny polka-dots and vertical stripes favored by designers for the fat. Instead I sought out clothes of a peculiar and offensive hideousness, violently colored, horizontally striped. Some of them I got in maternity shops, others at cut-rate discount stores; I was especially pleased with a red felt skirt, cut in a circle, with a black telephone appliquéd onto it. The brighter the colors, the more rotund the effect, the more certain I was to buy. I wasn't going to let myself be diminished, neutralized, by a navy-blue polka-dot sack.

Once, when I arrived home in a new lime-green car coat with toggles down the front, flashing like a neon melon, my mother started to cry. She cried hopelessly, passively; she was leaning against the banister, her whole body slack as if she had no bones. My mother had never cried where I could see her and I was dismayed, but elated too at this evidence of my power, my only power. I had defeated her: I wouldn't ever let her make me over in her image, thin and beautiful.

"Where do you find them?" she sobbed. "You're doing it on purpose. If I looked like you I'd hide in the cellar."

I'd waited a long time for that. She who cries first is lost. "You've been drinking," I said, which was true. For the first time in my life I experienced, consciously, the joy of self-righteous recrimination.

"What have I done to make you behave like this?" my mother said. She was wearing a housecoat and slippers, even though it was four-thirty in the afternoon, and her hair could have been cleaner. I stomped past her, up to my room, feeling quite satisfied with myself. But when I thought about it, I had doubts. She was taking all the credit for herself, I was not her puppet; surely I was behaving like this not because of anything she had done but because I wanted to. And what was so bad, anyway, about the way I was behaving?

"That's just the way I am," Aunt Lou said once. "If other people can't handle it, that's their problem. Remember that, dear. You can't always choose your life, but you can learn to accept it." I was accustomed to thinking of Aunt Lou as wise; she was certainly generous. The only trouble was that the bits of wisdom she dispensed could have several meanings, when you thought hard about them. For instance, was I supposed to accept my mother, or was she supposed to accept me?

In one of my daydreams I used to pretend Aunt Lou was my real mother, who for some dark but forgivable reason had handed me over to my parents to be brought up. Maybe I was the child of the handsome gambler, who would one day reappear, or Aunt Lou had had me out of wedlock when she was very young. In this case my father was not my real father, and my mother . . . but here it broke down, for what could have persuaded my mother to take me in if she hadn't been obliged to? When my father would comment on how fond Aunt Lou was of me, my mother would reply acidly that it was only because she didn't have me on her hands all the time. On her hands, in her hair, these were the metaphors my mother used about me, despite the fact that she seldom touched me. Her hands were delicate and long-fingered, with red nails, her hair carefully arranged; no nests for me among those stiff immaculate curls. I could always recall what my mother looked like but not what she felt like.

Aunt Lou however was soft, billowy, woolly, befurred; even her face, powdered and rouged, was covered with tiny hairs, like a bee. Wisps escaped from her head, threads from her hems, sweetish odors from the space between her collar and her neck, where I would rest my forehead, listening to the stories of her talking fox. In the summers, when I was small and we wandered the grounds of the Canadian National Exhibition, she would hold me by the hand. My mother didn't hold me by the hand, there were her gloves to think of. She held me by the arm or the back of the collar. And she would never take me to the Ex, which she said was not worthwhile. Aunt Lou and I thought it was worthwhile, we loved it, the shouting barkers and the pipe bands and the wads of pink cotton candy and greasy popcorn we would stuff into ourselves while rambling from one pavilion to another. We would head for the Pure Foods first every year to see the cow made of real butter; one year they made the Queen instead.

But there was something I could never quite remember. We went to the midway, of course, and on rides, the slower ones—Aunt Lou liked the Ferris wheel—but there were two tents Aunt Lou wouldn't let me visit. One had women in harem costumes and enormous jutting breasts painted on it, and two or three of these women would pose on a little stage outside the door in their gauzy pants with their midriffs showing, while a man with a megaphone tried to get people to buy tickets. The other was the Freak Show, and this tent had the fire-eater and the sword-swallower in it, as well as the Rubber Man and the Siamese Twins, JOINED HEAD TO HEAD AND STILL ALIVE, the man said, and the fattest woman in the world. Aunt Lou didn't want to go into this tent either. "It's wrong to laugh at other people's misfortunes," she said, sterner than usual. I found this unfair: other people laughed at mine, I should get a chance too. But then, nobody regarded being fat as a misfortune; it was viewed simply as a disgusting failure of will. It wasn't fated and therefore glamorous, like being a Siamese twin or living in an iron lung. Nevertheless, the Fat Lady was in that tent and I wanted to see her; but I never did.

What I couldn't remember was this: were there two tents, or was there only one? The man with the megaphone sounded the same for freaks and dancing girls alike. They were both spectacular, something that had to be seen to be believed.

Aunt Lou's favorite midway place was the one with the giant mouth on the outside, from which canned laughter issued in a never-ending stream. "Laugh in the Dark," it was called. It had phosphorescent skeletons, and distorting mirrors that stretched you and shrank you. I found those mirrors disturbing. I didn't want to be fatter than I already was, and being thinner was impossible.

I used to imagine the Fat Lady sitting on a chair, knitting, while lines and lines of thin gray faces filed past her, looking, looking. I saw her in gauze pants and a maroon satin brassiere, like the dancing girls, and red slippers. I thought about what she would feel. One day she would rebel, she would do something; meanwhile she made her living from their curiosity. She was knitting a scarf, for one of her rela-

tives who had known her from a child and didn't find
her strange at all.

Chapter Nine

I had one picture of Aunt Lou. I used to cart it
around with me and stand it on whatever bureau happened to be there, but when I escaped to Terremoto I
left it behind: Arthur might have noticed it was missing. It was taken on a hot August day on the grounds
of the Canadian National Exhibition, outside the Colosseum Building, by one of those roving photograph-
ers who snap your picture and hand you a slip of
paper with a number on it.

"Is that your mother?" Arthur asked once when I
was unpacking it.

"No," I said, "that's my Aunt Lou."

"Who's the other one? The fat one."

For a moment I hesitated, on the verge of telling
him the truth. "That's my other aunt," I said. "My
Aunt Deirdre. Aunt Lou was wonderful, but Aunt
Deirdre was a bitch."

"Looks like she had thyroid problems," Arthur
said.

"She didn't, she just ate too much. She worked as
a telephone operator," I said. "She liked that because
she could sit down all day and she had a loud voice.
She got promoted to one of those people who phone
you up to find out why you haven't paid the bill."
What lies I told him, and it wasn't just in self-defense:
already I'd devised an entire spurious past for this
shadow on a piece of paper, this woman of no dis-
cernible age who stood squinting at the camera, holding a cone of pink spun sugar, her face puffed and
empty as a mongoloid idiot's: my own shucked-off
body.

"She looks a bit like you," he said.

"A bit," I admitted. "I didn't like her. She was always trying to tell me how to run my life."

It hurt me a little to betray myself like that. The picture was an opening and I should have taken it, it was still early enough for such risks. Instead I retreated behind the camouflage of myself as Arthur perceived me. I suppose I couldn't trust him with all that discarded misery, I didn't think he would be able to handle it. He wanted me to be inept and vulnerable, it's true, but only superficially. Underneath this was another myth: that I could permit myself to be inept and vulnerable only because I had a core of strength, a reservoir of support and warmth that could be drawn on when needed.

Every myth is a version of the truth, and the warmth and support were there all right. I learned commiseration early, I gave dollar bills to the Salvation Army at Christmas and to legless men selling pencils on streetcorners, I was the sort children approach with lies about having lost their bus fare and I forked over every time. When I walked down Yonge Street I got hit by the Hare Krishna at each red light, it was like a parade, I don't know how they spotted me. I empathized with anything in pain: cats hit by cars, old women who fell on icy sidewalks and were mortified by their own weakness and displayed underpants, aldermen who wept on television when they lost an election. For this reason, as Arthur pointed out more than once, my politics were sloppy. I didn't like firing squads; I never felt that those toppled from power deserved what got done to them, no matter what they'd done in their turn. "Naive humanism," Arthur called it. He liked it fine when it was applied to him, though.

What he didn't know was that behind my compassionate smile was a set of tightly clenched teeth, and behind that a legion of voices, crying, *What about me? What about my own pain? When is it my turn?* But I'd learned to stifle these voices, to be calm and receptive.

I made it through high school on warmth and

supportiveness. In the *Braeside Banner,* under the
group pictures in which girls with dark mouths and
penciled brows and pageboys or ponytails were arranged in front of boys with crew cuts or oily duck's
asses, eyes front, feet crossed at the ankles, the epi-
gram for me always said, "Our happy-go-lucky gal
with the terrific personality!!!" or "A great pal!!!!" or
"Joanie's a laugh a minute!!" or "A swell kid who
never seems to get excited." For other girls they said
things like, "She likes them tall!!" or "Oh, those Don
Mills parties!!" or "Her main attraction is a certain
Simpson's Rep!" or even, "Good things come in small
packages." At home I was sullen or comatose, at the
movies I wept with Aunt Lou, but at school I was
doggedly friendly and outgoing, I chewed gum,
smoked in the washroom, and painted my lips Precious Pink or Sultry Red, my tiny cupid's mouth lost
in a sea of face. I was good at volleyball, though not
at basketball, in which you had to run around a lot. I
was elected to committees, usually as the secretary,
and I joined the United Nations Club and was part
of a delegation to the Model U.N., representing the
Arabs. I made quite a good speech on the plight of
the Palestinian refugees, as I recall. I helped with
decorations for the dances, stringing endless limp
wreaths of Kleenex flowers along the walls of the
sweaty gymnasium, though of course I never attended. My marks were reasonable but not so high as
to be offensive. More importantly, I played kindly
aunt and wisewoman to a number of the pancake-
madeup, cashmere-sweatered, pointy-breasted girls
in the class. It was for this reason that the yearbook
said such cozy things about me.

There were two other fat girls in the school. One
of these, Monica, was a year ahead of me. She had
greasy hair, cut short and combed back, like a boy's,
and she wore a black leather jacket with silver studs.
At noon hour she hung out with some of the tougher,
stupider boys in the parking lot, where they drank
from mickeys hidden in glove compartments and
exchanged dirty jokes. She was accepted by them,

more or less, but as another boy. They didn't seem to think of her as a woman at all. Theresa, the other one, was in the same year as I was but a different class. She was pallid and reticent; she never said much and had few friends. She waddled along the halls by herself, shoulders stooped and books clasped to her chest to hide some of her frontal bulk, peering shyly and myopically at her own feet. She wore cream-colored rayon blouses with discreet embroidery on them, like the forty-five-year-old office secretary's. Yet it was she rather than brazen Monica who had the traditional fat-girl reputation, it was Theresa at whom boys would shout from the other side of the street, "Hey Theresa, hey fatty! Wanta go out behind the field house with me?" for the benefit of other, less forthright boys. Theresa would turn her head away, blushing; no one knew whether or not the rumors were true, that she would "do it" under the right circumstances, but everyone believed them.

As for me, I had a terrific personality and my friends were nice girls, the kind boys wanted to take out to dances and movies, where they would be seen in public and admired. No one shouted things at me on the street; no one who went to our school, at any rate. These girls liked to walk home with me, asking my advice and confiding in me, for two reasons: if a boy who was not wanted approached them, there I was, a fat duenna, the perfect excuse, it was like having your own private tank; and if a more desirable boy turned up, how could my friends help but look good beside me? In addition, I was very understanding, I always knew the right moment to say, "See you tomorrow," and vanish into the distance like a blimp in a steady wind, leaving the couple gazing at each other on the sidewalk in front of those trim Braeside houses, those clipped lawns. The girls would phone me up later, breathlessly, and say "Guess what happened," and I would say "Oh, what?" as though I were thrilled and delighted and could hardly wait to find out. I could be depended upon not to show envy, not to flirt competitively, and not to wonder why I wasn't invited to the mixed-couples parties of these, my dearest friends. Though immersed in flesh, I was regarded as being above its desires, which of course was not true.

Everyone trusted me, no one was afraid of me, though they should have been. I knew everything about my friends, their hopes, their preferences, the brand of china and the style of wedding dress they had lined up for themselves already at the age of fifteen, the names of the unsuspecting boys on whom they wished to bestow these treasures, how they really felt about the boys they went out with, those drips and creeps, and about the other ones they would rather have gone out with, those living dolls. I knew what they thought about each other and what they said behind each other's backs. But they guessed nothing about me; I was a sponge, I drank it all in but gave nothing out, despite the temptation to tell everything, all my hatred and jealousy, to reveal myself as the duplicitous monster I knew myself to be. I could just barely stand it.

About the only advantage to this life of strain was that I gained a thorough knowledge of a portion of my future audience: those who got married too young, who had babies too early, who wanted princes and castles and ended up with cramped apartments and grudging husbands. But I couldn't foresee that at the time.

Monica dropped out of school as soon as she could. So did Theresa, in order to get married to a garage mechanic, an older man who didn't go to my school or any other. It was said she was pregnant, though as one of my friends remarked, how could you tell? I hung on, grimly; I wanted to graduate in order to be finished with it, but I had no idea what I was going to do next. My mother wished me to go to Trinity College at the University of Toronto, which was prestigious, and I almost wanted to myself, I wanted to study archaeology or perhaps history; but I couldn't bear the thought of four more years of acute concealed misery, with the horrors of sororities, engagements, football games and spring weddings thrown in. I started taking part-time jobs; I opened a bank account. I told Aunt Lou, but no one else, that as soon as I had enough money I was going to leave home.

"Do you think that's wise, dear?" she said.

"Do you think staying there would be wise?" I asked. She knew my mother, she should have sympathized with me. Perhaps she was worried about what would happen to me, out there in the world. I was worried about that too. I wanted to leave, but I was also afraid to.

I'd been feeling guilty about Aunt Lou: I hadn't been going to the movies with her as much as I used to. The truth was that I was afraid one of my friends, Barbara or Carole-Ann (who was a cheerleader) or Valerie, done up in a cashmere sweater, with little trussed breasts sticking out jaunty as cocked thumbs, a wreath of artificial flowers twined around the elastic band which held the ponytail, towing a boy wearing a jacket with the letter *B* on it, would turn up at the same movie and see me snivelling beside my fur-draped, hefty aunt.

"Don't go before you're ready," said Aunt Lou sagely, and as usual it could have meant anything.

The kinds of jobs I was able to get were unskilled and not very pleasant. Employers as a rule didn't want to hire anyone so fat, but some were too embarrassed to turn me away completely, especially when they'd advertised. I would look at them accusingly from between my bloated eyelids and say, "Here's the advertisement, right here," and they would take me on for a couple of weeks, making up a lie about one of their regular staff being away on holiday. Thus I worked in the five-and-dime for three weeks, as a theater usher for two, a cashier in a restaurant for three, and so on. Some employers welcomed me: I was as cheap as a woman but didn't cause the disruption among male employees and customers other women did. However, these were often hard, disagreeable jobs, like washing dishes, and I didn't stay at them long.

My mother was baffled by these jobs. "What do you have to work for?" she asked, many times. "We give you all the money you need." She found the jobs I took degrading to her personally, which was a bonus. They must have reminded her, also, of her own early life.

When sexual frankness became fashionable, I read a lot of accounts of other people's first sexual experiences: masturbation with doorknobs, water faucets and the handles of electric shavers, gropings in the back seats of cars at drive-in movies, scramblings among bushes and so forth. None of these were like mine. I myself did have two early sexual experiences, though for the most part I suppressed my interest in sex as completely as I suppressed my interest in war films. There was no available role for me, so I ignored the whole thing as much as possible. Although I pretended to, I didn't really join in my friends' collective passion for male singers. The most I would permit myself was an idealized lust for the figure of Mercury, with winged hat and sandals, impressive muscles and a telephone cable wrapped discreetly around his loins, that used to appear on the front of the Toronto telephone directory. It disappeared years ago. Perhaps the phone company discovered that he was the god of thieves and trickery as well as speed.

But I had vicarious access to the sexual mysteries through the Barbaras and Valeries with whom I ate lunch and walked home, though they tended to discuss such things more with each other than they did with me. They excluded me out of respect, as one would exclude a nun or a saint. Sexually they were prudish, doling themselves out in approved amounts, a kiss after the third date, more serious kissing only if you were going steady, protection below the neck. It was before the pill, and there were enough dismal examples held in front of their eyes, by mothers and

by gossip about girls who had to get married, or even
worse, who had to get married but couldn't, to keep
them rigid. If they went further than you were supposed to, they didn't tell.

My first sexual experience went like this. I was
walking home with Valerie, who has since made several guest appearances in the pages of my Costume
Gothics, once dressed in a farthingale, once in an
ersatz-Grecian dress of the Regency, cut low on the
bosom. This day, however, she was wearing a red
sweater with a poodle pin on it, a matching red plaid
skirt and penny loafers, with a navy-blue trench coat
over all. She was telling me about an important phone
call she'd had the evening before, when she was in
the middle of washing her hair. Several blocks before
the street where I usually turned off, we were inter-
cepted by a boy who had been trying to get Valerie to
go out with him for weeks. She wasn't interested—in
her opinion, as I knew, he was a pill—but etiquette
dictated that she not be too openly rude to him, as
that might get her the reputation of being stuck-up.
So he strolled along beside us, making nervous conversation to Valerie and ignoring me as much as he could.

Valerie gave me a significant look so I didn't turn
off down my street. Instead I walked with her all the
way to her house, knowing she would call later and
thank me for having caught on. At her driveway she
said goodbye, then turned and lilted up the walk,
her ponytail swinging. The back door closed behind
her. I stood there on the sidewalk, my feet bulging
over the sides of my penny loafers. My ankles hurt,
I'd gone three blocks out of my way and would now
have to retrace them, it was time for me to go home
and make myself a triple-decker Kraft Cheese and
peanut butter sandwich and get ready for my usher-
ette job at the Starlite Theater, where Natalie Wood
was playing in *Splendor in the Grass*. The boy, whom
even I judged unacceptable, was now supposed to
say, "See ya," and stride away from me as fast as he
could go. But instead he did a curious thing. He knelt
down in front of me, right in a mud puddle—it was

April and had been raining—and buried his face against my enormous stomach.

What did I do? I was stupefied; I was compassionate; I stroked his hair. My hand smelled of Brylcreem for days.

After a few minutes of this he got up, the knees of his pants dripping wet, and walked away. That was my first sexual experience. I went home and ate my sandwich.

As to why this particular boy, whose name I could never remember, though I could picture quite clearly the strained, even agonized expression on his face, performed this grotesque though almost ritual act on a muddy sidewalk in the suburb of Braeside Park in front of an ordinary house of red brick with white trim and two clipped cedars, one on either side of the front door, I had no clue. Perhaps it was sorrow over thwarted love and he was looking for consolation. Then again, it might have been an instinctive act of belly worship; or perhaps, judging from the way he threw his arms around me as far as they could go, his chemistry textbook lying forgotten on the sod, and dug in his fingers, he might have perceived me as a single enormous breast. But this is later speculation. At the time I was so shocked by the novelty of being touched by a boy that I forgot about the incident as soon as possible. It hadn't been very pleasant. I didn't even use it to make fun of him, as I might have if I had been thinner. On his part, he avoided me and didn't try to get Valerie to go out with him again.

My second sexual experience took place during one of my part-time jobs. It was when I was working as a cashier in a restaurant, a small, mediocre one called the Bite-A-Bit. It served hot dogs, hamburgers, milk shakes, coffee, pieces of pie; and if you wanted a full-course dinner, fried chicken and shrimp, minute steaks, grilled pork chops and roast beef. I worked from four-thirty to nine-thirty, when it closed, and part of my pay was a free meal, from the lower price ranges. I perched on a high stool behind the cash register and took in the money. I also looked after the customers who sat at the counter beside my stool, and for this purpose I had a telephone connected with the cooking area, over which I gave the orders.

The cooking area was at the back, with a pass-through hatchway decorated in fake-brick wallpaper and several copper pans which were never used. There were two cooks, a lethargic, resentful Canadian and a sprightly, bright-eyed foreigner, either Italian or Greek, I wasn't sure which. This was always the way, in my experience with jobs. The Canadians who had jobs like that didn't expect to rise any higher: despite the advantage of knowing the language and the terrain, this was the best they could do. The foreigners, on the other hand, were on the way up, they were saving money and learning, they didn't intend to stay on the menial level. The foreign cook took half the time of the other and was twice as polite. He beamed as he handed the waitresses their plates of food, he scampered around in his ovenlike enclosure like a baking chipmunk, humming snatches of exotic song, and you could see the other man would have liked to kill him.

My relationship with him began when he started to reach for the phone every time I called in an order. He had a clear view of me through the hatchway.

"Alloo," he would sing sweetly.

"A cheeseburger and a side of french fries," I would say.

"For you, I make it extra special."

I thought he was teasing me and ignored him, but one day he asked over the intercom, "You have coffee with me, eh? After work?"

I was too startled to say no. No one had ever asked me for coffee before.

He helped me on with my coat and opened the door for me, darting around me like a tugboat around the Queen Elizabeth; he was five inches shorter than I was and probably eighty pounds lighter. Once we were sitting across from each other in a nearby coffee shop, he got straight to the point.

"I require for you to marry me."

"What?" I said.

He leaned across the table, gazing at me with his sparkling black eyes. "I am serious. I want to meet with your father, and look, I show you my bank account." To my consternation he pushed a little blue bankbook towards me.

"My father?" I stammered. "Your bank account. . . ."

"See," he said, "I have right intentions. I wish to open restaurant of my own now soon, I have saved enough. You are a serious girl, you are not like many in this country, you are a good girl, I have watched you, and I do not know how to speak. You would work the cash register for me, and welcome the people. I would cook, much better things than in there." He gestured across the street towards the Bite-A-Bit. "I will serve the wine, who but a pig can eat without wine?"

"But," I said. Just for a moment I could not think of any reason why not. Then I imagined the expression on my mother's face as I loomed down the aisle in white satin with this tiny foreign man slung over my arm like a purse.

"I will give you babies," he said, "lots of babies, I see you like the babies. You are a good girl. Then, when we have enough money, we go and visit my country. You will like."

"But," I said, "I'm not the same religion as you."

He waved his hand. "You will change."

When I first visited Terremoto it was more obvious what he saw in me: I was the shape of a wife already, I was the shape it took most women several years to become. I had just started a little early, that was all. But at the time I couldn't overcome the suspicion that he was making fun of me; either that, or it was simply a commercial proposition. How easy it would be, though; for despite his size he was obviously used to making decisions, I myself would not have to make any ever again. However, I did not want to be a cashier for much more of my life. I wasn't good at adding.

"Thank you very much," I said, "but I'm afraid it's impossible."

He was not discouraged. Over the next few weeks he behaved as if he'd been expecting a rejection, as a matter of form. It was proper and modest of me to have refused him and now all I needed was persuasion; after the correct amount I would give in. He flirted with me through the hatchway when I went to pick up my orders, making cat's eyes and wiggling his small brown moustache at me, he called me over the intercom to sigh and plead, watching me all the while from his post at the griddle. When it was time for me to take my break and eat dinner he cooked expensive, forbidden things for me, piling my plate high with shrimps, which he knew I liked, and topping the mound with a sprig of parsley. My appetite, usually gargantuan, began to fall off, partly from the effects of being in contact with other people's food for hours at a time, but partly because at every meal I felt I was being bribed.

The whole thing had the air of a ceremony, a performance that it was necessary to go through before I gave in and did what he wanted; yet like all ceremonies that are believed in, it was sincere and oddly touching. I liked him, but he was disturbing me. I knew I didn't merit such attentions, and besides, there was something absurd about them; it was like being pursued by Charlie Chaplin. I was relieved when the permanent cashier returned and I could quit.

For a while I daydreamed about this man in school (I never did learn his real name; in his determination to become Canadian, he insisted that it was John). For the most part I saw him merely as a landscape, a region of blue skies and balmy climate, with white sand beaches and a stately classical ruin on a cliff, with pillars; a place that would be in marked contrast to dour Toronto and its gritty winter winds, its salt slush that decayed your boots, or its humid, oppressive summers; a place where I would fit in at last, where I would be the right shape. Sometimes I thought it would be pleasant to have married him, it would be as good as having a pet, for with his black eyes and his soft moustache he would be like a friendly animal, a squirrel or an otter, scurrying over my body, enormous to him as a peninsula. But gradually these images faded and as I tuned out the drone of the history teacher, talking monotonously about natural resources and other things that didn't interest me, I returned to an earlier fantasy.

In this one I was sitting in a circus tent. It was dark, something was about to happen, the audience was tense with expectation. I was eating popcorn. Suddenly a spotlight cut through the blackness and focused on a tiny platform at the top of the tent. Upon it stood the Fat Lady from the freak show at the Canadian National Exhibition. She was even fatter than I had imagined her, fatter than the crude picture of her painted on the hoarding, much fatter than me. She was wearing pink tights with spangles, a short fluffy pink skirt, satin ballet slippers and, on her head, a sparkling tiara. She carried a diminutive pink umbrella; this was a substitute for the wings which I longed to pin on her. Even in my fantasies I remained faithful to a few ground rules of reality.

The crowd burst out laughing. They howled, pointed and jeered; they chanted insulting songs. But the Fat Lady, oblivious, began to walk carefully out onto the high wire, while the band played a slow, stately melody. At this the crowd stilled, and a murmur of dismay arose. It was obvious this was a dangerous thing for her to be doing, she was so enormously fat, how could she keep her balance, she would topple and fall. "She'll be killed," they whispered, for there was no safety net.

Gradually, inch by inch, the Fat Lady proceeded along the wire, pausing to make sure of her balance, her pink umbrella raised defiantly above her head. Step by step I took her across, past the lumbering enterprises of the West Coast, over the wheatlands of the prairies, walking high above the mines and smokestacks of Ontario, appearing in the clouds like a pink vision to the poor farmers of the St. Lawrence Valley and the mackerel fishermen of the Maritimes. "Good Christ, what is it?" they muttered, pausing in the endless hauling-in of their nets. Several times she faltered and the crowd drew in its breath; the wire oscillated, she concentrated all her forces on this perilous crossing, for a fall meant death. Then, just before the bell went and the period was over—this was the trick—she would step to safety on the other side and the people would rise to their feet, the roar of their voices her tribute. A large crane would appear and lower her to the ground.

You'd think I would have given this Fat Lady my own face, but it wasn't so simple. Instead she had the face of Theresa, my despised fellow-sufferer. At school I avoided her, but I wasn't altogether a heartless monster, I wished to make reparation, I had good intentions.

I knew how Arthur would analyze this fantasy. What a shame, he'd say, how destructive to me were the attitudes of society, forcing me into a mold of femininity that I could never fit, stuffing me into those ridiculous pink tights, those spangles, those outmoded, cramping ballet slippers. How much better for me if I'd been accepted for what I was and had learned to accept myself, too. Very true, very right, very pious. But it's still not so simple. I wanted those things, that fluffy skirt, that glittering tiara. I liked them.

As for the Fat Lady, I knew perfectly well that after her death-defying feat she had to return to the freak show, to sit in her oversized chair with her knitting and be gaped at by the ticket-buyers. That was her real life.

Chapter Ten

When I was in my third year at Braeside High, Aunt Lou invited me to dinner one Sunday. I was surprised, as I knew she reserved Sunday evenings for Robert, the accountant from her company. But when she said, "Wear something nice, dear," I realized she was going to let me meet him. I didn't have anything nice to wear, but it was like Aunt Lou not to acknowledge this. I wore my felt skirt with the telephone on it.

I was prepared to be jealous of Robert. I'd pictured him as tall, overpowering and a little sinister, taking advantage of my Aunt Lou's affections. But instead he was small and dapper, the most trimly dressed man I'd ever seen. Aunt Lou had even cleaned up the apartment for him, more or less; though I could see the toe of a nylon stocking nosing out from under the best chair, where he sat sipping at the edge of his martini.

Aunt Lou was ornamented from head to toe. Things dangled from her, her wrists jingled, South Sea odors wafted from her. As she bustled about, putting the final touches to the feast she'd prepared, she seemed to warm and expand, filling the room. Robert watched her as if she were a gorgeous sunset. I wondered if any man would ever look at me like that.

"I don't know what your aunt sees in a dry old stick like me," he said, ostensibly to me but really to Aunt Lou.

Aunt Lou bellowed. "Don't let him fool you," she said. "Underneath it he's a devil."

After we'd finished the chocolate mousse, Aunt Lou said, "Joan, dear, we were wondering if you'd like to go to church with us."

This was even more of a surprise. My mother went to church for social reasons; she'd subjected me to several years of Sunday school, with white gloves and round navy-blue felt hats held on by elastic bands and patent-leather Mary Janes. Aunt Lou had sympathized when I said it was boring. She herself had occasionally taken me to a small Anglican church, though only on Easter Sundays, for the hymns, she said, but that was as far as it went. Now, however, she applied one of her astonishing hats to the top of her head, powdered her nose, and took her white gloves matter-of-factly in hand.

"It's not exactly a church," she said to me, "but Robert goes every Sunday."

We went in Robert's car, which he parked on a pokey side street north of Queen. The semi-detached houses were old two-story red brick with front porches; the neighborhood looked squalid and sagging. Dirty snow fringed the lawns. One of the houses stood out from the others because it had bright red window curtains, illuminated from behind so that they glowed, and it was this house we entered.

In the front hall there was a table with a large brass tray, a pile of paper slips and several pencils; beneath it, overshoes, rubbers and galoshes drained onto spread newspapers. Aunt Lou and Robert each wrote a number on one of the slips of paper, then placed the folded paper on the tray. "You write a number too, dear," Aunt Lou said. "Maybe you'll get a message."

"A message?" I said. "Who from?"

"Well, you never know," said Aunt Lou. "But you might as well try."

I thought I would wait and see what happened. When we'd gone through a pair of purple velvet curtains, we were in the Chapel, as I later learned to call it. It had once been the living room of the house, but now it contained five or six rows of folding bridge-table chairs, each with a hymnbook on it. In what had once been the dining room there was a raised stage with a pulpit covered in red velvet, and a small electric organ. Only a third of the chairs were occupied; the room filled up a little more before the service began, but on my subsequent visits I never saw it completely full. Most of the regular members of the congregation were quite old, and many had chronic coughs. Aunt Lou and Robert were among the youngest.

We settled into our front-row seats, Aunt Lou ruffling herself like a chicken, Robert sitting primly upright. Nothing happened for a while; from behind us came throat-clearings and shufflings. I opened the hymnbook, which was quite thin, not at all like the Anglican one. *The Spiritualist Hymnbook*, it was called; and, rubber-stamped below the title, *Property of Jordan Chapel*. I read two of the hymns, at random. One was about a joyous boat ride across a river to the Other Side, where loved ones were awaiting. The other was about the blessed spirits of those who've gone before, watching o'er us for our safety till we reach the other shore. This thought made me uncomfortable. Being told in Sunday school that God was watching you every minute of every hour had been bad enough, but now I had to think about all these other people I didn't even know who were spying on me. "What kind of a church is this?" I whispered to Aunt Lou.

"Shh, dear, they're starting," Aunt Lou said placidly, and sure enough the lights dimmed and a short woman in a brown rayon dress, with gold button earrings and a matching pin, crossed the stage and began to play the electric organ. A chorus of quavery voices rose around me, tiny and shrill as crickets.

Halfway through the hymn, two people entered from the door that led to the kitchen, and stood behind the pulpit. One, as I came to know, was the Reverend Leda Sprott, the leader. She was a stately older woman with blue eyes, blue hair and a Roman nose, dressed in a long white satin gown, with an embroidered purple band, like a bookmark, around her neck. The other was a skinny gray man who was referred to as "Mr. Stewart, our visiting medium." I later wondered in what sense he was visiting, since he was always there.

When the hymn had wavered to its close, Leda Sprott raised her hands above her head. "Let us meditate," she said, in a deep, resonant voice, and there was silence, broken only by the sound of uncertain footsteps, which went out through the purple curtains and then, very slowly, up the stairs. Leda Sprott began a short prayer, asking for the help of our loved ones who had gained the greater light for those of us still wandering in the mists on this side. Distantly, we heard a toilet flush, and the footsteps came back down.

"We will now have an inspiring message from our visiting medium, Mr. Stewart," said the Reverend Leda, stepping aside.

By the end of my time with the Spiritualists I'd practically memorized Mr. Stewart's message, since it was the same every week. He told us not to be downhearted, that there was hope; that when things seemed darkest, it was almost dawn. He quoted a few lines from "Say Not the Struggle Naught Availeth," by Arthur Hugh Clough:

> And not by eastern windows only,
>   When daylight comes, comes in the light;
> In front, the sun climbs slow, how slowly,
>   But westward, look, the land is bright.

And another line, from the same poem: "If hopes were dupes, fears may be liars." "Fears may indeed be liars, my friends; which reminds me of a little story I heard the other day, and which can be of help to us all at those moments when we are feeling down, when we're feeling nothing matters and what's the use of struggling on. There were once two caterpillars, walking side by side down a road. The pessimistic caterpillar said he'd heard that soon they would have to go into a dark narrow place, that they would stop moving and be silent. 'That will be the end of us,' he said. But the optimistic caterpillar said, 'That dark place is only a cocoon; we will rest there for a time, and after that we will emerge with beautiful wings; we will be butterflies, and fly up toward the sun.' Now, my friends, that road was the Road of Life, and it's up to each of us which we will choose to be, the pessimistic caterpillar, filled with gloom and looking forward only to death, or the optimistic caterpillar, who was filled with trust and hope and looked forward to the higher life."

The congregation never seemed to mind that the

message was always the same. In fact, they'd probably have felt cheated if it had varied.

After the message the collection was taken up by the brown rayon woman, and after that came the serious business. This was what everyone had come for, really: their own personal messages. The brown rayon woman brought in the brass tray, and Leda Sprott took up the pieces of paper one by one. She would hold each piece unopened in her hand, close her eyes, and give the message. Then she would open the paper and read the number. The messages were largely about health: "There's an old white-haired lady with light coming out from around her head, and she is saying, 'Be careful going down stairs, especially on Thursday'; and she's saying the word *sulphur*. She's warning you; she sends you love and greetings." "There's a man wearing a kilt, and he has a set of bagpipes; he must be Scottish; he has red hair. He's giving you a lot of love, and he's saying, 'Cut down on the sweet foods, they're not good for you.' He's telling you—I can't quite catch the word. It's a mat of some kind. 'Be careful of mats,' that's what he's saying."

After the pieces of paper were finished, Mr. Stewart took over and did free-form messages, pointing to members of the congregation and describing spirits which were standing behind their chairs. I found this much more disturbing than the numbers: Leda Sprott's messages seemed to come from inside her head, but Mr. Stewart did it with his eyes open, he could actually *see* dead people right there in the room. I slouched down in my chair, hoping he wouldn't point at me.

After this there were more hymns; then Leda Sprott reminded us about the Healing Hands session on Tuesday, the Automatic Writing on Wednesday, and the private sittings on Thursday, and that was all. There was some scuffling and crowding in the hall as several elderly men struggled with their galoshes. At the door people thanked her warmly; she knew most of them, and would ask, "Did you get what you wanted, Mrs. Hearst?" "How was that, Mrs. Dean?"

"I'll throw that medicine away right now," they'd say, or, "It was my Uncle Herbert, that was just the kind of coat he used to wear."

"Well, Robert," said Aunt Lou in the car. "I'm sorry she didn't come tonight."

Robert was visibly disappointed. "Maybe she was busy," he said. "I don't know who that other woman was, the one in the evening dress."

"A large woman," Aunt Lou said. "Hah. It sounded like me." She asked Robert up for a drink, but he said he was discouraged and should probably go home, so I went up instead and had a hot chocolate and some petit fours and a shrimp sandwich. Aunt Lou had a double Scotch.

"It's his mother," she said. "That's the third week in a row she hasn't turned up. She was always a little thoughtless. Robert's wife couldn't stand her, she refuses to go to church with him at all. 'If you ever do get to talk to that old horror,' she told him, 'I don't want to be there.' I think that's a bit cruel, don't you?"

"Aunt Lou," I said, "do you really *believe* all that stuff?"

"Well, you never can tell, can you?" she said. "I've seen them give a lot of accurate messages. Some of them don't mean all that much, but some of them are quite helpful."

"But it could just be mind reading," I said.

"I don't know how it's done," said Aunt Lou, "but they all find it very comforting. I know Robert does, and he likes me to take an interest. I feel you have to keep an open mind."

"It gives me the willies," I said.

"I keep getting messages from that Scotsman," Aunt Lou said musingly. "The one with the red hair and bagpipes. I wonder what he meant about the mats. Maybe he meant mutts, and I'm going to be bitten by a dog."

"Who is he?" I said.

"I haven't the faintest idea," Aunt Lou said. "Nobody I know of ever played the bagpipes. He's certainly not a relation."

"Oh," I said, relieved. "Have you told them that?"

"I wouldn't dream of it," said Aunt Lou. "I wouldn't want to hurt their feelings."

I fell into the habit of going regularly to the Jordan Chapel on Sunday nights. It was a way of seeing Aunt Lou which, by now, I preferred to the movies, as I was absolutely certain that nobody from Braeside High would ever see me there. I even spent a certain amount of time worrying about the Spiritualist doctrines: If The Other Side was so wonderful, why did the spirits devote most of their messages to warnings? Instead of telling their loved ones to avoid slippery stairs and unsafe cars and starchy foods, they should have been luring them over cliffs and bridges and into lakes, spurring them on to greater feats of intemperance and gluttony, in order to hasten their passage to the brighter shore. Some of the Spiritualists also believed in multiple incarnations, and some in Atlantis. Others were standard Christians. Leda Sprott didn't mind what you believed as long as you also believed in her powers.

I was willing to watch it all, with the same suspension of disbelief I granted to the movies, but I drew the line at putting a number on the tray. I didn't know any dead people and I had no wish to know any. One night, however, I did get a message, which was much more peculiar than anything I'd feared. It was during Leda Sprott's number session, and she was just about to process the last folded paper on the brass tray. As usual she'd closed her eyes, but then she opened them suddenly.

"I have an urgent message," she said, "for someone without a number." She was looking straight at me. "There's a woman standing behind your chair. She's about thirty, with dark hair, wearing a navy-blue suit with a white collar and a pair of white gloves. She's telling you . . . what? She's very unhappy about something. . . . I get the name *Joan.*

I'm sorry, I can't hear. . . ." Leda Sprott listened for a minute, then said, "She couldn't get through, there was too much static."

"That's my mother!" I said to Aunt Lou in a piercing whisper. "She's not even dead yet!" I was frightened, but I was also outraged: my mother had broken the rules of the game. Either that, or Leda Sprott was a fraud. But how could she know what my mother looked like? And if she'd snooped around, she wouldn't have made the mistake of using a living person.

"Later, dear," Aunt Lou said.

After the service was over I confronted Leda Sprott. "That was my mother," I said.

"I'm happy for you," said Leda. "I had the feeling she's been trying to contact you for some time. She must be very concerned about you."

"But she's still alive!" I said. "She isn't dead at all!"

The blue eyes wavered, but only for a moment. "Then it must've been her astral body," she said placidly. "That happens sometimes, but we don't encourage it; it confuses things, and the reception isn't always good."

"Her *astral body?*" I'd never heard of such a thing. Leda Sprott explained that everyone had an astral body as well as a material one, and that your astral body could float around by itself, attached to you by something like a long rubber band. "She must've come in through the bathroom window," she said. "We always leave it open a little; the radiator overheats." You had to be very careful about your rubber band, she said; if it got broken, your astral body could get separated from the rest of you and then where would you be? "A vegetable, that's what," said Leda Sprott. "Like those cases you read about, in the hospital. We keep telling the doctors that in some cases brain operations do more harm than good. They should be leaving the window open a bit, so the astral body can get back in."

I did not like this theory at all. I particularly

didn't like the thought of my mother, in the form of
some kind of spiritual jello, drifting around after me
from place to place, wearing (apparently) her navy-
blue suit from 1949. Nor did I want to hear that she
was concerned about me: her concern always meant
pain, and I refused to believe in it. "That's crazy," I
said, in as rude a voice as possible.

To my surprise, Leda Sprott laughed. "Oh, we're
used to being told *that*," she said. "We can certainly
live with that." Then, to my embarrassment, she took
hold of my hand. "You have great gifts," she said,
looking into my eyes. "Great powers. You should develop them. You should try the Automatic Writing, on
Wednesdays. I can't tell whether you're a sender or a
receiver . . . a receiver, I think. I'd be glad to help you
train; you could be better than any of us, but it would
take hard work, and I must warn you, without supervision there's some danger. Not all the spirits are
friendly, you know. Some of them are very unhappy. If they bother me too much, I rearrange the furniture. That confuses them, all right." She patted my
hand, then let go of it. "Come back next week and
we'll talk about it."

I never went back. I'd been shaken by the ap-
parition of my mother (who, when I returned that
Sunday night, didn't look at all as if she'd been astral-
traveling; she was the same as ever, and a little
tight). Leda Sprott's opinion of my great powers was
even more terrifying, especially since I had to admit
I found the thought appealing. Nobody had ever told
me I had great powers before. I had a brief, enticing
vision of myself, clad in a white flowing robe with
purple trim, looking stately and radiating spiritual
energy. Leda Sprott was quite fat . . . perhaps this
was to be my future. But I wasn't sure I really
wanted great powers. What if something went
wrong? What if I failed, enormously and publicly?
What if no messages would come? It was easier not to
try. It would be horrible to disappoint any congregation, but especially the one at the Jordan Chapel.
They were so trusting and gentle, with their coughs

and reedy voices. I couldn't stand the responsibility.

Several months later I confided in Aunt Lou. At the time, she'd seen I was upset and hadn't pressed for details. "Leda Sprott told me I had great powers," I said.

"Did she, dear?" Aunt Lou said. "She told me the same thing. Maybe we both have them."

"She said I should try the Automatic Writing."

"Do you know," Aunt Lou said thoughtfully, "I *did* try it. You'll probably think I'm silly."

"No," I said.

"You see, I've always wanted to know whether my husband is still alive or not. I felt that if he wasn't, he might have the, well, the politeness to let me know."

"What happened?" I asked.

"Well," Aunt Lou said slowly, "it was quite strange. She gave me a ballpoint pen, just an ordinary ballpoint pen. I don't know what I was expecting, a goose quill or something. Then she lit a candle and put it in front of a mirror, and I was supposed to stare at the candle—not the real one, the reflection. I did this for a while and nothing happened, except that I could hear a sort of humming noise. I think I fell asleep or sort of dozed off or something, just for a minute. After that it was time to go."

"Did you write anything?" I asked eagerly.

"Not exactly," said Aunt Lou. "Just a sort of scribble, and a few letters."

"Maybe he's still alive then," I said.

"You never can tell," said Aunt Lou. "If he is dead, it would be just like him not to say anything. He always wanted to keep me in suspense. But Leda Sprott said it was a good beginning and I should go back. She says it takes them a while to get through."

"So did you?"

Aunt Lou frowned. "Robert wanted me to. But you know, I'm not sure it's a good idea. I looked at the paper afterwards, and it wasn't at all like my handwriting. Not at all. I didn't like that feeling of being, well, taken over. I felt I should leave it alone, and I would too if I were you, dear. You can't fly on one wing. That's what I think."

Despite Aunt Lou's advice, I was strongly tempted to try some Automatic Writing myself, at home in my bedroom; and one evening when my parents were out, I did. I got one of the candles from the dining room downstairs, a red ballpoint pen, and my mother's Jot-a-Note from the telephone table. I lit the candle, turned out my bedroom light, and sat in front of the vanity-table mirror, staring at the small flame in the glass and waiting for something to happen. I was trying very hard to keep from moving my hand consciously: that would be cheating, and I wanted it to be real. Nothing happened, except that the candle flame seemed to get bigger.

The next thing I knew my hair was on fire: I'd leaned imperceptibly towards the candle. At that time I had bangs, and they'd started to sputter and frizzle. I slapped my hand over my forehead and ran to the bathroom; my front hair was badly singed, and I had to cut it off, which caused a scene with my mother the next day, as she'd just contributed five dollars towards a hairdo. I decided I'd better leave the Automatic Writing alone.

There was something on the notepad, though: a single long red line that twisted and turned back on itself, like a worm or a snarl of wool. I couldn't remember drawing it; but if that was all the Other Side had to tell me, why should I go to the trouble?

For a while I embroidered Leda Sprott's advice into a classroom daydream (I could do it if I wanted to; humble beginnings in unknown chapel; miraculous revelations; fame spreads; auditoriums packed; thousands helped; whispered comments, awe and admiration—"She may be a *large* woman, but what powers!"). After several months, however, it gradually faded away, leaving nothing but Mr. Stewart's sermon, indelibly engraved on my brain, to surface at inopportune moments: the pessimistic caterpillar and the optimistic caterpillar, inching their way along the Road of Life, involved in their endless dialogue. Most of the time I was on the side of the optimistic caterpillar; but in my gloomiest moments I would think, So what if you turn into a butterfly? Butterflies die too.

Chapter Eleven

The next job I got, after the Bite-A-Bit Restaurant, was at the Sportsmen's Show. This took place in March every year, down on the grounds of the Exhibition, in the Colosseum Building. It was like an auto show or a fall fair; speedboat, fiberglass canoe, and kayak peddlers all had booths, and fishing-rod and rifle companies did too. The Boy Scouts put on demonstrations of tent-pitching and fire-lighting, teams of them in their green uniforms grinding away at fire drills, with their pink bare knees sticking out of their short pants. Beside their platform the Ministry of Lands and Forests had a poster on forest-fire prevention. At stated times there were Indian dances, given by a group of bitter Indians in costumes that were too new to look real. I knew they were bitter because they ate hot dogs at the same hot-dog stand I did, and I overheard some of the things they said. One of them called me "Fatso."

There was a grandstand show too, with log-rolling contests and fly-casting competitions, and a Miss Outdoors pageant, and a seal named Sharky who could play "God Save the Queen" by tooting on a set of blowpipes.

I liked it better than any job I'd ever had. It was untidy and a little tawdry, and I could walk through the crowd without feeling too out of place. For all they knew I was an expert fly-caster or a female log-roller. I worked after school and all day Saturday and Sunday. On my dinner break I would eat five or six hot dogs and drink a few Honey Dews, then wander around, stopping to watch the ladies' outdoor fashion show, the latest in parkas and kapok life jackets, which Miss Outdoors would head off with a demonstration of her plug-casting technique; or perhaps I would go to one of the grandstand archways and look in while someone shot a balloon with an arrow, balancing on the gunwale of a canoe, or a man pushed another man off a spinning log into a plastic swimming pool.

My own job was fairly simple. I stood at the back of the archery range, wearing a red leather change apron, and rented out the arrows. When the barrels of arrows were almost used up, I'd go down to the straw targets, leaving the customers standing back of the rope barrier: a few children, some sports-minded younger men and their wives or girl friends, quite a few boys in black leather jackets who otherwise hung out around the shooting gallery. I'd pull the arrows out, drop them into the barrels, and start over again.

There were two other employees. Rob gave the spiel; he had experience as a huckster and carneyman, he worked the Ex in the summers—rides, cotton-candy stands, win-a-Kewpie-doll games. He stood with a foot on either edge of a barrel and called, "THREE for a dime, nine for a quarter, step right up and show your skill, break the balloon and you get one free, would the little lady like to try?" Bert, a shy first-year university student with glasses and crewneck sweaters, helped me pass out the arrows and rake in the quarters.

The difficulty was that we couldn't make sure all the arrows had actually been shot before we went to clear the targets. Rob would shout, "Bows DOWN please, arrows OFF the string," but occasionally someone would let an arrow go, on purpose or by accident. This was how I got shot. We'd pulled the arrows and the men were carrying the barrels back to the line; I was replacing a target face, and I'd just bent over to stick in the last target pin when I felt something hit me in the left buttock. There was a sound from behind, a sort of screaming laugh, and

Rob yelled, "Who did that?" before I had time to feel any pain. The fellow said he didn't mean to, which I didn't believe. The sight of my moonlike rump had probably been too much for him.

I had to go to the first-aid station to have the arrow taken out, and hitch up my skirt while the wound was plugged up and dressed. Luckily it was only a target arrow and it hadn't gone in very far. "Just a flesh wound," the nurse said. Rob wanted me to go home but I insisted on staying till closing time. Afterward he drove me back himself, in his ancient Volkswagen. He was very sweet. Although he was cynical about almost everything else, he was sympathetic to anyone who had been injured due to this kind of occupational hazard. He himself had nearly been killed once by a Mighty Mouse car that went off the track. When we stopped at a red light, he took his right hand off the wheel and patted me on the knee with it. "Too bad you can't piss standing up," he joked. That was my third sexual experience.

When I came in through the front door, my father's voice called to me from the living room, which was unusual. By that time my parents were letting me come and go as I pleased. They were sitting in their usual places. My father looked careworn and drained, my mother furious.

"We have some bad news for you, Joan," my father said gently.

"Your Aunt Lou died," said my mother. "Of a heart attack. I always knew she would." When it came to disasters, my mother's prophecies were discouragingly accurate.

At first I didn't believe it. My impulse was to sit down, which I did, heavily. I yelped with pain.

"What on earth," said my mother.

"Someone shot me with an arrow," I said. "In the behind."

My mother looked at me as if I was out of my mind. "Isn't that just like you," she said, as if it was my fault. "She left you some money," she continued belligerently. "It's the most idiotic thing I ever heard of.

It's a total and complete waste of time, if you ask me."

My mother, never one to beat around the bush, had gone over to Aunt Lou's apartment as soon as she'd heard the news from the apartment building superintendent, who had found poor Aunt Lou on the bathroom floor in her kimono. She'd slipped on the bath mat, either before or after the attack. The real will was with Aunt Lou's lawyer, but my mother had found a copy among Aunt Lou's papers. "A mess," she said. "The whole apartment's a mess. You'll have to come over and help me with it." For we were Aunt Lou's only relatives.

Aunt Lou had indeed left me some money. Two thousand dollars, in fact, which was a lot at that time, for someone of my age. But there was a condition: I could have it only if I reduced, and Aunt Lou had even picked the proper weight. I had to lose a hundred pounds.

This was what had made my mother so angry. She didn't think me capable of it. In her eyes, the money might as well have been thrown away. The only other person who got any was Aunt Lou's husband, the gambler, provided he could be found.

I spent the night mourning Aunt Lou, fitfully and noisily, though my tears were not yet completely felt, as I didn't yet believe she was dead. The finality of her disappearance didn't get through to me till the following morning, when, light-headed from lack of sleep, I limped after my mother into the now-empty apartment. It was much as I had last seen it, but without Aunt Lou's assurance and vitality it looked unkempt, grubby, shabby even. Aunt Lou always made you feel as though she had intended, even planned the disorder. Now it seemed like mere carelessness; or worse, as though someone had gone through it, searching for something that could not be found and throwing clothes and objects about with no regard for their owner. It was clear Aunt Lou hadn't expected to die or she would have been tidier. And yet she had expected it, or she wouldn't have left her curious will.

Now in her apartment I felt like an intruder, as

though we'd broken into her privacy without asking or were observing an intimate scene through a knot-hole in the wall. But it got worse. My mother started rifling her closets, pulling the clothes off the hangers, folding them and ramming them into a large brown Crippled Civilians donation bag she had brought, making remarks about them as she did so. "Look at that, will you," she said of Aunt Lou's best gold-sequinned evening dress. "Cheap." I saw Aunt Lou disappearing, piece by piece, into the brown paper bag which was swallowing her endlessly, her breezy clothes, her gay scarves and follies, her jokes about herself which my mother took seriously (that magenta blouse, for instance), and I couldn't stand it. I managed to save the fox, stuffing it surreptitiously into my purse while my mother's back was turned. Then I went into the kitchen, to commune with Aunt Lou one last time, via her refrigerator. My mother didn't comment, or complain that I wasn't helping her; I knew in some obscure way that I hadn't been brought along to help in any case, I'd been brought as a devious form of punishment for having loved Aunt Lou while she was alive.

I found a can of lobster in the cupboard and made myself a sandwich. Aunt Lou's purse was there, and I opened it. I felt like a spy, but I knew my mother would open it later and junk the contents. I took out Aunt Lou's wallet, her compact and one of her handkerchiefs with lace edging, which still had her characteristic smell, and put them in my own purse. It was not stealing, it was rescuing. I wanted to keep as much of her in existence as I could, for my mother was determined on obliteration.

My mother had been in a slump lately, but Aunt Lou's death perked her up again; it gave her some-thing to supervise. She made all the funeral arrange-ments, efficiently and with a certain grim relish. She sent out notices and replied to cards and telephone calls (from Aunt Lou's office, all of them) and placed an announcement in the paper. My father wasn't up to it. He took several days off from the hospital and wandered about the house in his maroon leather slippers, getting in my mother's way as she bustled about and saying, "Poor Lou," over and over, like some melancholy bird. The only other things he said to me were, "She practically brought me up," and, "She knit me a pair of socks during the war. They didn't fit." He had been fonder of her and closer to her than I had guessed, yet I couldn't help wondering how someone brought up by Aunt Lou could have turned out to be as inexpressive as my father. She used to say, "Still waters run deep," and, "If you can't say anything nice, don't say anything at all." Perhaps that explained it. She didn't leave him any money, though; he didn't need it and the gambler did, that would have been her reason.

Aunt Lou was put on display at O'Dacre's Funeral Home, surrounded by baskets of white chrysanthemums (ordered by my mother) and visited by equally middle-aged girls from the sanitary napkin company, who sniffed audibly, squeezed my mother's hand, and said what a wonderful personality she had. I disgraced myself at the funeral by crying too much and too loudly.

Robert the accountant was there, his eyes red and shrunken. After the service he pressed my hand. "She'll be in touch," he said. "We can count on her." But I couldn't believe it.

When we got back to the house my mother said, "Well, that's over with." The next thing I remembered was looking up at the ceiling of the living room. I'd fainted, knocking over an end table (scratched), a Swedish Modern lamp (broken), and a copper-enameled ashtray (undamaged).

It turned out that I had blood poisoning, from the arrow wound. The nurse at the first-aid station hadn't put enough disinfectant on it. The doctor said I must have been running a fever for days. It's true I'd been dizzy, my ears had been singing and objects had been shrinking and swelling around me, but I had attributed this to grief. I was put to bed and injected with penicillin. The doctor said it was a good thing I was so fat ("fleshy," he said); he seemed to hold a kind of blotter theory about fat and germs. My mother brought me chicken bouillon cubes dissolved in hot water.

I developed a raging fever, with delirium. One of the results of this was the notion that I'd been hit with the arrow at precisely the moment Aunt Lou died and that the shot had been guided by her departing spirit. She'd been letting me know, saying goodbye, in a rather eccentric manner, true—and she wouldn't have wanted me to get blood poisoning—but this was characteristic of her. I never quite got rid of this idea, although I knew it was farfetched. At the time it bothered me a lot; indeed it filled me with remorse, for I hadn't recognized this message from the dead, a cry for help perhaps. I should have dropped everything and rushed off to her apartment, not stopping even to remove the arrow. I might have been in time. I seemed to hear her voice, from a great distance, saying, "Most said soonest mended," and, "For want of a nail the man was lost," though I knew that both of these were wrong.

In my lucid moments, and when I was convalescing, I thought about her other message to me, the one in her will. How was I to interpret it? Did it mean she hadn't really accepted me for what I was, as I thought she had—that she too found me grotesque, that for her also I would not do? Or was it just pragmatism on her part, her realization that I would have an easier life if I were thinner? She'd offered me the money to get away, to escape from my mother, as she knew I wished to do; but on terms that would force me to capitulate, or so it seemed.

One day, while I was sitting up in bed, leafing through one of my father's detective novels, I happened to glance down at my body. I'd thrown the bedcovers off, as it was warm, and my nightgown had ridden up. I didn't usually look at my body, in a mirror or in any other way; I snuck glances at parts of it now and then, but the whole thing was too overwhelming. There, staring me in the face, was my thigh. It was enormous, it was gross, it was like a diseased limb, the kind you see in pictures of jungle natives; it spread on forever, like a prairie photographed from a plane, the flesh not green but bluishwhite, with veins meandering across it like rivers. It was the size of three ordinary thighs. I thought, That is really my thigh. It really is, and then I thought, This can't possibly go on.

When I was up and around again I told my mother I was going to reduce. She didn't believe me, but I went downtown to Richmond Street and weighed in, as the will stipulated, with Aunt Lou's lawyer, a Mr. Morrisey, who kept saying, "She was a character, your aunt." I'd already lost some weight during my illness, and I had only seventy pounds to go.

I had somehow expected that once I'd made my decision I would simply deflate, like an air mattress. I wanted it to happen suddenly and with little effort on my part, and I was annoyed when it didn't. I started taking my mother's miraculous remedies, all at once: a couple of fat pills in the morning, a dose of laxatives, half a box of Ayds, a little RyKrisp and black coffee, a waddle around the block for exercise. Of course I developed some spectacular side effects: blinding headaches, stomach cramps, accelerated heartbeat from the fat pills, and an alarming clarity of vision. The world, which I'd seen for so long as a blur, with the huge but ill-defined figure of my mother blocking the foreground, came sharply into focus. Sunshine and brilliant colors hurt my eyes. I suffered from fits of weakness and from alarming, compulsive relapses during which I would eat steadily, in a kind of trance, anything and everything in sight —I recall with horror consuming nine orders of fried chicken in a row—until my shrunken and abused stomach would protest and I would throw up.

I'd lost some time at school through sickness, and I couldn't catch up; it was too difficult to concentrate. I spent the mornings resisting the thought of lunch hour and the afternoons regretting it. I became listless and crabby; I snapped at my friends, I told them I didn't want to hear any more about their stupid boyfriends, I turned down requests to help with the decorations for the Senior Formal, which was to be called "April Antics." I was fed up with Kleenex flowers. My marks plummetted; my skin sagged into the loose folds of the chronically ill or aged, it flopped around me like a baggy sweat suit. Around May I was put through a surreal interview with the Guidance Counselor, during which I, bug-headed on diet speed, my mind zapping around like a mechanical mouse, stared walleyed at this non-credible bright-gray man while he said, "We know you have the ability, Joan. Is there something bothering you at home?" "My Aunt died," I said, and then began to giggle so hard I choked. The rest of the interview consisted of him whacking me on the back. I think he called my mother on the telephone.

At home I spent hours in front of the mirror, watching as my eyebrows, then my mouth, began to spread across my face. I was dwindling. The sight of a fat person on the street, which used to inspire fellow feeling, I now found revolting. The wide expanse of flesh that had extended like a sand dune from my chin to my ankles began to recede, my breasts and hips rising from it like islands. Strange men, whose gaze had previously slid over and around me as though I wasn't there, began to look at me from truck-cab windows and construction sites; a speculative look, like a dog eyeing a fire hydrant.

As for my mother, at first she was gratified, though she phrased it in her own way: "Well, it's about time, but it's probably too late." As I persevered, she said things like, "You're ruining your health," and, "Why do you have to go to extremes with everything?" and even, "You should eat something more than that, you'll starve to death." She went on baking sprees and left pies and cookies around the kitchen where they would tempt me, and it struck me that in a lesser way she had always done this. While I grew thinner, she herself became distraught and uncertain. She was drinking quite heavily now and she began to forget where she had put things, whether or not her dresses had been sent to the cleaners, what she had said or not said. At times she would almost plead with me to stop taking the pills, to take better care of myself; then she would have spasms of rage, a dishevelled piecemeal rage unlike her former purposeful fury. "You are the limit," she would say with contempt. "Get out of here, the sight of you makes me sick."

About the only explanation I could think of for this behavior of hers was that making me thin was her last available project. She'd finished all the houses, there was nothing left for her to do, and she had counted on me to last her forever. I should have been delighted by her distress, but instead I was confused. I'd really believed that if I became thinner she would be pleased; a smug, masterful pleasure, but pleasure nonetheless: her will being done. Instead she was frantic.

One afternoon when I'd dragged myself home from school, weak with hunger, and had gone into the kitchen for the single piece of RyKrisp which was my reward, she wandered in from the living room, a glass of Scotch in one hand, still in her pink dressing gown and furred mules.

"Look at you," she said. "Eat, eat, that's all you ever do. You're disgusting, you really are, if I were you I'd be ashamed to show my face outside the house." This was the sort of thing she used to say to me when I was fat and she was trying to browbeat me into reducing, but I felt this speech was not necessary any more.

"Mother," I said, "I'm on a diet, remember? I'm eating a piece of RyKrisp, if you don't mind, and I've lost eighty-two pounds. As soon as I lose eighteen more I'm going down to Mr. Morrisey's office and pick up Aunt Lou's money, and after that I'm moving out."

I shouldn't have given away my plans. She looked at me with an expression of rage, which changed quickly to fear, and said, "God will not forgive you! God will never forgive you!" Then she took a paring knife from the kitchen counter—I had been using it to spread cottage cheese on my RyKrisp—and stuck it into my arm, above the elbow. It went through my sweater, pricked the flesh, then bounced out and fell to the floor. Neither of us could believe she had done this. We both stared, then I picked up the paring knife, put it down on the kitchen table, and placed my left hand casually over the wound in my sweater, as if I myself had inflicted it and was trying to conceal it. "I think I'll make myself a cup of tea," I said conversationally. "Would you like one, Mother?"

"That would be nice," she said. "A cup of tea picks you up." She sat down unsteadily on one of the kitchen chairs. "I'm going shopping on Friday," she said as I filled the kettle. "I don't suppose you'd like to come."

"That would be nice," I said.

That evening, when there were no longer any sounds from my mother's room—she'd gone to bed early and my father was still at the hospital—I packed a suitcase and left. I'd been badly frightened, not so much by the knife (the scratch hadn't been deep and I'd washed it thoroughly with Dettol, to avoid blood poisoning) as by my mother's religious sentiments. After her mention of God I'd decided she was crazy. Though she'd forced me to go to Sunday school, she had never been a religious woman.

PART THREE

Chapter Twelve

The morning was bright with sunshine. It streamed through the windows, of the Library, where Charlotte sat, neatly attired in her modest gray gown, its white collar fastened at the throat with her mother's cameo brooch. The brooch aroused sad reveries: her mother, whose delicate pale features Charlotte had inherited, had pressed it into her hand moments before she died. She had smiled at Charlotte, a single tear rolling down her cheek, and had made her promise to always tell the truth, to be pure, circumspect and obedient. "When the right man appears, my darling," she had said, "you will know it; your heart will tell you. With my dying breath I pray for your safety." Charlotte had always treasured the picture of her mother's face, framed in the gently curling tresses of blonde hair fine as spiders' webs, and her sad but hopeful smile.

Charlotte shook off these unhappy thoughts. She bent again over her jeweler's glass; she was repairing the tiny clasp of an emerald bracelet. For a fleeting moment she pictured how the emeralds would look against Felicia's white skin, how their green would enhance her green eyes and complement her fiery hair. But she dismissed these thoughts too, they were unworthy of her, and concentrated on the work at hand.

There was a light laugh, like the drowsy twitter of some tropical bird. Charlotte glanced up. Through the gauzy white curtains she could see a couple strolling arm in arm at a short distance from the window, deep in what looked like a confidential conversation. By her red hair she recognized Felicia, who was wearing a very costly morning costume of blue velvet, trimmed with white ostrich feathers at the

127

throat and cuffs, with a dashing hat to match. Her hands were concealed in an ermine muff, and as she threw back her head to laugh once more, the sunlight glimmered on her milky throat and on her small teeth.

The man by her side, bending closer now to whisper something into her ear, was wearing a short cape; in his gloved left hand he carried a gold-handled riding crop, which he dangled nonchalantly. Charlotte thought it must surely be Redmond, and a pang of dismay shot through her; but as he straightened and turned his profile towards her, she realized that this man, although he certainly resembled Redmond, was not he. Redmond's nose was more aquiline.

Charlotte did not mean to eavesdrop, but she could not help overhearing part of the conversation. The man said something in a low voice, and Felicia replied, with a contemptuous toss of her head and another laugh:

"No, you are mistaken . . . Redmond suspects nothing. He is occupying himself completely these days with that whey-faced chit he hired to repair my emeralds, and has eyes for nothing else."

What could she mean? Charlotte was still gazing out the window at the departing couple when a slight sound made her turn. Redmond was standing in the doorway, regarding her with a fixed stare; his eyes burned like coals.

"How do you like my wife's new riding costume?" he asked her, with a sneer in his voice that let her know he had seen her looking through the window. A hot flush rose to Charlotte's cheek: was he accusing her of meddling, of spying and intruding?

"It becomes her very well," she answered with reserve. "I could not help seeing it, as she passed so very near the window."

Redmond laughed and came towards her. She rose from her chair and shrank back against the shelves of fine leather-bound books, each with Redmond's family crest stamped in gold on the spine. Her heart was beating with alarm. His face was flushed with drink, although it was still midmorning, and she recalled the strange stories she'd been hearing about his behavior from kindly Mrs. Ryerson, the housekeeper. His wife Felicia, Lady Redmond, also had a scandalous reputation. They could escape gossip because of their position, but Charlotte knew that if she herself once fell from virtue she would be doomed, fated to wander the polluted night streets of London or to find asylum only in a house of shame.

"I do not admire such fine plumage," he said. "That dress of yours now . . . that would be more fitting . . . in a wife. But you wear your hair too severely." He approached her and disengaged a tendril of her hair; then his hand crept towards her throat, his lips sought hers, his features distorted and savage. Charlotte pulled away, seeking wildly for some object with which to defend herself. She seized a weighty copy of Boswell's Life of Johnson: if he attempted to humiliate her in this way again, she would not scruple to strike him with it. He was not the first importunate nobleman she'd had to fend off, and it was not her fault she was young and pretty.

"I beg you to remember, sir," she cried, "that I am alone and unprotected under your roof. Remember your duty!" Redmond looked at her with a new respect; but before he could reply, there was a low laugh. In the doorway stood Felicia in all her opulent splendor, dangling her plumed hat in one dainty hand. Beside her stood the cloaked stranger.

"Prettily spoken," said the stranger, grinning at Charlotte. "Redmond, I hope you take it to heart."

Felicia ignored her and addressed herself to Redmond.

"It seems to me, Redmond, that your little Miss Jeweler is overly long about my emeralds. Surely it does not take such a time to repair a few broken catches and mount a few gems. When will she be done?"

Charlotte flinched at being thus spoken of in the third person, but Redmond bowed to his wife, an ironic bow. "You must ask her yourself, my dear," he said. "The ways of a professional are unfathomable, like the ways of a woman." He strode towards the doorway. "Good of you to ride over, Otterly," he said, shaking hands with the tall stranger. "You know I am always glad to see you for luncheon, even when unannounced."

"I like a little brisk exercise of a morning," the man replied. The two strolled away. Felicia remained a moment, studying Charlotte with an appraising glance, as if she were a piece of furniture.

"I would not remain here too long, if I were you," she said. "The drains in this house are not good; for those with sensitive natures, such as your own, they have been known to have a bad effect on the health, and even on the mind. If you care for some outdoor exercise, however, you might enjoy a stroll in our maze. I'm told it's interesting." She swept away in a swirl of velvet.

Charlotte sat in a whirl of confused emotions. How dare these people treat her like this! But yet with Redmond, though he could be so disagreeable, she had found herself wishing that his hand had remained on her throat just a moment longer. . . . And the cloaked stranger, he must be Redmond's half brother, the Earl of Otterly. The things she had heard about him from Mrs. Ryerson had not been pleasant.

She was too upset to continue working. She locked the emeralds back into their box, locked the box into the room as Redmond had instructed her, and went upstairs to her own room to compose herself.

But when she opened the door of her bedroom, it was all she could do to keep from uttering a scream. There, spread out on her bed, was her good black silk dress, viciously slashed to ribbons. Great gashes had been cut into the skirt, the bodice had been mutilated beyond repair, the sleeves were in shreds. It looked as though some sharp instrument had been employed, a knife or a pair of scissors.

Charlotte entered the room and closed the door

behind her. Her knees felt weak and she was a little dizzy. Who had done this? She knew she had left the dress in the wardrobe when she had gone down to commence her work on the jewels. She opened the wardrobe door. . . . All of her other clothes had been treated in similar fashion: her travelling cloak, her one other dress, her nightrail, her petticoats, her tippet. She had nothing left to wear but the clothes she had on her back.

But why? she asked herself, as she sank, trembling, onto her small, hard bed. It occurred to her that someone wanted to frighten her away, someone wanted her to leave Redmond Grange . . . or perhaps it was a warning, a sign left by a well-wisher. She had looked for a note but there had been none. Only those ominous slashes.

She had left her room at nine o'clock; she had breakfasted, then worked alone until eleven-thirty, when she had overheard the conversation between Felicia and Otterly. In that time, anyone in the household—or someone from beyond it!—could have entered her room, unseen by her, and committed the deed. Redmond, Felicia, Otterly, kindly Mrs. Ryerson . . . the maids, the cook, William the gardener, Tom the coachman, with his ratlike smile. It could have been any of them.

Fearfully, she recalled Felicia's remark about the badness of the drains. Had it been a threat? And if she disobeyed the warning, to what lengths would her unknown enemy be prepared to go in order to rid Redmond Grange of her . . . forever?

I wrote this in Terremoto with my apple-green felt pen. It took me four days, which was far too slow. Usually I wrote my Costume Gothics on the typewriter, with my eyes closed. It was somehow inhibiting to have to see what I'd put on the page, and in apple-green it was more lurid than I'd intended.

I decided I'd have to make the trip to Rome for the typewriter and the hair dye. I'd never be finished with Charlotte at the rate I was going, and my own financial future depended on hers. The sooner she could be safely established the better.

Meanwhile she was in peril, my eternal virgin on the run, my goddess of quick money. The house was after her, the master of the house as well, and possibly the mistress. Things were closing in on her, though so far she was being sensible. She was a plucky girl who refused to be intimidated. Otherwise she'd take the next coach out. I myself didn't have the least idea who'd slashed up her clothes. Redmond, of course, would buy her a new wardrobe, which would fit perfectly, unlike the shabby discards she'd been wearing. She'd hesitate to accept, but what could she do? She didn't have a stitch to her name. Bad things always happened to the clothes of my heroines: bottles of ink got poured over them, holes were burned in them, they got thrown out of windows, shredded, ripped. In *The Turrets of Tantripp* someone stuffed them full of hay, like a scarecrow or a voodoo effigy, and floated them down a river. Once they were buried in a cellar.

Felicia wouldn't like Charlotte's new wardrobe though. "If you're going to set this girl up as your mistress, Redmond," she'd say, within Charlotte's hearing, "I wish you'd do it somewhere else." She was a cynical woman, and used to his escapades.

I replaced the manuscript in my underwear drawer, put on my disguise, and set out for Rome, locking the door carefully behind me.

Driving in Italy made me nervous. People steered cars as if they were horses. They didn't think in terms of roads but in terms of where they wanted to go: a road was where someone else wanted you to go, a road was an insult. I admired this attitude, as long as I wasn't driving. When I was it made me jumpy. The road from the town was a series of zigzags, with no fences or posts on the drop side. I beeped the horn all the way down, and chickens and children scattered.

I made it to Tivoli without accidents, then down

the long hill to the plain. Rome hovered in the distance. The closer I came to it, the more raw earth there was, the more huge pipes and pieces of red, blue and orange machinery lay strewn like dinosaur bones beside the highway. Men were digging, excavating, tearing down, abandoning; it was beginning to look like North America, like any big junk city. The road was now crowded with trucks, small ones and large ones with trailers carrying more pipes, more machines, in and out, but I couldn't tell whether it was evidence of growth or of decay. For all I knew the country was teetering on the edge of chaos, it would be plunged into famine and revolt next week. But I couldn't read the newspapers, and the disasters of this landscape were invisible to me, despite the pipes and machines; I floated along serenely as through a movie travelog, the sky was blue and the light golden. Huge blockish apartment buildings lined the road to Rome, their balconies festooned with washing, but I couldn't guess what kind of life went on inside them. In my own country I would have known, but here I was deaf and dumb.

I pushed my way through the stifling traffic and found a place to park. The American Express office was crowded; long lines of women in sunglasses like mine and men in rumpled summer suits jammed the wickets. The American dollar was unstable and banks were refusing to cash traveler's checks. I should've taken Canadian, I thought. After waiting my turn I was given some fresh money and went out to search for a typewriter.

I found a secondhand portable Olivetti and bought it, using my limited vocabulary and finger signals. I came out of the store weighed down by the typewriter but nevertheless feeling light as a dancer, anonymous and unwatched in the procession of sidewalk people I would never have to know.

Then suddenly I remembered Arthur. He'd been there with me, we'd been on this very same street together, I could feel him still beside me, real as touch. We'd been holding hands. We'd stopped to consult our map, right here in front of this store, it even smelled the same. Had it happened or was I making it up? Had we really walked through the maze of Roman streets together, did we meander in a rented Fiat, did we drive along the Appian Way with its tombs and rumored ghosts, did we descend into the Catacombs, stuffed with the dried shells of Christians, were we guided by a short Bulgarian priest, did we rise again after thirty minutes? Did we go round and round the Colosseum, unable to find the right exit while thunderous trucks swayed past on either side, loaded with metal and cement, pillars, lions for the games, loot, slaves? My feet hurt a lot but I'd been happy. Arthur had been with me, he wasn't with me now, we had been walking along a street like this one and then the future swept over us and we were separated. He was in the distance now, across the ocean, on a beach, the wind ruffling his hair, I could hardly see his features. He was moving at an ever-increasing speed away from me, into the land of the dead, the dead past, irretrievable.

Chapter Thirteen

I first met Arthur in Hyde Park. It was an accident: I collided with him between an anti-vivisectionist speaker and a man who was predicting the end of the world. I was living with a Polish Count in London at the time, and I still wasn't sure how I'd gotten into it.

When I'd walked out my mother's front door two years earlier, closing it gently behind me so as not to wake her up, I had no such plans. In fact I had no plans at all. I had a suitcase in one hand and my purse in the other. The suitcase contained the few clothes that would still fit me, skirts with belts that could be pulled in, blouses that could be gathered

and tucked; I'd had to discard a whole wardrobe over
the year I'd been deflating. It was the end of June,
almost my nineteenth birthday. I'd written the grade
thirteen examinations and I knew I'd failed at least
four papers, but the results wouldn't be available till
August. In any case I didn't care.

Aunt Lou's fox was in my suitcase, and in my
purse I had her birth certificate and the picture of us
at the National Exhibition. I had about thirty dollars,
seventeen of my own and thirteen from the petty cash
box my mother kept in the kitchen; I would repay it
later. I could not yet collect Aunt Lou's legacy as I
was still overweight, but I had money in the bank
from my various jobs and I could get some out in the
morning.

I took a bus downtown, where I checked into the
Royal York Hotel. This made me nervous: I'd never
stayed in a hotel before in my life. I used Aunt
Lou's name, as I didn't want my mother to trace me.
That was stupid, she would have recognized Aunt
Lou's name at once, but I didn't think of that. Instead
I was prepared to be challenged by the desk clerk for
being underage, and I would then have been able
to whip out Aunt Lou's birth certificate and demon-
strate that I was forty-nine.

But all he said was, "Anyone with you?"

"No," I said. He looked over my shoulder and
around the gilded lobby to make sure I was telling the
truth. It didn't strike me at the time that he might
have suspected I was a prostitute. I attributed my
success not to the fact that the lobby was empty, but
to the white gloves I'd worn as a symbol of adulthood
and social status. "A lady never goes out of the house
without putting on her gloves," said my mother. Aunt
Lou lost gloves continually.

(Perhaps it was to the Royal York Hotel, that
bogus fairyland of nineteenth-century delights, red
carpeting and chandeliers, moldings and cornices,
floor-to-ceiling mirrors and worn plush sofas and brass-
trimmed elevators, that the first stirrings of my creative impulse could be traced. To me, such a building

seemed designed for quite other beings than the
stodgy businessmen and their indistinct wives who
were actually to be found there. It demanded ball
gowns and decorum and fans, dresses with off-the-
shoulder necklines, like those on the Laura Secord
chocolate boxes, Summer Selection, crinolines and
dapper gentlemen. I was upset when they remodeled
it.)

Once the bellhop was finally gone—he hung
around for a long time turning the lights on and off
and opening and closing the venetian blinds until I
remembered what I'd read about tipping—I opened
all the bureau drawers. I longed to write an elegant
note on the aristocratic stationery, but there was no
one at all I could write to. I took a bath, using up all
the monogrammed towels. I washed my hair and
rolled it up in a set of plastic-mesh-covered rollers.
All the time I was fat I'd worn my hair cropped short,
which emphasized the roundness of my face. My
mother kept making proposals for improvement;
she'd wanted me to wear a pageboy, then a poodle
cut, but I'd rejected everything. Now, however, I'd
been growing my hair for a year and it was shoulder-
length, dark red and straight. I didn't wear it loose
but kept it back with a bobby pin behind each ear.
When my hair was neatly rolled, I stood in front of
the full-length mirror on the back of the bathroom
door and examined myself, much as a real estate
agent might examine a swamp, with an eye to future
development. I was still overweight and I was still
baggy. There were stretch marks on my thighs, and
my face was that of a thirty-five-year-old housewife
with four kids and a wandering husband: I looked
worn down. But I had green eyes and small white
teeth, and luckily I didn't have pimples. I had only
eighteen pounds to go.

In the morning I bought a paper and went
through the want ads, looking for a room. I found one
on Isabella Street, called up the landlady and represented myself over the phone as a twenty-five-year-
old office girl, non-drinking and non-smoking. I

pinned my hair back, put on my white gloves and went off to inspect it. I gave my name as Miss L. Delacourt, and I used this name also when I opened a new bank account later in the day. I withdrew all my money from my other account and closed it; I didn't want my mother tracking me down. This was the formal beginning of my second self. I was amazed at how easily everyone believed me, but then, why should they suspect?

That afternoon I went to the hospital to see my father. I'd never been inside it before, so I had no idea how to find him. I asked receptionists and they asked each other until they discovered he was in an operating room. They wanted me to make an appointment or stay in the reception area—I hadn't told them I was his daughter—and I said I would. But I'd heard the floor number, and when none of them was watching I got up quietly and went to the elevator.

I stood outside the door, waiting, and finally he came out. I'd never seen him dressed in his official uniform: he had a white cap on and a gown, and a mask over the lower half of his face, which he was in the act of pulling down. He looked much more impressive than he ever had at home, he looked like someone with power. He was talking with two other doctors. I had to call out to him before he noticed me.

"Your mother's been worried sick," he said without annoyance.

"She's been worried sick all my life," I said. "I just wanted to tell you that I'm all right. I'm not coming back, I have a room and enough money."

He stared down at me with an expression I could not place then because I'd rarely had it directed my way. It was admiration, and perhaps even envy: I had done what he couldn't bring himself to do, I had run away. "Are you sure you're all right?" he said. When I nodded, he said, "I don't suppose I could persuade you to go around and see her?"

"She tried to kill me," I said. "Did she tell you that?" I was exaggerating, as the knife hadn't gone in very far, but I wanted to impress on him the fact

that it wasn't my fault. "She stuck a knife in my arm."
I rolled up my sleeve to show him the scratch.

"She shouldn't have done that," he said, as if
she'd made a left-hand turn where a right was required. "I'm sure she didn't mean to."

I agreed to keep in touch with him—I kept this
promise, more or less—but I refused to have anything more to do with my mother. He understood
my position. He said it in those words exactly, like a
man who has spent a lot of time understanding people's positions. I've remembered that phrase, and it
occurred to me a long time afterwards that no one
ever understood his position; not me, not my mother or Aunt Lou, not anyone. I don't think it was because he didn't have one. His position was the position of a man who has killed people and brought
them back to life, though not the same ones, and
these mysteries are hard to communicate. Other than
that, his position was that of a man who wears maroon leather slippers and fiddles with house plants on
weekends, and for this reason is thought of as an in-
consequential fool by his wife. He was a man in a
cage, like most men; but what made him different
was his dabbling in lives and deaths.

For the next couple of months I lived in my Isabella Street room, for which I paid fourteen dollars a
week. That included a change of sheets and towels
and a hot plate, on which I boiled cups of tea and prepared low-calorie snacks. The house itself was a red-
brick Victorian one—they've torn it down since and
built a highrise—with dark, creaky wooden-floored
hallways, a staircase which has been useful to me on
several occasions ("She glided up the staircase,
one hand on the banister . . ."), and a smell of furniture polish. Undercutting the furniture polish was another smell, probably vomit. Both the house and the
neighborhood had gone downhill; but the landlady
was a Scot and severe, so whatever vomiting went on
was done behind closed doors.

Other people lived in the house but I seldom
saw them, partly because I was out a lot. I trotted

briskly down the steps every morning as if I had a
job, but actually I was starving myself so I would be
able to collect Aunt Lou's money. In the evenings I
would return to my room and boil up a package of
peas or some corned beef on the single hot plate.
While I ate I mourned Aunt Lou. Now that she was
dead I had no one to talk to; I'd get out her fox fur,
which smelled of mothballs, and stare at it, hoping it
would miraculously open its mouth and speak, in the
voice of Aunt Lou, as it had during my childhood. I
tried going to the movies, by myself, but it only depressed me more, and with Aunt Lou absent I had to
deal with the attentions of strange men, which interrupted the films. In August I went to the Canadian
National Exhibition, a melancholy pilgrimage. I
hadn't been there with Aunt Lou for three years—
she must've felt I was getting too old for it—and it
seemed different, shoddier somehow, the gaiety
forced and raucous.

I went to the museum a lot, and the art gallery,
places where I could walk around and look as if I was
doing something, places where I would not be
tempted by food. I took bus trips: to St. Catharines,
to London, Ontario, to Windsor, and to Buffalo and Sy-
racuse and Albany. I was searching for a city I could
move to, where I would be free not to be myself. I
didn't want anything too different or startling, I just
wanted to fit in without being known.

It was on these bus trips that I first discovered
there was something missing in me. This lack came
from having been fat; it was like being without
a sense of pain, and pain and fear are protective, up
to a point. I'd never developed the usual female fears:
fear of intruders, fear of the dark, fear of gasping
noises over the phone, fear of bus stops and slowing
cars, fear of anyone or anything outside whatever
magic circle defines safety. I wasn't whistled at or
pinched on elevators, I was never followed down
lonely streets. I didn't experience men as aggressive
lechers but as bashful, elusive creatures who could
think of nothing to say to me and who faded away at

my approach. Although my mother had warned me about bad men in the ravine, by the time I reached puberty her warnings rung hollow. She clearly didn't believe I would ever be molested, and neither did I. It would have been like molesting a giant basketball, and secretly, though I treasured images of myself exuding melting femininity and soft surrender, I knew I would be able to squash any potential molester against a wall merely by breathing out. So when I shrank to normal size I had none of these fears, and I had to develop them artificially. I had to keep reminding myself: Don't go there alone. Don't go out at night. Eyes front. Don't look, even if it interests you. Don't stop. Don't get out of the car. Keep going.

I would be sitting near the center of the bus. Behind me would be a man smoking a cigar, beside me a stranger. Every couple of hours we would stop at a roadside restaurant where I would make sleepwalking trips to the Ladies', which smelled always of disinfectant and liquid soap. There I would wipe from my face with dampened paper towels the bus fumes, oily and brownish; and later, when the side of my head was bumping against the cold metal of the window frame and my body itched with the desire to sleep, a hand would appear on my thigh, stealthy, not moving, an exploratory hand, tense with the knowledge of its solitary mission.

When the hands appeared I couldn't cope with them. They took me by surprise. Men didn't make passes at fat girls, so I had no experience, and I was acutely uncomfortable. The hands didn't frighten or arouse me, they simply made me aware that I didn't know what to do. So I would pretend I didn't notice the hand; I would gaze out the window at the pitch-black landscape, while deft fingers crept up my thigh. At the next stop I would excuse myself politely and stumble off the bus, without much idea of what to do next.

Sometimes I would look for a motel; more often, though, I'd head for the bus-station restaurant and eat all the dry doughnuts and pieces of fish-glue pie I could afford. At these times I felt very lonely; I also longed to be fat again. It would be an insulation, a cocoon. Also it would be a disguise. I could be merely an onlooker again, with nothing too much expected of me. Without my magic cloak of blubber and invisibility I felt naked, pruned, as though some essential covering was missing.

Despite these relapses I dwindled. Suddenly I was down to the required weight, and I was face to face with the rest of my life. I was now a different person, and it was like being born fully grown at the age of nineteen: I was the right shape, but I had the wrong past. I'd have to get rid of it entirely and construct a different one for myself, a more agreeable one. And I decided against any of the places I'd visited. Living in a rented room in Albany would be the same, finally, as living in a rented room in Toronto, except that there would be less chance of running into my mother on the street. Or anyone else who might recognize me.

The thought of going on with the same kind of life for ever and ever depressed me. I wanted to have more than one life, and when at last I stepped triumphantly down from the scales in Mr. Morrisey's office and collected the money, I went straight to a travel agency and bought a plane ticket for England.

Chapter Fourteen

"You have the body of a goddess," the Polish Count used to say, in moments of contemplative passion. (Did he rehearse?)

"Do I have the head of one too?" I replied once, archly.

"Do not make such jokes," he said. "You must believe me. Why do you refuse to believe in your own beauty?"

But which goddess did he mean? There was more than one, I knew. The one on the Venus pencil package, for instance, with no arms and all covered with cracks. Some goddesses didn't have bodies at all; there was one in the museum, three heads on top of a pillar, like a fire hydrant. Many were shaped like vases, many like stones. I found his compliment ambiguous.

The Polish Count was an accident. I met him first when I fell off a double-decker bus near Trafalgar Square. Luckily I didn't fall from the upper deck; I had one foot halfway to the ground, but I wasn't used to having the bus start before people were safely off it and it leapt from under me, sending me sprawling onto the sidewalk. The Polish Count happened to be passing by, and he picked me up.

At the time I was living in a damp bed-sitter in Willesden Green. I found it through Canada House, which was the first place I went when I got to London. I was homesick already. I knew no one, I had nowhere to stay, and I was disappointed by what I'd seen of England on the bus from the airport. So far it was too much like what I had left, except that everything looked as though two giant hands had compressed each object and then shoved them all closer together. The cars were smaller, the houses were crowded, the people were shorter; only the trees were bigger. And things were not as old as I'd expected them to be. I wanted castles and princesses, the Lady of Shalott floating down a winding river in a boat, as in *Narrative Poems for Juniors,* which I studied in Grade Nine. I'd looked up *shalott,* fatally, in the dictionary: *shalot, kind of small onion.* The spelling was different but not different enough.

> *I am half-sick of shadows, said*
> *The Lady of Small Onion.*

Then there was that other line, which caused much tittering among the boys and embarrassment among the girls:

The curse is come upon me, cried
The Lady of Shalott.

Why did boys think blood running down a girl's leg
was funny? Or was it terror that made them laugh?
But none of it put me off, I was a romantic despite
myself, and I really wanted, then, to have someone,
anyone, say that I had a lovely face, even if I had to
turn into a corpse in a barge-bottom first.

Instead of the castles and ladies, though, there
was only a lot of traffic and a large number of squat
people with bad teeth.

Canada House, when I got there, was a marble
mausoleum, impressive but silent. A woman behind a
dark wooden counter in a cavernous, dimly lit room,
in which a few dour Canadians were reading week-
old Toronto newspapers and collecting their mail,
handed me a list of rooms to let. Since I knew nothing
about the topography of London I took the first one
I could get. Unfortunately it was an hour's ride
from the center via the underground, which was like
a traveling front parlor lined in purple plush; I kept
expecting to see footstools and potted palms. Toronto's new subway, on the other hand, with its pastel
tiles and smell of Dust-Bane, was more like a traveling bathroom. Already I was feeling provincial.

When I came up from the underground, I
walked along a street lined with tiny shops; an un-
healthy number of them were candy stores. The
woman at Canada House had drawn me a rough map;
she had also advised me to purchase a small Maple
Leaf and wear it on my lapel, so as not to be mistaken for an American.

The house was a Tudor cottage, the same as all
the others on the street, fake Tudor, fake cottage,
with a walled front garden. The landlord was a surly
man in shirtsleeves and braces who seemed to be
afraid I would have orgiastic parties and skip without
paying the rent. The room itself was on the ground
floor and smelled of rotting wood; it was so damp
that the furniture actually was rotting, though very

slowly. As I lay in my clammy bed the first night, wondering if I had taken off so much weight and come so far for nothing, a black man climbed in through the front window. But all he said was, "Wrong window, sorry," and climbed out again. I could hear faint sounds of a lively party going on farther down the street. I was disgustingly lonely. I was already thinking about moving somewhere else, a flat would be better, I would have more space; but this room was inexpensive and I wanted Aunt Lou's money to last as long as possible. When it was gone I would have to make a decision, choose what I was going to do, get a job (I could touch-type) or go back to school (perhaps I could be an archaeologist after all), but I wasn't ready yet, I wasn't adjusted. I'd spent all my life learning to be one person and now I was a different one. I had been an exception, with the limitations that imposed; now I was average, and I was far from used to it.

I wasn't supposed to cook in my room—the landlord felt his tenants were conspiring to set his house on fire, though this would have been difficult as it was so damp—but I was permitted to boil a kettle on the single gas ring. I took to drinking tea and eating Peek Frean biscuits, in bed, with all the covers pulled up around me. It was the end of October and piercingly chilly, and the heat in my room was controlled by shillings in the slot. So was the hot water in the shared bathroom; I took few baths. I began to understand why people on the underground smelled the way they did: not dirty exactly, but cooped-up. Aside from the tea and biscuits, I ate in cheap restaurants and soon learned to avoid the things I would ordinarily have eaten. "Hot dog," I found out, meant a reddish, thin object fried in lamb fat. "Hamburger" was a square, sawdusty-beige thing between two halves of a hard bun, and "milk shakes" tasted like chalk. I ate fish and chips, or eggs, peas and chips, or sausage and mash. I bought an undershirt.

I began to feel I should be doing something besides watching my stash of traveler's checks dwindle.

Travel was supposed to be broadening; why did I feel narrower? So I bought a map of England and picked out names that sounded familiar from high school, like York, or names that intrigued me, like Ripon. I would go to these places on the British Railway, stay overnight in a second-rate inn or a bed-and-breakfast, and come back the next day. I looked at historic buildings. I inspected churches and collected the pamphlets they had on racks with a slot for a six-pence, which I didn't always contribute. I learned what a "clerestory" was, and bought postcards, which made me feel I had been somewhere. These postcards I sent to my father, addressed to the hospital, with cryptic notes on them like, "Big Ben's not so big," and, "Why do they call it the Lake District? They should call it the Puddle District, ha ha." I began to feel that England was a message in code which I didn't know how to decipher, and that I would have to read a lot of books in order to understand it.

I'd been in England about six weeks when I fell off the bus. The Polish Count helped me up, and I thanked him. It was a simple enough beginning.

He was slightly shorter than I was, with wispy light-brown hair receding from his forehead, sloping shoulders, and rimless spectacles, which were not fashionable at the time. He was wearing a navy-blue overcoat, a little frayed and shiny, and carrying a briefcase. In order to help me up he set down the briefcase, placed a hand under each of my arm-pits, and gave a gallant heave. I almost toppled him over but we regained our balance, and he picked up his briefcase.

"Are you all right?" he asked, in a vaguely English accent. If I had been English I might have been able to tell he was a Polish Count; as it was, I could not.

"Thank you very much," I said. I had ripped a stocking and scraped my knee, and my ankle was badly twisted.

"You must sit down," he said. He steered me across the road and into a restaurant called, as I re-

member, The Golden Egg, and brought me some tea
and a black-currant tart, slightly squashed. His manner was warm but patronizing, as if I were an un-
usually inept child. "There," he said, beaming. I noticed that he had an aquiline nose, though it didn't
achieve its potential due to his height. "This tea is the
English remedy for everything. They are a strange
people."

"Aren't you English?" I asked.

His eyes—which were greenish-gray, or perhaps
grayish-green—clouded over behind his spectacles, as
if I'd asked a rude personal question. "No," he said.
"But in these days, one must adapt. You, of course,
are American."

I explained that I wasn't, and he seemed disappointed. He asked me if I liked to ski, and I replied
that I had never learned. "I owe my life to skis," he
said enigmatically. "All Canadians ski. How else would
one get around, over the snow?"

"Some of us use toboggans," I said. The word
puzzled him, and I explained.

I finished my tea. This was the moment, I felt,
when I should thank him graciously for his kindness
and leave. Otherwise we would have to exchange the
stories of our lives and I was too depressed about
mine to want to do that. So I thanked him and stood
up. Then I sat back down again. My ankle had swollen and I could barely walk.

He insisted on taking me all the way back to Willesden Green, supporting me as I hobbled to the underground station and along the street past the candy stores.

"But this is appalling," he said when he saw my
rooming house. "You can't live here. *Nobody* lives
here." Then he volunteered to wrap my ankle in
towels wrung out in cold water. He was doing this,
kneeling in front of me while I sat on the bed, when
the landlord appeared and gave me a week's notice.
The Polish Count informed him that the lady had
sprained her ankle. The landlord replied that he
didn't care what I had sprained, I was out come Thurs-

day, as he couldn't have that kind of carryings on in his house. It was the sight of my naked, tumescent foot that had offended him.

When he had gone, the Polish Count shrugged. "They are a small-minded people, the English," he said. "A nation of shopkeepers." I didn't know this was a quotation and thought it was very clever of him. I had been shocked to find Stonehenge surrounded by a fence, with a gate in it for taking tickets. "You have seen the Tower of London?" he asked. I hadn't. "We will go there tomorrow."

"But I can't walk!"

"We will go in a taxi, and by boat." He had not asked me, he had told me, so I didn't think of saying no. Also, he seemed old to me; in fact he was forty-one, but I put him in the category of aged and therefore harmless men.

On this excursion, he told me the story of his life. He requested mine first, as politeness demands. I said I'd come to London to study art at the art school, but I'd decided I had no talent. He sighed. "You are a wise girl," he said, "to have made this discovery so early in life. You will not delude yourself with false hopes. I myself once wished to be a writer, I wished to be like Tolstoy, you understand; but now I am exiled from my own language, and this one is fit for nothing but to make hoardings with. It has no music, it does not sing, it is always trying to sell you something."

I didn't know who Tolstoy was; I nodded and smiled. He went on to relate his personal history. His family had belonged to the upper class, before the war; he wasn't a Count exactly, but he was something or other, and he showed me a signet ring he wore on his little finger. It was a mythical bird, a griffin or a phoenix, I forget which. The family had scrabbled along under the Germans, but when the Russians invaded he knew he had to get out or be shot.

"Why?" I said. "You hadn't done anything."

He gave me a pitying look. "It is not what you do," he said, "but who you are."

He and a party of six others had skied to the border, where a guide was to meet them and take them across. But he became ill. He insisted the others go on without him, and crawled into a cave, certain he would die. The others were caught at the border and executed. He recovered and made his own way across, travelling at night and taking the direction from the stars. When he first arrived in England, he washed dishes in Soho restaurants to make a living; but once he had learned enough English, he obtained a position as a clerk in a bank, working in the foreign exchange department. "I am the last," he said, "of a dying race. The last of the Mohicans." In fact he had a daughter back in Poland, as well as a mother; but he had no son, and this weighed on him.

My first reaction to this story was that I had met a liar as compulsive and romantic as myself. But my usual impulse was to believe everything I was told, as I myself wished to be believed, and in this case it was the right impulse, since his story was essentially true. I was very impressed. He seemed to belong to a vanished and preferable era, when courage was possible. I limped through the Tower of London on his rather stringy arm with a mixture of emotions new to me: I felt sorry for him because of the sufferings he had undergone, I admired his daring, I was flattered by the attention he was paying to me and grateful for it, and especially I was pleased to be thought wise. I later found that almost anyone would tell you you were wise if you confessed you had no talent.

That was a Sunday. On Monday he had to work at the bank in the daytime, but in the evening he took me to dinner at a club for Polish expatriates, which was full of one-eyed Generals and other Polish Counts. "We are the few that are left," he said. "The Russians killed off the others."

"But weren't you both against the Germans?" I asked. He laughed gently and explained, at some length.

My own ignorance amazed me. All sorts of things had been happening behind my back, it appeared:

treacheries and famines, diplomatic coups, ideological murders and doomed heroic exploits. Why had no one told me? They had, perhaps, but I hadn't been listening. I had been worrying about my weight.

On Tuesday he took me to a chamber music concert, a benefit for some Polish political organization I had never heard of. I mentioned that I hadn't yet found another room.

"But you will live with me!" he exclaimed. "I have a nice place, very nice, very charming, with lots of room. Of course you must do this." He had the entire second floor of a house in Kensington, which was owned by a nonagenarian English Lord who was usually in a nursing home. The third floor was occupied by three working girls, but of a good class, he assured me: they worked in offices.

I thought it was very considerate and kind of him to offer to share his apartment with me. As he had never touched me, except to help me across the street or along it, because of my ankle, and had never made any suggestive remarks, I was quite surprised when, after I had brushed my teeth and was about to climb into bed (wearing, I believe, a heavy sack-shaped flannel gown I'd bought at Marks & Spencer's the week before), there was a discreet knock at my door and this man, whose first name I didn't even know, appeared in the doorway, dressed in a pair of blue-and-white-striped pajamas. He understood that he was getting into bed with me, and he understood that I understood this also.

The story I told Arthur later, about being seduced under a pine tree at the age of sixteen, by a summer camp sailing instructor from Montreal, was a lie. I was not seduced at all. I was a victim of the Miss Flegg syndrome: if you find yourself trapped in a situation you can't get out of gracefully, you might as well pretend you chose it. Otherwise you will look ridiculous. Innocence has its hazards, and in my case one of them was that the Polish Count couldn't conceive of anyone being as simpleminded as I was. If you ask a woman to move into your apartment and she consents, naturally she is consenting to be your mistress. It's an odd term, "mistress," but that was how he thought of me, these were the categories into which his sexual life was arranged: wives and mistresses. I was not the first mistress. For him there was no such thing as a female lover.

When describing the episode with the Montreal sailing instructor to Arthur, I took care to include some salacious details. I added a few convincing small touches as well, the pine needles sticking into my bum, his Jockey undershorts, the smell of Brylcreem; I was good at things like that. Of course I never went to summer camp in my life. My mother wanted me to, but it meant being shut up for two months with a pack of sadistic overgrown Brownies, with no escape. So I spent the summers lying about the house, eating and reading trashy books, some of which had salacious details. It was these I used in the story of my life; I had to borrow, because the first experience with the Polish Count was not at all erotic. My ankle hurt, the pajamas turned me off, and he looked weird without his spectacles. Also it was painful; and although he was patient and instructive later, though inclined to give performance points—it was almost like taking tap-dancing lessons—he wasn't on this occasion.

When he discovered I wasn't the easygoing art student manquée he'd thought I was—when he realized he had deprived me of my virginity—the Polish Count was filled with remorse. "What have I done?" he said mournfully. "My poor child. Why didn't you say something?" But anything I could have said would have been implausible. This was the reason I fabricated my life, time after time: the truth was not convincing.

So I said nothing, and he patted my shoulder anxiously. He felt he'd injured my chances for a good marriage. He wanted to make it up to me and couldn't understand why I wasn't more upset. I was sitting up in bed, pulling my flannel gown back on (for it was just as cold and damp in his flat as it had

been in mine) and watching his long, melancholy face
with the green-gray eyes slightly askew. I was glad it
had happened. It proved to me finally that I was normal, that my halo of flesh had disappeared and I
was no longer among the untouchables.

Chapter Fifteen

I often wondered what would have happened if I'd
stayed with the Polish Count instead of moving in
with Arthur. Maybe I would be fat and content, sitting in his apartment during the day, wearing a flowered negligee, doing a little embroidering, a little
mending, reading trashy books and eating chocolates;
in the evenings we would dine out at the Polish
Officer's Club and I would be treated with respect,
more or less; I would have an acknowledged position,
I would be "Paul's mistress." But it wouldn't have
worked, he was too methodical. His first name was
Tadeo but he preferred to be called Paul, his third
name, after Saint Paul, who was a systematic man,
no loose ends. His idea of the good life was that it
should be tidy.

Even his escape over the Polish border had been
tidy. ("But it was chance that saved your life!" I exclaimed. "No," he said, "I would have been dead anyway if I had not used my head.") He calculated his
course precisely and emerged from the forest at the
exact point he intended. To keep himself awake and
to dispel the hallucinations he was having, he recited
the multiplication tables as he plodded through the
snow and the darkness (plodded, for he had given his
skis to a member of the doomed party). He didn't
panic, as I would have done; he paid no attention to
the vivid geometrical shapes and, later, the menacing
faces that appeared before him in the air. I too had
seen the shapes and the faces, during my attack of

blood poisoning, and I knew that my response, especially in the depths of that Polish forest, dense as hair, cold as despair, would have been to sit down in the snow and let disaster overtake me. Details would distract me, the candle stubs and bones of those who had gone before; in any labyrinth I would have let go of the thread in order to follow a wandering light, a fleeting voice. In a fairy tale I would be one of the two stupid sisters who open the forbidden door and are shocked by the murdered wives, not the third, clever one who keeps to the essentials: presence of mind, foresight, the telling of watertight lies. I told lies but they were not watertight. My mind was not disciplined, as Arthur sometimes pointed out.

So did Paul. He was compulsive about time, he had to leave the house at precisely eight-fifteen, and before that he spent ten minutes by the clock polishing his shoes and brushing his suit. He found my lack of order charming, but not for long; soon he was making speeches about how much easier it was to hang up one's clothes at the time, rather than leaving them in a heap on the floor till the next morning. He didn't expect much of me—after all, I was only a mistress—but those few things he expected absolutely. I think he considered training me to live with him a minor and tedious challenge, sort of like training a dog: a limited number of tricks, learned thoroughly.

With the exception of that first surprising night he confined sex to weekends. He believed in separate rooms, so I slept on a fold-out bed in the room he called the library. He was not stingy or repressive by nature, but he was a man with a mission, and because I slept in the library I soon discovered what it was.

The first day, after he left for the bank, I slept in till eleven. Then I got up and browsed around the flat, opening the kitchen cupboards, looking for something to eat but also exploring the personality of this man who the night before had, as they say, violated my honor. I was curious, and you can tell a lot about a person from their kitchen cupboards. Paul's were very well-organized; tinned goods prevailed, with some utilitarian dried soups and a package of water biscuits. The foods were of two kinds, bare necessities and exotica: squid, I recall, and some seal meat (which we had later; it was rank and oily). Next I did the refrigerator, which was spotless and almost empty. I ate several water biscuits with some tinned sardines, then made myself a cup of tea and went into Paul's room to go through his closet and bureau drawers. I was careful not to disturb anything. There were some tinted photos on the bureau, the lips purplish, the hair yellowish-gray. Boxer shorts; all his pajamas were striped except for a pair of silk ones. Under the boxer shorts there was a revolver, which I didn't touch.

I went back to the library, intending to get dressed, but I thought I'd go through the bookshelves first. The books were mostly old, cloth- and leather-bound with marbled endpapers, the kind you find on secondhand book tables. A number of them were in Polish, though there were English ones too: Sir Walter Scott, quite a lot of that, and Dickens and Harrison Ainsworth and Wilkie Collins; I remember the names because I subsequently read most of them. But there was one shelf that puzzled me. It consisted of nurse novels, the mushy kind that have a nurse on the cover and a doctor in the background gazing at her with interest and admiration, though never pop-eyed with desire. They had titles such as *Janet Holmes, Student Nurse; Helen Curtis, Senior Nurse;* and *Anne Armstrong, Junior Nurse.* Some had more daring titles, such as *Romance in Paradise* and *Lucy Gallant, Army Nurse.* They were all by a woman with the improbable name of Mavis Quilp. I skimmed through a couple, remembering them well. I'd read dozens, back in my fat days. They were standard fare, each ending with nurse and doctor wrapped in each other's arms as firmly and antiseptically as elastic bandages. There was something odd about the language, the clichés were a little off, distorted just slightly. For instance, someone said, "They're selling like pancakes" instead of "hotcakes," someone else said, "Keep a stiff upper jaw," and Anne Armstrong "trombled" rather than trembled when the doctor brushed past her, though that could have been a typo. Other than this, however, they weren't remarkable; but they were so out of place in Paul's library that I asked him about them that evening.

"Paul," I said, when we were seated opposite each other at the kitchen table, eating the tinned seal meat and drinking the half-bottle of champagne he had brought back as a propitiation offering, "why do you read those trashy books by Mavis Quilp?"

He gave me a peculiar, twisted smile. "I never read those trashy books by Mavis Quilp."

"Then why do you have fourteen of them in your library?" Perhaps Paul was a secret agent—which would explain the revolver—and the Quilp books were messages in code.

He was still smiling. "I write those trashy books by Mavis Quilp."

I dropped my fork. "You mean, *you're* Mavis Quilp?" I started to laugh, but was stopped by the offended look on his face.

"I have a mother and a daughter on the inside," he replied stiffly.

The story he told me was this. On first arriving in England, he had still fancied himself a writer. He had written a three-volume epic dealing with the fortunes of a petit-aristocratic family (his) before, during and after the war, laboring away at it with the help of a dictionary in the intervals between his ten-hour stints as a dishwasher. He would rather have written in Polish, but felt it was no use. His novel had thirteen major characters, all of them related, and each with an entourage of wives, mistresses, friends, children and uncles. When he'd finished his book at last and had typed it, painfully, himself, he took it to a publisher. He knew nothing of publishers; inadvertently, he had chosen one that did nothing but Westerns, nurse novels and historical romances.

They rejected his novel, of course, but they were impressed by the quality and especially the quantity of his work. "You can turn it out, all right, mate," the man had told him. "Here's a story line for you, write it up and keep it simple, a hundred quid. Fair enough?" He had needed the money.

While his three-volume epic went the rounds of other, more respectable publishers—it never did get accepted—he churned out junky novels, using at first the story lines provided for him, later supplying his own. He was now receiving between two and three hundred pounds a book, no royalties. With his new job at the bank he earned exactly enough to support himself, so the nurse-novel money was extra, and he sent it to his mother and daughter in Poland. He had a wife there too, but she had divorced him.

The publisher had offered him Westerns and historical romances, but he stuck to his specialty. For Westerns you had to use words like "pard," which he didn't feel comfortable with; and historical romances would depress him, they would remind him of his old, privileged life. (Escape literature, he told me, should be an escape for the writer as well as the reader.) With nurse novels he didn't need to learn anything extra or use any strange words except a few medical terms easily found in a first-aid handbook. He had chosen his pseudonym because he found the name Mavis to be archetypically English. As for Quilp. . . .

"Ah, Quilp," he sighed. "This is a character from Dickens, it is a deformed, malicious dwarf. This is what I see myself to be, in this country; I have been deprived of my stature, and I am filled with bitter thoughts."

Status, I thought; but I did not say it. I was learning not to correct him.

"What about something more like you," I suggested. "Spy stories, you know, with intrigue and international villains. . . ."

"That would be too much like life," he sighed.

"For nurses, nurse novels may be too much like life," I said.

"Nurses do not read the nurse novels. They are read by women who wish mistakenly to be a nurse.

In any case, if the nurses wish to avoid the problems of their life, they must write spy stories, that is all. What is gravy for the goose will be misplaced on the gander, such is fate." Paul believed in fate.

It was to Paul, then, that I owed my choice of career. Aunt Lou's money was running out, much faster than I'd anticipated, though I was trying to be economical, and I didn't like the thought of getting a job. Nobody likes that thought, really, they only do it because they have to. I could touch-type, but it seemed to me I could make money faster by typing at something of my own, and other people's business letters are very boring. Also, there was nothing much for me to do on weekday evenings while Paul sat bashing away at his current book, *Judith Morris, Arctic Expedition Nurse*, chain-smoking Gauloises stuck in a short gold cigarette holder he kept clenched between his teeth, and drinking one glass of tawny port per evening. At such times, contempt for his readers and for himself hovered in the room like a cloud of smoke, and his temper after one of these sessions was foul but cold, like smog.

I asked Paul to get me some samples of historical romances from Columbine Books, his publisher, and I set to work. I joined the local library and took out a book on costume design through the ages. I made lists of words like "fichu" and "paletot" and "pelisse"; I spent whole afternoons in the costume room of the Victoria and Albert Museum, breathing in the smell of age and polished wood and the dry, sardonic odor of custodians, studying the glass cases and the collections of drawings. I thought if I could only get the clothes right, everything else would fall into line. And it did: the hero, a handsome, well-bred, slightly balding man, dressed in an immaculately tailored tweed cloak, like Sherlock Holmes's, pursued the heroine, crushing his lips to hers in a hansom cab and rumpling her *pelisse*. The villain, equally well-bred and similarly clad, did just about the same thing, except that in addition he thrust his hand inside her *fichu*. The rival female had a lithe body like that of a jungle animal beneath her exquisitely stitched corset, and like all such women, she came to a bad end. I wasn't as good at bad ends as I later became: I think she merely tripped on her *paletot*, going downstairs. But she deserved this, as she'd attempted to reduce the heroine to a life of shame by tying her up and leaving her in a brothel, under the supervision of a madam to whom I gave the features of Miss Flegg.

But I had aimed too high. My first effort came back with instructions to the effect that I could not use words like "fichu" and "paletot" and "pelisse" without explaining what they meant. I made the necessary revisions and received my first hundred pounds, with a request for more material. Material, they called it, as if it came by the yard.

I was quite thrilled when two copies of *The Lord of Chesney Chase* arrived in a brown-paper parcel, with a dark-haired woman in a plum-colored traveling cloak on the cover and my pen name in white lettering: Louise K. Delacourt. For of course I used Aunt Lou's name; it was a kind of memorial to her. Several years later, when I'd switched to a North American publisher, I was asked for a photograph. It was for the files, they said, to be used for publicity; so I sent them the shot of Aunt Lou at the Ex, with me standing beside her. This picture was never used. The women who wrote my kind of book were supposed to look trim and healthy, with tastefully grayed hair. Unlike the readers, they had brisk shoulders and were successful. They weren't supposed to squint into the sun, displaying both rows of teeth and holding a cone of spun sugar. The readers preferred not to think of their fairy godmothers, the producers of their delicate nightly masquerades, as overblown and slightly frowsy, with slip straps that showed and necklines that gaped, like Aunt Lou's. Or my own.

Initially Paul encouraged me, partly because of the money. He liked the idea of having a mistress, but he couldn't really afford to keep one. After the first five or six months, when I started earning more per book than he did, he even began to charge me rent, though having me sleeping in his library didn't cost him any extra. I was grateful for his belief, not in my talent exactly, for he didn't feel that writing this kind of book required any, but in my perseverance: I could think up plots almost as fast as he could, and I was a better typist, so I could equal him page for page on a good night. At first he was paternal and indulgent.

In some ways he reminded me of the man with the bouquet of daffodils who had exposed himself in that chivalrous and touching way on the wooden bridge when I was a young Brownie. Paul too had that air of well-meaning but misplaced gallantry; they were both, I thought, gentle and harmless beneath their eccentricities, asking only simple gratifications that didn't impose too much on the partner or watcher. And both of them had rescued me, perhaps, though the identity of the daffodil man was still not clear to me.

I couldn't tell about Paul's identity either, for as time went on he began to change. Or possibly I merely learned more about him. For instance, he viewed the loss of my virginity as both totally his fault—thus making him responsible for me—and a fall from grace which disqualified me from ever being a wife, or his wife at any rate. He thought my lack of guilt was a sign of barbarism. Anyone from across the Atlantic Ocean was a kind of savage to him, and even the English were questionable, they were too far west. So he ended by being angry with me for my failure to cry, though I told him over and over that this wasn't the sort of thing I cried about.

Then there were his views on the war. He seemed to think that the Jews were in some obscure metaphysical way responsible for it, and thus for the loss of his family chateau.

"But that's ridiculous," I said, outraged; he couldn't mean it. "That's like saying a rape victim is responsible for being raped, or a murder victim. . . ."

He drew imperturbably on his Gauloise. "This

also is true," he said. "They have brought it upon themselves."

I thought about the revolver. I couldn't ask him about it without revealing that I'd snooped in his room, and I knew by now he would find this unforgivable. I began to feel a little like Eva Braun in the bunker: what was I doing with this madman, how did I get into this thoroughly sealed place, and how could I get out? For Paul had an end-of-the-world fatalism: civilization for him had either already collapsed or was about to. He thought there would be another war, in fact he hoped there would; not that he thought it would solve or improve anything, but so that he himself might fight in it and distinguish himself by acts of bravery. He hadn't resisted enough in the last one, he felt; he'd been too young to know that he should've stayed and perished in the forest with the rest of the slaughtered army. To have lived, to have survived, to have escaped was a kind of disgrace. But he didn't picture war as tanks, missiles and bombs, he pictured it as himself on horseback, with a sabre, charging against impossible odds. "Women do not understand these things," he'd say, clenching his teeth down on the end of his cigarette holder. "They believe that life is babies and sewing."

"I can't sew," I said, but he would merely say, "Later you will sew. You are so young," and go on to prophesy more doom.

I recited slogans of hope, in vain; he would only smile his twisted little smile and say, "You Americans are so naive, you have no history." I'd given up trying to tell him I was not an American. "It is all the same thing, isn't it?" he would say. "The lack of one kind of history is the same as the lack of another."

Ultimately our differences were: I believed in true love, he believed in wives and mistresses: I believed in happy endings, he in cataclysmic ones; I thought I was in love with him, he was old and cynical enough to know I wasn't. I had merely been deluded into this belief by my other belief, the one in true love. How could I be sleeping with this peculiar man, who was no Bell Telephone Mercury, without being in love with him? Surely only true love could justify my lack of taste.

Because Paul knew I was not in love with him, because he thought of me as a mistress and of mistresses as unfaithful by nature, he began to have fits of jealousy. It was all right as long as I did nothing but loll around the flat, reading and typing out my Costume Gothics and going nowhere except with him. He didn't even mind my trips to the Victoria and Albert; he didn't notice them much, because I was always home before he was and I didn't go there on the weekends. It was over the Portobello Road that we came to the parting of the ways. He himself introduced me to it, and it quickly became an obsession with me. I would pore for hours over the stalls of worn necklaces, sets of gilt spoons, sugar tongs in the shape of hen's feet or midget hands, clocks that didn't work, flowered china, spotty mirrors and ponderous furniture, the flotsam left by those receding centuries in which, more and more, I was living. I had never seen things like this before; here there was age, waves of it, and I pawed through it, swam in it, memorized it—a jade snuffbox, an enameled perfume bottle, piece after piece, exact and elaborate —to fix and make plausible the nebulous emotions of my costumed heroines, like diamonds on a sea of dough.

What amazed me was the sheer volume of objects, remnants of lives, and the way they circulated. The people died but their possessions did not, they went round and round as in a slow eddy. All of the things I saw and coveted had been seen and coveted previously, they had passed through several lives and were destined to pass through several more, becoming more worn but also more valuable, harder and more brilliant, as if they had absorbed their owners' sufferings and fed on them. How difficult these objects are to dispose of, I thought; they lurk passively, like vampire sheep, waiting for someone to buy them. I myself could afford almost nothing.

After these excursions I would return to the flat exhausted, my energy drained, while back in their stalls the coral rose brooches, the cairngorm pins, the cameos with their ivory profiles would be glowing in the dusk, sated as fleas. No wonder Paul began to suspect I had a lover and was sneaking off to visit him. Once he followed me; he thought I didn't see him, dodging in and out of the racks of used evening gowns and feather boas, like a comic private eye. It was beneath his dignity, of course, to actually accuse me of anything. Instead he threw tantrums because I wanted to go to the Portobello Road on Saturday, the good day, and he felt this day should be reserved for him. He began to attack my novels too, calling them cheap and frivolous, and it infuriated him when I agreed with him pleasantly. Of course they were cheap and frivolous, I said, but I had never claimed I was a serious writer. He took this as a dig at his own previous ambitions. Probably he would rather have found out I had a lover than discovered I didn't. A lover would have been less humiliating.

Paul was beginning to frighten me. He would wait for me at the top of the stairs after my orgies in the Portobello Road, standing there like a newel post, not saying anything, and as I came up the steps he would fix me with a reproachful, vindictive stare. "I saw a wonderful Victorian jack-in-the-box today," I would begin, but my voice would sound false, even to myself. I'd always found other people's versions of reality very influential and I was beginning to think that maybe he was right, maybe I did have a secret lover. I certainly began to want one, for making love with Paul had begun to resemble a shark fight, he was no longer gentle, he was pinching and biting and coming into the library on weekdays. It would have been all right except for the baleful glances and the oppressive silences, and the revolver, which was making me anxious.

Also, he'd just announced that the Polish government had agreed to let his mother out of Poland.
He had saved up for it and at last it would happen,
it was easier to get the old ones out than the young
ones, he said. But I didn't want a Polish Countess
living with us—where would she sleep?—discussing
me in Polish and siding with Paul against me and
ironing his boxer shorts, which I refused to do. He
was devoted to his mother, which was tolerable only
at a distance. But when I mentioned moving out, to
give them more space, I said, he wouldn't hear of it.

Chapter Sixteen

I never told Arthur about Paul, which was perhaps
a mistake. Not that he would have minded the fact
that I was living with another man; but he would
have been horrified by Paul's title, such as it was, and
by his politics. Any woman who could live with such
a man would have been stamped *wrong* by Arthur
right away, and this was obvious to me fifteen minutes after I met him.

I was walking in Hyde Park, in July 1963. From
either side came the sound of orations, doom-laden
as the Old Testament, but I only half heard them.
It was almost my twenty-first birthday, but I wasn't
thinking about that either. I was pacing out the route
which was about to be taken by Samantha Deane,
the heroine of *Escape from Love*, as she fled from the
illicit attentions of Sir Edmund DeVere. He'd just
tried to take advantage of her in the children's schoolroom while everyone else had gone off to the Crystal
Palace for the day.

*As Samantha hurried down the stairs, her cheeks
burned with the memory of what had just occurred.*

She'd been sitting alone in the schoolroom, working on the piece of crewelwork she kept for her few leisure moments. She hadn't heard the door open, hadn't heard Sir Edmund approach until he was within two yards of her chair. With an exclamation of surprise, she had risen to her feet. Sir Edmund was flushed and dishevelled. His usual iron control had vanished. As he gazed at her, his eyes flamed like those of some wild animal that scents its quarry.

"Sir Edmund," Samantha said, trying to keep her voice level. "What is the meaning of this intrusion? Why are you not at the Crystal Palace with the others?" Yet despite her efforts her knees were weak, either with fright or with a response she tried in vain to deny.

"I knew you were alone," he said, moving closer. "I slipped away. You must take pity upon me, you must know that my life is hell." Yet he was not pleading, he was demanding. He seized her by the wrist and drew her toward him, pressing his hard mouth against hers. In vain she struggled, fighting both him and her own unbidden desires. His avid hands were already at her throat, tearing aside her fichu. . . .

"Remember who you are!" she managed to gasp. "You are a married man!" His only answer was a harsh laugh. Desperately she remembered the short thick needle she still grasped in her right hand. She lifted it and raked it across his cheek. More in surprise than in pain, he released her, and she made use of this moment to run for the door, to slam it behind her and twist the heavy key in the lock. She was too terrified to think of taking a cloak or even a shawl.

Now she was hurrying through the Park, without knowing how she'd gotten there. Her thin black dress was little protection against the chill air of evening. Where was she to go, what to do? What explanation would Sir Edmund give the others, especially Lady Letitia, when they returned to find him locked in the schoolroom and the governess gone? Whatever he said would be to her discredit, she was sure; she

could not return; and after that he would seek her
out, hunt her down. . . . She had only a few pennies
in her reticule. Where was she to spend the night?

Dark shapes flitted by on either side, and from
time to time she heard low, mocking laughter. . . .
Daughters of sin, vile abandoned creatures such as
she herself might have become had she not struggled.
. . . But perhaps she was now in even more danger.
Alone, weak, unprotected—to what dissolute reveler
might she not fall prey? She had not forgotten the
lecherous advances of the Earl of Darcy, Sir Ed-
mund's uncle. Then she had fled from his residence
to Sir Edmund's, seeking protection; but the protec-
tor had failed her. . . .

There were footsteps behind her. She shrank into
the shade of a tree, hoping to escape notice, but a
shadow loomed against the setting sun, there was a
hand on her arm, and a voice, hoarse with passion,
breathed her name. . . .

At this point in my rehearsal I felt something
on my arm. I looked down at it; there *was* a hand on
it. I screamed, quite loudly, and the next thing I knew
I was lying on top of a skinny, confused-looking
young man. Pieces of paper were scattered over us
like outsized confetti. Then I was being helped to my
feet by several members of the crowd that had immediately gathered.

"Tryin' to molest yer, was he, love?" said one,
burly and beer-scented. "Bleedin' agitators."

"I was just handing her a leaflet," said my assailant. To my horror I saw that he had a slight cut on his
cheek. I felt like an idiot.

"Want to call a bobby, love? They should be put
away, they should, bothering young girls."

"No, thank you," I said. An anti-vivisectionist
and a prophet of doom had both come over from
their soap boxes to help. They were almost identical,
saintly refined old men with pale-blue Ancient Mari-
ner eyes. When they saw I wasn't hurt, each gave me
a pamphlet.

"It was entirely my fault," I told everyone. "It was a mistake. I thought he was someone else. I just panicked, that's all. Here, let me get you a Kleenex," I said to the young man. "I'm sorry I scratched you." I rummaged in my purse but was unable to find one.

"It's all right," he said stoically. He was on his knees, gathering up his leaflets, and I knelt to help him. The leaflets had a black-and-white drawing of an atomic bomb explosion, and the motto, KEEP THE WORLD FROM GOING UP IN SMOKE. "Banning the bomb?" I asked.

"Yes," he said gloomily. "Not that it's doing any good. But you have to keep on."

I looked at him more closely. He was wearing a black crew-neck sweater, which I found quite dashing. A melancholy fighter for almost-lost causes, idealistic and doomed, sort of like Lord Byron, whose biography I had just been skimming. We finished collecting the pamphlets, I fell in love, and we went for a drink at the nearest pub. That wasn't hard to maneuver: all I had to do was express interest in the cause, I would've preferred it if he'd had a British accent; unfortunately he was only a Canadian, like me, but I overlooked this defect.

While Arthur stood in line at the bar for my double Scotch and his Guinness—when he drank at all, he tended to drink things that were supposed to have health giving minerals in them—I felt anxiously through my brain for whatever scraps of political lore might have lodged there inadvertently, like bits of spinach among front teeth. I'd presented myself as someone who was at least semi-informed; now I'd have to come across. I even took out the pamphlets I'd been handed and glanced rapidly through them, hoping for some hint or topic. *Do you know that* DOG *spelled backwards is* GOD? one of them began. DOG, apparently, was the fourth member of the Holy Trinity, and was going to be in on the Last Judgment. The other pamphlet was more orthodox: Armageddon was at hand and if you wanted to come out of it you had to lead a pure life.

When Arthur returned with the drinks I was ready for him. Whenever the conversation got too specific, I switched the subject to the plight of the Palestinian refugees. I knew quite a lot about this from my days in the U.N. Club at Braeside High. At the time, this area was obscure enough to catch Arthur's attention, and I was ashamed to see that he was moderately impressed.

I let him walk me as far as the Marble Arch tube station. I couldn't invite him home with me, I explained, because I shared a flat with a clerk-typist who was very fat and homely, and who became quite unhappy and depressed if I asked any men into the flat for whatever reason. It was best to avoid phoning, I told him, but if he could give me his number. . . . He didn't have a phone, but, even better, he invited me to a rally the next day. Faint with lust, I went to the public library—the same one where I got my costume books—and took out all of Bertrand Russell's books I could find, which caused some difficult moments with Paul when he came across them. "Communistic trash," he raged. "I will not allow them within my household."

"I was only doing research," I said. "I thought I might do something a little more modern this time, set in the twenties."

"It will not sell," said Paul. "If you raise the skirts and cut the hair, it will not sell. They prefer it if the woman should retain her mystery. As I do," he added, kissing me on the collarbone.

At one time I would have found remarks like this very European and charming, but they were beginning to irritate me. "Some mystery," I said, "if all it takes is a few yards of cloth and a wig. Men are mysterious too, you know, and I don't notice them wearing ringlets and waltz-length ballgowns."

"Ah, but the mystery of man is of the mind," Paul said playfully, "whereas that of the woman is of the body. What is a mystery but a thing which is remaining hidden? It is more easy to uncover the body than it is the mind. For this reason, a bald man is not looked upon as an unnatural horror, but a bald woman is."

"And I suppose a moronic woman is more socially acceptable than an idiot man," I said, intending sarcasm.

"Just so," said Paul. "In my country they were often used as the lowest form of prostitute, whereas a man with no mind, for him there was no use." He smiled, feeling he'd proved his point.

"Oh, for heaven's sake," I said. I stomped out to the kitchen to make myself a cup of tea. Paul was puzzled. He was also suspicious: he still couldn't understand my sudden interest in Bertrand Russell.

I had a lot of trouble with these books, and, I discovered, with theories and politics in general. I didn't want to be blown up by an atomic bomb, but on the other hand I couldn't believe that anything I could do would prevent it. I might as well be trying to abolish the automobile: if I got run over by one, I'd be just as dead, I reasoned. I thought Lord Russell had a very appealing face, though, and I immediately gave him a bit part in *Escape from Love* as a benevolent old eccentric who rescues Samantha Deane in Hyde Park by beating her assailant over the head with his umbrella. (*"Take that, sir! Are you all right, my dear?" "How can I ever express my gratitude?" "I see you are well brought up, and I believe your explanation. Allow me to offer you asylum for the night. . . . My housekeeper will lend you a nightgown. Mrs. Jenkins, a cup of tea, if you please, for this young lady."*) I even supplied him with a hobby—he raised guppies—which made me feel quite friendly towards all his frontispieces and able to tolerate his policies and the awe-tinged admiration with which Arthur regarded him.

If Arthur had known about my little dramatization of Lord Russell, he would've been appalled. "Trivializing," he would have called it, and did call it in later years, when I was less able to conceal this particular habit of mine. Also when I was less willing to simulate adoration of Arthur's hero-of-the-day: Arthur was fickle, he changed allegiances, and after I'd been through this a few times I became wary. "What about *Mrs.* Marx?" I would say, or, "I bet Marx's wife wanted him to be a doctor." All I would get would be a disgusted look, so I would go into the kitchen and fantasize about the home life of Marx. "Not tonight, dear, I have a headache, you intellectuals are all the same, mooning around, why don't you get out there and make something of yourself if you're so smart, god knows you have the talent."

I thought of Castro as a tiger in bed though, with those cigars and that beard, which would explain his vogue in North America. But Mao was my favorite, you could tell he liked to eat. I pictured him wolfing down huge Chinese meals, with relish and no guilt, happy children climbing all over him. He was like an inflated Jolly Green Giant except yellow, he wrote poetry, he had fun. He was fat but successful and he didn't take any shit about it. The home life of Stalin was boring, too much was known about it, he was such a puritan anyway. But Mao, what a garden of delights. He encouraged jugglers and spectacles, he liked the color red and flags and parades and table tennis; he knew the people needed food and escape, not just sermons. I liked to think about him in the bathtub, all covered with soap, like an enormous cherub, beaming away and very appreciative while some adoring female—me!—scrubbed his back.

As far as I was concerned, it was impossible to love a theory. I didn't love Arthur for his theories, although they lent him a kind of impersonal grandeur, like a crimson-lined opera cloak. I loved him for the way his ears stuck out, just slightly; for the way he pronounced certain words—"aunt," for instance, and "grass." Being from the Maritimes, he said *ahnt* and *grahss*, whereas I was from Ontario and said *ant* and *graass*. I found this exotic. I loved his deliberate threadbareness, his earnest idealism, his ridiculous (to me) economies—he used tea bags twice—the way he stuck his finger in his ear, his farsightedness and the battered reading glasses he had to wear for it. Once I said, "I guess that's why you like me, you can't see what I look like up close." It was a little early to make this joke; he said, "No, that isn't the reason." Then there was a long, awkward pause, as if he was trying to think very hard about the reason he did like me. Or perhaps, I thought with a sinking of the stomach, about whether he liked me at all.

This was a problem. I couldn't tell what Arthur felt about me, if anything. He seemed to enjoy discussing the philosophy of civil disobedience with me, or rather telling me about it, for I was wise enough not to reveal my ignorance and mostly nodded. He allowed me to go around handing out leaflets with him, and ate with relish the sandwiches I would bring on these occasions. He told me about his background, his father the judge, his mother the religious nut. His father had wanted him to be a lawyer, his mother had insisted he be a medical missionary at the very least. He'd thwarted both of them by going into Philosophy, but he hadn't been able to stick it through all the syllogisms ("A bald man is bald," he said, "what does that have to do with the human condition?" and for once I could agree without hypocrisy ... until I started thinking about it; what if you *were* a bald man?). He'd left after his third year, to take a break and meditate on the true path. (That was the difference between us: for Arthur there were true paths, several of them perhaps, but only one at a time. For me there were no paths at all. Thickets, ditches, ponds, labyrinths, morasses, but no paths.)

Then he'd gotten involved in the ban-the-bomb movement, which had absorbed him for two years. He'd devoted a lot of time and energy to the movement, but somehow he was still on the fringes, a leaflet man. Perhaps it was because he was a Canadian.

I radiated sympathy and understanding. We were sitting in a cheap restaurant, which smelled of lamb fat, eating plates of fried eggs, chips and peas, which was what Arthur mostly ate. He was running out of money; soon he'd have to take another occasional job, sweeping floors or folding napkins or, worst of all, washing dishes; either that or accept what he considered his parents' bribery and go back to school at the University of Toronto, which he hated with a cool, abstract passion.

His Earlscourt flat had a small kitchen, but he didn't like cooking, and the kitchen itself was a shambles. He shared the flat with two other men, a New Zealander who was studying at the London School of Economics and who ate cold, ketchup-covered canned baked beans and left the unwashed plates around like the scenes of tiny slaughters, and a gazelle-eyed radical from India who cooked brown rice and curries for himself and also left the plates around. Arthur was fastidious; he didn't like messes. But he was so fastidious he wouldn't clean them up, so we ate out. Once or twice I went over and tidied the kitchen for them, but this had no good effects and a couple of bad ones. Arthur was given another false impression about me: I wasn't at heart a kitchen-tidier, and he was disappointed later when he found this out. The New Zealander, whose name was Slocum, pursued me around the kitchen with pleas ("Be a sport, I haven't had one bit since I got to this bleeding cold-hearted country, not one bit"), and the Indian radical lost the initial respect he'd had for me as a politico of sorts and began to make cow-eyes and flare his nostrils. One could not, apparently, be both a respected female savant and a scullery maid.

Meanwhile, I couldn't get any further with Arthur than holding hands; and life with Paul was becoming more and more insupportable. What if he were to follow me, find me handing out leaflets with Arthur, and challenge him to a duel, or something equally upsetting? It was Arthur I loved, not Paul, I decided. I took drastic measures.

I waited till Paul had left for the bank; then I packed everything I owned, including my typewriter and the half-finished manuscript of *Escape from Love*. I scribbled a note for Paul. I wanted to say, "Darling, it's better this way," but I knew this was not dramatic enough, so instead I wrote, "I have been making you unhappy and we cannot go on like this. It was not to be." I didn't think he would be able to trace me, and I didn't really think he would try. Still, he was a great one for points of honor. Perhaps he would materialize in the doorway one evening with some grotesque, theatrical weapon, a paper knife or a straight razor. I didn't see him using the revolver; it was too modern. Before I could lose my nerve, I bundled all my luggage into a taxi, and unbundled it onto Arthur's doorstep. He would be home, I knew, I'd checked it out the day before.

"I've been evicted," I told him.

He blinked. "Just like that?" he said. "I think that's illegal."

"Well, it's happened," I said. "Because of my political sympathies. The landlord found some of those leaflets . . . he's violently right-wing, you know. There was a terrible row." (This was a version of the truth, I felt. Paul was the landlord, sort of, and he was right-wing. Nevertheless I was an impostor, and I felt like one.)

"Oh," said Arthur. "Well, in that case. . . ." I was a political refugee. He invited me in so we could consider what I should do, and he even helped me carry the luggage up the stairs.

"I don't have any money," I said, over a cup of tea which I'd made myself in the filthy kitchen. Neither did Arthur. Neither did either of his roommates, he knew for a fact. "I don't know anyone else in London."

"I guess you can sleep on the sofa," he said, "until you get a job." What else could he say? We both looked at the sofa, which was ancient and lumpy; stuffing dripped from its mangled side.

I slept on the sofa for two nights; after that I slept with Arthur. We even made love. I'd been expecting fervor of a kind, because of his politics, but the first few times it was a lot more rapid than I was used to. "Arthur," I said tactlessly, "have you ever slept with a woman before?" There was a pause, during which I could feel his neck muscles tense. "Of course I have," Arthur said coldly. It was the only direct lie he ever consciously told me.

Once I was there, installed in his own house under his very nose, Arthur began to pay more attention to me. He even became affectionate, in his own way; he would brush my hair for me, clumsily but with concentration, and he would sometimes come up behind me and hug me, apropos of nothing, as if I were a teddy bear. I myself was bliss-filled and limpid-eyed: the right man had come along, complete with a cause I could devote myself to. My life had significance.

There were difficulties, though: the Indian and the New Zealander were ubiquitous, opening our door in the mornings to borrow shillings from Arthur, the New Zealander leering, the Indian remote with the ascetic disapproval he'd assumed as soon as he found out we were sleeping together. Or the New Zealander would sit on the sofa, listening to his transistor radio and doing rapid calculations under his breath, while the Indian took baths, leaving the wet towels on the floor; he was fond of saying that no one understood the evils of the class system the way he did, since he'd been raised in it, but he couldn't get over the habit of regarding anyone who picked up a towel as a servant. Both resented my presence; or rather, they resented what they regarded as Arthur's good fortune. Arthur himself wasn't conscious of their resentment, or of his good fortune either.

The other difficulty was that I could find neither time nor space to work on *Escape from Love*. When Arthur went out, he expected me to go with him; and if by any chance I could avoid that, one of the others was sure to be there. I kept the manuscript in a locked suitcase, as I suspected the New Zealander of snooping in our room. One day I returned to find that the Indian had hocked my typewriter. He'd repay me later, he promised, but after that I resented every grain of brown rice he ate. I didn't have enough money left to get it out of the pawnshop myself, and I'd counted on at least two hundred pounds for the finished work. I grew daily and secretly more desperate. Arthur didn't know about this problem; he kept wondering why I hadn't yet got a job as a waitress. In the fictitious past I'd constructed for his benefit I'd included a few items of truth, and I'd told him I had once been a waitress. I also told him I'd once been a cheerleader, and we laughed together over my politically misguided past.

When I'd been with them three weeks I was almost broke. Nevertheless, one day I blew a few precious shillings on some remnant material for bathroom curtains, a red-and-orange floral print. They'd make the bathroom less chilly and cavernous, I thought. I was going to sew them myself, by hand. I'd never sewn anything before in my life. I came up the stairs, humming to myself, and unlocked the door of the flat.

There, standing in the middle of the parlor floor, was my mother.

Chapter Seventeen

How had she found me?

She was standing, very upright, on the clay-colored rug, dressed in her navy-blue suit with the white collar; her white gloves, hat and shoes were immaculate, and she was clutching her purse under her arm. Her face was made up, she'd drawn a bigger mouth around her mouth with lipstick, but the shape of her own mouth showed through. Then I saw that she was crying, soundlessly, horribly; mascara was running from her eyes in black tears.

Through her back I could see the dilapidated sofa; it looked as though the stuffing was coming out of her. The hair on the back of my neck bristled, and I leapt back through the front door, shut it behind me, and leaned against it. It was her astral body,

I thought, remembering what Leda Sprott had told me. Why couldn't she keep the goddamned thing at home where it belonged? I pictured my mother floating over the Atlantic Ocean, her rubber band getting thinner and thinner the farther it was stretched; she'd better be careful or she'd break that thing and then she'd be with me forever, lurking around in the parlor like a diaphanous dustball or a transparent Kodak slide of herself taken in 1949. What did she want from me? Why couldn't she leave me alone?

I opened the door again, to confront her and have it out finally; but she was gone.

I immediately rearranged all the furniture, which was difficult as it was old and heavy. Then I went through the flat, checking for open windows, but there weren't any. How had she gotten in?

I didn't tell the others about this visitation. They were a little put out about the furniture; not that they cared, but they felt I should have consulted them. "I was trying to save you the trouble," I said. "I just think it looks better this way." They put it down to housewifely instincts and forgot about the incident. I didn't, though: if my mother had managed to get her astral body across the Atlantic Ocean once, she'd be able to do it again, and I didn't welcome the next visit. I wasn't sure that rearranging the furniture would keep her out. Leda Sprott had used it for unfriendly spirits, but my mother wasn't a spirit.

I got the telegram five days later. It had been sitting in Canada House for four days; I'd continued to get my mail there and I'd used it as my return address on the infrequent postcards I'd been sending my father, in case my mother should ever have taken it into her head to sleuth me out and hunt me down. I didn't pick up my mail very often, because all I ever got was the occasional postcard from my father, with a picture of the Toronto skyline as seen at night from Centre Island—he must've bought several dozen of them at once—and the message, "Everything all right here," as if he were sending me a report card.

The telegram said: YOUR MOTHER DIED YESTERDAY. RETURN PLEASE. FATHER.

I read it three times. At first I decided it was a trap: my mother had sent it herself, she'd got the address off one of my postcards left carelessly lying around by my father, she was trying to lure me back within striking distance. But in that case she would have said YOUR FATHER DIED YESTERDAY. However, she might have realized that I wouldn't want to return while she was still alive, and sent the telegram as a false all-clear signal.

But what if she really was dead? In that case she'd turned up in my front parlor to tell me about it. I didn't at all want this to be true, but I suspected it was. I would have to go back.

When I reached the flat, the Indian radical was sitting crosslegged on the floor, explaining to Arthur, who was on the sofa, that if he had sexual intercourse too much he would weaken his spirit and thereby his mind, and would become politically useless. The thing to do, he said, was to draw the seminal fluid up the spinal column into the pituitary gland. He used the example of Gandhi. I listened to this conversation for a couple of minutes through the half-opened door (listening outside doors was a habit I'd retained), but since I couldn't hear what Arthur was answering, if anything, I walked in.

"Arthur," I said, "I have to go back to Canada. My mother died."

"If she's dead already," he said, "why go back? There's nothing you can do."

He was right, but I needed to know she was really dead. Even if I phoned the house long-distance and spoke with my father, I couldn't be sure. . . . I would have to see her. "I can't explain," I said, "it's a family thing. I just have to go back."

Then we both remembered that I didn't have any money. Why hadn't my father sent me some? He'd assumed that I was competent and solvent; he always assumed that there was nothing the matter with me, I was a sensible girl. My mother would have known better. "I'll think of something," I said. I sat on the bed and chewed my fingers. My typewriter was in hock, *Escape from Love* was locked in my suitcase, untouched since I'd moved in with Arthur; it was only half done. I had hardly enough money for the paper to complete it. I could write my father for money, but that would be a precious pound, and besides, my bank account here was in the name of Louisa K. Delacourt. That would be hard to explain to my father, especially by telegram. It might hurt his feelings.

I slipped the manuscript into my bag. "I'm going to the library," I told Arthur. Before I left, I pinched one of the New Zealander's cheap yellow notepads and a ballpoint pen. No use to borrow: there would have been an inquisition.

For the next two days I sat in the library reading room, laboriously block-printing and tuning out the rustlings, creakings, wheezings and catarrhal coughs of the other occupants. Samantha Deane was kidnapped precipitously from her bedroom in the house of the kindly guppy man; threatened with rape at the hands of the notorious Earl of Darcy, the hero's disreputable uncle; rescued by the hero; snatched again by the agents of the lush-bodied, evil-minded Countess of Piedmont, the jealous semi-Italian beauty who had once been the hero's mistress. Poor Samantha flew back and forth across London like a beanbag, ending up finally in the hero's arms, while his wife, the feeble-minded Lady Letitia, died of yellow fever, the Countess, now quite demented, plunged to her death off a battlement during a thunderstorm and the Earl was financially ruined by the Pacific Bubble. It was one of the shortest books I'd ever written. Fast-paced though, or, as the jacket put it, event followed event to a stunning climax. I picked up a copy in Toronto when it came out. Samantha was charming in blue, her hair rippling like seaweed against an enormous cloud; Castle DeVere turreted with menace in the background.

But I got less for it than usual, partly because of

the length—Columbine paid by the word—and partly because the bastards knew I needed the money. "The conclusion is a little *unresolved*," said the letter. But it was enough for a one-way airplane ticket.

My mother was dead, all right. Not only that, I'd missed the funeral. I didn't think to telephone from the airport, so as I walked up the front steps of the house in Toronto I didn't know whether or not anyone would be there to welcome me.

It was evening and the lights in the house were on. I knocked; no one answered so I tried the door, found it open, and walked in. I could see she was dead right away because some of the plastic covers were on the chairs and some were off. My mother would never have done a thing like that. For her, they were either on or off: the living room had two distinct and separate personalities, depending on whether or not she was entertaining. The uncovered chairs looked faintly obscene, like undone flies.

My father was sitting in one of the chairs, wearing his shoes. This was another clue. He was reading a paperback book, though abstractedly, as if he no longer needed to absorb himself in it completely. I saw this just for an instant before he noticed me.

"Your mother's dead," he said. "Come in and sit down, you must have had a long trip."

His face was more furrowed than I'd remembered it, and also more defined. Previously it had been flat, like a coin, or even like a coin run over by a train; it had looked as though the features had been erased, but not completely, they were smudged and indistinct as if viewed through layers of gauze. Now however his face had begun to emerge, his eyes were light blue and shrewd, I'd never thought of him as shrewd; and his mouth was thin, even a little reckless, the mouth of a gambler. Why had I never noticed?

He told me that he'd found my mother at the bottom of the cellar stairs when he'd returned from the hospital one evening. There was a bruise on her temple and her neck was oddly twisted, broken, as he recognized almost immediately. He had called an ambulance for form's sake although he knew she was dead. She was wearing her housecoat and pink mules, and she must have tripped, my father said, and fallen down the stairs, hitting her head several times and breaking her neck at the bottom. He hinted at the amount she had been drinking lately. The verdict at the inquest was accidental death. It could not have been anything else, as there were no signs of anyone having been in the house and nothing had been taken. This was the longest conversation I ever had with him.

I was overcome by a wave of guilt, for many reasons. I had left her, walked out on her, even though I was aware that she was unhappy. I had doubted the telegram, suspecting a plot, and I hadn't even made it back for the funeral. I had closed the door on her at the very moment of her death—which, however, couldn't be determined exactly, as she had been dead for five or six hours at least by the time my father found her. I felt as if I'd killed her myself, though this was impossible.

That night I went to the refrigerator, *her* refrigerator, and gorged myself on the contents, eating with frantic haste and no enjoyment half a chicken, a quarter of a pound of butter, a banana cream pie, storebought, two loaves of bread and a jar of strawberry jam from the cupboard. I kept expecting her to materialize in the doorway with that disgusted, secretly pleased look I remembered so well—she liked to catch me in the act—but despite this ritual, which had often before produced her, she failed to appear. I threw up twice during the night and did not relapse again.

My suspicions began the next day, when my father said to me at breakfast, looking at me with his new, sly eyes and sounding as if he'd rehearsed it, "You may find this difficult to believe, but I loved your mother."

I did find it difficult to believe. I knew about the

twin beds, the recriminations, I know that in my mother's view both I and my father had totally failed to justify her life the way she felt it should have been justified. She used to say that nobody appreciated her, and this was not paranoia. Nobody did appreciate her, even though she'd done the right thing, she had devoted her life to us, she had made her family her career as she had been told to do, and look at us: a sulky fat slob of a daughter and a husband who wouldn't talk to her, wouldn't move back to Rosedale, that stomping ground of respectable Anglo-Saxon money where his family had once lived, was he ashamed of her? The answer was probably yes, although during these conversations my father would say nothing; or he would say that he hadn't liked Rosedale. My mother would say that my father didn't love her, and I believed my mother.

Stranger still was his need to say to me, "I loved your mother." He wanted to convince me, that was clear; but it was also clear that he hadn't really been expecting me to come back from England. He'd already given my mother's clothes to the Crippled Civilians, he'd made footmarks all over the rug, there were dirty dishes in the sink at least three days old, he was systematically violating all the rules. He said an even more suspicious thing on the second day. He said, "It isn't the same without her," sighing and looking at me as he did so. His eyes pleaded with me to believe him, join the conspiracy, keep my mouth shut. I had a sudden image of him sneaking out of the hospital, wearing his white mask so he would not be recognized, driving back to the house, letting himself in with his key, removing his shoes, putting on his slippers and creeping up behind her. He was a doctor, he'd been in the underground, he'd killed people before, he would know how to break her neck and make it look like an accident. Despite his furrows and sighs he was smug, like a man who'd gotten away with something.

I told myself, in vain, that this was not the sort of thing he would do. Anything is the sort of thing anyone would do, given the right circumstances. I began to hunt for motives, another woman, another man, an insurance policy, a single overwhelming grievance. I examined my father's shirt collars for lipstick, I sifted through official-looking papers in his bureau drawers, I listened in on the few phone calls he received, crouching on the stairs. But nothing turned up, and I abandoned my search a lot sooner than I would have if I'd been convinced. Besides, what would I have done if I'd found out my father was a murderer?

I switched to speculations about my mother; I could afford to speculate about her, now that she was no longer there. What had been done to her to make her treat me the way she did? More than ever, I wanted to ask my father whether she was pregnant before they got married. And what about that young man in her photograph album, with the white flannels and expensive car, the one she said she'd been more or less engaged to? More or less. Some tragedy lurked there. Had he thrown her over because her father had been a stationmaster for the CPR? Was my father second-best, even though he was a step up for her?

I got out the photograph album to refresh my memory. Perhaps in the expressions of the faces there would be some clue. But in all the pictures of the white-flannelled man, the face had been cut out, neatly as with a razor blade. The faces of my father also were missing. There was only my mother, young and pretty, laughing gaily at the camera, clutching the arms of her headless men. I sat for an hour with the album open on the table before me, stunned by this evidence of her terrible anger. I could almost see her doing it, her long fingers working with precise fury, excising the past, which had turned into the present and betrayed her, stranding her in this house, this plastic-shrouded tomb from which there was no exit. That was what she must have felt. It occurred to me that she might have committed suicide, though I'd never heard of anyone committing suicide by throwing themselves down the cellar stairs. That would explain my father's furtiveness, his wish to be believed, his eagerness to get rid of her things, which would remind him perhaps that he was partly to blame. For the first time in my life I began to feel it was unfair that everyone had liked Aunt Lou but no one had liked my mother, not really. She'd been too intense to be likable.

It was partly my failure as well. Had I been wrong to take my life in my own hands and walk out the door? And before that I had been the fat mongoloid idiot, the defective who had shown her up, tipped her hand: she was not what she seemed. I was a throwback, the walking contradiction of her pretensions to status and elegance. But after all she was my mother, she must once have treated me as a child, though I could remember only glimpses, being held up by her to look at myself in the triple mirror when she'd brushed my hair, or being hugged by her in public, in the company of other mothers.

For days I brooded about her. I wanted to know about her life, but also about her death. What had really happened? And especially, if she'd died in her pink housecoat and mules, why had she turned up in my front parlor wearing her navy-blue suit from 1949? I decided to find Leda Sprott and ask her for a private sitting.

I looked her up in the phone book, but she wasn't there. Neither was the Jordan Chapel. I took a streetcar to the district where it had stood, and walked up and down the streets, searching for it. Finally I found the house; no doubt about it, I remembered the gas station on the corner. But a Portuguese family lived there now, and they could tell me nothing. Leda Sprott and her tiny band of Spiritualists had vanished completely.

I stayed with my father for nine days, watching my mother's house disintegrate. Her closets and dresser drawers were empty, her twin bed stood made but unused. Dandelions appeared on the lawn, rings around the bathtub, crumbs on the floor. My father did not exactly resent my presence, but he didn't urge me to stay. We had been silent conspirators all our lives, and now that the need for silence was removed, we couldn't think of anything to say to each other. I used to imagine that my mother was keeping us apart and if it weren't for her we could live happily, like Nancy Drew and her understanding lawyer Dad, but I was wrong. In fact she'd held us together, like a national emergency, like the Blitz.

Finally I got a room by myself, on Charles Street. I couldn't really afford it, but my father told me he was planning to sell the house and move into a one-bedroom apartment on Avenue Road. (He eventually married again, a nice legal secretary he met after my mother's death. They moved to a bungalow in Don Mills.)

For a while after my mother's death I couldn't write. The old plots no longer interested me, and a new one wouldn't do. I did try—I started a novel called *Storm over Castleford*—but the hero played billiards all the time and the heroine sat on the edge of her bed, alone at night, doing nothing. That was probably the closest to social realism I ever came.

The thought of Arthur contributed to my depression. I should never have left, I told myself. We'd kissed goodbye at the airport—well, not the airport exactly, but he'd seen me to the BOAC bus terminal —and I'd told him I'd come back as soon as I could. I'd written him faithfully every week, and I'd explained that I couldn't return just yet as I didn't have the money. For a while he'd answered; odd letters, full of news about his leaflet activities, which he signed "Yours sincerely." (I signed mine, "Love and a thousand kisses, XXXX.") But then there was silence. I didn't dare to think about what had happened. Was there another woman, some pamphlet-distributing chippy? Maybe he'd simply forgotten about me. But how could he, when I'd left most of my luggage in his apartment?

I got a job as a makeup demonstrator at the

cosmetics counter in Eaton's, selling mascara. But I cried a lot at night and my eyes were puffy, so they switched me to wigs. Not even the good wigs, the synthetic ones. It wasn't very interesting work, and the customers' fruitless quest for youth and beauty depressed me. Occasionally when no one was looking I would try on the wigs myself, but it was mostly the gray ones. I wanted to see how I would look when I was older. I would soon be old, I felt, and nothing would happen to me in the meantime because I wasn't interested in anything or anyone. I'd been deserted, I was convinced of it now. I was miserable.

Chapter Eighteen

I sat in exile on the Roman curb, on top of my portable Olivetti in its case, and wept. Pedestrians paused; some said things to me. I wanted Arthur back, I wanted him right here, with me. If I explained, how could he be angry? I'd handled things very badly. . . .

I stood up, wiped my face with a corner of my scarf, and looked around for a newsstand. I bought the first postcard I could find and wrote on the back of it, *I'm not really dead, I had to go away. Come over quickly. XXX.* I didn't sign my name or put any address: he would know who it was and where to find me.

After I'd mailed it I felt much better. Everything would be all right; as soon as he got the postcard Arthur would fly across the ocean, we would embrace, I'd tell him everything, he would forgive me, I would forgive him, and we could start all over again. He would see that I couldn't possibly go back to the other side, so he would change his name. Together we would bury all his clothes and buy new ones, once I'd sold *Stalked by Love*. He would grow a beard or a moustache—something distinguished and pointed, not the amorphous frizz that made men look like out-of-control armpits—and he might even dye his hair.

I remembered the hair dye. I located the equivalent of a drugstore and spent some time going through the rinses, tints, washes and colorings. I finally settled for Lady Janine's "Carissima," a soft, glowing chestnut, autumn-kissed, laced with sunlight and sprinkled with sparkling highlights. I liked a lot of adjectives on my cosmetic boxes; I felt cheated if there were only a few.

To celebrate the birth of my new personality (a sensible girl, discreet, warm, honest and confident, with soft green eyes, regular habits and glowing chestnut hair), I bought myself a *fotoromanzo* and sat down at an outdoor café to read it and eat a *gelato*.

If Arthur were here he'd be helping me to read the *fotoromanzo*. We practiced our Italian that way, reading the speeches from the rectangular voice balloons out loud to each other, looking up the hard words in our pocket dictionary and figuring out the meanings from the black-and-white photos. Arthur found this faintly degrading; I found it fascinating. The stories were all of torrid passion, but the women and men never had their mouths open and their limbs were arranged like those of mannequins, their heads sat on their necks precise as hats. I understood that convention, that sense of decorum. Italy was more like Canada than it seemed at first. All that screaming with your mouth closed.

In this one the mother was secretly the lover of the daughter's fiancé, *fidanzato*. "I love you," she said, plaster-faced; *Ti amo*. She was wearing a negligee. "Do not despair," he said, gripping her shoulders. They never seemed to say anything I really needed, like "How much are the tomatoes?" In the next square the woman's negligee was slipping off her shoulder.

A shadow loomed over me. I started and looked up: it was only a stranger though, white teeth and overpressed suit, nylon tie, pink and green. I knew that single women weren't supposed to sit alone in bars, but this wasn't a bar and it was the middle of the day. Perhaps it was the *fotoromanzo* that had attracted him. I closed it, but he'd already sat down at my table.

"*Scusi, signora.*" He asked me a question; I had no idea what it meant. I smiled weakly and said, "*Inglese, no parlo Italiano,*" but he grinned even more intensely. In his eyes our clothes fell to the floor, we fell to the floor, the white glass-topped table overturned and there was broken glass everywhere. Don't move, Signora, not even your hand with the wedding ring, where is your husband? Or you will cut yourself and there will be a lot of blood. Stay here on the floor with me and let me run my tongue over your belly.

I scrambled to my feet, gathering up my purse, hoisting the typewriter. The man behind the counter grinned as I paid my bill. How could I have allowed it, a man with such pointed shoes and a pink-and-green nylon tie? He reminded me of the vegetable man in the market square, with his grape-colored eyes, caressing the furry peaches, hefting the grapefruits possessively as breasts. My hand slid through his lambswool hair, we surged together on a wave of plums and tangerines, grapevines twined around us. . . .

Arthur, I thought, you'd better get my postcard fairly soon or something regrettable is going to happen.

It was midafternoon by the time I got back to Terremoto. I went to the post office, as I'd been doing every day, hoping for news from Sam. So far there had been nothing. "Louisa Delacourt," I said as usual, but this time the woman behind the counter turned her whole body, like the wax fortune-teller at the Canadian National Exhibition, who would pick out a card for you if you gave her a dime. Her hand came through the slot in the window, holding a blue airmail letter.

Outside, beyond the eyes of the lounging policemen, I tore it open and read a single word: BETHUNE. That was the code word for success. If there had been a fiasco, the letter would have said TRUDEAU. Sam was convinced the Mounties examined his mail; not only the mail he received but also the mail he sent out. "That'll fix the buggers," he said. "Let them try to figure that one out."

I crumpled the thin blue letter and stuffed it into my purse. Relief flooded through me, I was really free now; the inquest had gone all right, the stories of Sam and Marlene had been believed, I'd had a boating accident. I was officially dead even though no body had been found.

Charlotte was having tea with Mrs. Ryerson, the plump, friendly housekeeper. So far, she was the only person in the entire household that Charlotte could trust. A fire was blazing on the hearth, shedding warmth and rosy reflections. Nevertheless, Charlotte did not feel quite safe. She wondered whether she should tell Mrs. Ryerson about her destroyed wardrobe; but she decided not to, not just yet. . . .

"Mrs. Ryerson," Charlotte said, buttering a scone, "what is the maze?"

A shadow crossed Mrs. Ryerson's face. "What maze, miss?"

"Tom, the coachman, warned me not to go near it."

"And I wouldn't if I was you, miss," Mrs. Ryerson said emphatically. "It's not a good place, the maze, especially for young girls."

"But what is it?" Charlotte asked, puzzled.

"It's one of them mazes, miss, as was planted by the Master's forebears, hundreds of years ago, in the reign of Good Queen Bess it was, or so they say. The Master won't talk of it, ever since the first Lady

Redmond was lost there, and the second one too, in broad daylight it was. Some say the Little Folk dance there and they don't like intruders, but that's just superstition. The first Lady Redmond, she said so too, and she went into it just to prove it was harmless, but she never did come out. They searched it later but nothing was found, nothing but one of her gloves, white kid it was."

Charlotte was astonished. "You mean . . . there's been more than one Lady Redmond?" she asked.

Mrs. Ryerson nodded. "This one's the third," she said. "The second one, a sweet girl she was too, she got so curious about what happened to the first, she went in as well. That time they heard her screaming, but when they went in—Tom the coachman it was and two of the grooms—she was gone. Spirited right away, as you might say. It's all overgrown, you know, miss."

In spite of herself, Charlotte shivered. "Why. . . . That's extraordinary," she murmured. She felt a strong desire to visit the maze, to look at it, if only from the outside. She didn't believe in supernatural agencies. "What about . . . the present Lady Redmond?" she asked.

"She don't go near it, as I know of," Mrs. Ryerson replied. "Some say as how there's no center to the maze and that's how they get lost, they gets into it and can't find their way out. Some say as how the first Lady Redmond and the second one are still in there, wandering around in circles." Mrs. Ryerson glanced over her shoulder; despite the warmth of the room, she drew her shawl more closely about her.

Charlotte finished the scone and licked her fingers fastidiously. "Why, that's ridiculous," she said. "Who ever heard of a maze without a center?" But she was thinking uneasily of the events of the night before. . . . She'd been in her bedroom, and she'd heard a sound . . . a sound that came from outside, below, on the terrace . . . the sound of footsteps . . . and then, surely she was not mistaken, the sound *of someone calling her name. An icy tremor of fear shot through her. She arose and went to the window. There, below her, clearly visible in the eerie light from the moon, which had just appeared from behind a wisp of gauzy cloud, stood a figure . . . a figure swathed in a dark cloak, its features concealed.*

As Charlotte gazed, the figure turned and stalked away with measured steps. Who was trying to mystify her? Anger replaced her fear, and curiosity: she would get to the bottom of this. Hastily she made her way down the back stairs, which terminated, she knew, in a side door opening onto the terrace.

She was just in time to see the figure plunge into a yawning portal at the end of the terrace walk. Charlotte followed rashly; she hurried down a flight of stone steps. Before her was the lawn, with its formal Elizabethan flower plots, and beyond that . . . the entrance to the maze. The cloaked figure plunged into the entranceway and disappeared; from somewhere came a low laugh.

Charlotte stood still. . . . Suddenly she was terrified. She felt drawn towards the maze, irresistibly, against her will, yet she knew that if she went in, something terrible would happen to her.

A hand on her arm made her start and scream, and she was looking up into the dark, enigmatic face of Redmond.

"A little late to be out walking, is it not?" he said mockingly. "Or perhaps you were intending to . . . meet someone. You seem dressed for some such occasion."

Charlotte blushed crimson. She realized she was wearing nothing but her nightrail; beneath its snowy covering her breasts moved with agitation.

"I . . . I must have been walking in my sleep," she said in confusion. "I do not recall ever having done so before."

"A dangerous custom," Redmond remarked, tightening his grip on her arm—for she had attempted to pull away—"and dangerous customs must

*be paid for." His face bent closer to her own; his
eyes were gleaming in the light from the crescent
moon. "And now. . . ."*

I'd been typing at the table, with my eyes closed;
but as I paused to consider how Charlotte was going
to get away this time (there were no library books
around, no candelabra, no pokers from the fireplace
she could hit him with; perhaps a good swift knee
in the groin? But that was out of bounds in my books;
it would have to be an interruption by a third party),
I heard a sound.

There was someone outside, on the path. I could
hear stealthy footsteps, coming down towards me. A
shoe slid on gravel. The footsteps paused.

"Arthur?" I said in a small voice. But it wasn't
Arthur, it couldn't be, so soon. I wanted to scream,
to rush into the bathroom and shut and bolt the
door, I could squeeze through the small window and
run up the hill to my car, where did I put the
keys? Faces formed and disintegrated in my head.
. . . What did they want?

I realized how visible I must be, back-lit behind
the picture window. I froze, listening, then turned
out the light and crouched down behind the table.
Was it Mr. Vitroni, come back for some dubious reason in the middle of the night? Was it a stranger,
someone, some man, who'd heard I lived alone? I
couldn't remember whether or not I'd locked the
door.

For a long time I huddled behind the table, listening for a sound, feet coming toward me, feet
retreating. I could hear insects, a distant whine, a
car winding up the hill toward the square . . . but
nothing else.

Finally I got up and looked out the front window
onto the balcony, then out the kitchen window,
then out the bathroom window. Nothing and nobody.

It was nerves, I told myself. I would have to
watch that. I climbed into bed, taking my *fotoromanzo* with me to calm myself down. I could read it

without a dictionary, almost, since there were a lot of words and phrases I already knew. *I am not afraid of you. I don't trust you. You know that I love you. You must tell me the truth. He looked so strange. Is something the matter? Our love is impossible. I will be yours forever. I am afraid.*

PART FOUR

Chapter Nineteen

"So!" cried Felicia, breaking in upon them. "This is how you disport yourself when my back is turned. Really, Redmond, I wish you would have more consideration." She was wearing a dark cloak, thrown loosely over a sumptuous costume of flaming orange silk, with blue velvet trim. In an instant Charlotte was certain that it was Felicia who had called her name, lured her out of the house in her nightrail. It was Felicia who had written BEWARE in blood across her yellowing, warped bedroom mirror. . . . Perhaps it was a conspiracy between the two of them. But Felicia seemed in earnest and her surprise appeared genuine. Charlotte's conviction wavered as she watched them confront each other.

"First it was the upstairs maid," Felicia stormed. "Then that girl you hired to repair the leather bindings in the Library. If you must behave this way, you might have a little more taste. Next time have the goodness to select someone from your own class."

"Of what do you accuse me, madam?" Redmond growled. Despite herself, Charlotte felt a surge of sympathy toward him. Surely he only behaved this way because of the unhappiness of his marriage; surely if he were truly loved, unselfishly and purely instead of with Felicia's jealous possessiveness, he would be a different man. But she quickly suppressed this thought.

"Of carrying on in a shameless manner with this . . . this. . . ."

"May I ask what you yourself are doing out at this time of night?" Redmond asked, his voice a menacing purr.

Before Felicia could answer, Charlotte found her own anger coming to her rescue. "I refuse to stand *here any longer. You may believe me or not, both of you, as you choose." She turned and ran back toward the house, holding back the tears that she knew would come unbidden as soon as she could reach the safety of her room. She felt humiliated and degraded. Behind her, she could hear Felicia laughing, and perhaps Redmond was laughing too. She hated both of them.*

As she ran along the terrace, a heavy stone jar, one of the ornaments of the balcony above, toppled over and crashed on the balustrade beside her, breaking into pieces, missing her by inches. Charlotte stifled a scream; she glanced up into the darkness. She knew now, it was beyond a doubt, she'd seen a black-cloaked shape whisking away, someone was trying to kill her. . . .

I'd set up the typewriter on the table. It worked all right, but there was no letter *k* in the Italian alphabet: I substituted *x*. And the keyboard was different, which meant I had to look. It was distracting, like some curious Martian code. I began to write the *k*'s in by hand, wondering what "xill" meant. I stared at the word. . . . A kind of Aztec lizard, a Roman numeral?

Arthur would have known. He was good at crossword puzzles. But Arthur wasn't there.

Arthur, I thought, my eyes filling with tears, where are you? Why won't you come and find me? At any moment he might appear at the door, unexpectedly. He had done it once.

He had arrived at night, in the middle of a rainstorm. The landlady knocked at the door of my room. "Miss Delacourt," she said, "it's ten o'clock. You know you aren't supposed to have visitors after seven." I was lying on the bed, staring at the ceiling.

"I don't have any visitors in here," I said, opening the door to show her it was true. I never had any visitors.

"There's one downstairs," she said. "I told him he couldn't come in. Said his name was Arthur something," she said, as she slopped off down the hall in her kimono and shower thongs.

I ran down the front stairs, clutching the banister. It couldn't be Arthur, I'd given him up for lost. His last letter was dated September 8; it was now November. But if by some miracle it was Arthur and the landlady had sent him away. . . . I flung open the front door, prepared to gallop down the street after him in my terrycloth bathrobe. He was just turning to go back down the steps.

"Arthur," I screamed, throwing my arms around him from behind. He was wearing a yellow plastic raincoat with the collar turned up about his ears; his head was cold and soaking wet. We teetered on the edge of the top step; then I let go and he turned around.

"Where the hell have you been?" he said.

I couldn't ask him in, since the landlady was keeping watch around the corner of the upstairs hall, so I got my umbrella and rubber boots and went off into the night with him. We had some granular coffee in a late-night hamburger-and-chile place and unravelled the past.

"Why didn't you write?" I said.

"I did but the letters got returned." He'd sent them to my father's address; he, of course, was no longer there.

"But I sent you my new address," I said, "as soon as I moved. Didn't you get it?"

"I've been back here since the middle of September," he said. "Slocum was supposed to be forwarding my mail, but I didn't get any of it till today."

How unjust I'd been to doubt him. I was overjoyed to see him, I felt we should immediately go somewhere to celebrate and then hop into bed. "It's great that you're back!" I said.

Arthur didn't think it was great. He was quite depressed, and looked it: all his corners were turned down, eyes, mouth, shoulders. "What's the matter?" I asked, and he told me, at some length.

The Movement had fallen to pieces. He dropped dark hints, but I could never figure out whether it had been crushed by a show of force from without, had been infiltrated and destroyed from within, or had disintegrated through general lack of morale and squabbles among its members. Whatever the reason, something he'd believed in and worked for had failed, and this failure had plunged him into a state of existential gloom. He'd spent some time being torpid, and then in despair he'd agreed to accept money from his parents—surely I must see how bad things had been —and return to the University of Toronto. He was supposed to be writing a paper on Kant.

So it wasn't purely a longing to see me that had brought him across the ocean. It was inertia and the absence of a sense of purpose. I didn't mind that much, so long as he was there, and he had gone to a lot of trouble to find me. He'd walked at least three blocks in the rain: that meant dedication of a sort.

We spent the rest of the evening, and many evenings that followed, discussing whether or not it was ethical for him to stay in Toronto and go to the university on money that he considered tainted. "But if it's for a good end—" I would say. I didn't care whether it was ethical or not: I wanted him to stay with me, and the alternative he was proposing was a trip to northern British Columbia to work in an asbestos mine. "It's not for a good end," he would reply mournfully. "What use is Kant anyway? It's all abstract bullshit. . . ." But he lacked the willpower to quit.

All that winter I devoted myself to cheering Arthur up. I took him to movies, I listened to his complaints about the university, I typed his papers for him, complete with footnotes. We ate hamburgers at Harvey's Hamburgers and went for walks in Queen's Park, and on jaunts to the Riverdale Zoo, about the only entertainments, aside from the movies, that we could afford. We slept together, when we could. Arthur was living in residence, and that sort of thing was tolerated only if you did it furtively; my landlady, on the other hand, would tolerate nothing, no matter how furtive.

Sometimes during these nights I would wake up to find Arthur clinging to me as if the bed was an ocean full of sharks and I was a big rubber raft. Asleep he was desperate, he sometimes talked to people who weren't there and ground his teeth. But awake he was apathetic and unresponsive, or coldly dialectical. Without his political enthusiasms he was quite different from the way he'd been in England. He allowed me to do things for him, but he didn't participate.

None of this bothered me very much. His aloofness was even intriguing, like a figurative cloak. Heroes were supposed to be aloof. His indifference was feigned, I told myself. Any moment now his hidden depths would heave to the surface; he would be passionate and confess his long-standing devotion. I would then confess mine, and we would be happy. (Later I decided that his indifference at that time was probably not feigned at all. I also decided that passionate revelation scenes were better avoided and that hidden depths should remain hidden; façades were at least as truthful.)

In the spring Arthur proposed. We were sitting on a Queen's Park bench, eating take-out hamburgers and drinking milk shakes.

"I have a good idea," Arthur said. "Why don't we get married?"

I said nothing. I couldn't think of any reasons why not. Arthur could, though, and he proceeded to analyze them: neither of us had much money, we were probably too young and unsettled to make such a serious commitment, we didn't know each other very well. But to all these objections he had the answers. He'd been giving it quite a lot of thought, he said. Marriage itself would settle us down, and through it, too, we would become better acquainted. If it didn't work out, well, it would be a learning experience. Most importantly, we could live much more cheaply together than we could separately. He'd move out of residence and we'd both move into a larger rented room than the one I had, or even a small flat. I would keep my job, of course; that way he wouldn't have to accept so much money from his parents. He'd been thinking of switching into political science, which would mean several more years at school, and he wasn't too sure his parents would support him through that.

I chewed the rest of my hamburger and swallowed it thoughtfully; then I slurped up the rest of my milk shake. Now or never was the time for courage, I thought. I longed to marry Arthur, but I couldn't do it unless he knew the truth about me and accepted me as I was, past and present. He'd have to be told I'd lied to him, that I'd never been a cheerleader, that I myself was the fat lady in the picture. I would also have to tell him that I'd quit my job as a wig-seller several months before and was currently finishing *Love Defied*, on the proceeds of which I expected to live for at least the next six months.

"Arthur," I said, "marriage is serious. There are a few things I think you should know about me, in advance." My voice was trembling: surely he would be horrified, he would find me unethical, he would be disgusted, he would leave. . . .

"If you mean you were living with another man when you met me," he said, "I already know that. It doesn't bother me in the least."

"How did you find out?" I asked. I thought I'd been very careful.

"You didn't expect me to believe that story about your fat roommate, did you?" he said indulgently. He smiled and put his arm around me. "Slocum followed you home," he said. "I asked him to."

"Arthur," I said, "you sneaky old spy." I was delighted that he'd been jealous or curious enough to have done this; I also saw that he was pleased at having penetrated my disguise. But how annoyed he'd be if he discovered he'd only made it as far as the first layer. . . . I decided to postpone my revelations to some later date.

The only difficulty with the actual wedding was that Arthur refused to be married in a church, since he disapproved of religion. He also refused to be married in a city hall, because he disapproved of the current government. When I protested that these were the only choices, he said there had to be some other way. I went through the Yellow Pages, under "Bridal" and "Weddings," but these departments covered only gowns and cakes. Then I looked under "Churches." There was one division labeled "Interdenominational."

"Will this do?" I said. "If they'll marry anyone to anyone else, they can't have very strict religious convictions." I talked him into it, and he phoned the first name on the list, a Reverend E. P. Revele.

"It's all set," he told me, coming out of the pay phone. "He says we can have it at his house, he'll supply the witnesses, and it'll only take ten minutes. He says they like to do a little ceremony, nothing religious."

That was fine with me. I didn't want to be done out of a ceremony, I wouldn't feel married without one. "What did you say?"

"As long as he keeps it short."

Arthur also told me that it would only cost fifteen dollars, which was lucky since we didn't have very much money. I was torn between asking him to postpone the wedding—I'd think of some excuse, but really so I could finish *Love Defied* and buy a good wedding dress—and rushing to the Interdenominationalists right away, before Arthur found out the truth. Fear prevailed over vanity, and I bought a white cotton dress with nylon daisies on it at Eaton's Budget Floor. It would be a little disappointing, but I could stand the disappointment of a cheap cotton wedding a lot better than I could stand the thought of no wedding at all. I was terrified that I'd be exposed at the last minute as a fraud, liar and impostor. Under the strain I started to eat extra helpings

of English muffins covered with butter, loaves of
bread and honey, banana splits, doughnuts, and secondhand cookies from Kresge's. Though these in-
dulgences were not obvious to Arthur, I was gaining
weight; the only thing that saved me from bloating
up like a drowned corpse was the wedding date itself, and even so, I'd gained thirteen pounds by
the time it arrived. I could just barely get my zipper
done up.

No one we knew came to our wedding, for the
simple reason that we knew no one. Arthur's parents
were out of the question: Arthur had written them
an aggressively frank letter saying that we'd been
sleeping together for a year, so they needn't think
his marriage was a capitulation to convention. They,
of course, denounced both of us and cut off Arthur's
funds. I thought of inviting my father but he might
reveal more of my past than I wanted Arthur to
know. I sent him a postcard afterward, and he sent
me a waffle iron. Arthur didn't like any of the philosophy students, and I hadn't become friends with any
of my fellow wig demonstrators, so we wouldn't even
get any wedding presents. I went out and bought
myself a soup kettle, a pair of oven mitts and, on
impulse, a gadget for taking the stones out of cher-
ries and the pits out of olives, to make myself feel
more like a bride.

On the day itself, Arthur picked me up at my
rooming house and we got on the northbound subway together. We sat on the black leatherette seats
and watched the pastel tiles flash by; we held hands.
Arthur seemed apprehensive. He'd lost weight and
was skinny as a funeral brass; our reflections in the
subway-car windows had deep hollows under the
eyes. I didn't see how he was possibly going to be
able to carry me over the threshold. We didn't even
have a threshold: we hadn't rented an apartment yet,
because I still had two paid-in-advance weeks left at
my rented room, and Arthur said there was no point
wasting money.

We got off the subway and transferred to a bus.

It wasn't till after it had started that the name on the front of it registered. "Where did you say this man lives?" I said. Arthur handed me the piece of paper on which he'd scribbled the address and told me. It was in Braeside Park.

I began to sweat. The bus went past the stop where I used to get off; up a side street I glimpsed my mother's house. My face must have been white, for when Arthur glanced at me, squeezing my hand to reassure me or for reassurance, he said, "Are you all right?"

"Just a little nervous, I guess," I said, with a ducklike laugh.

We got off the bus and walked along the sidewalk, into the dank interior of upper Braeside Park, past the trim, respectable, haunted fake-Tudor dwellings of my obese adolescence. My terror was growing. Surely the minister would be someone I knew, someone whose daughter I'd gone to school with, someone who would recognize me despite my change of shape. He wouldn't be able to contain himself, he would exclaim at my transformation and tell humorous stories about my former size and weight, and Arthur would know—on our very wedding day!—how deeply I'd deceived him. He'd know I hadn't gone steady with a basketball player, or been third runner-up in the Rainbow Romp queen-of-the-prom contest. The maple trees were heavy with drooping green leaves, the air was humid as soup, laden with car fumes which had drifted in from the nearest thoroughfare. Moisture beaded our upper lips; I could feel the sweat spreading under my arms, staining the purity of my white dress.

"I think I'm having a sunstroke," I said, leaning against him.

"But you haven't been in the sun," Arthur said reasonably. "That's the house, right up there, we'll get inside and you can have a drink of water." He was pleased in a way that I was reacting with such distress; it camouflaged his own.

Arthur helped me up the cement front steps of

Number 52 and rang the bell. There was a small, or-
nately lettered sign on the door that said "Paradise
Manor"; I read it without comprehension. I was
trying to decide whether or not to faint. Then, even if
there was a revelation, I could exit with dignity, in an
ambulance. The aluminum screen door had the sil-
houette of a flamingo on it.

The door was opened by a tiny old woman in
pink gloves, pink high-heeled shoes, a pink silk dress
and a pink hat decorated with blue cloth carnations
and forget-me-nots. There was a round circle of rouge
on each of her cheeks, and her eyebrows were two
thinly penciled arcs of surprise.

"We're looking for the Reverend E. P. Revele,"
Arthur said.

"Oh, what a lovely dress!" the old woman
chirped. "I love weddings; I'm the witness, you know,
my name is Mrs. Symons. They always have me for
the witness. Here comes the bride," she called to the
house in general.

We went in. I was recovering; surely this was
no one I knew. Thankfully I breathed in the smell of
upholstery and warm furniture polish.

"The Reverend does the ceremonies in the parlor," said Mrs. Symons. "It's such a lovely ceremony,
I'm sure you'll like it." We followed her, and found
ourselves in a grotto.

It was the standard Braeside living room, poorer
section, with a dining room opening onto it, which in
turn opened into the kitchen; however, the walls contained, not the traditional soothing landscapes (Brook
in Winter, Country Lane in Fall), but several peacock fans, some framed pieces of embroidery, a picture of a ballet dancer that lit up from behind
ornamented with sprays of dried leaves, a painting of
a North American Indian woman smiling winsomely,
a shellwork picture—flowers in a vase, the petals of
each made from a different kind of shell—and a number of fading photographs, also in frames, with signa-
tures across the bottom. The chesterfield and matching easy chairs were of plum-colored velvet and each

easy chair had a matching footstool; all were smothered in many-colored doilies crocheted in wool. The mantel of the fireplace was crowded with objects: little Buddhas, Indian gods, a china dog, several brass cigarette cases and a stuffed owl under a glass bell.

"Here comes the Reverend," said Mrs. Symons in an excited whisper. There was shuffling noise behind us. I turned, then collapsed into a plum-colored armchair; for there, standing in the doorway in her long white gown with the purple bookmark, leaning now on a silver-headed cane and surrounded by a nimbus of Scotch whiskey, was Leda Sprott.

She looked me straight in the face, and I could tell she knew exactly who I was. I moaned and closed my eyes.

"Wedding nerves," shrilled Mrs. Symons. She grabbed my hand and began chafing my wrist. "I fainted three times during my own wedding. Get the smelling salts!"

"I'm all right," I said, opening my eyes. Leda Sprott hadn't said anything; maybe she'd keep my secret.

"Are you all right?" Arthur said to me. I nodded. "We were looking for a minister named E. P. Revele," he said to Leda Sprott.

"I am E. P. Revele," she said. "Eunice P. Revele." She smiled, as if she was used to incredulity.

"Are you qualified?" Arthur asked.

"Of course," said Leda. She waved at an official-looking framed certificate on the wall. "They wouldn't let me perform weddings if I weren't. Now, what will you have? I specialize in mixed marriages. I can do Jewish, Hindu, Catholic, five kinds of Protestant, Buddhist, Christian Scientist, agnostic, Supreme Being, any combination of these, or my own specialty."

"Maybe we should take the specialty," I said to Arthur. I wanted it over and done with as soon as possible, so I could get away.

"That is the one I myself prefer," said Leda. "But first, the picture." She went to the hall, where she called, "Harry!" I took this chance to look at the certificate. "Eunice P. Revele," it said, right enough. I was confused: either she was really Leda Sprott, in which case the ceremony would be invalid, or she was really Eunice P. Revele; if so, why had she used another name at the Jordan Chapel? But then, I thought, men who changed their names were likely to be con-men, criminals, undercover agents or magicians, whereas women who changed their names were probably just married. Beside the certificate was a photo of Leda, much younger, shaking hands with Mackenzie King. It was signed, I noticed.

Mrs. Symons was trying to get Arthur to put a plastic wreath of flowers around his neck, with no success. She put one on me, though, and a man in a gray suit came in with a Polaroid camera. It was Mr. Stewart, the visiting medium. "Smile," he said, squinting through the viewfinder. He himself smiled broadly.

"Look," Arthur said, "this isn't. . . ." But there was a flash, and Mrs. Symons whipped off my wreath.

"When the gong sounds, you stand to attention," Mrs. Symons said. She was very excited. "You look lovely, dear."

"It sounded all right over the phone," Arthur said to me in a low voice.

"Who were you talking to?" I asked. "You said it was a man."

"I thought it was," Arthur said.

The gong sounded and Leda paced in, wearing a different robe, a purple one, trimmed in red velvet. I recognized the remains of the Jordan Chapel curtains and pulpit: times were evidently hard. With the help of Mr. Stewart, she got up onto the footstool that stood in front of the fireplace.

"Arthur Edward Foster," she intoned. "Joan Elizabeth Delacourt. Advance." She broke into a fit of coughing as, hand in hand, we approached her.

"Kneel," she said, stretching out her arms in front of her as if about to dive off the stool. We did. "No, no," she said irritably, "on either side. How can I join you together if you're already joined?" We got up, kneeled again, and Leda placed a slightly trembling hand on each of our heads.

"For true happiness," she said, "you must approach life with a feeling of reverence. Reverence for life, for those loved ones who are still with us, and also for those who have gone before. Remember that all we do and all that is in our hearts is watched and recorded, and will someday be brought to light. Avoid deception and falsehood; treat your lives as a diary you are writing and that you know your loved one will someday read, if not here on this side, then on the other side, where all the final reconciliations will take place. Above all, you should love each other for what you are and forgive each other for what you are not. You have a beautiful aura, my children; you must work to preserve it." Her voice dropped to a mumble; I think she was praying. She swayed dangerously and I hoped she would not fall off the stool.

"Amen," said Mrs. Symons.

"You may rise," said Leda. She asked for our rings—I'd insisted on double rings, and we'd got them in a pawn shop—and circled them three times around the statue of the Buddha, though it might have been the stuffed owl; from where I was standing, I couldn't see. "For wisdom, for charity, for tranquillity," she said. She gave Arthur's ring to me and my ring to Arthur.

"Now," she said, "holding the rings in your *left* hands, place your *right* hands on each other's hearts. When I count to three, *press.*"

"Three is the mystical number," Mrs. Symons said. "Four is too, but. . . ." By this time I'd recognized her: she was one of the old Jordan Chapel regulars. "My name comes out to five," she continued. "That's numerology, you know."

"There's a story I heard recently that would be appropriate for this occasion," said Mr. Stewart. "There were once two caterpillars who were walking down the Road of Life, the optimistic caterpillar and the pessimistic. . . ."

"Not now, Harry," Leda Sprott said sharply. The ceremony was getting out of hand. She told us to put the rings on each other's fingers, hastily pronounced us man and wife, and clambered down off the footstool.

"Now the presents!" cried Mrs. Symons. She scurried from the room. Leda produced a certificate, which we were all supposed to sign.

"There's someone standing behind you," Mr. Stewart said. His eyes were glazed and he seemed to be talking to himself. "She's a young woman, she's unhappy, she has on white gloves . . . she's reaching out towards you. . . ."

"Harry," Leda said, "go and help Muriel with the presents."

"We don't want any presents, really," I said, and Arthur agreed, but Leda Sprott said, "A wedding isn't a wedding without presents," and pink Mrs. Symons was already hurrying in from the hall with several packages wrapped in white tissue paper. We thanked them; we were both acutely embarrassed because these well-meaning, rather pathetic old people had gone to so much trouble and we were secretly so ungrateful. Mr. Stewart gave us the Polaroid snapshot, in which our faces were a sickly blue and the sofa was brownish-red, like dried blood.

"Now I have something to say to the bride and groom . . . separately," said Leda Sprott. I followed her into the kitchen. She shut the door and we sat down at the kitchen table, which was an ordinary one covered with checked oilcloth. She poured herself a shot from a half-empty bottle, then looked at me and grinned. One of her eyes, I could see now, was not quite focused; perhaps she was going blind.

"Well," she said. "I'm pleased to see you again. You've changed, but I never forget a face. How is your aunt?"

"She died," I said, "didn't you know?"

"Yes, yes," she said, waving one of her hands impatiently, "of course. But she must still be with you."

"No, I don't think so," I said.

Leda Sprott looked disappointed. "I can see you haven't taken my advice," she said. "That's unfortunate. You have great powers, I told you that before, but you've been afraid to develop them." She took my hand and peered at it for some moments, then dropped it. "I could tell you a lot of mumbo jumbo, which would probably mean just as little to you as the truth," she said. "But I liked your aunt, so I won't. You do not choose a gift, it chooses you, and if you deny it it will make use of you in any case, though perhaps in a less desirable way. I used my own gift, as long as I had it. You may think I'm a stupid old woman or a charlatan, I'm used to that. But sometimes I had the truth to tell; there's no mistaking it when you do. When I had no truth to tell, I told them what they wanted to hear. I shouldn't have done that. You may think it's harmless, but it isn't." She paused, staring down at her fingers, which were knotted with arthritis. Suddenly I believed in her. I wanted to ask her all the questions I'd saved up for her: she could tell me about my mother. . . . But my belief faded: hadn't she just hinted that the Jordan Chapel was fraudulent and her revelations guesswork and playacting?

"People have faith in you," Leda said. "They trust you. That can be dangerous, especially if you take advantage of it. Everything catches up to you sooner or later. You should stop feeling so sorry for yourself." She was looking at me sharply with her one good eye, her head on one side, like a bird. She seemed to expect some reply.

"Thank you," I said awkwardly.

"Don't say what you don't mean," she said irritably. "You do enough of that already. That's really all I have to say to you, except . . . yes, you should try the Automatic Writing. Now, send in your new husband."

I didn't want Arthur to be alone with her. If she'd been this blunt with me, what was she likely to say to him?

"You won't tell him, will you?" I said.

"Tell him what?" Leda asked sharply.

It was hard to put into words. "What I was like," I said. What I meant was: *What I looked like.*

"What do you mean?" Leda said. "You were a perfectly nice young girl, as far as I could tell."

"No, I mean . . . my shape. I was, you know." I couldn't say "fat"; I used that word about myself only in my head.

She saw what I meant, but it only amused her. "Is that all?" she said. "To my mind it's a perfectly proper shape. But don't worry, I won't give away your past, though I must say there are worse tragedies in life than being a little overweight. I expect you not to give mine away, either. Leda Sprott owes a little money here and there." She laughed wheezily, then started to cough. I went to get Arthur.

Five minutes later he came out of the kitchen. As we left, Mrs. Symons teetered along the hall after us, down the steps and along the walk, throwing handfuls of rice and confetti at us and chirping gaily. "Good luck," she called, waving her pink-gloved hand.

We walked to the bus stop, carrying the packages. Arthur didn't say anything; his jaw was grim.

"What's the matter?" I asked. Had Leda told him about me after all?

"The old fraud ripped me off for fifty bucks," he said. "On the phone she told me fifteen."

When we got back to my rented room we opened the tissue-paper packages. They contained a plastic punch bowl with matching cups, a ninety-eight-cent book on health-food cookery, a framed print of Leda, shaking hands with Mackenzie King, and some government pamphlets about the health-giving properties and correct use of yeast. "She must make quite a profit," Arthur said.

Surely we would have to go through it all over again at the City Hall, I thought; the ceremony with the footstool and the stuffed owl couldn't possibly be legal. "Do you think we're really married?" I asked.

"I doubt it," Arthur said. But strangely enough we were.

Chapter Twenty

We went on our honeymoon four years later, in 1968. It was Arthur's Quebec separatist incarnation, so he insisted on going to Quebec City, where he confused all the waiters by trying to speak *joual* to them. Most of them found it insulting; the ones who really were separatists sneered at his pronunciation, it was too Parisian for them. We spent the first night watching the funeral of Robert Kennedy on the bunny-eared television set in the cheap motel where we were staying. It wouldn't work unless you held onto the bunny ears with one hand and put your other hand on the wall. I did the wall-touching, Arthur did the watching. By that time I was feeling truly married.

It took me a while. At first our life was unsettled. We had no money except what I could earn by writing Costume Gothics and pretending to take odd jobs, and we lived in rooming houses instead of the tawdry apartments we later sought out. Sometimes there would be a kitchen alcove concealed by a bamboo curtain or a plastic accordion door, but more often there would be only a single-burner hot plate. I would cook dinners of vegetables in boilable plastic packages, or tins of ravioli, and we would eat them sitting on the edge of the bed and trying not to get any more tomato sauce on the sheets. After the meal I would scrape the plates into the rooming-house toilet and rinse them in the bathtub, as these rooms rarely had sinks. This meant that during baths, which we took together, with me soaping Arthur's back, his ribs sticking out like Death's in a medieval woodcut, we would often be surprised by the odd noodle or pea, floating in the soap scum like an escaped fragment of Sargasso Sea. I felt it added a welcome touch of the tropics to those otherwise polar bathrooms but Arthur didn't like it. Although he denied it, he had a thing about germs.

I complained a lot about the inconvenience of this improvised suitcase life, and after two years of it, when Arthur was a teaching assistant in Political Science and had a salary of sorts, he broke down and we got a real apartment. It was in a slum—which has since become fashionably white-painted and coach-lamped—but at least it had a full kitchen in addition to the cockroaches. I then discovered to my dismay that Arthur expected me to cook, actually cook, out of raw ingredients such as flour and lard. I'd never cooked in my life. My mother had cooked, I had eaten, those were our roles; she wouldn't even let me in the kitchen when she was cooking, for fear I would break something, stick my germ-laden finger in a sauce, or tread too heavily, causing her cake to fall. I hadn't taken Home Economics in high school; I took Business Practices instead. I wouldn't have minded the cooking, though from the other girls' accounts it was mostly about nutrition; but I shrank from the thought of sewing. How could I possibly sit there, sewing a huge billowing tent for myself, while the others worked away at their trim tailored skirts and ruffled blouses?

But for Arthur's sake I would try anything, though cooking wasn't as simple as I'd thought. I was always running out of staples such as butter or salt and making flying trips to the corner store, and there were never enough clean dishes, since I hated washing them; but Arthur didn't like eating in restaurants. He seemed to prefer my inedible food: the Swiss fondue which would turn to lymph and balls of chewing gum from too high a heat, the poached eggs which disintegrated like mucous membranes and the roast chickens which bled when cut; the bread that refused to rise, lying like quicksand in the bowl; the flaccid pancakes with centers of uncooked ooze; the rubbery pies. I seldom wept over these failures, as to me they were not failures but successes, they were secret triumphs over the notion of food itself. I wanted to prove that I didn't really care about it.

Occasionally I neglected to produce any food at all because I had forgotten completely about it. I would wander into the kitchen at midnight to find Arthur making himself a peanut-butter sandwich and be overwhelmed with guilt at the implication that I'd been starving him. But though he criticized my cooking, he always ate it, and he resented its absence. The unpredictability kept him diverted; it was like mutations, or gambling. It reassured him, too. His view of the world featured swift disasters set against a background of lurking doom, and my cooking did nothing to contradict it. Whereas for me these mounds of dough, these lumps burning at the edges, this untransformed blood, represented something quite different. Each meal was a crisis, but a crisis out of which a comfortable resolution could be forced to emerge, by the addition of something . . . a little pepper, some vanilla. . . . At heart I was an optimist, with a lust for happy endings.

It took me a while to realize that Arthur enjoyed my defeats. They cheered him up. He loved hearing the crash as I dropped a red-hot platter on the floor, having forgotten to put on my oven mitt; he liked to hear me swearing in the kitchen; and when I would emerge sweaty-faced and disheveled after one of my battles, he would greet me with a smile and a little joke, or perhaps even a kiss, which was as much for the display, the energy I'd wasted, as for the food. My frustration and anger were real, but I wasn't that bad a cook. My failure was a performance and Arthur was the audience. His applause kept me going.

That was all right with me. Being a bad cook was much easier than learning to be a good one, and the extra noise and flourishes didn't strain my powers of invention. My mistake was in thinking that these expectations of Arthur's were confined to cooking. It only looked that way at first, because as far as he could tell I attempted nothing else.

It wasn't that Arthur was dishonest: what he thought and what he said he thought were the same. It was just that both of these things were different from what he felt. For years I wanted to turn into what Arthur thought I was, or what he thought I should be. He was full of plans for me, ambitions, ways in which I could exercise my intelligence constructively, and there I would be, lying lumpishly in bed in the mornings while he was up and making himself black coffee and pursuing one of his goals. That was what was wrong with me, he told me, I didn't have any goals. Unfortunately I was unable to think of this word except in connection with hockey, a game I didn't much enjoy.

But Arthur wasn't always an early riser. He had his down moments too. After his disillusionment with the atom-bomb people he'd stayed out of politics for a while. But soon he was on the upswing. This time it was civil rights: he went down to the States and almost got shot. But then that came apart and he was into another period of depression. In quick succession he went through Vietnam and sheltering draft dodgers, student revolt, and an infatuation with Mao. Every one of these involved extensive reading, not just for Arthur but for me. I made a real effort, but somehow I was always out of date, perhaps because I found it so hard to read theories. By the time I'd adjusted my views to Arthur's, his had already changed. Then I would have to be converted anew, improved, made to see the light once more. "Here," he would say, "read this book," and I'd know the cycle had begun again.

The trouble with Arthur was that he meant well, he meant too well, he wanted everyone to mean as well as he did. When he would find out they didn't, that not all of them burned with his own pure flame but some had pride, others were self-interested and power-hungry, he would become angry. He was a prisoner of conscience.

Once I'd thought of Arthur as single-minded, single-hearted, single-bodied; I, by contrast, was a sorry assemblage of lies and alibis, each complete in itself but rendering the others worthless. But I soon discovered there were as many of Arthur as there were of me. The difference was that I was simultaneous, whereas Arthur was a sequence. At the height of his involvement with any of these causes, Arthur would have the electricity of six, he'd scarcely sleep at all, he'd rush about stapling things and making speeches and carrying signs. But at the low points he'd barely be able to make it out of bed, he'd sit in a chair all day, chain-smoking and looking out the window, watching television, or doing crosswords or jigsaw puzzles of Jackson Pollock paintings and Oriental rugs. It was only on the way up or the way down that I existed for him as any kind of distinct shape; otherwise I was just a kind of nourishing blob. We made love only during the middle periods. When he was way up he had no time, when he was way down he had no energy.

I admired and envied his purity of conscience, despite its drawbacks: when Arthur was going down, overcome by disillusionment and clouds of doom, he'd write letters to all the people he'd worked with during the up period, denouncing them as traitors and scoundrels, and I was the one who would get the phone calls from them, outraged, puzzled or hurt. "Well, you know how Arthur is," I'd say to them. "He hasn't been feeling very well, he's been discouraged."

I wished he would do his own explaining, but he specialized in ambushes. He never had fights with people, he never talked things out with them. He would simply decide, by some dark, complicated process of evaluation, that these people were unworthy. Not that they'd done something unworthy, but that unworthiness was innate in them. Once he'd made his judgment, that was it. No trial, no redress. I once told him that I thought he was behaving a little like Calvin's God, but he was offended and I didn't press it. Secretly I was afraid of this same kind of judgment being applied to me.

I often hoped Arthur would find some group that would be able to sustain the overwhelming burden of his trust. It wasn't just that I wanted Arthur to be happy, though I did. I had two other reasons. One was that his depressions made me miserable, because they made me feel inadequate. The love of a good woman was supposed to preserve a man from this kind of thing, I knew that. But at these times I wasn't able to make him happy, no matter how badly I cooked. Therefore I was not a good woman.

The other was that I couldn't write Costume Gothics when Arthur was depressed. He hung around the house much of the time, and when he wasn't doing anything he didn't want me to do anything either. If I went into the bedroom and closed the door, he would open it, stand in the doorway looking at me reproachfully, and say he had a headache. Or he would want me to help him with his crossword puzzle. It was very hard to concentrate on my heroine's tumultuous breasts, my hero's thin rapacious mouth, with this kind of thing going on. I would have to pretend I was going out to look for a job, and from time to time I would really get one, in self-defense.

It was only after I got married that my writing became for me anything more than an easy way of earning a living. I'd always felt sly about it, as if I was getting away with something and nobody had found me out; but now it became important. The really important thing was not the books themselves, which continued to be much the same. It was the fact that I was two people at once, with two sets of identification papers, two bank accounts, two different groups of people who believed I existed. I was Joan Foster, there was no doubt about that; people called me by that name and I had authentic documents to prove it. But I was also Louisa K. Delacourt.

As long as I could spend a certain amount of time each week as Louisa, I was all right, I was patient and forbearing, warm, a sympathetic listener. But if I was cut off, if I couldn't work at my current Costume Gothic, I would become mean and irritable, drink too much and start to cry.

Thus we went on from year to year, with Arthur's frenzied cycles alternating with my own, and it was fine really, I loved him. Every once in a while I'd suggest that perhaps it was time for us to settle down somewhere, a little more permanently, and have children. But Arthur wasn't ready, he would say, he had work to do, and I had to admit that I myself had mixed feelings. I wanted children, but what if I had a child who would turn out like me? Even worse, what if I turned out to be like my mother?

All this time I carried my mother around my neck like a rotting albatross. I dreamed about her often, my three-headed mother, menacing and cold. Sometimes she would be sitting in front of her vanity table, sometimes she would be crying. She never laughed or smiled.

In the worst dream I couldn't see her at all. I would be hiding behind a door, or standing in front of one, it wasn't clear which. It was a white door, like a bathroom door or perhaps a cupboard. I'd been locked in, or out, but on the other side of the door I could hear voices. Sometimes there were a lot of voices, sometimes only two; they were talking about me, discussing me, and as I listened I would realize that something very bad was going to happen. I felt helpless, there was nothing I could do. In the dream I would back into the farthest corner of the cubicle and wedge myself in, press my arms against the walls, dig my heels against the floor. They wouldn't be able to get me out. Then I would hear the footsteps, coming up the stairs and along the hall.

Arthur would shake me awake. "What's the matter?" I would say.

"You were grunting."

Grunting? Humiliation. Screaming would be one thing, but grunting. . . . "I was having a nightmare," I'd say. But Arthur couldn't understand why I would have nightmares. Surely nothing that terrible had ever happened to me, I was a normal girl with all kinds of advantages, I was beautiful and intelligent, why didn't I make something of myself? I should try to be more of a leader, he would tell me.

What he failed to understand was that there were really only two kinds of people: fat ones and thin ones. When I looked at myself in the mirror, I didn't see what Arthur saw. The outline of my former body still surrounded me, like a mist, like a phantom moon, like the image of Dumbo the Flying Elephant superimposed on my own. I wanted to forget the past, but it refused to forget me; it waited for sleep, then cornered me.

Chapter Twenty-One

When I stopped to think about it, I felt our marriage was happier than most. I even became a little smug about it. In my opinion, most women made one basic mistake: they expected their husbands to understand them. They spent much precious time explaining themselves, serving up their emotions and reactions, their love and anger and sensitivities, their demands and inadequacies, as if the mere relating of these things would get results. Arthur's friends tended to be married to women like this, and these women, I knew, thought of me as placid, sloppy and rather stupid. They themselves made it from crisis to crisis, with running commentaries, on a combination of nerve ends, cigarettes, bludgeoning honesty and what used to be called nagging. Because I didn't do this, Arthur's friends envied him a bit and confided to me in the kitchen. They were beleaguered and exhausted; their wives had a touch of the shrill self-righteousness familiar to me from my mother.

But I didn't want Arthur to understand me: I went to great lengths to prevent this. Though I was tempted sometimes, I resisted the impulse to confess. Arthur's tastes were Spartan, and my early life and innermost self would have appalled him. It would be like asking for a steak and getting a slaughtered cow. I think he suspected this; he certainly headed off my few tentative attempts at self-revelation.

The other wives, too, wanted their husbands to live up to their own fantasy lives, which except for the costumes weren't that different from my own. They didn't put it in quite these terms, but I could tell from their expectations. They wanted their men to be strong, lustful, passionate and exciting, with hard rapacious mouths, but also tender and worshipful. They wanted men in mysterious cloaks who would rescue them from balconies, but they also wanted meaningful in-depth relationships and total openness. (The Scarlet Pimpernel, I would tell them silently, does not have time for meaningful in-depth relationships.) They wanted multiple orgasms, they wanted the earth to move, but they also wanted help with the dishes.

I felt my own arrangement was more satisfactory. There were two kinds of love, I told myself; Arthur was terrific for one kind, but why demand all things of one man? I'd given up expecting him to be a cloaked, sinuous and faintly menacing stranger. He couldn't be that: I lived with him, and cloaked strangers didn't leave their socks on the floor or stick their fingers in their ears or gargle in the mornings to kill germs. I kept Arthur in our apartment and the strangers in their castles and mansions, where they belonged. I felt this was quite adult of me, and it certainly allowed me to be more outwardly serene than the wives of Arthur's friends. But I had the edge on them: after all, when it came to fantasy lives I was a professional, whereas they were merely amateurs.

And yet, as time went by, I began to feel something was missing. Perhaps, I thought, I had no soul; I just drifted around, singing vaguely, like the Little Mermaid in the Andersen fairy tale. In order to get a soul you had to suffer, you had to give something up; or was that to get legs and feet? I couldn't remember. She'd become a dancer, though, with no tongue. Then there was Moira Shearer, in *The Red Shoes*. Neither of them had been able to please the handsome prince; both of them had died. I was doing fairly well by comparison. Their mistake had been to go public, whereas I did my dancing behind closed doors. It was safer, but. . . .

It was true I had two lives, but on off days I felt that neither of them was completely real. With Arthur I was merely playing house, I wasn't really working at it. And my Costume Gothics were only paper; paper castles, paper costumes, paper dolls, as inert and lifeless finally as those unsatisfactory blank-eyed dolls I'd dressed and undressed in my mother's house. I got a reputation for being absentminded, which Arthur's friends found endearing. Soon it was expected of me, and I added it to my repertoire of deficiencies.

"You apologize too much," one of the strident wives told me, and I began to wonder about that. It was true, I did apologize. But why did I feel I had to be excused? Why did I want to be exempted, and what from? In high school you didn't have to play baseball if you had your period or a pain in your stomach, and I preferred the sidelines. Now I wanted to be acknowledged, but I feared it. If I brought the separate parts of my life together (like uranium, like plutonium, harmless to the naked eye, but charged with lethal energies) surely there would be an explosion. Instead I floated, marking time.

It was September. Arthur was in one of his slumps, having just written a batch of letters de-

nouncing everyone connected with the Curriculum
Reform movement, which had been his latest cause.
I'd just started a new book; *Love, My Ransom* was
the working title. With Arthur hanging around the
apartment it was hard to close my eyes and drift off
into the world of shadows; also, the old sequence of
chase and flight, from rape or murder, no longer held
my attention as it once had. I needed something new,
some new twist: there was now more competition,
Costume Gothics were no longer regarded as mere
trash but as money-making trash, and I felt I was in
danger of being crowded out. From scanning the
works of my rivals, as I did every week, anxiously,
in the corner drugstore, I could see that the occult
was the latest thing. It was no longer enough to have
a hero with a cloak; he had to have magical powers
as well. I went to the Central Reference Library and
read up on the seventeenth century. What I needed
was a ritual, a ceremony, something sinister but deco-
rative. . . .

When Penelope awoke, she found she was blind-
folded; she could move neither hand nor foot. They
had tied her to a chair. The two of them were whis-
pering together at the opposite end of the room; she
strained to catch their words, knowing that her life
and that of Sir Percy might depend upon it.

"We can use her to gain access to the knowledge,
I tell you," Estelle was saying. She was a tempestuous
beauty with gypsy blood.

"It would be better to put her out of the way,"
muttered François. "She has seen too much."

"Yes, yes," said Estelle, "but first we can use her.
It is not often that one with such great but unde-
veloped powers comes into my hands."

"Have your way," François said, between his
teeth, "so long as you will then allow me to have
mine." His flashing eyes swept over Penelope's trem-
bling and helpless young body. "Hush . . . she is
awake."

Estelle approached, moving with savage, un-

tamed grace. Her small white teeth flashed in the semidarkness, and she threw back her long, dishevelled red hair. "So, my child," she said with false friendliness. "You are awake. Now you will perform a small service for us, hein?"

"I will do nothing for you," Penelope said. "I know you for what you are."

Estelle laughed. "Such courage, little one," she said. "But you will not be able to help yourself. Drink this." She forced some liquid from an exotic flask between Penelope's teeth. Then she removed Penelope's blindfold and placed a small table with a mirror on it before her, lit a candle, and set the candle in front of the mirror.

Penelope felt an aura of evil gather in the room; it grew thick around her. Despite herself, she felt her gaze being drawn to the flame; her mind fluttered, fascinated, helpless as a moth, her own reflection disappeared . . . further into the mirror she went, and further, till she seemed to be walking on the other side of the glass, in a land of indistinct shadows. Ahead of her, voices murmured in the mist.

"Do not be frightened," Estelle's voice said from a great distance. "Tell us what you see. Tell us what you hear."

I'd been typing with my eyes closed, as usual, but at this point I opened them. I'd come up against a blank wall: I hadn't the least idea what Penelope would see or hear next. I thought about it for half an hour, with no result. I'd have to act it through. This was a long-standing habit of mine: when I came to a dead end, I tried to simulate the scene as much as possible and block out the action, like a stage director.

It was risky, since Arthur was watching television in the next room. Also, I didn't think we had any candles. I went out to the kitchen, rummaged through the drawers, and came up with a short, dust-covered stub which had once gone with the chafing dish I'd bought in a moment of delusion and thrown out in a moment of rage. I stuck it to a saucer, found the matches, and went back into the bedroom, closing the door. Arthur thought I was writing an essay on the sociology of pottery for the university extension course I claimed to be taking.

I lit the candle end and set it in front of my dressing-table mirror. (I'd recently bought a three-sided one, like my mother's.) It was only when I was sitting in front of the mirror that I remembered my previous experiment with Automatic Writing, back in high school. That time I'd set fire to my bangs. I pinned my hair back from my face, just in case. I wasn't expecting to get any messages, only to set the scene for my book, but I felt I should have a pen or a pencil handy.

Penelope, of course, was a natural medium. She was easily hypnotized. She had also just had some liquid from an exotic flask, which would help. I went out to the kitchen again, poured myself a Scotch and water, and drank it. Then I sat myself in front of the mirror and tried to concentrate. Maybe Penelope should get a message from Sir Percy, telling her that he was in danger. Maybe she should transmit one. . . . Was she a sender or a receiver? Bell Telephone would go out of business if this method could be perfected. . . .

My attention was wandering. *You are Penelope,* I told myself sternly.

I stared at the candle in the mirror, the mirror candle. There was more than one candle, there were three, and I knew that if I moved the two sides of the mirror toward me there would be an infinite number of candles, extending in a line as far as I could see. . . . The room seemed very dark, darker than it had before; the candle was very bright, I was holding it in my hand and walking along a corridor, I was descending, I turned a corner. I was going to find someone. I needed to find someone.

There was movement at the edge of the mirror. I gasped and turned around. Surely there had been a figure, standing behind me. But there was no one.

I was wide awake now, I could hear a faint roar from the television in the next room, and the voice of the announcer, "He shoots, he scores! A blistering drive from the point. There may have been a rebound. . . . Here comes the replay. . . ."

I looked down at the piece of paper. There, in a scrawly handwriting that was certainly not my own, was a single word:

Bow

I blew out the candle and turned on the overhead light. *Bow*. What the hell was that supposed to mean? I got out the paperback Roget's Thesaurus I kept for synonyms of words I used often, such as "tremble"—*v. flutter, throb* (SHAKE); *quiver, shiver, shudder* (FEAR)—and looked it up.

bow—n. curtsey, obeisance, salaam (RESPECT, GESTURE); prow, stem, nose (FRONT); longbow, crossbow (ARMS); curve, bend, arch (CURVE, BEND).

bow—v. nod, salaam, curtsey (RESPECT, GESTURE); arch, round, incline (CURVE, BEND); cringe, stoop, kneel (SLAVERY); submit, yield, defer (SUBMISSION).

What a dumb word, I thought; there was no way that was going to help out with Penelope and Estelle. But then I felt the impact of what had happened. I had actually written a word, without being conscious of doing it. Not only that, I'd seen someone in the mirror, or rather in the room, standing behind me. I was sure of it. Everything Leda Sprott had told me came back to me; it was real, I was convinced it was real and someone had a message for me. I wanted to go down that dark, shining corridor again, I wanted to see what was at the other end. . . .

On the other hand, I didn't want to. It was too frightening. It was also too ridiculous: what was I doing playing around with candles and mirrors, like

one of Leda Sprott's octogenarian Spiritualists? I
needed a message for Penelope, true, but I didn't
have to run the risk of setting myself on fire to get
one.

I went out to the kitchen and poured myself
another drink.

That was how it began. The mirror won, curiosity prevailed. I set Penelope aside, I left her sitting
in her chair: I would attend to her later. The word
hadn't been for her, it had been for me, and I wanted
to find out what it meant. The next morning I went
to the nearest Loblaws and bought six pairs of dinner
candles, and that evening, when Arthur was watching a football game, I went again into the mirror.

The experience was much the same as before,
and it remained the same for the three months or
so during which I continued with this experiment.
There was the sense of going along a narrow passage
that led downward, the certainty that if I could only
turn the next corner or the next—for these journeys
became longer—I would find the thing, the truth or
word or person that was mine, that was waiting for
me. Only one thing changed: the feeling that someone was standing behind me was not repeated. When
I would emerge from the trance, as I suppose it
could be called, there would usually be a word, sometimes several words, occasionally even a sentence, on
the notepad in front of me, though twice there was
nothing but a scribble. I would stare at these words,
trying to make sense of them; I would look them up
in Roget's Thesaurus, and most of the time, other
words would fill in around them:

> Who is the one standing in the prow
> Who is the one voyaging
> under the sky's arch, under the earth's arch
> under the arch of arrows
> in the death boat, why does she sing
>
> She kneels, she is bent down
> under the power
> her tears are dark

her tears are jagged
her tears are the death you fear
Under the water, under the water sky
her tears fall, they are dark flowers

I wasn't at all sure what this meant, nor could I ever get to the end of the corridor.

However, the words I collected in this way became increasingly bizarre and even threatening: "iron," "throat," "knife," "heart." At first the sentences centered around the same figure, the same woman. After a while I could almost see her: she lived under the earth somewhere, or inside something, a cave or a huge building; sometimes she was on a boat. She was enormously powerful, almost like a goddess, but it was an unhappy power. This woman puzzled me. She wasn't like anyone I'd ever imagined, and certainly she had nothing to do with me. I wasn't at all like that, I was happy. Happy and inept.

Then another person, a man, began to turn up. Something was happening between the two of them; cryptic love letters formed on the pages, obscure, frightening. This man was evil, I felt, but it was hard to tell. Sometimes he seemed good. He had many disguises. Occasionally there would be passages that looked as if they came from somewhere else, and some rather boring prosy sermons about the meaning of life.

I kept all the words, and the longer sections I worked out from them, in a file folder marked *Recipes*. I'd sometimes hidden notes for Costume Gothics in the same file, though I stored the manuscripts themselves in my underwear drawer.

Between these sessions, in the daytime, when I was doing the dishes or coasting along the aisles of the supermarket, I would have moments of sudden doubt about this activity. What was I doing, why was I doing it? If I was going to hypnotize myself like this, shouldn't it be for some good end, like giving up drinking? Was I going (perhaps) just a little crazy? What would Arthur think if he found out?

I don't know what would have happened if I'd kept on, but I was forced to stop. I went into the mirror one evening and I couldn't get out again. I was going along the corridor, with the candle in my hand as usual, and the candle went out. I think the candle really did go out and that was why I was stuck there, in the midst of darkness, unable to move. I'd lost all sense of direction; I was afraid to turn around even, in case I ended up going farther in. I felt as though I was suffocating.

I don't know how long it was; it felt like centuries, but then Arthur was shaking me. He sounded angry.

"Joan, what're you doing?" he said. "What's the matter with you?"

I was back in our bedroom. I was so thankful I threw my arms around Arthur and started to cry. "I've had the most terrible experience," I said to him.

"What?" he said. "I found you in here with the lights out, staring into the mirror. What happened?"

I couldn't tell him. "I saw someone outside the window," I said. "A man. He was looking in."

Arthur rushed over to the window to look, and I quickly checked the piece of paper. There was nothing on it at all; not a mark, not a scratch. I vowed I would stop this stupidity right then and there. Leda Sprott had said you needed training, and now I was ready to believe it. The next day I threw out my remaining candles and went back to Penelope and Sir Percy Somerville. I wanted to forget all about this little adventure into the extranatural. I wasn't cut out for the occult, I told myself. I scrapped Penelope's mirror scene: she would have to make do with rape and murder like everyone else.

But I was left with the collection of papers. Several weeks later, I got them out and looked through them. They seemed to me to be as good as a few similar books I'd seen in bookstores. I thought maybe one of the small experimental publishing houses might be interested in them, so I typed them up and sent them off to Black Widow Press. I got back what I thought was a rather rude letter, almost by the next post:

Dear Ms. Foster:

Quite frankly, these reminded us of a cross between Kahlil Gibran and Rod McKuen. Though some of the pieces are not without literary merit, unfortunately the whole collection is uneven in tone and unresolved. Perhaps you should begin with submissions to the literary magazines. Or you might try Morton and Sturgess; it might be their kind of thing.

This depressed me for a while. Maybe they were right, maybe it wasn't any good. I didn't suppose it would help if I said the manuscript had been dictated by powers beyond my control. Why did I want to publish it anyway? Who did I think I was? "Who do you think you are?" my mother used to ask me, but she would never wait for an answer.

But I had as much right to try as the next person. I screwed up my nerve and bundled the pages off to Morton and Sturgess. I wasn't at all prepared for what happened.

The decisive meeting took place in the bar at the Inn on the Park. I'd never been in this place before: it wasn't the sort of place Arthur would ever go. It was too expensive, for one thing, and it was obviously for capitalists. Despite myself, I was impressed.

There were three of them at the meeting: John Morton, the original owner of the company, who was distinguished-looking; Doug Sturgess, his partner and the one in charge of promotion, who struck me as an American; and a haggard-eyed young man, introduced to me as an editor, Colin Harper. "A poet himself," said Sturgess heartily.

They all ordered martinis. I wanted a double Scotch, but I didn't want to be thought unladylike, not right away. They would find out soon enough, I felt. So I ordered a Grasshopper.

"Well," said John Morton, looking at me benevolently, with the tips of his fingers pressed together.

"Yes, indeed," said Sturgess. "Well, Colin, you might as well begin."

"We thought it was—ah—reminiscent—of a mixture of Kahlil Gibran and Rod McKuen," said Colin Harper unhappily.

"Oh," I said. "It's that bad, is it?"

"*Bad?*" said Sturgess. "Is she saying bad? You know how many copies those guys *sell?* It's like having the *Bible,* man." He was wearing a suit with a safari jacket top.

"You mean you want to do it?" I said.

"It's dynamite," said Sturgess. "And isn't she a great little lady? We'll have a great cover. Four-color, the works. Do you play the guitar?"

"No," I said, surprised. "Why?"

"I thought we might do you as a sort of female Leonard Cohen," said Sturgess.

The other two were slightly embarrassed by this. "Of course, it will need a little editing," said Morton.

"Yes," said Colin. "We might take out the more, well. . . ."

"A bit of it could come out, here and there," said Sturgess. "I mean, there's some of it I don't understand too much: for instance, who's the man with the daffodils and the icicle teeth?"

"I sort of like that," Colin said. "It's, you know, Jungian. . . ."

"But the part about the Road of Life, well. . . ."

"I like that," Sturgess said. "That's clear, that's something you can get your teeth into."

"Well, gentlemen, those are details," said Morton. "We can clear all that up later. It's evident that this is a book that has something for everyone. My dear," he said, turning to me, "we would be most happy to publish your book. Now, do you have a title for it?"

"Not yet," I said. "I haven't thought much about it. I guess I didn't really think it would ever get published. I don't know much about these things."

"What about this bit, right here," Sturgess said,

thumbing through the manuscript. "This sort of caught my eye. Section Five:

> *She sits on the iron throne*
> *She is one and three*
> *The dark lady   the redgold lady*
> *the blank lady   oracle*
> *of blood, she who must be*
> *obeyed   forever*
> *Her glass wings are gone*
> *She floats down the river*
> *singing her last song*

and so forth."

"Yes," said Morton, "that's resonant. That reminds me of something."

"What I mean is, here's your title," said Sturgess. *"Lady Oracle.* That's it, I have a nose for them. The women's movement, the occult, all of that."

"I don't want to publish this book if it isn't really any good," I said. I was on my third Grasshopper, and I was beginning to feel undignified. I was also beginning to wonder about Arthur. What was he going to think about it, this unhappy but torrid and, I was feeling now, slightly preposterous love affair between a woman in a boat and a man in a cloak, with icicle teeth and eyes of fire?

"Good," said Sturgess. "Don't you worry your pretty little head about good. We'll worry about good, that's our business, right? I know just the way to handle this. I mean, there's lots of good, but this is *terrific.*"

Chapter Twenty-Two

"Arthur," I said, "I'm having a book published." I said this while Arthur was watching the eleven P.M. *Na-*

tional News on the CBC, hoping he wouldn't quite hear me. But he did.

"What?" he said. "A book? You?"

"Yes," I said.

Arthur looked dismayed. He turned down the volume on the news. "What's it about?" he said.

"Well, it's sort of, you could say it's about the male-female roles in our society." I was uneasy about this; I was thinking of Section Fourteen, which had the embrace between the Iron Maiden, smooth on the outside but filled with spikes, and the man in the inflated rubber suit. But I was trying to think of something he'd find respectable, and this seemed to be all right, as he stopped frowning.

"That's good," he said. "I've always told you that you had the ability. I could look it over for you, if you like. Fix it up for you."

"Thank you, Arthur," I said, "but it's already been edited." This was true: poor Colin Harper had been over the manuscript several times, scratching things out and writing *delete* in the margins. He had tried to be tactful, but the book obviously embarrassed him. He'd used the word "melodramatic" twice, and once he'd said "Gothic sensibility," which gave me a fright —*he knew.* But it was only a coincidence. "It's already at the printer's," I told Arthur. "They want me to be on television," I added, I suppose to impress him.

Arthur was displeased again, as I knew he would be. "Why didn't you tell me sooner?"

"You've been so busy," I murmured. "I didn't want to bother you." This was true enough, as Arthur had met a whole new group of people and was into a fresh upward spiral of activity.

"Well, that's wonderful," he said. "I'll have to read it. We should go out to celebrate; there're some people I've been wanting you to meet anyway."

Arthur's idea of going out to celebrate was the Young Lok Gardens on Spadina. "It's the way Sai Woo's used to be," said Arthur, "before it got famous." What he meant was that it was cheap. We'd eaten there once before, and the food was good; but for me a celebration should have drinks at least, and candles if possible. Young Lok Gardens didn't have a liquor license.

But Arthur was feeling touchy, so I didn't suggest anything else. We walked over to Spadina and took a bus. Arthur still refused to let us have a car; wasteful, he said. I knew he was morally right; he was always morally right. This was admirable, but it was beginning to be a strain.

The people we were going to meet, Arthur told me, were Don and Marlene Pugh. Arthur and Don taught in the same university department and shared the same views. Arthur respected Don's mind, he told me. He was very good at respecting people's minds, initially. But he would always manage to find some flaw, some little corner of dry rot. "Nobody's perfect," I would tell him. Not even you, I increasingly wanted to add.

We walked into the Young Lok Gardens, which was crowded, as usual. A couple sitting against the far wall waved at us, and we squeezed ourselves through the tables to reach them.

"Joan, this is Don Pugh and his wife Marlene," Arthur said, and I suddenly felt sick to my stomach. I knew Marlene. I'd gone to Brownies with her.

She hadn't changed that much, she was still a lot thinner than I was. She was wearing a faded-denim jacket and jeans, with a flower embroidered on the jacket pocket; she had sparse blonde hair, worn raggedly about her shoulders, and round silver-rimmed glasses. She was slim and muscular, with chunky silver rings on all four fingers of her left hand, like knuckle dusters. I could tell she'd flown up to Guides, covered her sleeves with badges, gone on to take modern dancing, Gestalt therapy, karate, carpentry. She smiled up at me, cool and competent. I, of course, was wearing fringes: a shawl, a dangly necklace with which I could easily be strangled, a scarf. My hair needed washing, my fingernails were dirty, my shoelaces felt untied, although I wasn't wearing any.

Wads of fat sprouted on my thighs and shoulders, my belly bulged out like a Hubbard squash, a brown wool beret popped through my scalp, bloomers coated my panic-stricken loins. Tears swelled behind my eyes. Like a virus meeting an exhausted throat, my dormant past burst into rank life.

"Great to meet you," Marlene said.

"Excuse me," I said. "I have to go to the bathroom."

I headed for the ladies', followed by their astonished eyes. Once there, I locked myself into a cubicle, where I sat, helpless with self-pity, snorting and blowing my nose. Some celebration. Marlene my tormentor, who'd roped me to a bridge and left me there, a living sacrifice, for the monster of the ravines; Marlene the ingenious inquisitor. I was trapped again in the nightmare of my childhood, where I ran eternally after the others, the oblivious or scornful ones, hands outstretched, begging for a word of praise. She hadn't recognized me, but when she did I knew what would happen: she would have a smile of indulgence for her former self, and I would be overcome with shame. Yet I hadn't done anything shameful; she was the one who'd done it. Why then should I be the one to feel guilt, why should she go free? Hers was the freedom of the strong; my guilt was the guilt of those who lose, those who can be exposed, those who fail. I hated her.

I couldn't stay in there all night. I wiped my face with a damp paper towel and repaired my makeup. I would just have to tough it out.

When I came back to the table, they were eating a whole sweet-and-sour fish, complete with bulging, baked eyes. They hardly noticed my return: they were deep into a discussion of United States cultural imperialism. Another man had joined them, sad-eyed, sandy-haired and balding. I gathered that his name was Sam, though no one bothered to introduce me.

I sat and listened as they batted their ideas back and forth like Ping-Pong balls, scoring their various points. They were deciding the future of the country.

Should it be nationalism with a socialist flavor, or socialism with a nationalist flavor? Don, it appeared, had all the statistics; Arthur had the fervor. Sam seemed to be the theoretician; it came out that he'd trained as a rabbinical student. Marlene pronounced the judgments. Self-righteousness was hers, I thought. She was even more self-righteous than Arthur. She had all the aces, she'd once worked in a factory, which impressed hell out of the others. No one said anything to me; Arthur might have mentioned my book, I felt, but maybe he was protecting himself. He didn't want to say anything about it before he'd read it; he didn't trust me. The only one at the table I had any hope of communicating with was the baked fish, now reduced to a spine and a head.

"Let's get some fortune cookies," I said with forced cheerfulness. "I love them, don't you?" Arthur ordered some, with the air of indulging a spoiled child. Marlene gave me a look of contempt.

I decided to tackle her head-on. I might as well know the worst, right now. "I think we went to the same Brownies," I said.

Marlene laughed. "Oh, Brownies," she said. "Everyone went to Brownies."

"I was a Gnome," I said.

"I really can't remember what I was," she said. "I can't remember much about it at all. We used to hide in the cloakroom afterwards though, and phone people up on the church phone. When they answered we would say, 'Is your refrigerator running?' and when they'd say yes, we'd say, 'Then you better catch it.' That's about all I remember."

I could recall this game very well, since they would never let me play. I was astonished at how much I still resented this. But I resented even more the fact that she hadn't recognized me. It seemed very unjust that an experience so humiliating to me hadn't touched her at all.

The fortune cookies came. Don and Arthur ignored theirs, but the rest of us opened them. I got *A new love awaits you*. Sam got one that promised riches, and Marlene's said, *It is often best to be one-self.*

"I obviously got the wrong one," Sam said.

"I don't know," Marlene said. "You've always been a closet capitalist." They seemed to know each other better than I'd thought.

"I got the wrong one too," I said. Marlene's, I felt, was meant for me. *It is often best to be oneself,* whispered the small, crumby voice, like a conscience. But which one, which one? And if I was ever to begin, think how appalled they would be.

"What was wrong with you?" Arthur said when we were back at the apartment.

"I don't know," I said. "To be perfectly honest, I didn't go for Marlene all that much."

"Well, she liked you, a lot," Arthur said. "She told me when you were in the can."

"The first time?" I said.

"No," he said, "I think it was the third."

Thank God for toilet cubicles, I thought, the only places left for solitary meditation and prayer. What had I been praying for? I'd prayed, with all my heart, that Marlene would fall down a hole.

During the following week, Marlene and Don, with Sam in their wake, practically moved in with us. Marlene became Arthur's Platonic ideal. Not only did she have a mind he could respect, she was also a tip-top cook, mostly vegetarian. Don and Marlene had two young children, and despite the fact that it was Arthur who'd festooned our bedroom with every known form of birth-control device, urged me to take the Pill, grouched when it made me throw up, and turned guacamole-green every time my period was late, I was now silently reproached for not having any.

Marlene was the managing editor of *Resurgence*, a small Canadian-nationalist left-wing magazine, of which Don was the editor and Sam the assistant editor. Arthur quickly became a contributing editor, and wrote a carefully researched article on branch plants, which Marlene read, chain-smoking (her only vice), nodding thoughtfully, and saying things like, "Good point you've got there," while Arthur beamed. The Muse, I thought angrily; she never bothered to help me make the coffee, I did it all. It was the least I could do, as Arthur said, and I was determined to do the least.

I was jealous of Marlene, but not in the ordinary way. It didn't occur to me that Arthur would ever think of laying a hand on her skinny little rump, any more than a devout Catholic would palpate the Madonna. And it was soon obvious to me that Marlene was having an affair with Sam, although Don didn't know. I decided not to tell anyone, not yet. I was immediately more good-natured; I bought cookies, which I served with the coffee, and began to sit in on the editorial sessions. I was especially friendly to Sam; I could see that he was under a lot of pressure. Although one side of him was as dedicated and earnest as Arthur, he had a less intimidating side which he revealed only in the kitchen while he helped with the coffee. I liked the fact that he helped with the coffee, and that he was much clumsier than I was.

Meanwhile, the galley proofs of *Lady Oracle* had come from the publisher. I corrected them, with growing apprehension. On rereading, the book seemed quite peculiar. In fact, except for the diction, it seemed a lot like one of my standard Costume Gothics, but a Gothic gone wrong. It was upsidedown somehow. There were the sufferings, the hero in the mask of a villain, the villain in the mask of a hero, the flights, the looming death, the sense of being imprisoned, but there was no happy ending, no true love. The recognition of this half-likeness made me uncomfortable. Perhaps I should have taken it to a psychiatrist instead of a publisher; but then, I remembered the psychiatrist my mother had sent me to. He hadn't been much help, and no one would understand about the Automatic Writing. Perhaps I shouldn't have used my own name, Arthur's name rather; then I wouldn't have had to show him the book. More and more I dreaded this. He hadn't mentioned the book since I'd first told him about it, and neither had I. Though I resented his lack of interest, I welcomed the chance to postpone the day of judgment. Arthur wouldn't like the book, I was certain of it, and neither would anyone else.

I called up Mr. Sturgess, of Morton and Sturgess. "I've changed my mind," I said. "I don't want the book published."

"What?" said Sturgess. "Why not?"

"I can't explain," I said. "It's personal."

"Look," Sturgess said, "you've signed a contract, remember?"

But not in blood, I thought. "Couldn't we just sort of call the whole thing off?"

"We're in production," Sturgess said. "Why don't you meet me for a drink and we'll discuss it."

He patted me on the back, figuratively, and told me it would be all right. I allowed myself to believe him. After that he began making special phone calls, to keep my morale bolstered.

"We're revving up the engines," he would say one day. Then, "We've got you on a couple of key spots." Or, "We're sending you on tour, trans-Canada." This last made me think of the Queen, standing on the back platform of a train, waving. Would I have to do that? It also made me think of Mr. Peanut, who would come to the Loblaws parking lot on special Saturdays. He had ordinary legs and arms, with spats and white gloves, but his body was a huge peanut; he would dance in a blind, shambling way while girl attendants sold coloring books and packages of peanuts. As a child I'd loved him, but suddenly I saw what it was like to be the peanut: clumsy, visible and suffocating. Maybe I shouldn't have signed the contract, so carelessly, so recklessly, after my fifth Grasshopper. As the publication date approached, I would wake every morning with a sense of unspecified foreboding, before I remembered.

I was reassured by the advance copies of the book, though. It looked like a real book, and there was my picture on the back, like a real author's. Louisa K. Delacourt never got her picture on the back. I was a little alarmed by the jacket blurb: "Modern love and the sexual battle, dissected with a cutting edge and shocking honesty." I didn't think the book was about that, exactly; but Sturgess assured me he knew what he was doing. "You write it, you leave it to us to sell it," he said. He also told me jubilantly that he'd "placed" the most important review.

"What does that mean?" I said.

"We made sure the book went to someone who'd like it."

"But isn't that cheating?" I asked, and Sturgess laughed. "You're incredible," he said. "Just stay that way."

UNKNOWN BURSTS ON LITERARY SCENE LIKE COMET, said the first review, in the *Toronto Star*. I cut it out with the kitchen scissors and pasted it into the new scrapbook I'd bought from Kresge's. I was beginning to feel better. The *Globe* review called it "gnomic" and "chthonic," right in the same paragraph. I looked these words up in the dictionary. Maybe it wasn't too bad, after all.

(But I didn't stop to reflect on the nature of comets. Lumps of cosmic debris with long red hair and spectacular tails, discovered by astronomers, who named them after themselves. Harbingers of disaster. Portents of war.)

Chapter Twenty-Three

I gave Arthur a copy of *Lady Oracle*, inscribed in the front, *For Arthur, With All My Love, XXXX, Joan*. But he didn't say one word about it, and I was afraid to ask him what he thought. His manner became distant, and he began to spend a lot of time at the uni-

versity, or so he said. I would catch him giving me
hurt looks when he thought I wasn't watching. I
couldn't figure it out. I'd been expecting him to tell
me the book was bourgeois or tasteless or obscure or a
piece of mystification, but instead he was acting as
though I'd committed some unpardonable but un-
mentionable sin.

I complained to Sam, who was in the habit now
of dropping over for a beer or two in the afternoons.
He knew I knew about Marlene, so he could complain
to me.

"I'm in deep shit," he said. "Marlene's got me by
the balls, and she's twisting. She wants to tell Don.
She thinks we should be open and honest. That's
okay in theory, but . . . she wants to move in with me,
kids and all. It'd drive me crazy. Also," he said, with
a return to sanctimoniousness, "think what it would
do to *Resurgence*, it'd fall apart."

"That's too bad," I said. "I have a problem."

"*You* have a problem?" Sam said. "But you never
have problems."

"This time I do," I said. "It's about Arthur and my
book. I mean, he hasn't even told me it's bad," I said.
"It's not like him at all. He's acting as though it just
doesn't exist, but at the same time he's hurt by it. Is
it really that terrible?"

"I'm not a metaphor man, myself," Sam said,
"but I thought it was a pretty good book. I thought
there was a lot of truth in it. You got the whole marriage thing, right on. It isn't how Arthur would've
struck me, but another guy can never see that side,
right?"

"Oh my God," I said. "You think that book is
about Arthur?"

"So does Arthur," Sam said. "That's why he's hurt.
Isn't it?"

"No," I said. "Not at all."

"Who's the other fellow then?" Sam wanted to
know. "If he finds out it's someone else, he's going to
be even more pissed off, you know."

"Sam, it isn't about anyone. I don't have any secret lover, I really don't. It's all sort of, well, imaginary."

"You're in deep shit," Sam said. "He's never going to believe that."

This was what I feared. "Maybe you could have a talk with him."

"I'll try," said Sam, "but I don't think it'll work. What am I supposed to tell him?"

"I don't know," I said. Sam must have said something though, because Arthur's attitude modified a little. He continued to look at me as though I'd betrayed him to the Nazis, but he was going to be a good sport and not mention it. The only thing he said was, "When you write your next book, I'd appreciate it if you'd let me see it first."

"I'm not going to write any more books," I said. I was hard at work on *Love, My Ransom*, but he didn't have to know about that.

I had other things to worry about. Sturgess' battle plan was now in full swing, and my first television show was coming up. After that, Morton and Sturgess were throwing a party for me. I was very nervous. I put on a lot of Arrid Extra-Dry and a long red gown, and tried to remember what Aunt Lou's etiquette booklet had said about sweaty palms. Talcum powder, I thought. I sprinkled some on my hands and set off in a taxi for the television station. Just be yourself, Sturgess had told me.

The interviewer was a man, a young man, very intense. He joked with the technicians while they put the noose around my neck; a microphone, they said. I swallowed several times. I felt like Mr. Peanut, big and cumbersome. The strong lights went on and the intense young man turned towards me.

"Welcome to *Afternoon Hot Spot*. Today we have with us Joan Foster, author, I guess that's author*ess*, of the runaway bestseller *Lady Oracle*. Tell me, Mrs. Foster—or do you prefer to be called *Ms*. Foster?"

I was taking a drink of water, and I set it down so

quickly I spilled it. We both pretended the water was not running across the table and into the interviewer's shoes. "Whichever you like," I said.

"Oh, then you're not in Women's Lib."

"Well, no," I said. "I mean, I agree with some of their ideas, but. . . ."

"Mrs. Foster, would you say you are a happily married woman?"

"Oh *yes*," I said. "I've been married for years."

"Well, that's strange. Because I've read your book, and to me it seemed very angry. It seemed like a very angry book. If I were your husband, I'm not sure I'd like it. What do you think about that?"

"It's not about my *marriage*," I said earnestly. The young man smirked.

"Oh, it's not," he said. "Then perhaps you'll tell us what inspired you to write it."

At this point I told the truth. I shouldn't have done it, but once I'd started I couldn't stop. "Well, I was trying some experiments with Automatic Writing," I said. "You know, you sit in front of a mirror, with a paper and pencil and a lighted candle, and then. . . . Well, these words would sort of be given to me. I mean, I'd find them written down, without having done it myself, if you know what I mean. So after that . . . well, that's how it happened." I felt like a total idiot. I wanted another drink of water, but there wasn't any, I'd spilled it all.

The interviewer was at a loss. He gave me a look that clearly said, You're putting me on. "You mean these poems were dictated to you by a spirit hand," he said jocularly.

"Yes," I said. "Something like that. You might try it yourself, when you get home."

"Well," said the interviewer. "Thank you very much for being with us this afternoon. That was the lovely Joan Foster, or should I say Mrs. Foster—oh, she'll get me for that one!—*Ms.* Joan Foster, authoress of *Lady Oracle*. And this is Barry Finkle, signing off for *Afternoon Hot Spot*."

At the party, Sturgess took my elbow and steered me around the room as if I were a supermarket push-cart.

"I'm sorry about the interview," I told him. "I shouldn't have said that."

"What do you mean?" he crowed. "It was sensational! How'd you think it up? You sure put him in his place!"

"I didn't mean to," I said. No use to tell him that what I'd said was true.

There were a lot of people at the party, and I was bad at remembering names. I made a mental note not to drink too much. I'd made a fool of myself once that day, I felt. I had to keep calm.

When Sturgess finally let go of my elbow, I backed up against the wall. I was hiding from a newspaper columnist who'd seen the television program and wanted to have a conversation about psychic phenomena. I felt like crying. What was the use of being Princess-for-a-day if you still felt like a toad? Acted like one, too. Arthur would be humiliated. What I'd said, coast to coast, was way off the party line. Not that he had a party. This was a party, some party. I finished my double Scotch and went for another.

When I was getting my drink at the bar, a man came up beside me.

"Are you Lady Oracle?" he said.

"It's the name of my book," I said.

"Terrific title," he said. "Terrible book. It's a left-over from the nineteenth century. I think it's a combination of Rod McKuen and Kahlil Gibran."

"That's what my publisher thought, too," I said.

"I guess you're a publishing success," he said. "What's it like to be a successful bad writer?"

I was beginning to feel angry. "Why don't you publish and find out?" I said.

"Hey," he said, grinning, "temper. You've got fantastic hair, anyway. Don't ever cut it off."

This time I looked at him. He too had red hair, and he had an elegant moustache and beard, the moustache waxed and curled upward at the ends, the beard pointed. He was wearing a long black cloak and spats, and carrying a gold-headed cane, a pair of white gloves, and a top hat embroidered with porcupine quills.

"I like your hat," I said.

"Thanks," he said. "I got a girl to do it for me. A girl I knew. She did some gloves to match, but I kept getting stuck on things—people in breadlines, dead dogs, nylon stockings, stuff like that. This is my dress uniform. Why don't you come home with me?"

"Oh, I couldn't," I said. "Thank you anyway."

He didn't seem disappointed. "Well, at least you can come to my show," he said. He handed me an invitation, slightly smudged. "The opening's tonight. It's just a couple of blocks from here; that's how come I crashed this party, I got tired of my own."

"All right," I said. There didn't seem any harm in it, I thought. Secretly I was flattered: it was a long time since anyone had propositioned me. Also I found him attractive. Him or the cape, I wasn't sure which. And I wanted to get away from the columnist.

The opening was at a minor art gallery, The Takeoff, and the show itself was called SQUAWSHT. "It's a pun, like," he told me as we walked across to Yonge Street. "*Squaw* and *squashed*, get it?"

"I think so," I said. I was studying the invitation, in the light from a store window. "The Royal Porcupine," it said. "Master of the CON-CREATE POEM." There was a picture of him in full dress, flanked by a shot of a dead porcupine, taken from underneath so its long front teeth were showing.

"What's your real name?" I said.

"That is my real name," he said, a little offended. "I'm having it changed legally."

"Oh," I said. "What made you happen to pick that particular one?"

"Well, I'm a Royalist," he said. "I really dig the Queen. I felt I should have a name that would reflect that. It's like the Royal Mail or the Royal Canadian

Mounted Police. Also I thought it would be memorable."

"What about the porcupine?"

"I've always figured the beaver was wrong, as a national symbol," he said. "I mean, the beaver. A dull animal and too nineteenth-century; all that industry. And you know what they used to be hunted for? The skin was for hats, and then they cut the nuts off for perfume. I mean, what a fate. The porcupine though, it does what it likes, it's covered with prickles so nobody messes with it. Also it has strange tastes, I mean beavers chew trees, porcupines chew toilet seats."

"I thought they were easy to kill," I said. "You hit them with a stick."

"Propaganda," he said.

As we arrived, a number of people were leaving; outside, the SPCA was picketing with signs that read SAVE OUR ANIMALS. The show itself consisted of several freezers with glass tops and fronts, like the display cases for ice cream and frozen juice in supermarkets. Inside these freezers there were a number of dead animals, all of which had apparently been run over by cars. They were quick-frozen in exactly the poses they'd been discovered in, and attached to the side of each one, in the position usually reserved for the name of the painting, the size and the materials— Composition #72, 5′ × 9′, acrylic and nylon tubing— there was a little card with the species of the animal, the location where it had been found, and a description of its injuries: RACOON AND YOUNG, DON MILLS AND 401, BROKEN SPINE, INTERNAL HEMORRHAGE, for instance; or DOMESTIC PUSSYCAT, RUSSELL HILL ROAD, CRUSHED PELVIS. There were a skunk, several dogs, a fawn and a porcupine, as well as the usual cats, groundhogs and squirrels. There was even a snake, mangled almost beyond recognition.

"What do you think of it?" asked the Royal Porcupine when we'd made the rounds.

"Well," I said, "I don't know. . . . I guess I don't know much about art."

"It's not art, it's poetry," the Royal Porcupine said, slightly offended. "Con-create poetry, I'm the man who put the creativity back in concrete."

"I don't know much about that either."

"That's obvious from the stuff you write," he said. "I could write that stuff with my toes. The only reason you're so famous is your stuff is obsolete, man, they buy it because they haven't caught up with the present yet. Rearview mirror, like McLuhan says. The new poetry is the poetry of *things*. Like, this has never been done before," said the Royal Porcupine, looking morosely over towards the front door of the gallery, where another bunch of queasy first-nighters was making a green-faced exit. "Do you realize that?"

"Have you sold anything?" I asked brightly.

"No," he said, "but I will. I should take this show to the States, people up here are so cautious, they're unwilling to take a chance. That's how come Alexander Graham Bell had to go south."

"That's what my husband says," I offered.

The Royal Porcupine looked at me with new interest. "You're married," he said. "I didn't know that. You've got the sexiest elbows I've ever seen. I'm thinking of doing a show on elbows, it's a very unappreciated part of the body."

"Where would you get them?" I asked.

"Around," he said. He took me by the elbow. "Let's get out of here."

As we went past the group of SPCA picketers outside the front door, he muttered, "They missed the *point*. I don't squash them, I just recycle them, what's wrong with that?"

"Where are we going?" I asked the Royal Porcupine, who still had hold of my elbow.

"My place," he said.

"I'm hungry," I said evasively.

So we went to Mr. Zums on Bloor Street, where I had a Zumburger with the works and the Royal Porcupine had a chocolate milk shake. I paid—he didn't have any money—and we debated the pros and cons of going back to his place.

"I want to make love to your elbow," he said. "With fringe benefits."

"But I'm married," I said, chewing thoughtfully on my Zumburger. I was resisting temptation, and it was a temptation. Arthur had frozen me out; as far as he was concerned I might as well have been a turnip. I'd been finding myself attracted to the most inappropriate men lately: CBC news commentators, bus conductors, typewriter repairmen. In my fantasies I wasn't even bothering with the sets and costumes, I was going straight to the heavy breathing. Things must have been bad.

"That's okay," said the Royal Porcupine, "I prefer married women."

"My husband might not prefer it," I said.

"He doesn't have to know, does he?"

"He'd know. He has intuition." This wasn't true; what was really worrying me was: even if Arthur did know, would he care? And what if he didn't care, what then? "He'd think you're decadent, he'd think you were bad for my ideology."

"He can have your ideology, I'll take the rest, fair enough? Come on, let me sweep you off your feet. You're the type, I can tell."

I finished my Zumburger. "It's impossible," I said.

"Have it your way," he said, "you win one, you lose one. You're missing something though."

"I don't have the energy," I said.

He said he'd walk me home, and we set off along Bloor, heading west toward the street of old three-story red-brick houses, with porches and gables, where Arthur and I were living at that time, temporarily as ever. The Royal Porcupine seemed to have forgotten about his proposition already. He was worrying about the success of his show. "The last one I did, there was only one review. The old fart said it was an unsuccessful attempt to be disgusting. You can't even shock the bourgeoisie any more; you could put on a show of amputated orphans' feet and someone would ask you to sign them."

We passed the Museum and the Varsity Stadium and continued west, through a region of tiny, grubby old stores which were turning into boutiques, past a wholesale truss concern. On Brunswick we turned north, but after several houses the Royal Porcupine stopped and shouted. He'd found a dead dog, quite a large one; it looked like a husky.

"Help me get it into the bag," he said, for he'd taken a green plastic garbage bag out from under his cloak. He jotted down the location in a notebook he carried for the purpose. Then he lifted the hind end and I slid the garbage bag over it. The bag wasn't big enough and the dog's head stuck out the top, its tongue lolling.

"Well, goodnight," I said, "it was nice meeting you."

"Just a minute," he said, "I can't get this thing back by myself."

"I'm not going to carry it," I said. The blood was still wet.

"Then take my cane."

He hoisted the dog and concealed it under his cloak. We smuggled it into a taxi, for which I ended up paying, and went to the Royal Porcupine's lair. It was in a downtown warehouse that had been converted into artists' studios. "I'm the only one who lives here though," he said. "I can't afford not to. The others have real houses."

We went up the heavy industrial elevator to the third floor. The Royal Porcupine didn't have very much furniture, but he did have a large freezer, and he took the dog over to it immediately and lowered it in. Then he tied the limbs so the corpse would freeze in the position in which we'd found it.

While he was doing this, I explored. Most of the space was empty. In one corner was his bed, a mattress on the floor, no sheets; on top of it were several mangy sheep-skin rugs, and over it hung a tattered red velvet canopy with tassels. He had a card table and two card chairs; on both the table and the chairs there were used plates and cups. On one wall was a blow-up of himself, in costume, holding a dead mouse by the tail. Beside it was a formal portrait of the Queen and Prince Philip, with decorations and tiaras, in a heavy gilt frame like the kind in the principal's office at high school. Against the other wall stood a kitchen counter, with none of the plumbing installed. It held a collection of stuffed animals. Some were toys, teddy bears and tigers and bunnies. Some were real animals, expertly finished and mounted, birds mostly: a loon, an owl, a bluejay. Then there were a few chipmunks and squirrels, not done well at all. The stitches were visible, they had no bead eyes, and they were long and fat, like liverwursts, their legs sticking straight out.

"I tried taxidermy first," said the Royal Porcupine, "but I wasn't any good at it. Freezing's a lot better, that way they don't get moths."

He had taken off his cloak, and as I turned I saw that he was now taking off his shirt as well. The dog blood left red stains as he unbuttoned; his chest emerged, covered with auburn hair.

His green eyes lit up like a lynx's, and he walked towards me, growling softly. The backs of my knees were weak with lust, and I felt a curious tingling sensation in my elbows.

"Well, I guess I'd better be going now," I said. He said nothing. "How do you work the elevator?"

"For Christ's sake," I said a minute later, "wash your hands!"

"I've always wanted to know what it was like to fuck a cult figure," the Royal Porcupine said reflectively. He was lying on his mattress, watching me as I scrubbed the dog blood off my belly with a corner of his shirt, dipped in the toilet. He didn't have a sink.

"Well," I said a little sharply, "what's it like?"

"You have a nice ass," he said. "But it's not that different from anyone else's ass."

"What were you expecting?" I said. Three buttocks. Nine tits. I felt like a moron for wanting to get the dog blood off, I felt I was violating one of his rituals, I was letting him down. I hadn't risen to the occasion, and already I was feeling guilty about Arthur.

"It's not what there is," he said, "it's what you do with it."

He didn't say whether what I did with it would pass his standards or not, and at that moment I didn't care. I just wanted to go home.

Chapter Twenty-Four

This was the beginning of my double life. But hadn't my life always been double? There was always that shadowy twin, thin when I was fat, fat when I was thin, myself in silvery negative, with dark teeth and shining white pupils glowing in the black sunlight of that other world. While I watched, locked in the actual flesh, the uninteresting dust and never-emptied ashtrays of daily life. It was never-never land she wanted, that reckless twin. But not twin even, for I was more than double, I was triple, multiple, and now I could see that there was more than one life to come, there were many. The Royal Porcupine had opened a time-space door to the fifth dimension, cleverly disguised as a freight elevator, and one of my selves plunged recklessly through.

Not the others, though. "When can I see you again?" he asked.

"Soon," I said. "Don't call me, though, I'll call you. Okay?"

"I'm not applying for a job, you know," he said.

"I know. Please understand." I kissed him goodnight. Already I was beginning to feel that I couldn't see him again. It would be too dangerous.

When I got back to the apartment Arthur wasn't there, although it was almost twelve o'clock. I threw myself on the bed, stuck my head under the pillow, and began to cry. I felt I'd ruined my life, again. I would repent, I would turn over a new leaf, I wouldn't call the Royal Porcupine, although I was longing to. What could I do to make it up to Arthur? Perhaps I could write a Costume Gothic, just for him, putting his message into a form that the people could understand. Nobody, I knew, read *Resurgence* except the editors, some university professors, and all the rival radical groups who edited magazines of their own and spent a third of each issue attacking each other. But at least a hundred thousand people read my books, and among them were the mothers of the nation. *Terror at Casa Loma*, I'd call it, I would get in the evils of the Family Compact, the martyrdom of Louis Riel, the horrors of colonialism, both English and American, the struggle of the workers, the Winnipeg General Strike. . . .

But it would never work. In order for Arthur to appreciate me I'd have to reveal the identity of Louisa K., and I knew I couldn't do that. No matter what I did, Arthur was bound to despise me. I could never be what he wanted. I could never be Marlene.

It was two in the morning when Arthur came back.

"Where have you been?" I asked, snuffling.

"At Marlene's place," Arthur said, and my heart dropped. He'd gone for consolation, and. . . .

"Was Don there?" I asked in a small voice.

It turned out that Marlene had told Don about Sam, and Don had hit her in the eye. Marlene had called up the entire editorial staff of *Resurgence*, including Sam. They'd come over to Marlene's house, where they'd had a heated discussion about whether or not Don had been justified. Those in favor said the workers often hit their wives in the eye, it was an open and direct method of expressing your feelings. Those against it said it was degrading to women. Marlene had announced she was moving out. Sam said she couldn't move in with him, and another debate began. Some said he was a prick for not letting Marlene move in with him, others felt that if he didn't really want her to he was right to say so. In the middle of this, Don, who'd been out getting drunk at Grossman's Tavern, came back and told them all to get the hell out of his house.

I was secretly glad of this uproar. Arthur could no longer consider Marlene the paragon he once had, and it took some of the heat off me.

"What about Marlene?" I said, with false concern. "Was she all right?"

"She's outside the door," Arthur said heavily, "sitting on the stairs. I thought I should check with you first. I couldn't just leave her there, not with him in that condition."

He didn't say anything about the television interview though, and for this I was grateful. Perhaps he hadn't seen it. It would have been a terrible humiliation to him. I hoped no one would tell him about it.

Marlene slept on the chesterfield that night, and the next night, and the next. It appeared she'd moved in with us. I couldn't do anything about it, for wasn't she in trouble, wasn't she a political refugee? That was how she saw it, and Arthur did too.

During the days she negotiated over the phone with Don and, strangely enough, with Sam. Between these conversations she sat at my kitchen table, chain-smoking and drinking my coffee and asking me what she should do. She was no longer neat and tidy; her eyes were dark-circled, her hair stringy, her nails ragged from biting. Should she keep on seeing Sam, should she go back to Don? Don had the children, temporarily. As soon as she got a place of her own, she'd get them away from him if she had to go to court to do it.

I refrained from asking her when she was going to get a place of her own. "I don't know," I said, "which of them do you love?" I sounded exactly like the friendly housekeepers in my own Costume Gothics, I thought, but what else could I say?

"Love," Marlene snorted. "Love isn't the *point*.

The point is, which of them is up to having a truly equal relationship. The point is, which is the least exploitive."

"Well," I said, "offhand I'd say Sam was." He was my friend, Don wasn't, so I was putting in my plug for Sam. On the other hand, I still didn't like Marlene very much, so why was I wishing her on my friend? "But I'm sure Don's very nice, too," I added.

"Sam is a swine," Marlene said. When Women's Lib had appeared, Marlene had dismissed it as bourgeois; now she was a convert. "It takes a personal experience to really open your eyes," she told me. She kept implying I hadn't suffered enough; in this too I was deficient. I knew I shouldn't feel defensive about it, but I did.

When Marlene was off visiting Sam, Don would drop by to consult me. "Well, maybe you should move to another city," I said. That was what I would have done.

"That would be running away," Don said. "She's my wife. I want her back."

Then, in the evenings, when Marlene was seeing her children, Sam would come over and I'd make him a drink. "God, it's driving me crazy," he'd say. "I'm in love with her, I just don't want to live with her all the time. I tell her we can spend *important* time together, significant time, much better if we live in separate houses. And I don't see why we can't have other relationships, as long as ours is the main one, but she can't see it. I mean, I'm not the jealous type."

With all the coming and going, I began to feel I was living in a train station. Arthur was hardly ever there, since Marlene and Don had resigned from *Resurgence* and he himself was trying to keep it going. Marlene was too distraught to help much with the cooking and cleaning up, and she was no help with the rest of my life either. Increasingly, I was daydreaming about the Royal Porcupine. I hadn't called him yet, but any moment now I knew I would give in. I searched the papers for reviews of SQUAWSHT, and found one in the Saturday entertainment supplement. "A telling and incisive commentary on our times," it said.

"How would you like to go to an art show?" I asked Marlene. The show was still on, it wouldn't hurt just to walk through it.

"That pretentious bourgeois shit?" she said. "No thanks."

"Oh, have you seen it?" I asked.

"No, but I read the review. You can tell."

Meanwhile there was my literary career. The day after the television show, the phone calls had begun. They were mostly from people who'd believed me and who wanted to know how to get in touch with the Other Side, though some were hate calls from people who thought I'd been making fun of the interviewer, or Spiritualism, or both. Some thought I could foretell the future and wanted me to foretell theirs. None of them asked for love potions or wart remover, but I felt it would come to that.

Then there were the letters, which Morton and Sturgess forwarded to me. They were mostly from people who wanted help getting published. At first I tried answering them, but I soon discovered that these people did not want their fantasies destroyed. When I explained that I had no surefire contacts in the publishing world, they were outraged to be told I was powerless? It overwhelmed me with guilt that I couldn't live up to their expectations, so after a while I started throwing the letters out unanswered, and after that, unread. Then the people started arriving at the apartment, demanding to know why I hadn't answered their letters.

New articles were appearing every week, with titles like "The Selling of *Lady Oracle*" and *"Lady Oracle*: Hoax or Delusion?" And because of that first, calamitous television interview, which had made the papers—AUTHOR CLAIMS SPIRIT GUIDANCE—the other interviewers Sturgess had lined up wouldn't leave the subject alone. It did no good for me to say I didn't want to talk about it; that only whetted their curiosity.

"I hear *Lady Oracle* was written by angels, sort of like the Book of Mormon," they'd say.

"Not exactly," I'd say. Then I'd try to change the subject, hoping that Arthur wasn't watching. Sometimes they would be seriously interested, which was even worse. "So you think there *is* a life after death," they'd say.

"I don't know. I guess no one really knows that, do they?"

After these shows I would phone up Sturgess, in tears, and beg to be excused from the next one. Sometimes he would bolster up my sagging self-confidence: I was great, I was doing fine, sales were terrific. Sometimes he would act hurt and say it was our understanding when we signed the contract that I'd do a certain number of shows, didn't I remember?

I felt very visible. But it was as if someone with my name were out there in the real world, impersonating me, saying things I'd never said but which appeared in the newspapers, doing things for which I had to take the consequences: my dark twin, my funhouse-mirror reflection. She was taller than I was, more beautiful, more threatening. She wanted to kill me and take my place, and by the time she did this no one would notice the difference because the media were in on the plot, they were helping her.

And that wasn't all. Now that I was a public figure I was terrified that sooner or later someone would find out about me, trace down my former self, unearth me. My old daydreams about the Fat Lady returned, only this time she'd be walking across her tightrope, in her pink tutu, and she'd fall, in slow motion, turning over and over on the way down. . . . Or she'd be dancing on a stage in her harem costume and her red slippers. But it wouldn't be a dance at all, it would be a striptease, she'd start taking off her clothes, while I watched, powerless to stop her. She'd wobble her hips, removing her veils, one after another, but no one would whistle, no one would yell *Take it off baby*. I tried to turn off these out-of-control fan-

tasies, but couldn't, I had to watch them through to
the end.

After Sam left one afternoon, I sat at the kitchen
table, drinking Scotch. Marlene was out seeing a lawyer; she'd left her breakfast dishes on the table, a
mound of orange peels and a bowl half full of water-
logged Rice Krispies. Her healthy eating habits had
gone down the drain. So had mine. I was a nervous
wreck, I realized, and I'd been one for some time. My
home was a campground littered with other people's
garbage, physical, emotional; Arthur was never there,
for which I didn't blame him; I'd been unfaithful to
him but I didn't have the courage either to tell him or
to do it again, as I wished to. It wasn't willpower that
was keeping me away from the Royal Porcupine, it
was cowardice. I was inept, I was slovenly and hollow, a hoax, a delusion. Tears trickled down my face,
onto the crumb-strewn table.

Pull yourself together, I told myself. You've got
to get out.

Marlene came back from her lawyer, teeth
clenched, eyes glinting; visits to her lawyer usually
had this effect on her. She sat down and lit a cigarette.

"I've got that prick," she said.

I wasn't sure which one she meant, but I wasn't
interested. "Marlene," I said, "I have a wonderful
idea. This place is really too small for the three of us."

"You're right," she said. "It's a little crowded. I'll
be moving out as soon as I can find a place of my
own."

"No," I said, "*we'll* move out. Term's almost over.
Arthur and I will go away for the summer and you
can stay here. It'll help you get things sorted out."

Arthur wasn't enthusiastic when I told him. At
first he said we couldn't afford it, but I told him my
aunt had died and left me some money.

"I thought your aunt died a long time ago," Arthur said.

"That was my other aunt, that was Aunt Lou.

This was Aunt Deirdre. We never got on that well, but I guess she didn't have anyone else to leave it to." The truth was that I'd sold *Love, My Ransom* for a reasonable sum. My own life was a mess, but Louisa K. was doing all right.

"What about the magazine?" Arthur asked. "I can't just dump it."

"You need a rest," I told him. "Marlene will take it over again. She needs something to get her mind off everything else."

I told Sturgess my mother was dying of cancer and I had to go to Saskatchewan to look after her.

"What about all those appearances," he said, aggrieved, "and the trans-Canada tour?"

"Postpone them," I said. "I'll do it when I get back."

"Could you at least do an interview in Regina?"

"My mother's dying, remember?" I said, and he had to make do with that.

It was Sam who suggested Italy and gave us Mr. Vitroni's address. He'd got it from a friend. Arthur wanted to go to Cuba, but we couldn't get visas in time.

We took a plane to Rome and rented a red Fiat, which we drove to Terremoto. I navigated, using Sam's friend's directions and a map. The gearshift knob came off a few times, but Arthur always had trouble with cars. We moved into the flat, and there we were, away from everyone, ready to sort out our life.

I suppose I'd been hoping for a reconciliation, or at least for a return to the way things had been before *Lady Oracle*, and in a way this did happen. My tortuous Fat-Lady fantasies disappeared. Away from the *Resurgence* group, Arthur was sweeter, more pensive. I made coffee in the mornings and passed it out to him through the kitchen window. Then we would sit among the pieces of broken glass on the balcony, drinking it and practicing our Italian from the *fotoromanzi* or just gazing out over the valley. We went for walks on the hills above the town and admired the view. Arthur wanted to do some field work, as he called it, dealing with the system of land ownership, but his Italian wasn't good enough, so he let the project drop. From time to time he scratched away at an article for *Resurgence,* on the difficulty of making feature films in Canada; but he seemed to have lost his fervor. We made love a lot and visited ruins.

One day we went to Tivoli. We bought some ice-cream cones, then went to see the Cardinal's gardens, with the famous waterwork statues. We went down a staircase bordered with sphinxes, water shooting from their nipples, and wandered from grotto to grotto. At the end we came to Diana of Ephesus, the guidebook said, rising from a pool of water. She had a serene face, perched on top of a body shaped like a mound of grapes. She was draped in breasts from neck to ankle, as though afflicted with a case of yaws: little breasts at the top and bottom, big ones around the middle. The nipples were equipped with spouts, but several of the breasts were out of order.

I stood licking my ice-cream cone, watching the goddess coldly. Once I would have seen her as an image of myself, but not any more. My ability to give was limited, I was not inexhaustible. I was not serene, not really. I wanted things, for myself.

Chapter Twenty-Five

Almost as soon as we got back from Italy, I called the Royal Porcupine. He didn't sound surprised. "What took you so long?" he said.

"I was away," I said ambiguously. "I tried to call you before I left, but you weren't there."

We met at the Red Hot stand in Simpson's Basement. The Royal Porcupine explained that he was even poorer than usual and this was the cheapest place in town to have lunch, as you could get two hot dogs and an orange drink for a dollar. I found his cape a little incongruous in Simpson's Basement, and the sexual fantasies I'd been having about him drooped slightly. Still, there was something Byronic about him. Byron, I remembered, had kept a pet bear in his rooms and drunk wine from a skull.

He borrowed a subway token from me and we went back to his place. "I have to explain something first," I said in the freight elevator. "We have to keep this light." Arthur, I said, was very important to me and I didn't want to do anything that would hurt him.

The Royal Porcupine said that was fine with him, and the lighter things were, the better.

At first they were very light. Finally I had someone who would waltz with me, and we waltzed all over the ballroom floor of his warehouse, he in his top hat and nothing else, I in a lace tablecloth, to the music of the Mantovani strings, which we got at the Crippled Civilians. We got the record player there, too, for ten dollars. When we weren't waltzing or making love, we frequented junk shops, combing them for vests, eight-button gloves, black satin Merry Widows and formal gowns of the fifties. He wanted a sword cane, but we never did find one. We did find a store in Chinatown which had button boots for sale, left over from 1905. They hadn't sold because they were odd sizes, and I had to sit down on the curb and let the Royal Porcupine try to cram my feet into each pair, beautiful half-tones, white glacé kid, pearl gray. I felt like Cinderella's ugly sister. The only pair I could get on were black lace-ups with steel toes, washerwoman boots, but even these were desirable. We bought them, and later a pair of black net stockings to go with them.

I soon discovered that my own interest in nineteenth-century trivia was no match for the Royal Porcupine's obsession with cultural detritus. Whereas I liked antique silver and snuffboxes, he lusted after green Coca-Cola bottles, worn Captain Marvel comic books, Mickey Mouse watches, Big Little Books and movie star paper dolls from the twenties. He didn't have very much money, so he couldn't buy everything he wanted, but he was a walking catalog of ephemera, of the irrelevant and the disposable. Everything, for him, was style; nothing was content. Beside him I felt almost profound.

Unfortunately the lace-up black ankle boots gave me severe pains in the feet if I wore them for more than half an hour; but it was enough for a couple of good waltzes. When we'd tired ourselves out we'd go to the Kentucky Fried Chicken place on the corner and order a bucket and two Cokes. These we would eat in the warehouse. The Royal Porcupine wanted to save the chicken bones, boil them, and glue and wire them into a sculpture, which he would call "Joan Foster Kentucky Fried"; he wanted to exhibit it at his next show. It was a terrific idea, he said. The black shoes would be called "Foster Dances #30," and he'd cover a Mantovani record with clumps of my hair and call it "Hairy Foster Music." And if he could have a pair of my Weekend Set underpants, he could. . . .

"That's very creative," I said, "but I don't think it's a good idea."

"Why not?" he said, a little hurt.

"Arthur would find out."

"Arthur," he said. "It's always Arthur."

He was beginning to resent Arthur. He made a point of telling me about his two other women. They were both married, one to a psychologist, the other to a chemistry professor. He said they were both very dumb and no good in bed. The chemistry professor's wife used to leave baked goods for him beside the freight elevator, without warning. We would lie on his grubby mattress, eating the damp pumpkin cakes and the flat high-protein bread (she was a health-food freak) while the Royal Porcupine talked about her deficiencies. I began to wonder whether he did the same with both of them, about me. I minded, but I couldn't afford to.

"Why do you see them, if they're so boring?" I asked.

"I have to do something when you're not here," he said petulantly. Already he'd decided they were my fault.

Occasionally I would have an attack of guilt about Arthur and cook special meals for him, which failed even more miserably than the meals I usually cooked. I even toyed with the idea of telling him, trying openness and honesty as Marlene had; but then, it hadn't done any wonders for her, and I was fairly sure it wouldn't do much for me either. I was afraid that Arthur would laugh, denounce me as a traitor to the cause, or kick me out. I didn't want that: I still loved him, I was sure of it. "Maybe we should have an open marriage," I said to Arthur one night as he was hacking his way through a pork chop that I'd put under the broiler and then forgotten about. But he didn't even answer, which might've been because his mouth was full, and that was as far as I got.

When we'd returned from Italy, Marlene was no longer in our apartment. She'd gone back to Don. They'd "worked it out," they said; but she was still seeing Sam. Nobody was supposed to know, but of course Sam told me immediately.

"Where does that leave you?" I said.

"Back where we started," he said, "but with more experience."

That was where Arthur and I seemed to be also. The trouble with me, I thought, was that I had experience all right, but I couldn't seem to learn from it.

Arthur was back at his teaching job, and the *Resurgence* group had reunited, which should have made him happy. He wasn't happy though, I could tell. Once I would have made a big effort to cheer him up, but I was beginning to resent the gray aura he gave off constantly, like a halo in reverse. Some days I felt his unhappiness was all my fault, I was neglecting him. But more often I tried to dismiss it. Perhaps he simply had a talent for unhappiness, as others had a talent for making money. Or perhaps he was trying to destroy himself in order to prove to me that I was destructive. He was beginning to accuse me of not taking enough interest in his work.

From this soggy domestic atmosphere the Royal Porcupine was a welcome escape. He didn't make many demands; with him it was easy come, easy go. I began to get careless. I started calling him from the apartment when Arthur was out, and then when Arthur was merely in the next room. My work was suffering too: I'd completely lost interest in Costume Gothics. What did I need them for now?

When I finally went on Sturgess' trans-Canada tour, the Royal Porcupine came along, and we had a lot of fun smuggling him into the motel rooms. Sometimes we dressed up in middle-aged tourist outfits, bought at the Crippled Civilians, and registered under assumed names. In Toronto I started going to parties, not exactly with him, but five minutes before or after. We'd get other people to introduce us to each other. These games were childish, but a relief.

It was at one of these parties that I met Fraser Buchanan. He came up to me, glass in hand, and stood smirking while I asked the Royal Porcupine what he did for a living.

"I'm a mortician," he said. We both thought this was funny.

"Excuse me, Ms. Foster," Fraser Buchanan said, extending his hand. "My name is Fraser Buchanan. Perhaps you've heard of me." He was a short man, tidily dressed in a tweed jacket and turtle-neck sweater, with sideburns that he obviously found daring, as he turned his head often to give you the benefit of a side view.

"I'm afraid I haven't," I said. I smiled at him; I was feeling good. "This is the Royal Porcupine, the con-create poet."

"I know," said Fraser Buchanan, giving me an oddly intimate smile. "I'm familiar with his . . . work. But really, Ms. Foster, I'm more interested in you." He sidled closer, wedging himself between me and the Royal Porcupine. I leaned backward a little.

"Tell me," he said in a half-whisper, "how is it that I never saw any of your work in print before *Lady Oracle?* Most poets, or should I say poetesses, go through an, ah, an apprentice period. In the little magazines and so forth. I follow them closely, but I never saw anything of yours."

"Are you a journalist?" I asked.

"No, no," he said. "I used to write a little poetry myself." His tone suggested that he had since outgrown this. "You might call me an interested observer. A lover," he smirked, "of the arts."

"Well," I said, "I guess I just never thought any of my stuff was good enough to be published. I never sent any of it in." I gave what I hoped was a modest laugh and looked over his shoulder at the Royal Porcupine, hoping for rescue. Fraser Buchanan's thigh was resting ever so lightly against my own.

"So then you sprang fully formed, like Athena from the head of Zeus," he said. "Or rather, from the head of John Morton. That man certainly has a nose for young talent."

I couldn't put my finger on it, but there was some very unpleasant insinuation going on. I laughed again and told him I was going to get another drink. It occurred to me that I'd seen him before, front row center at a television talk show, taking notes in a little book. Several talk shows. Several out-of-town talk shows. A motel lobby.

"Who is that strange little man?" I asked the Royal Porcupine later, as we lay exhausted on his mattress. "What does he do?"

"He knows everyone," he said. "He used to be with the CBC, I guess everyone did. Then he started a literary magazine called *Reject;* the idea was that it would print only stuff that'd been rejected by other literary magazines, the more the merrier, plus the rejection slips. He was going to give a prize for the best rejection slip, he said it was an art. But it flopped because nobody wanted to admit they'd been rejected. He printed a lot of his own stuff in the first issue, though. I think he's English. He goes to all the parties, he goes to every party he can get into. He used to go around saying, 'Hello, I'm Fraser Buchanan, the Montreal Poet.' I think he once lived in Montreal."

"But how come you know him?"

"I submitted stuff to *Reject*," the Royal Porcupine said. "That was when I was still doing words. He rejected it. He hates my stuff, he thinks it's too far out."

"I think he's been following me around," I said. What I thought was worse: he's been following *us* around.

"He's freaky," said the Royal Porcupine. "He has this thing about celebrities. He says he's writing a history of our times."

That evening I took a taxi home early. I was suffering again from self-doubt. The difficulty was that I found each of my lives perfectly normal and appropriate, but only at the time. When I was with Arthur, the Royal Porcupine seemed like a daydream from one of my less credible romances, with an absurdity about him that I tried to exclude from my fictions. But when I was with the Royal Porcupine, he seemed plausible and solid. Everything he did and said made sense in his own terms, whereas it was Arthur who became unreal; he faded to an insubstantial ghost, a washed out photo on some mantelpiece I'd long ago abandoned. Was I hurting him, was I being unfaithful? How could you hurt a photograph?

When I walked into the apartment that evening, I was still thinking about this. The *Resurgence* crowd was there in force; something exciting was going on. Sam was the only one who said hello. They had a captive union organizer there, a real one, backed into the corner. He called them "you kids."

"If you kids want to get involved, okay," he was saying, "but if the workers want to spit on policemen, let *them* spit on policemen. It's *their* jobs. You kids can go to jail, you don't have steady jobs, you can miss some time, but for them it's different."

Don started to argue that this was precisely why they and not the workers should do it, but the union organizer waved his hand in dismissal. "No, no," he said. "I know you kids mean well, but believe me. Sometimes the wrong kind of help is worse than no help at all."

"What's going on?" I asked Sam.

"It's a strike down at a mattress factory," Sam said. "Trouble is, most of the workers are Portuguese, and they don't buy our line all that much. Canadian nationalism means bugger all to them, you know? Not that we can get it across to them, we're still looking for an interpreter."

"Who spit on a policeman?"

"Arthur did," Sam said, and I could tell from the smug yet chastised look on Arthur's face that indeed he had. For some reason this annoyed me.

If I hadn't just come from the Royal Porcupine's, I wouldn't have said anything; but he thought politics were boring, especially Canadian nationalism. "Art is universal," he'd say. "They're just trying to get attention."

When I was with Arthur, I believed in the justice of his cause, his causes, every one of them; how could I live with him otherwise? But the Royal Porcupine took the edge off causes. It was the Cavaliers and the Roundheads all over again.

"Oh, for heaven's sake," I said to Arthur. "I suppose you can hardly wait to be arrested. But what'll that solve, not a damn thing. You don't live in the real world, you won't join any kind of a political party and go out there and really change things, instead you sit around and argue and attack each other. You're like the Plymouth Brethren, all you're interested in is defining your own purity by excluding everyone else. And then you go out and make some useless, *meaningless* gesture like spitting on a policeman."

No one said anything; everyone was too stunned. I was the last person they'd have expected such a tirade from, and come to think of it, who was I to talk? I was hardly saving the world myself.

"Joan's right," Marlene said, in a voice cold with tactics. "But let's hear what kind of useful, meaningful gesture she'd like to suggest instead."

"Oh, I don't know," I said. I immediately started backing up and apologizing. "I mean, it's really none of my business, I don't know all that much about politics. Maybe you could blow up the Peace Bridge or something."

I was horrified to see that they were taking me seriously.

The next evening a small deputation arrived at the apartment. Marlene, Don, Sam and a couple of the younger Resurgenites.

"We've got it out there in the car," Marlene said.

"Got what?" I asked. I'd just washed my hair, I hadn't been expecting them. Arthur was off teaching his night class in Canadian Literature; he'd barely spoken to me that day, and I wasn't happy about that.

"The dynamite," she said. She was quite excited. "My father's in construction, it was easy to pinch it, plus the detonator and a couple of blasting caps."

"Dynamite? What're you doing with dynamite?"

"We talked over your idea," she said. "We decided it wasn't such a bad one. We're going to blow up the Peace Bridge, as a gesture. It's the best one to blow up, because of the name."

"Wait a minute," I said, "you might hurt someone."

"Marlene says we'll do it at night," Don said quickly. "We won't blow it all up anyway, it's more like a symbol. A gesture, like you said."

They wanted me to hide the dynamite for them. They'd even thought out a plan. They wanted me to buy a used car, under an assumed name, using a fake address, the apartment of a new Resurgenite who was going away for a couple of months anyway.

Then I had to put the dynamite in the trunk of the car and move the car around every day, from one street to another, from one all-night parking lot to the next.

"A used car costs money," I said slowly.

"Look, it was your idea," Marlene said. "The least you can do is help us out. Besides, you can get a cheap one for a couple of hundred."

"Why me?"

"They'd never suspect you," Marlene said. "You don't look much like the dynamite type."

"How long will I have to do this?" I asked.

"Only till we get the plan together. Then we'll take over the car."

"All right, I'll do it," I said. "Where's the dynamite?"

"Here," Don said, handing me a cardboard carton.

I never had any intention of carrying out their plan. The next day I took a taxi to the Royal Porcupine's and stowed the box in the cellar. There were a lot of crates and boxes there anyway. I told him it was an ugly statue I'd got for a wedding present and I couldn't bear to have it in the house any longer.

"I'd rather you didn't open it," I said. "For sentimental reasons."

Chapter Twenty-Six

The Royal Porcupine couldn't let well enough alone. That was one of the things I liked about him: he didn't believe in well enough, he believed in cataclysmic absolutes.

"Where'd you get the dynamite?" he said. We were lying on his mattress; he always kept serious questions till afterwards.

"I asked you not to open that box," I said.

"Come on, you knew I would. You know I love ugly statues. Where'd you get it?"

"It's not my dynamite," I said. "It belongs to some other people."

"I've never seen any of that stuff go off," he said thoughtfully. "I always like Victoria Day though, that was my favorite holiday. That and Hallowe'en."

"If you're thinking of blowing anything up," I said, "forget it. You'd get me in deep trouble if they found out it was missing."

"We could replace it," he said, "with other dynamite."

"No," I said. I was remembering the time he'd almost electrocuted us. He'd heard from one of his friends, also a con-create artist, that if you got a string of Christmas tree lights, plugged it in, unscrewed one of the lights, and stuck your finger in the socket at the moment of ejaculation, not only you but your partner would have the greatest orgasm in the world. His friend's recipe also included several joints, but the Royal Porcupine had given up dope. "Jejune," he called it. "Fred Astaire didn't smoke dope, right?" He'd spent days trying to persuade me to perform this act, or "art-if-act," as he called it; the "if" stood for the element of chance. He'd even bought a third-hand string of Christmas tree lights. "I refuse to turn myself into an electric toaster to satisfy one of your demented whims," I told him; so he'd hidden the lights under the mattress and plugged them in just before my next visit. He was planning to sneak his finger into the socket without my knowing, at the crucial moment; but we'd hardly begun before wisps of smoke began to curl out from under the mattress. I was afraid something similar would happen with the dynamite.

As usual, the more I resisted, the more excited he became. He got up off the mattress and started pacing the room. He put his fur hat on, a recent one, with Mountie earflaps. "Come *on*," he said, "it would be terrific! We wouldn't blow anything up, we'd just set it off, at night somewhere, and watch it go. Wow, it'd be sensational. It would be, like, an *event,* and we'd be the only audience, it would be all for us. *Ka-boom.* It's the only chance you'll ever get, how could you pass up something like that?"

"Easily," I said. "I don't like loud meaningless noises."

"Then you're with the wrong man," he said. He started licking my ear.

"Chuck, be reasonable."

"Reasonable," he said sullenly. "If I was reasonable, you wouldn't love me. Everyone else is reasonable." He took off his fur hat and flung it across the room. "And don't call me *Chuck.*" (I'd recently found out that his real name was Chuck Brewer, and he even had a job: he was a part-time commercial artist, specializing in layout and design. He told me this in deepest confidence, as if it were disreputable.)

Five days later we were walking across High Park, looking for a suitable place. It was eleven at night, it was the middle of March; there was still ice on the ponds and snow under the trees, it was a late spring. The Royal Porcupine had on one of his fur coats and his fur hat with the earflaps down. Under his coat he was carrying the dynamite in the cardboard box, with the fuse and detonator. He said he'd found out how to work it. I didn't believe him; also I didn't trust his motives.

"I'm not going along with this if you blow up any people," I said.

"I told you, I won't."

"Or any animals. Or any houses, or any trees."

"You still don't get it," he said impatiently. "The point isn't to blow anything up, it's just to blow up the dynamite. It's a pure act."

"I don't believe in pure acts," I said.

"Then you don't have to come with me," he said craftily, but I felt if I didn't he might break his promise and blow up something important, like a reservoir or the Gzowski Memorial down by the lakefront, which he'd mentioned in passing.

After inspecting a few likely sites, he settled on a stretch of open ground near a medium-sized pond. There didn't seem to be any structures nearby and it was quite far from the road, so I approved it. I crouched shivering in a clump of bushes while he fiddled with the dynamite, attaching the blasting cap and unraveling the wire.

"Are we far enough away?" I asked.

"Oh, sure," he said. Though when he set off the charge, it made an impressive enough *WHUMP*, and we were showered with bits of earth and a few small stones.

"Hah!" cried the Royal Porcupine. "Did you see that!"

I hadn't seen anything, as I'd closed my eyes and covered them with my mittened hands. "It was great," I said admiringly.

"Great," he said. "Is that all you can say? It was fuckin' *terrific*, it's the best art-if-act I've ever done!" He pulled me into his fur coat and began undoing buttons.

"We've got to get out of here," I protested. "Someone must've heard it, the police will come, they patrol this park."

"Come on," he begged, and I couldn't refuse, it was obviously so important to him. We made seismographic love inside his coat, listening for the sound of sirens, which never arrived.

"You're one in a million," he said. "Nobody else would've done that. I think I'm in love with you." I should've felt ironic about this, but I didn't. I kissed him gratefully, I must admit.

He was a little disappointed that the explosion didn't make the front page. For a whole day it didn't even make the newspapers, but on the second day he located a paragraph buried in the *Star*.

MYSTERIOUS EXPLOSION IN HIGH PARK

Police were puzzled by a small blast Wednesday, apparently caused by dynamite. No one was injured, although the sewer system of a nearby park restaurant was temporarily disrupted. There was no apparent reason for the blast; vandalism is suspected.

The Royal Porcupine was enthralled by this report, which he read out loud to me several times. "No apparent reason," he crowed. "Fabulous!" He took the clipping to a photo blow-up service, had it enlarged, framed it in a carved frame from the Crippled Civvies, and mounted it beside the Queen.

For weeks after the explosion, Marlene and Don and the rest believed that I was moving the dynamite around the city, in a 1968 powder-blue Chevy. Meanwhile they were debating their contemplated act. Not how to do it, for they never got that far. They didn't even get as far as maps and strategy, they were stuck at the level of pure theory: would they be blowing up the right thing? It would be a nationalist act, true, but was it nationalist enough, and if so, would it serve the people? Some decisive act was necessary, Don argued; otherwise they would be outflanked. Already ideas they'd thought were theirs alone were beginning to appear in newspaper editorials, and the Gallup poll showed a swing in their direction. They viewed these developments with alarm: the revolution was getting into the wrong hands.

I didn't mind moving their imaginary dynamite around the city. It gave me a perfect chance to leave the apartment any time I felt like it. "Time to move the dynamite," I'd say cheerfully, and there wasn't much Arthur could say. In fact he was even proud of me. "You've got to admit she's intrepid," Sam said. They felt I was being very cool.

Most of the time I'd go over to the Royal Porcupine's. But something was changing. The lace tablecloth in which I waltzed with him was turning itself back into a lace tablecloth, with a rip in it; the black pointed boots were no longer worth the pain they in-

flicted. Motels became motels, and what they meant
to me now was hard work and embarrassment. Sturgess was sending me on yet more trips, to Sudbury, to
Windsor, and it was costing me more and more to get
through the interviews.

Afterward I would go back to the motel and
wash out my underwear and pantyhose in the bathroom sinks, squeezing them in towels and draping
them over coat hangers. In the mornings they were
never quite dry but I would put them on anyway,
feeling the clammy grub-gray touch against my skin.
It was like dressing in the used breath of other people. While the Royal Porcupine sat on the bed's edge,
white and skinny as a root, and asked me questions.

"What's he like?"

"Who?"

"You know, Arthur. How often do you. . . ."

"Chuck, it's none of your business."

"It is my business," he said. He didn't pick up on
the name; he was becoming less and less like the
Royal Porcupine and more and more like Chuck. "I
don't ask you those things about your lady friends."

"I made those other women up," he said sulkily.
"There's no one but you."

"So who leaves the pumpkin cakes?"

"My mother," he said. I knew this was a lie.

He'd always lived in his own unwritten biography, but now he started seeing the present as
though it was already the past, bandaged in gauzy
nostalgia. Every restaurant we ate in he left with a
sigh and a backward glance; he spoke of things we'd
done the week before as if they were snapshots in
some long-buried photograph album. Each of my ges-
tures was petrified as I performed it, each kiss
embalmed, as if he was saving things up. I felt like
a collectable. "I'm not dead yet," I told him more
than once, "so why are you looking at me like that?"

This was one of his moods. In another he would
be openly hostile towards me. He began to take a

morbid interest, not in his own newspaper clippings, which weren't numerous, but in mine. He'd cut them out and use them to belabor me.

"It says here you're a challenge to the male ego."

"Isn't that silly," I said.

"But you are a challenge to the male ego," he said.

"Oh, come on," I said. "Who've I ever challenged?"

"It says here you're a threat."

"What the hell do you mean?" I said. I'd been especially nice all afternoon, I felt.

"You stomp all over people's egos without even knowing you're doing it," he said. "You're emotionally clumsy."

"If we're going to have this conversation, would you please put on your clothes?" I said. My lower lip was trembling; somehow I couldn't argue with a naked man.

"See what I mean?" he said. "You're telling me what to do. You're a threat."

"I am not a threat," I said.

"If you aren't a threat," he said, "why are you screaming?"

I began to cry. He put his arms around me, I put my arms around him, oozing tears like an orphan, like an onion, like a slug sprinkled with salt. "I'm sorry," he said. "I don't have a male ego anyway, I probably have the ego of a wombat."

"I thought we were going to keep it light," I said, between damp snorts.

"It's light, it's light," he said. "Wait'll it gets heavy. I'm just depressed because it's raining and I don't have any money."

"Let's go out for some Kentucky Fried," I said, wiping my nose. But he wasn't hungry.

One rainy afternoon when I arrived at his warehouse, he was waiting for me all dressed up in his cape and a tie I'd never seen before, a Crippled Civilians maroon one with a mermaid on it. He

grabbed me by the waist and whirled me around
the floor; his eyes sparkled.

"What is it?" I said when I'd caught my breath.
"What's gotten into you?"

"A surprise," he said. He led me over to the bed:
lying on it was a truly grotesque white pancake hat
from the fifties, with a feather and a veil.

"Where did you get *that?*" I said, wondering
what new fantasy had gripped him. The fifties had
never been his favorite period.

"It's your going-away hat," he said. "I got it at
the Sally Ann, eighty-nine cents."

"But what's it for?"

"Going away, of course," he said, still elated. "I
thought we might, you know, go away together.
Elope."

"You must be crazy," I said. "Where would we
go?"

"How about Buffalo?"

I started to laugh, then saw that he was serious.
"That's very sweet of you," I said, "but you know that
I can't."

He wanted me to leave Arthur and move in with
him. That's what it amounted to, and finally he admitted it. We sat side by side on the bed, staring
at the floor. "I want to live a normal life with you,"
he said.

"I don't think we could," I said. "I'm a terrible
cook. I burn things."

"I want to wake up in the morning and eat
breakfast with you and read *The Globe and Mail.*"

"I could come over for breakfast," I said. "A late
breakfast."

"I want to brush your hair."

I began to snivel. I'd once told him Arthur liked
brushing my hair; or used to.

"What's he got that I haven't got?"

I didn't know. But I didn't want him to spoil
things, I didn't want him to become gray and multi-
dimensional and complicated like everyone else. Was

every Heathcliff a Linton in disguise? What did I want, adventure or security, and which of them offered what? Perhaps neither of them offered either, they both wanted me to offer these things, and once more I was deficient. The Royal Porcupine lay with his head against my stomach, waiting for the answer.

"I don't know," I said. "It isn't that."

He sat up again. "That's the trouble with you, you have no motives. Don't you know how dangerous that is? You're like an out-of-control school bus."

"I don't mean to be," I said. To make up for it, I bought him a bottle of One-A-Day vitamin pills and a pair of socks and dusted off his stuffed animals. I even gave him my fox, the one that had been Aunt Lou's. This was a real gift: I valued it. Once it would have delighted him, but he barely glanced at it.

"At least you could tell him about us," he said. "Sometimes I think you're ashamed of me."

But I drew the line at that. "I can't," I said, "it would ruin everything. I love you."

"You're afraid to take a chance on me," he said mournfully. "I can see that. I'm not much now, I admit it, but think of the potential!"

"I like you the way you are," I said, but he couldn't believe me. It wasn't that I didn't love him. I did, in a peculiar way, but I knew I couldn't live with him. For him, reality and fantasy were the same thing, which meant that for him there was no reality. But for me it would mean there was no fantasy, and therefore no escape.

The next time I stepped out of the freight elevator, there was an ambush waiting for me. The Royal Porcupine was there, but he was no longer the Royal Porcupine. He'd cut his hair short and shaved off his beard. He was standing in the middle of the floor, no cape, no cane, no gloves; just a pair of jeans and a T-shirt that said *Honda* on it. He was merely Chuck Brewer; had he always been, underneath his beard? He looked plundered.

"My God," I said, almost screamed. "What did you do that for?"

"I killed him," Chuck said. "He's over with, he's finished."

I started to cry. "Oh, I forgot these," he said. He ripped down his picture of the Queen, then his dynamite poster, and threw them onto the pile he'd made of his costumes.

"What about your animals?" I said stupidly.

"I'm getting rid of them," he said. "They aren't any good to me now."

I was staring at his chin; I'd never seen it before. "Now will you move in?" he said. "It doesn't have to be here, we could get a house."

It was horrible. He'd thought that by transforming himself into something more like Arthur he could have Arthur's place; but by doing this he'd murdered the part of him that I loved. I scarcely knew how to console the part that remained. Without his beard, he had the chin of a junior accountant.

I hated myself for thinking this. I felt like a monster, a large, blundering monster, irredeemably shallow. How could I care about his chin at a time like this? I threw my arms about him. I couldn't do what he wanted, it was all wrong.

"I can tell you aren't going to," he said, disengaging my arms. "Well, I guess there's only one thing to do. How about a double suicide? Or maybe I could shoot you and then jump off the Toronto Dominion Centre with your body in my arms." He managed a white smile, but he didn't fool me. He was completely serious.

Chapter Twenty-Seven

The freight elevator ponderously descended. I imagined the Royal Porcupine pounding down three flights of stairs, shedding his clothes, to confront me on the ground floor, stark naked; but when the door grated open he wasn't there. I ran three blocks to the Kentucky Fried Chicken, ducked inside and ordered a Family Bucket. Then I took a taxi back to the apartment. I would tell all, I would cry. I would be forgiven, I would never do it again, if only Arthur would pardon me and take me back to safety.

I climbed the stairs to the apartment and flung open the door, breathing hard. I was ready for the scene. It wouldn't be just a confession, it would be an accusation too: why had Arthur driven me to it, what did he propose to do about it, shouldn't we discuss our relationship to find out what had gone wrong? For some complicated and possibly sadistic reason of his own he'd allowed me to become involved with a homicidal maniac, and it was time he knew about it. I didn't ask much, I only wanted to be loved. I only wanted some human consideration. Was that so terrible, was that so impossible, was I some kind of mutation?

Arthur was watching television. His back was toward me, and the nape of his neck was vulnerable. I noticed that he needed a haircut, and this hurt me. He was like a child, whole in his beliefs and trusts. What was I doing?

"Arthur," I said, "there's something I have to discuss with you."

He said, without turning, "Could you wait till it's over?"

I sat down on the floor beside his chair and opened the Family Bucket. Silently I offered it to him. "How can you eat that American crap?" he said, but he took a breast and began to chew. He was watching the Olympic doubles figure-skating championships; once he would watch only the news, but now it was anything he could get, situation comedies, hockey games, police series, talk shows. The television set had vertical foldover on the lower third of the screen, so that the people on the talk shows had four hands, like Indian gods and goddesses, and the chase sequences on the police shows appeared upside down, with two sets of cops and two sets of robbers; but Arthur wouldn't get it fixed because of the expense. He said he knew someone who could fix it.

The Austrian skaters, in long white sleeves, the girl in a dark bodice, glided backwards around the rink at incredible speed, completely synchronized. Each of them had four legs. They turned and the girl flew up into the air and posed, upside down, two-headed, while the man held her with one arm. Down she came—"Her right foot touched," said the commentator—and they both fell, multiplying as they hit the ice. They got up and continued their routine, but it wasn't quite the same. Canada's pair fell down too, although they were daring at first.

The Fat Lady skated out onto the ice. I couldn't help myself. It was one of the most important moments in my life, I should have been able to keep her away, but out she came in a pink skating costume, her head ornamented with swan's-down. With her was the thinnest man in the world. She smiled at the crowd, nobody smiled back, they didn't believe what they were seeing because she was whirling around the rink with exceptional grace, spinning like a top on her tiny feet, then the thin man lifted her and threw her and she floated up, up, she hung suspended . . . her secret was that although she was so large, she was very light, she was hollow, like a helium balloon, they had to keep her tethered to her bed or she'd drift away, all night she strained at the ropes. . . .

There's something I have to tell you, I thought of saying during the commercial. But Arthur was rooting through the Family Bucket for an unconsumed piece, his fingers were covered with grease, and he had a little piece of chicken on his chin. Tenderly I wiped it off. This was a defenseless moment: how could I violate it? Arthur would need dignity.

A famous figure-skater praised margarine, unconvincingly, her eyes hypnotized by the cue cards. Then the competition came back on. The Fat Lady was still there, bobbing against the ceiling. The U.S. team scooted across the bottom of the screen like a centipede, but no one paid any attention, they were all distracted by the huge pink balloon that bobbed with such poor taste above their heads. . . . The Fat Lady kicked her skates feebly; her tights and the huge moon of her rump were visible. Really it was an outrage. "They've gone for the harpoon gun," I heard the commentator say. They were going to shoot her down in cold blood, explode her, despite the fact that she had now burst into song. . . .

Why am I doing this? I thought. *Who's doing this to me?* "I'm going to bed," I told Arthur. I couldn't act, I couldn't even think straight; at any moment the Royal Porcupine might come hammering at the door, or scream some terrible message over the phone, the moment before he jumped, and I was paralyzed, there was nothing I could do. I could only wait for the ax to fall and, knowing him, it wouldn't even be an ax, it would be a rubber turkey from some joke shop; that or a huge explosion. He had no sense of proportion. Russia won the title, again.

The next morning I got the first of the phone calls. No voice, nothing, though I said hello three times. Just some breathing and a click. I knew it had to be him, but I was surprised by his lack of originality. The second phone call came at six, and the third one at nine. The next day I got a letter from him, or I felt it had to be from him. It was just a blank sheet of paper with a little woodcut of Death, holding a scythe, and the caption, MAY I HAVE THIS WALTZ? The letters and words had been cut from the Yellow Pages and pasted on; Death was from a magazine. I crumpled it up and threw it into the garbage. He'd certainly gone to work fast, but I wasn't going to let him see he was getting to me.

What I really expected was an anonymous letter to Arthur. I started censoring his mail, though to do it I had to get up early and make it to the downstairs hallway in time to snatch the mail as it came through the letter slot. I'd ponder the envelopes, and if the contents weren't obvious I would save them to steam open later. I did this for five days, but nothing happened. The phone calls continued. I didn't know whether Arthur got any; if so, he didn't mention it.

Everything depended on whether the Royal Porcupine wanted me back—if so, he wouldn't tell Arthur—whether he wanted to kill me, which I doubted, or whether he just wanted revenge. I thought of phoning to ask him; he might tell me the truth if I got him at the right moment. I should never have given him this power, the power to ruin my life; for it wasn't yet completely ruined, something could still be salvaged. I hinted to Arthur that it might be a nice change for us to move to another city.

On the sixth day I got another letter. The address was typewritten; there was no stamp, it must've been delivered by hand. Inside there was another cut-out message: OPEN THE DOOR. I waited half an hour and opened it. On the doorstep there was a dead porcupine with an arrow stuck into it. A label attached to the arrow read JOAN.

"Oh, for Christ's sake," I said. If the landlord, or Arthur, had found it first there would have been an uproar or at least an inquisition. I had to get rid of it in a hurry. It was a large porcupine, with extensive wounds, and it was already beginning to rot. I pulled it to the side of the porch and dumped it among the hydrangeas, hoping that none of the neighbors was watching. Then I went upstairs, got a green plastic Glad Bag, stuffed the porcupine into it, and managed to get it into the garbage can labeled "Tenants" in the hinged bin at the back. I pictured the Royal Porcupine unfreezing all his animals, one by one, and leaving them on my doorstep. He had a lot of them, they'd last for weeks.

I felt he was going too far. In the afternoon I went out to a pay phone and called him. "Chuck, is that you?" I said when he answered.

"Who is this," he said, "Myrna?"

"You know bloody well it's not Myrna, whoever she may be," I said. "It's Joan, and I want you to know I don't think you're funny at all."

"What do you mean?" he said. He really did sound surprised.

"You know," I said. "Your little notes. I suppose you thought you were being very clever, cutting the letters out of the Yellow Pages like that so I wouldn't know it was you."

"No, I didn't," he said. "I mean, what notes? I've never sent you any notes."

"What about that *thing* you left on my doorstep this morning? I suppose that wasn't one of your precious mangled animals."

"What are you talking about?" he said. "You must be crazy. I haven't done a thing."

"And you can stop phoning and breathing at me over the phone, too."

"I swear to God I haven't called you once. Has someone been calling you?"

I felt defeated. If he was lying, that meant he was going to continue. If he wasn't, then who was doing it? "Chuck, be honest," I said.

"I thought I asked you not to call me that," he said coldly. "I haven't done anything to you. Why should I? You told me it's over. Okay, I was mad at the time, but I thought about it, and if you say it's over, it's over. You know me, here today, gone tomorrow. Easy come, easy go. Why should I worry?"

I was hurt that he was taking it so calmly. "So that's really all I meant to you," I said.

"Look, you were the one who backed out, not me. If you don't want to live with me, what do you expect me to do? Stick my head in the oven?"

"Maybe I was wrong," I said, "maybe we should talk about it."

"Why prolong the agony?" he said. "Besides, I've got company."

Then he hung up on me. I slammed down the phone and jiggled the coin return; I felt I should definitely get my dime back, he owed me that. But from the black machine, no satisfaction.

I ran back to the apartment, closed myself into the bedroom, got out my typewriter, and shut my eyes. A tall man in a cloak, that was what I needed. All the time I'd been with the Royal Porcupine I hadn't written a word. Was this why my creatures seemed more real than usual, nearer to me, charged with an energy greater than I gave them?

But it was no good; I couldn't stop time, I could shut nothing out.

That night there was another call, and the next day another note: COME INTO THE FUNERAL PARLOR, with a picture of a spider glued to it. The day after that, a dead bluejay on the doorstep. That night I thought I heard someone climbing the fire escape.

I began to hesitate before picking up the phone. I thought of getting a shrill whistle, the kind you were supposed to use on obscene phone callers. Once I screamed "Stop it!" into the phone before realizing it was only Sam. I wasn't afraid, exactly; I still thought of it as a prolonged and revengeful practical joke, and the Royal Porcupine for I was still convinced he was the one—probably thought of it as a work of art. Maybe he was taking pictures of me opening the door and finding his smelly little tokens of esteem, maybe he'd put the prints on exhibition. I thought about going over to his warehouse and trying to reason with him. . . .

The phone rang. I let it ring three times, then picked it up, prepared for the breathing and maybe even a threatening laugh. "Hello," I said.

"This is Joan Delacourt?" A man's voice, thick and odd somehow.

"Yes," I said automatically, before I'd had time to think about this use of my maiden name. Everyone called me Joan Foster now.

"Joan. At last I have founded you."

"Who is this?" I said.

"You cannot guess?" the voice said coyly. Now it

was sounding familiar. "This is your friend Mavis." A flirtatious laugh.

"Paul," I said. "Oh, my God."

"I have read about you in the newspaper," Paul said, undaunted by my dismay, "I have recognized the picture, though it is not so beautiful as you. I have been so happy about your success, you do not need to write the Gothic Romance any more, you are a true writer. I have read your book. It is promising, I think, for a first book, by a woman."

Behind me I could hear Arthur coming in the door. I had to get Paul off the phone, but I didn't want to hurt his feelings. "Paul," I said, "I must see you. I'd like to see you."

"This, too, is what I desire," said Paul. "I know of a good restaurant. . . ."

I met him at it the next day, for a late lunch. Zerdo's, the restaurant was called. There never used to be restaurants in Toronto with names like Zerdo's, but now there were many. It was like Paul to pick a restaurant with a name like some sort of drain cleaner, I thought as I opened the door. It was a narrow darkened room with tables covered with checked cloths and lamps in the shape of candles. Artificial grapevines festooned the walls. At the back of the room was a pass-through hatchway covered with fake brick wallpaper and hung with copper pans. . . . The maître d' bustled toward me, short and alert, gold-tasselled menus under his arm.

"John," I said involuntarily. I'd know that soft moustache anywhere. . . .

"I beg your pardon, madame," he said. "My name is Zerdo."

Paul was already walking toward me. Ceremoniously he kissed my hand and led me with gentle melancholy towards a table. When we were seated he did not speak, but gazed at me with reproachful eyes from behind his glasses, which were now, I noticed, tinted: a pale mauve.

"This used to be called the Bite-A-Bit," I said. I didn't say I'd been the cashier, but there was my

double behind the cash register, a heavy woman
with bunned hair, wearing a black dress which
showed her rippling elbows but not her bosom. One
of my once-potential futures, in the flesh; Mrs. Zerdo, no doubt. At this moment I envied her.

"Joan," said Paul. "Why have you fleed from
me?" He'd taken the plastic rose out of its vase
and was twirling it between his fingers, apparently
unaware that it wasn't real. What could I say that
would be appropriate?

"It was all for the best," I said.

"No, Joan," he said sadly. "It was not. You know
I have loved you. I have wished to marry you, once
you were older; I planned that, I should have told
you. Yet you run away from me. You have made me
very unhappy." He said this, yet I didn't altogether
believe him. I noticed his suit, which was certainly
a more expensive one than he'd once been able to
afford; and he had an air of confidence that was new
to him. The bitter, threadbare aristocrat had been
blurred a little; superimposed on that was a layer of
successful businessman.

Zerdo appeared with the wine list. He was def-
erential to Paul, who ordered flawlessly. Paul took
out a Gauloise, offered me one, and inserted one for
himself in his cigarette holder, which was new and
sumptuous.

"I am pleased I have discovered you," Paul said,
as we sipped our lemon soup. "Now we will have
to think what to do, as I see you have married."

"Paul," I said to change the subject, "do you live
here now? Have you moved to Canada?"

"No," he said, "but I am here often. On business.
I am no longer with the bank since six years, I have
another business. I am—" he hesitated "—importer."

"What do you import?" I asked.

"Many things," he said vaguely. "Wood carvings,
the chess sets and the boxes for cigarettes, from
Czechoslovakia; garments from India, they are popular now, and from Mexico. It is helpful to have a
knowledge of many languages. I do not speak all my-

self, but one can always arrange." He didn't really want to talk about it. I remembered the revolver. Was that a slight bulge under his arm, could he possibly be wearing a shoulder holster? I thought, in rapid succession, of heroin, opium, atomic weapons, jewels and state secrets.

"I have extracted my mother," he said, "from Poland, but she has died."

We talked about that, and about his daughter, during the moussaka.

"I read in the paper that your husband is some sort of a Communist," he said when we'd reached the baklava. "Joan, how could you marry a man like this? I have told you what they are like."

"He's not exactly a Communist," I said. "It's hard to explain, but it's different here. Besides, it doesn't mean anything here, it's respectable, sort of. They don't *do* anything; they just have meetings and talk a lot, sort of like the Theosophists."

"Talk is dangerous," said Paul darkly. "All such things begin by talk. They are good at talk, they are like the Jesuits. Poor child, this is how he made you marry him. You have had your brain washed out by him."

"No," I said, "it wasn't like that," but Paul was convinced.

"I can tell you are very unhappy," he said.

This was true enough, and I didn't deny it. In fact I was enjoying the sensation of all this sympathy lapping around me, like warm washcloths. I'd thought Paul would be angry with me, but he was being so nice. I drank another glass of wine and Paul ordered brandy.

"You can trust me," he said, patting my hand. "You were a child, you did not know your own mind. Now you are a woman. You will leave this man, you will divorce, we will be happy."

"Paul, I can't leave," I said. He swam before me in a haze of nostalgia. Was this my lost love, my rescuer? My eyes filled with tears, and so did my nose. I blotted myself with the table napkin. Any minute now I was really going to cry.

Paul's jaw tightened. "He will not let you. I see," he said. "They are like that. If you tell him it is I you love, he will. . . . But I have friends. If necessary I shall steal you."

"No," I said, "Paul, you can't do that. That would be dangerous. Besides, people don't do things like that here."

Paul patted my hand. "Do not worry," he said. "I know what I am doing. I will wait, and then, at the right moment, I will strike." His eyes gleamed; it was a challenge, he wanted to win.

I couldn't tell him I didn't want to be stolen; that would be too rude, and painful for him as well. "Well," I said, "it's important that you don't tell anyone you've seen me. And you shouldn't phone. . . . Paul, did you phone me before, without saying anything?"

"Maybe once," he said. "I thought it was wrong number." So it wasn't him.

We got up to leave. Paul took my arm. "Do you still write Mavis Quilps?" I said, remembering. "I guess you don't have to any more."

"I continue to write them, as a recreation," Paul said. "It is soothing to the mind, after a hard day's work." He paused for a moment, searched an inside pocket. "Here," he said. "I have brought a gift, for you. You are a specialty. I am alone in my life, no one else would care. But I know you would like it."

He handed me the book. *Nurse of the High Arctic*, it said on the cover. By Mavis Quilp. The pink-cheeked nurse smiled winsomely from the nimbus of her parka.

"Oh, Paul," I said, "thank you so much." I was touched, ludicrously; it was like the end of the whale movie, he was so sad, so trusting, so hopeless, consolation was so impossible. I threw my arms around his neck and burst into tears.

Now you've done it, I thought as I sobbed

against his shoulder. I had to stoop a little to do this. He was wearing Hai Karate shaving lotion, which made me cry even harder. How could I get out of it? I had been too encouraging, again.

Chapter Twenty-Eight

Paul wanted to put me into a taxi. It was part of his image that I should go off in a taxi, but I said I wanted to walk, so he got into the taxi himself. I watched as he was swept away, north on Church Street in the glinting metal traffic. Then I started to walk home.

My eyes were still swollen and I was numbed and depressed. Paul's wish to rescue me was gallant but futile, as all gallantry now seemed to me futile. Besides, I didn't want to be rescued by him, but hadn't had the courage to tell him. Sullenly I would iron his boxer shorts and eat his caviar, in some tacky hideout, pretending to be happy and grateful; sullenly I would escape again, leaving him punctured and perhaps, this time, vengeful. I'd once thought I was in love with him. Maybe I had been.

"There's magic in love and smiles. Use them every day, in all you do, and see what wonderful things happen," Brown Owl used to say chirpily, reading it from her little book. I'd believed that slogan, I'd believed that the absence of wonderful things happening had been due to my own failure, my insufficient love. Now it seemed to me that the name of a furniture polish could be substituted for "love" in this maxim without at all violating its meaning. Love was merely a tool, smiles were another tool, they were both just tools for accomplishing certain ends. No magic, merely chemicals. I felt I'd never really loved anyone, not Paul, not Chuck the Royal Porcupine, not even Arthur. I'd polished them with

my love and expected them to shine, brightly
enough to return my own reflection, enhanced and
sparkling.

At that moment it seemed to me impossible that
anyone could ever really love anyone, or if they
could, that anything lasting or fine would come of it.
Love was the pursuit of shadows, and I was a shadow
for Paul, doomed to flee before him, evanescent
as a cloud. Some cloud, I thought, already my feet
hurt. He probably didn't want me at all, he wanted
the adventure of kidnapping me from what he
imagined to be a den of fanged and dangerous Com-
munists, armed to the teeth with brain-suction de-
vices and slaughterous rhetoric, I in their midst
bound hand and foot by jargon. Once he had me he
wouldn't know at all what to do with me. He hadn't
been able to live with me before, he couldn't stand
the mess, and the years hadn't made me any neater.
I was not the same as my phantom.

When I got home there was another anonymous note, something about coffins, but I scarcely
glanced at it. I climbed the stairs to the apartment,
slowly; I had a blister on one foot. I hoped Arthur
would be there so I'd have at least the comfort of a
familiar body; but he wasn't, and I remembered he'd
said he'd be at a meeting. The apartment was empty
and desolate, as it would be, I thought, without him.
I'd better get used to it; any day now the Royal
Porcupine would get tired of his game and escalate
it.

I went into the bathroom, ran the tub full of
warm water, added some Vitabath and climbed in
with my Mavis Quilp. The bathroom had always been
my refuge, it was the only room in the house, all the
houses, where I could lock the door. I'd wallow in
the tub like a steamy walrus while my mother
cleared her throat discreetly outside the door, torn
between the grunts and shouts of the body she refused to admit she possessed and her unwillingness to
be explicit.

"Joan, what are you doing in there?"

Long pause. "Taking a bath."

"You've been in there for an hour. Other people might want to use the bathroom too, you should be more considerate."

I covered myself with bubbles and submerged myself in *Nurse of the High Arctic*. Why had Sharon ever left her comfortable hospital in England to come up north where there were no conveniences and where the handsome doctor sneered at her every time she dropped a scalpel? She sped over the ice floe in her runaway dogsled, pursued on foot by the grouchy doctor. *Stop, you silly little fool. I can't, I don't know how.* I knew what would happen, I was familiar with Paul's style. . . . Only when the doctor saw her upside down and covered with fur would he realize how much he loved her, and after that he would have to earn her love in return. He would have an accident, or she would have an accident, one or the other. Pure ice, pure snow, chaste kiss.

I longed for the simplicity of that world, where happiness was possible and wounds were only ritual ones. Why had I been closed out from that impossible white paradise where love was as final as death, and banished to this other place where everything changed and shifted?

The phone rang, but I let it ring. I wasn't going to get out of the bathtub and leave puddles on the floor to listen to someone breathe; I would stay here with Sharon and Doctor Hunter. *He touched her cheek, brushing away a strand of hair. Brusquely he told her that she should keep her hair pinned back: didn't she remember her training?* Seductive ringlets, tendrils and strands, they always featured in Paul's books, as in Milton's. *Sharon blushed and turned away to hide it.*

Three quarters of an hour later, as the helicopter with the rescued Eskimo was touching down (any moment now, the declaration, the embrace), as the water was getting tepid for the second time, I thought I heard someone in the next room. I listened, careful not to make a ripple: there were definite footsteps, crossing the main room and heading towards my bedroom.

I froze in the bathtub; I went rigid with fear. For a moment I lay there like a giant popsicle; visions of knife-wielding rapists, their fangs dripping blood, flashed before me, visions of burglars, dope-crazed and lethal, visions of perverts who would chop me into pieces and leave choice cuts in every trash bin in the city. There was no bathroom window. Perhaps if I stayed quiet he would simply take what he could find, which wouldn't be much, and leave the way he had come. I could have sworn I'd put the catch on the window that opened onto the fire escape, and he hadn't come in the door, it squeaked so much I would have heard it.

Slowly I eased myself out of the bathtub. I didn't pull the plug, it would've gurgled. I spread out the bath mat, then knelt on it and applied my eye to the keyhole. At first I could see nothing. The mysterious visitor was out of sight in the bedroom. I waited, and he crossed the doorway. His face was turned the other way, but he was short and he looked familiar.

It was Paul, I decided. I hadn't been expecting him quite so soon. There were some rummaging sounds, a few mutterings: what was he doing? He was supposed to be looking for me, not going through my closet. I felt like calling out, "Oh, for heaven's sake, Paul, I'm in here." I wrapped my torso in a bath towel; I'd have to go out and have a serious talk with him, apologize to him, tell him I was sorry but he'd misunderstood me, I was happy with my husband and the past was the past. He could hardly carry me off after that. Then we would become old friends.

I unlocked the door and padded in my bare feet across to the bedroom. "Paul," I said, "I want to. . . ."

The man turned around, and it wasn't Paul. It was Fraser Buchanan, in his tweed jacket with the leather patches and a trendy turtle-neck sweater, plus a pair of black gloves. He'd been going through my bureau drawers, and it was obvious from his thoroughness and air of method that this wasn't the first time he'd done this sort of thing.

"What are you doing in here?" I shouted at him.

I'd startled him, but he recovered quickly. He bared his teeth like a cornered chinchilla.

"I'm doing research," he said, very cool. Obviously it wasn't the first time he'd been caught.

"I could have you arrested," I said. I can't have looked too dignified: I was holding the towel together at the back.

"The fact is, I know a good deal more about you than you think. I know things I'm sure you would rather keep . . . private. Just between us two."

What had he found out? Who would he tell? *Arthur*, I thought. *Arthur will know*. My hidden selves, my other lives, unworthy. I couldn't let that happen.

"What?" I managed to squeak. "What are you talking about?"

"I think you understand me well enough, Mrs. Foster. Or should I say Miss Delacourt, Miss Louisa K. Delacourt, author of *Love Defied* and others?"

He'd got as far as my underwear drawer, then.

"I've read a number of your books," he continued, "though I didn't know at the time they were yours. They aren't bad, for that kind of thing. But they don't exactly go with *Lady Oracle*, do they? Wrong image, I should think. I don't expect your Women's Libber fans will be too overjoyed when they hear the news, though some other people I could think of might find it amusing. Not to mention the *Braeside Banner*. Those pictures of you are really fine. Tell me, how did you manage to lose all that avoirdupois?"

"What do you want?" I said.

"Well, that depends," he said crisply, "on what you've got to offer. In exchange, you might say."

"Let me put on some clothes," I said, "and we'll talk it over."

"I prefer you this way," said Fraser Buchanan.

I was furious, but I was also frightened. He'd discovered at least two of my secret identities, and I was so confused at that point I couldn't remember whether I had any more. If I hadn't become a culture heroine it wouldn't have mattered quite so much, though I couldn't stand the thought of Arthur knowing about my previous life as Pneumatic Woman. And if he told the media people the truth about Louisa K. Delacourt, my brief interlude of being taken seriously would be over. Unpleasant as it had been, I'd discovered it was much better than not being taken seriously. I would rather dance as a ballerina, though faultily, than as a flawless clown.

I put on my apricot velvet gown, piled my hair on top of my head with a few seductive tendrils twining around my neck, and attached some dangly gold earrings. I put on makeup, I even put on some perfume. Something would have to be done about Fraser Buchanan, but I hadn't yet figured out what. I decided to admire him. As I entered the living room, I smiled at him. He was sitting on the chesterfield with his hands on his knees, as if waiting for the dentist.

I suggested we go out for a drink, as there was nothing to drink in the apartment (a lie). He agreed readily, as I thought he would. He felt he had won and there was nothing to be discussed but the terms. The bar he chose was the Fourth Estate. He hoped a lot of journalists would see him with me. I ordered a Dubonnet on the rocks with a twist of lemon, he a double Scotch. I offered to pay, but he didn't go for that.

"I also know about your little fling with that fraudulent artist, or poet, or whatever he calls himself," he confided, leaning across the chic round mirror-topped table. "I've been following you around."

My stomach went cold. This was the thing I had feared the most. I'd been so careful; had Chuck told him? If he'd wanted to really hurt me, of course that's what he would've done.

"Everybody knows about that. Even my husband knows about *that*," I said, with enough contempt to dismiss it as a negotiable item. "The man practically issued press releases. He sold two of my shopping lists in a sealed envelope to a university; he swore they were love letters. He filched them from my purse. Didn't you know that?" Selling samples of my handwriting was something Chuck had often threatened to do—he needed the bread, as he put it—but as far as I knew he'd never done it.

Fraser Buchanan's face fell like a section of badly engineered land fill: if Arthur already knew, he could gain nothing by threatening to tell him.

"How did you get in?" I asked conversationally, to smooth over his confusion. I was interested, too: I'd met a lot of amateur con-men but never a professional. "It couldn't have been the window over the fire escape."

"No," he said, "it was the one next to it. I swung myself across."

"Really?" I said. "That's quite a distance. And I suppose that was you phoning me and then not saying anything."

"Well, I had to make sure you weren't there, so I could get in."

"Sort of backfired though," I said.

"Yes, but you would've found out sooner or later."

He explained how he'd tracked down my maiden name, which had never appeared in an interview, by combing the records of marriages. "Were you really married by someone called Eunice P. Revele?" he said. Then he'd searched through high-school yearbooks until he'd found me. Matching me with Louisa K. Delacourt had been a guess, which he'd needed to substantiate by finding evidence. The Royal Porcupine had been the easiest; he'd also thought that was his ace in the hole, but to my relief he conceded it wasn't. "Marriage isn't what it used to be," he said with disgust. "A few years ago that would've been worth a bundle. Now everybody tells everything, you'd think it was a competition."

I asked him about the dead animals, also about the notes. "Why would I do a thing like that?" he asked with genuine surprise. "There's no percentage in that. I'm a businessman."

"Well, if you've been following me around, you might have seen who left them. The woodchucks and things."

"I don't work in the mornings, love," he said. "Only at night, I'm a night person."

We had another drink and then got down to brass tacks. "What do you want out of all this?" I asked.

"Simple," he said. "Money and power."

"Well, I don't have much money," I said, "and I don't have any power at all."

But this he refused to believe. He hated celebrities, he felt they diminished him. All of them, however ephemeral, had money and power, according to him. Not only that, none of them had any talent really, at least not any more than the next fellow. Therefore they had got where they had through chicanery and fraud and they deserved to be relieved of some of their cash. He was especially contemptuous of *Lady Oracle* and of my publisher, and he was convinced that I'd got the book published by using my feminine wiles. "He's always launching young unknown ladies, that man," he said, during his fourth drink. "With big pictures of them on the back of the book, just the face and neck and down to the tits. Flash in the bedpan, most of them. No talent."

"You should take up literary criticism," I said.

"What," he said, "and give up my practice? Doesn't pay enough." He never used the word "blackmail," and he referred to the others he had the goodies on, as he put it, as his clients.

"Who else?" I said, my eyes wide and appreciative. I was letting him bask.

It was here that he made his mistake. He took out his black notebook, thereby letting me know of its existence. "Of course, I can't tell you those things they'd rather people didn't know," he said, "same as I'll never tell yours. But just to give you an idea—" He read out seven or eight names, and I was suitably impressed. "Here's one, now," he said. "Clean as a whistle, you'd think. It took me six months on him. But it was worth it. Little boys' bottoms, that was his. All right if you like that sort of thing, I suppose. You can always find something if you keep at it long enough. Now, back to business."

I had to have that notebook. My only hope was to keep him in the bar long enough to get him drunk and snitch it out of his jacket pocket. I'd noted which one it was in. Unfortunately, I was getting a little drunk myself.

After a long involved conversation, which got slower and more circuitous with every drink, we sawed off at twenty percent of my income. I'd have to send him duplicates of my royalty statements, he said, so he'd know I wasn't cheating. "Think of me as a sort of agent," he said. He had the same arrangement with several other authors.

As we got up to leave, he placed his hand discreetly on my ass.

"Your place or mine?" he said, lurching.

"Yours, by all means," I said. "I'm married, remember?"

It was a lot easier than I'd thought. I tripped him going up the steps to his fancy apartment building, and got the book while helping him up. I got into the elevator with him and waited till the door was closing. Then I slipped out and ran from the building. I fell down myself, once, ripping my hem, but it wasn't serious. I hopped into a taxi and that was that. Slick as television, almost.

Arthur was home when I got back. I could hear him typing away in his study, *rat-a-tat-tat*. I locked myself in the bathroom, took off my velvet dress, and went through Fraser Buchanan's notebook. Black leather binding, no name or title, gilt edges. The writing inside was tiny, like cockroach tracks. I scarcely bothered with the quite astonishing revelations he'd put down; I was looking, compulsively, for myself.

The book was organized like a diary, by dates. Useful items were starred; the rest was Buchanan's somewhat rambling notation. Most of the time he used only initials.

> J.F.—"celebrated" authoress of *Lady Oracle*. Met at party, pretentious artists. Built like a brick nuthouse. Red hair, dyed no doubt, big tits; kept pointing them at me. Played stupid, inane laugh, looked over her shoulder a lot. Underneath it a ball-stomper, could tell at once. Evasive about the book, should look into it. Married to Arthur Foster, writes for *Resurgence*. Pompous bugger.

And later:

> Estimated income: ?? Not that much, but she can get some from Foster. *Check maiden name.

And later:

> She's having it off with C. B. That's the most expensive fuck she'll ever have. The wages of sin is monthly installments to yours truly. *Hotel records. Get pictures if possible.

And even later:

> *Louisa K. Delacourt.

He was systematic, all right. What did I ever say to offend him? I wondered. Was it hatred I was reading, or just hardheaded mercenary cynicism? Did I point my tits at him that night, or not? I supposed a short man would experience it that way. Was my laugh inane? He did hate me, I felt. I was a little hurt, as we'd just had a pleasant evening.

But it didn't matter, since I had the book and I intended to keep it. No doubt he would try to get it back; he'd be desperate, it was his living. It was also incriminating evidence: it was in his handwriting, it had his name on it, the address was inside the cover, it was undeniable. I was surprised no one had tried to steal it before. But then, he may not have told anyone else about it.

I tore out a choice page and sealed it into an envelope. I would send it to him in the morning, like the ear of a kidnap victim, just to let him know I had the book. I enclosed a note as well: *If anything happens to me the book is in good hands. One word from you and it goes to the police.* Stalemate, I felt.

I went to bed before Arthur did, but I lay awake long after he went to sleep, trying to undo the tangle that my life had become. At any moment Paul might swoop down on me, figurative sword in hand, and perpetrate some disastrous rescue that would ruin my life. Now Fraser Buchanan would be trying to get his book back. I'd have to think of a good place to hide it; a locker in the subway station, or maybe I could keep mailing it back and forth to myself . . . no, that wouldn't do. I might get a safe-deposit box in a bank.

Malevolence was flowing towards me, around me, someone was sending me absurd but threatening notes, phoning me up and breathing; Fraser Buchanan accounted for only some of those calls. Someone was leaving dead animals on the doorstep, and if it wasn't the Royal Porcupine it was someone who knew about him. Who could possibly have found out? Perhaps one person was doing the animals, another the notes, a third the phone calls . . . but I couldn't believe that. It had to be a single person, with a plan, a plot that had some end in view. . . .

Then all at once I knew. It was Arthur. The whole thing was Arthur. He'd found out about the Royal Porcupine, he must've known for some time. He'd been watching me all along, not saying anything; it would be like him not to say anything. But he'd made a decision about me finally, a pronouncement, thumbs down. I was unworthy, I would have to go, and this was his plan to get rid of me.

I thought about how he could have done it all.

The anonymous letters would be easy. I could check our Yellow Pages to see if anything had been cut out, but he wouldn't be that careless. Most of the phone calls had been made when he wasn't home, though it was true that for some of them he'd been there. But he could have got a friend to help him. (Who?) The animals, anyone could find dead animals. Planting them on the doorstep would be more difficult, especially since I'd made a point of getting up first lately. But he could have put them there at night.

He was the one, he must be; he was working up to something and I didn't at all want to know what it was. The easy explanation would be that he'd gone crazy, in some very deep and undetectable way. But it didn't have to be that at all. Every man I'd ever been involved with, I realized, had had two selves: my father, healer and killer; the man in the tweed coat, my rescuer and possibly also a pervert; the Royal Porcupine and his double, Chuck Brewer; even Paul, who I'd always believed had a sinister other life I couldn't penetrate. Why should Arthur be any exception? I'd known he had phases, but I hadn't suspected this completely different side to his personality; not until now. The fact that I'd taken so long to discover it made it all the more threatening.

Arthur was someone I didn't know at all. And he was right in the bed beside me. I was afraid now, almost afraid to move; what if he woke up, eyes glittering, and reached for me . . . ? For the rest of the night I listened to him breathe. He sounded so peaceful.

I had to get away, as quickly as possible. If I simply went to the airport and got on a plane, anyone at all would be able to trace me. My life was a snarl, a rat's nest of dangling threads and loose ends. I couldn't possibly have a happy ending, but I wanted a neat one. Something terminal, like scissors. I would have to die. But for this I needed help. Who could be trusted?

Chapter Twenty-Nine

In the morning I waited till Arthur was out of the house. Then I phoned Sam.

"I have to see you," I said, "it's important."

"What's up?" he said. Marlene had answered the phone, and Sam sounded as if he was still asleep.

"I can't talk about it over the phone." It was an article of faith with Sam that his phone was bugged by the CIA, or at the very least the Mounties, and he was probably right. Also, I wanted to sound paranoid enough from the very beginning to convince him.

"Should I come over?" he said, perking up.

"No," I said. "I'll meet you in front of Tie City on Bloor Street in half an hour." Sam lived in the Annex, I knew he could make it if he rushed. I wanted him to rush; it would make him feel more urgent. Then I hung up, mysteriously.

I'd thought very carefully about the story I was going to tell them, for of course it would be both of them; there was no chance that Marlene wouldn't come along too. The truth was out of the question, as usual. If I told them the truth they'd feel they couldn't help me, since according to the ideology merely personal problems weren't supposed to be very significant. If I could get each of them alone it would be different, but together they were each other's witnesses and potential accusers. I needed the right villains, persecuting me for a cause they'd consider important. I felt a little cheap about this. Sam, like most of the group members, was essentially honest, in a devious sort of way; whereas I was essentially devious, with a patina of honesty. But I was desperate.

I waited nervously in front of Tie City, looking at the ties in the window and glancing from time to time over my shoulder, until Sam and Marlene appeared. They'd actually taken a taxi, which gave me hope: ordinarily they never took taxis.

"Look normal," I told them in a low, furtive voice. "Pretend you're walking along the street." We walked along the street, heading west, and I told them the place and time of the real meeting. "I thought I saw one of them at the corner," I said. "Don't let yourself be followed." Then we separated.

That afternoon at three-thirty we met in the Roy Rogers, the one on Bloor west of Yonge. I ordered a vanilla milk shake. Sam had a Roy with the works. Marlene ordered a Dale Evans.

We carried our trays to a round table beside a plate-glass window, through which we could see a small back yard with an enormous Coca-Cola billboard in it, boy and girl linking healthy eyes and swilling.

"You picked a great place," Sam said. "They'd never suspect this joint."

"Did you know you can get authentic Trigger Shit by sending away for it?" Marlene asked.

"Authentic, balls," Sam snorted. "There's more of that around than pieces of the True Cross. Besides, the real Trigger was stuffed and mounted years ago." Marlene looked put down.

I checked the underside of the table, as if for hidden mikes. Then I leaned toward them. "They've found out about the dynamite," I said.

Sam didn't say anything. Marlene rolled a cigarette. She'd taken to rolling them lately; the tobacco ends stuck out and flamed when she lit up, but she held the cigarette gamely in the corner of her mouth while she talked. "Who has?" she said. "How do you know?"

"I'm not sure," I said. "It could be the Ontario Provincial Police or the Mounties; maybe even the CIA. Anyway it's someone like that. When I went to move the car the day before yesterday I saw two men watching it. I didn't go near it, I just walked right by as though I had nothing to do with it. When I went back yesterday they were still there, or maybe it was two other men. That time I didn't even go down the street, I crossed over and went down a side street."

"That means they haven't traced it to you yet," Marlene said. "Otherwise they wouldn't bother watching the car, they'd watch you instead."

"They haven't *yet*," I said. "But they're going to. They'll trace me to the apartment; I gave that address when I bought the car. They'll get a description from the landlord. If they pick me up, they'll find out my real name and they'll get Arthur, and then they'll get you."

Sam was shaken. His escape fantasy had come to life at last, and he didn't like it. Marlene, however, was very cool. Her eyes narrowed, partly because of the smoke. "You think it's the Mounties?" she said.

"If we're lucky," I said. "If it is, they might never find me, and if they do at least we'd get a trial. But if it's the others, the CIA or maybe someone worse, they might just, you know, get rid of us. They always make it look like a suicide, or an accident."

"Holy shit," Sam said. "I'm sorry we got you into this. But it can't be the CIA, we're small potatoes."

"I think you're wrong," Marlene said. "They hate nationalist organizations, they want to keep this country *down*."

"Well, there's one good thing," I said. "Right now they can't trace it any further than that apartment, until they find out who I am."

"We better get you out of the country," Marlene said.

"Yes," I said, perhaps a little too quickly. "But I can't simply hop on a plane. If I disappear, they'll keep looking till they find me. I think we should arrange a sort of dead end for them."

"What did you have in mind?" said Sam.

I gave it some thought. "Well, I think we should stage my death; that way, when they start nosing around, they'll find out I'm dead and that will be that. There's not really anything to connect the rest of you with that car and the dynamite. We'll just leave it where it is and let them worry about it."

They were both impressed by this idea, and we began discussing ways and means. Sam came up with a plan for a fake car accident, using a body mangled beyond recognition. He watched a lot of prime-time television.

"So where do we get the body?" Marlene asked, and that was the end of that.

Sam's face lit up. "Hey . . . what about a vat of lime sprinkled with your teeth? Nothing identifies you positively like your teeth. That's what they use in airplane crashes, to identify the victims. They'd think the rest of you was eaten away."

"Where are we going to get my teeth?" I asked.

"You have them all pulled out, of course," Sam said, a little hurt by my negative reaction. "You can get a set of false ones, they're more hygienic anyway."

"No," I said. "They'd torture the dentist. He'd tell them everything. I might consider one or two teeth," I conceded.

Sam sulked. "If you're serious about this, you have to do it right."

"What I need is something very neat," I said. "What about this?" I pulled a newspaper clipping out of my purse. It was about a woman who had drowned in Lake Ontario, very simply, no frills. She had merely sunk like a stone, and her body had never been recovered. She'd made no attempt to catch the life preserver thrown to her. It was one of the first times, said the paper, that an inquest had been held and a death certificate issued with no corpse present. I sometimes clipped items like this out of the newspaper, thinking they might come in handy as plot elements. Luckily I'd saved this one.

"But it's been done already," said Sam.

"They won't notice," I said. "At least I hope they won't notice. Anyway, it's my only chance."

"What about Arthur?" Marlene asked. "Shouldn't he know?"

"Absolutely not," I said. "Arthur can't act, you know that. He'll be interviewed by the police, he's sure to be, and if he knows I'm really alive he'll either be so phoney they'll know something's wrong or so calm and collected they'll think he did me in himself. He wouldn't convince anyone. We can tell him later, after it's all over. I know it's cruel, but it's the only way." I went over this point with them several times; the last thing I wanted was Arthur on my trail.

Finally they agreed. In fact, they were flattered that I thought they'd be able to put on a much more convincing act than Arthur. "Just don't overdo the grief," I told them. "Some guilt, but not too much grief."

They thought I should have some forged documents to get out of the country with, but I said a friend of mine would take care of that, and the less they knew about it, the better. I was glad I'd kept my Louisa K. Delacourt passport and identification up to date.

Marlene said she had to go to a meeting, so Sam walked me to the subway. He was worried about something. Finally he said, "Joan, are you sure about those men? Are you sure they were watching?"

"Yes, why?"

"They just aren't that inefficient. If they've been at it for two days, they'd have got to you by now."

"Sam," I said, "I'm not really sure at all. Maybe it's them, maybe I'm mistaken. But that's not the only reason I want to get away."

"What is it then?" said Sam.

"Promise you won't tell Marlene?" He promised. "I'm being blackmailed."

"You're kidding," Sam said. "What for?"

I wanted to tell him, I was about to tell him, but I thought better of it. "It's not political," I said. "It's personal."

Sam didn't push for details; he knew when to back off. "I'm being blackmailed too," he said. "By Marlene. She wants to tell Don about us."

"Sam, does she have to come along?"

"Yes," he said. "We need two witnesses. Anyway, she'll be terrific with the police. She's a terrific liar."

"Sam, it's very good of you to do this for me," I said. It was a lot to ask, I was beginning to see that. "If you get into any real trouble, I'll come back and bail you out."

He squeezed my hand reassuringly. "It'll go like clockwork, you'll see," he said.

I didn't tell him about the other things, the dead animals and the phone calls and letters. That would be too complicated, I felt. Nor did I mention my suspicions about Arthur. Sam had known Arthur for a long time, and he wouldn't be able to believe he would do such things. He'd think I was imagining it.

The accident was to take place in two days, provided the weather held. I used the intervening time to make the arrangements. First I bought a skirt and blouse so I'd be wearing clothes on the plane that no one had ever seen me in. I went out to the airport, by subway and bus, and got a ticket to Rome, using my Louisa K. Delacourt identification. I said I was going on a four-week vacation. I bought the pink Mountie scarf and some dark glasses, changed into my new outfit in the ladies' can, covered up my hair, and got a Hertz Rent-A-Car, a bright-red Datsun. I said I'd be returning it to the airport in two days. I went to the ladies' can again, changed back to my old clothes and drove away.

I parked around the corner from our apartment, checked to make sure Arthur wasn't there, dug an old suitcase out of the cupboard, and packed a few essentials. I wrapped the suitcase up in brown paper and carried it like a parcel to the car, where I stowed it in the trunk.

The next morning I told Arthur I had a headache and was going to stay in bed for a while. I asked him to get me an aspirin and a glass of water. I thought he'd leave the house as soon as possible—he never liked it when I was sick—but to my surprise he hung around, brought me a cup of tea, and asked if he could do anything. I was touched: perhaps I'd misjudged him, perhaps I should tell him everything, it wasn't too late. . . . But he might be acting this way because he could tell I was up to something. I reminded him of the article he had to finish for *Resurgence,* and at last he left.

I jumped out of bed, put on a respectable dress, and stuffed my T-shirt and jeans into my oversized purse. Because of Arthur I was already three-quarters of an hour behind schedule. I drove the rented car east and went past the city and along the shore of Lake Ontario, looking for a spot where I could make a landing without running into a cliff or a crowd of people. I found a stretch of beach with some scrubby trees and a few picnic tables, which were empty. I hoped they'd stay empty; I thought they would, as it was a weekday in early June and the roadside families hadn't yet burst into full flower. I would leave the car here and rendezvous with it later. The trees would screen me as I washed ashore.

I drove back to the nearest pay phone, which was outside a service station, and called a taxi, explaining that my car had broken down and I was late for an appointment in the city. I described the spot and said I'd be standing beside a red Datsun. I drove back to my beach, locked the car, with my suitcase in the trunk and my ticket and Louisa K. identification in the glove compartment, and buried the car keys in the sand under the right front wheel. When the taxi came I took it to the Royal York Hotel, went in the front door and down to the lower level, changed into my T-shirt and jeans, crammed the dress I'd been wearing into my purse, and walked out the side door. The ferry dock was only a few blocks away. Sam and Marlene were already there.

"Were you followed?" Marlene asked.

"I don't think so," I said. We rehearsed again the story they were to tell Arthur: they'd run into me on the street and on impulse we'd all decided to go sailing over at the Island. Sailing rather than canoeing, we felt: it was easier to fall off a sailboat, whereas if it was a canoe, we'd all have to tip into the lake, and I told them there was no reason for them to get wet, too.

We took the ferry to the Island. Marlene had brought a camera; she felt there should be a pictorial record showing me as happy and carefree, so I posed with Sam, then with Marlene, leaning against the railing of the ferry and grinning like a fool.

Once on the Island, we strolled up and down past the boat-rental places, trying to decide which outfit would be likely to be the least suspicious of us. We picked the most slovenly-looking one and were granted a boat without any trouble, five dollars down and the rest when we brought it back. It was quite small and the attendant said that really there should only be two people on it, but he'd stretch a point as long as we didn't take it out of the harbor.

"You know how to sail," he said, more as a statement than a question.

"Of course," I said quickly. The attendant went back inside his hutch and we were left alone with the boat.

Sam began to untie it briskly from the dock. We all got in and pushed out into the Toronto harbor, where other sailboats, their white wings flapping, were tacking competently back and forth.

"Now what?" I said.

"Now we just run up the sails," Sam said. He undid various ropes and tugged at them, this way and that, until a sail began to move experimentally up the mast.

"You do know how to sail?" I asked him.

"Sure. I used to do it all the time, at summer camp."

"How long ago was that?" Marlene asked.

"Well, I remember the basics," he said defensively, "but if you'd rather take over. . . ."

"I've never been in a sailboat in my life," Marlene said, with that shade of contempt women reserve for men who have been caught out in a fraudulent display of expertise. By this time we were moving steadily into the course of an island ferry.

"Maybe we should go back," I said, "and get a canoe."

"We can't," Sam said. "I don't know how."

We ended up with Marlene at the tiller, while Sam and I scrambled around, ducking the boom and trying to control the ropes which somehow in turn controlled the sails. This worked, after a fashion, but my spirits had plunged. Why had I concocted this trashy and essentially melodramatic script, which might end by getting us all killed in earnest? Meanwhile we wobbled across the Toronto harbor, past the causeway they seemed to be constructing out of dumped garbage, and out into the lake. With the boat more or less under control, I crouched on the deck, peering into my compact mirror and trying to cover my face with eye shadow from a pot of Midnight Blue. The blue face was Marlene's suggestion: that way, she said, my white face wouldn't be easily seen from the shore. It was for this reason too that I was wearing jeans and a blue T-shirt.

Outside the harbor it was windier, and there were real waves. We sped east with the wind behind us. My face was now blue enough, and I was scanning the shoreline, which looked quite different when seen from the water, trying to remember where I'd left the car.

"We're too far out," I shouted to Sam, "can't you get us farther in?" I could swim, but I was not a strong swimmer. I didn't want to have to float a mile on my back.

Marlene handed me Don's binoculars, which she'd thought to bring, that old Brownie training. She'd brought everything but semaphore flags. I scanned the shoreline with them and there were the sandbar and the picnic tables and, yes, the car, receding at a fast clip behind us.

"It's back there," I called to Sam, pointing. "How do we get back?"

"Tack," Sam yelled, diving for a rope.

"What?"

"I'll have to take the tiller," he screamed, and began to crawl back towards us.

"Oh, God, I just remembered something," Marlene said; screeched rather, as otherwise we couldn't hear above the wind and the waves, which were beginning to look frightening. They had white foam streaks on them and were splashing over the sides of the boat.

"What?"

"Don . . . this will be all over the papers, and he'll know we were together."

"Tell him you're just friends now!" I screamed.

"It won't work," Marlene said, pleased that the thing she wanted revealed was going to be brought to light with no intervention by her; and in her despair or joy, she let go of the tiller. The boat swung, the sail collapsed, Sam ducked, and the flailing boom hit me in the small of the back and knocked me overboard.

I was unprepared and got a mouthful of unprocessed Lake Ontario water as I sank. It was much colder than I'd expected, and it tasted like stale fins and old diapers. I rose to the surface, coughing and gasping.

Sam had dropped the sails and the boat was wallowing uncertainly a little farther on. Marlene was yelling, "Oh, my God," very authentically, as if I really had fallen overboard and was drowning. She reached out her hands towards me, leaning dangerously, and called, "Over here! Joan!" but Sam caught hold of her.

I couldn't climb back into the boat and do it again the right way; I would have to proceed from here. I made a feeble dive and attempted to swim under the boat, as we had planned. I was supposed to come up on the other side, where I would be out of sight from the shore in case anyone was watching, and this move was necessary as I'd spotted a family at one of the picnic tables. I made it on the second try, but Marlene and Sam were still looking on the side

where I had disappeared: they seemed to have forgotten all about the plan. I tore the binoculars off my
neck—they were weighing me down—and attempted
to heave them into the boat, with no success; they
sank forever. Then I remembered my dress, which
was in my bag, stowed in the bow. "My dress," I
yelled, "remember to ditch it," but they'd drifted
downwind from me and didn't hear. They were trying to regain control of the boat.

I spat out more of the lake and lay back as flat
as I could; if there's one thing I knew how to do it
was float. I pointed myself towards the shore and
kicked my feet under the water; I hoped I was waft-
ing unobtrusively toward the sand spit, helped by
the waves, which broke occasionally over my head.
We had bungled, but that wasn't so bad. It would
look better than if I had simply dived off the boat.
I stared up at the blue sky with its white drifting
clouds and concentrated on the next move.

Luckily I ran aground out of sight of the picnic
tables, which were screened by the clump of bushes.
I was only about five hundred yards from where I
should have been. I pulled myself onto the shore and
lay there, catching my breath, while orange peels,
dead smelts and suspicious-looking brown lumps ed-
died around me, sucked in and out by the waves.
My hair was full of sand and little pieces of seaweed.
When I was ready I squelched as quietly as I could
along the shore and crouched behind the bushes. My
car was on the other side of them, I knew, but so
was the picnicking family. I couldn't risk getting close
enough to watch them, but I could hear the whining
of the children and the grunts of the father.

I lurked in the underbrush for at least half an
hour, dripping and shivering and avoiding the poison
ivy and the drying mounds of human shit and melting toilet paper, the wads of crumpled sandwich
wrap, bits of salami and old pop bottles, and wondering whether they were going to stay all day and if
so whether I would miss my plane. Finally I heard

the sound of a car motor and the crunch of wheels on gravel.

I gave them time to get away, then walked to the car, dug the keys out from where I'd buried them, took my stuicase from the trunk and changed into my skirt and blouse in the back seat, covering my wet hair with the Mountie scarf. My face in the rearview mirror looked startling; genuinely drowned, almost. I wiped the blue eye shadow off with Kleenex, which I threw into the bushes. I wrung out my jeans and T-shirt, rolled them into a ball, stuffed them into a green plastic Glad Bag which I'd brought for this, and packed the bag at the bottom of the suitcase. As I drove off I caught a glimpse of Marlene and Sam; they'd got the sail back up but hadn't managed to turn around, and they were scudding towards Kingston with all sails set.

I made it to the airport, returned the rent-a-car, and caught the plane with twenty minutes to spare. Sitting on the plane waiting for it to take off was the worst part; I couldn't quite believe that I hadn't been followed. But I was safe.

PART FIVE

Chapter Thirty

What price safety, I asked myself. I was sitting on the balcony in my underwear, covered with towels, taking a steamy sunbath in the middle of nowhere. The Other Side was no paradise, it was only a limbo. Now I knew why the dead came back to watch over the living: the Other Side was boring. There was no one to talk to and nothing to do.

Maybe I really did drown, I thought, and this whole thing, the hours on the plane—I'd watched *Young Winston*, without the earphones—the Hertz Rent-A-Car, the flat, my trip to Rome for the hair dye, was a kind of joke perpetrated by the afterlife. The soul sticks around the body for a while after death because it's confused, or that's what the Spiritualists said. In that case I should've been hovering somewhere near the oily surface of Lake Ontario, slightly east of Toronto Island, not allowing for the currents. Or they'd fished me out, I was unidentified, I was lying on a public slab; or I'd been cut up for spare parts and this panorama was going on because some other body got my eyes. My entire life didn't flash before me the way it was supposed to, but it would, I was always a late bloomer.

Learn to live in the present, take life as it comes, that's what they told you in the improve-your-head manuals. But what if the present was a washout and the life to come was a bog? I was feeling marooned; the impulse to send out messages, in bottles or not, grew every day. *I am still alive. Stuck here, have not sighted a ship for days. Am tired of talking to the local flora and fauna and the ants. Please rescue.* I was here, in a beautiful southern landscape, with breezes and old-world charm, but all the time my own country was embedded in my brain, like a metal plate left over from an operation; or rather, like one of those pellets you drop into bowls of water, which expand and turn into garish mineral flowers. If I let it get out of control it would take over my head. There was no sense trying to get away, I'd brought them all with me, I could still hear their voices, murmuring like a faraway but angry mob. It was too late to rearrange the furniture, I couldn't keep them out.

Where was the new life I'd intended to step into, easily as crossing a river? It hadn't materialized, and the old life went on without me, I was caged on my balcony waiting to change. I should take up a hobby, I thought, make quilts, grow plants, collect stamps. I should relax and be a tourist, a predatory female tourist, and take snapshots and pick up lovers with pink nylon ties and pointy shoes. I wanted to unclench myself, soak in the atmosphere, lie back and eat the flapdoodles off the tree of life, but somehow I couldn't do it. I was waiting for something to happen, the next turn of events (a circle? a spiral?). All my life I'd been hooked on plots.

I wondered whether Arthur had gotten my postcard yet. Would he join me, would we start again, would there be a fresh beginning, a new life? Or would he still be angry, had he really been the one . . . ? Perhaps I should never have sent that postcard. On the other hand, he might just tear it up, ignore my plea for rescue.

I lay back in my chair and closed my eyes. There was the vegetable man standing in the doorway, his arms full of, what else, vegetables; overgrown zucchinis, artichokes, onions, tomatoes. He smiled, I ran over to him, he crushed me in his short-sleeved olive arms, there was tomato juice all over the floor, we slipped in it and tumbled in a heap among the squashed zucchinis, it was like making love with a salad, crisp and smooth at the same time. But it wouldn't be like that, he'd appear in the doorway and instead of running over to him I'd remember my underwear draped on the chairback.

"Excuse me while I pick up a few things." What would he think of me? I'd scuttle around the room, gathering, concealing. "Won't you have a cup of tea?" Incomprehension. His smile would fade. What did I ask him here for anyway? And besides, he would tell everyone in the village, the men would leer and creep around my house at night, the children would throw stones.

I sat up in the plastic chair and opened my eyes. It was no use, I was jumpy as a flea on a skillet, I couldn't even have a sexual fantasy without anxiety. I needed a drink and I was out of Cinzano. And the children were already throwing stones; yesterday one had almost hit me.

I got up and wandered into the flat. I still had no routine, and there seemed less and less reason to do anything at any given time. I went into the kitchen, shedding towels along the way. I was hungry, but there was nothing to eat except some cooked pasta, drying out already, and a yellowing bunch of parsley in a glass of water on the windowsill. There was something to be said for refrigerators. Although they inspired waste, they created the illusion that there would always be a tomorrow, you could keep things in them forever. . . . Why had the media analysts never done any work on refrigerators? Those who had refrigerators surely perceived life differently from those who didn't. What the bank was to money, the refrigerator was to food. . . . As these thoughts dribbled through my head I began to feel that my whole life was a tangent.

I noticed that something was wrong with the ants. I examined their saucer of sugar-water: I'd forgotten to add water and the solution had thickened to a syrup. Some of the ants were nibbling at the edges but others had ventured out onto the surface and were trapped, like saber-toothed tigers in the tar pits. Now they were dead or waving their antennae feebly. I tried to rescue the still-living ones with a matchstick, fishing them out and leaving them on the side of the saucer; but mostly it was no use, they

were hopelessly glued. I was always bad with pets.
SOS, I wrote in sugar-water. *Do something.*

I went back into the main room to put on one of
my baggy dresses. I no longer needed the scarf with
the pink Mounties: I'd dyed my hair the day after I'd
gone to Rome, and it was now mud brown. It had
none of the promised sparkling highlights. In fact it
looked terrible. Why hadn't I bought a wig instead? I
knew why not, they were too hot, I'd cook my head.
But a nice gray wig would've looked better than the
hair dye.

I walked up the hill to the market square. The
road was scattered with handbills; perhaps there
was an election going on, I'd heard sound trucks
winding up to the square almost every day, playing
catchy tunes and broadcasting slogans. I was outside it though, I was a foreigner, and there was
something beyond that, something wrong. I was passing through a corridor of hostile eyes, the old black-
draped women with their sausage legs no longer returning my *bongiorno,* they didn't even nod, they
stared through me or averted their eyes. One put her
hand over the eyes of the little girl sitting beside her
and made the sign of the cross. What had I done,
what taboo had I violated?

I went to the *macelleria* and pushed in through
the many-colored plastic streamers that covered the
entranceway like seaweed. The butcher and his wife
were a comforting couple, round as dumplings, both
of them, wrapped in big white aprons and smeared
with blood. The trays in the glass display case weren't
filled ostentatiously like those in the butcher shops
in Toronto. What they sold was scarce enough: a few
small pieces of veal-like beef, a lone organ: liver, a
heart, a kidney or two; three or four oval white objects that I suspected of being testicles. Usually the
butcher and his wife would lift, offer, suggest incom-
prehensible things, beaming all the while.

But today they weren't beaming. When they saw
me come in their faces went still and watchful. Was
I making this up or did they seem a little afraid of

me? They didn't help me out with the terminology the way they usually did, and I was reduced to pointing. Even though I bought five tiny squares of tissue-paper beef, an extravagant number, they weren't mollified. And I couldn't even ask them what I'd done to offend or frighten them like this. I didn't know the words.

To the bakery, the grocery store, the vegetable stand, money dripping from my wounded purse, and it was the same, something was wrong. Had I committed some crime? I scarcely had the courage to walk over to the post office, as I knew the policemen would be there. But I'd done nothing, I told myself, it must be a misunderstanding of some kind. It would be cleared up later. I would ask Mr. Vitroni about it.

"Delacourt," I shouted bravely at the post office. There was no change in the woman behind the counter, since she was never friendly anyway. Soundlessly she extended a fat envelope. Brown manilla, Sam's typewriter.

Outside I tore it open. It was stuffed with newspaper clippings, arranged neatly in order, the oldest one on top, and a typed note from Sam. "Congratulations. You've become a death cult." I thumbed quickly through the clippings. SUICIDE SUSPECTED IN AUTHORESS DEATH. INVESTIGATION CALLED FOR, the top one read, and it went on from there. Some had the photo off the back of *Lady Oracle*, some the grinning boatside snapshots Marlene had taken on the day of my death. There was a lot of talk about my morbid intensity, my doomed eyes, the fits of depression to which I was apparently subject (though not a word about the Royal Porcupine, nothing about Louisa Delacourt . . . Fraser Buchanan was keeping a low profile). Sales of *Lady Oracle* were booming, every necrophiliac in the country was rushing to buy a copy.

I'd been shoved into the ranks of those other unhappy ladies, scores of them apparently, who'd been killed by a surfeit of words. There I was, on the bottom of the death barge where I'd once longed to be, my name on the prow, winding my way down the river. Several of the articles drew morals: you could sing and dance or you could be happy, but not both. Maybe they were right, you could stay in the tower for years, weaving away, looking in the mirror, but one glance out the window at real life and that was that. The curse, the doom. I began to feel that even though I hadn't committed suicide, perhaps I should have. They made it sound so plausible.

My next thought was: I can never go back now. Here were all these people spewing out words like flowers on a coffin, collecting their usual fee for doing so, and being very serious. If I rose from the dead, waltzed back and announced that it was all a deception, what were they supposed to do? They'd be stuck with egg on their faces, they'd hate me forever and make my life a nightmare. Women scorned to the contrary, nothing matched the fury of a deceived death cultist. It would be like the reappearance of James Dean, thirty years older and pot-bellied, or Marilyn walking down Yonge Street in curlers, having put on fifty pounds. All those who were expressing regret and remembering my ethereal beauty would be extremely upset if I were to materialize in the flesh. I'd have to stay safely buried on the Other Side, perhaps forever. In fact, my death was becoming so profitable to so many people that they'd probably have me bumped off and cemented and sunk in the Toronto harbor the moment I stuck my snout above water.

What had become of my neat, quiet, well-planned death by misadventure? Evidence had come to light—whose? how?—that I did not fall, but jumped. This was ridiculous. It *was* true I had meant to jump, but in fact I fell, prematurely. And some reporter got to Marlene, who overdid it. She said they threw me a life preserver but I made no attempt to reach it and went down with barely a struggle. Of course there wasn't any life preserver, she shouldn't have invented one. But who had interviewed my father, and why did he tell them I was a strong swimmer? He never saw me swim in his life. I wasn't a bad swimmer. I learned in high school gym class, it was one of the sports I didn't mind, because I was mostly out of sight. My specialty was floating on my back, that and the breast stroke. I wasn't much good at the crawl.

So they thought I jumped on purpose, refused the life preserver, and sank intentionally, and there was nothing I could do to prove them wrong, though an anonymous informant had volunteered the information that it wouldn't have been like me to commit suicide, I loved life. And it wasn't like me, at all.

Well, I thought, maybe I really did want to die or I wouldn't have pretended to do it. But that was wrong; I pretended to die so I could live, so I could have another life. They were being perverse and it made me angry.

I walked back down the hill, carrying my bundles. I loved life, it said this right in the newspaper. So why would I want to do a thing like that?

Chapter Thirty-One

I decided to ignore my suicide, since there was nothing I could do about it. For the next three days I tried to work. I sat in front of the typewriter with my eyes closed, waiting for the plot to unroll itself effortlessly behind my eyes, like a movie. But something was blocking it, there was static. I'd taken Charlotte through several narrow escapes: twice she'd been on the verge of rape, and she'd almost been murdered once (arsenic in the Spotted Dick pudding, causing severe vomiting). I knew what had to happen. Felicia, of course, would have to die; such was the fate of wives. Charlotte would then be free to become a wife in her turn. But first she would have a final battle with Redmond and hit him with something (a candelabrum, a poker, a stone, any hard sharp object would do), knocking him out and inducing brain fever with hallucinations, during which his features and desires would be purified by suffering and he would murmur her name. She would nurse him with cold compresses and realize how deeply she loved him; then he would awaken in his right mind and propose. That was one course of action. The other would be a final attempt on her life, with a rescue by Redmond, after which he would reveal how deeply he loved her, with optional brain fever on her part. These were the desired goals, but I was having trouble reaching them.

For one thing, Felicia was still alive, and I couldn't seem to get rid of her. She was losing more and more of her radiant beauty; circles were appearing beneath her eyes, lines between her brows, she had a pimple on her neck, and her complexion was becoming sallow. Charlotte, on the other hand, had roses in her cheeks and a spring in her step, even though she was afraid to walk beneath the parapets because of the falling objects. The life of danger agreed with her; also, her sixth sense told her she would be awarded the prize, the prizes in fact, for in addition to Redmond she would get the emeralds, the family silver, deeds of land stowed away in attics, she would rearrange the furniture and give Felicia's clothes to the Crippled Civilians, she would sack the evil servants like Tom the coachman and reward the virtuous ones like Mrs. Ryerson and generally throw her weight around. All she had to do was stick it out until the murderer's hands were actually around her throat.

Charlotte stood looking out the Library window. Two figures, a man's and a woman's, were entering the maze. She was trying to see who they were; not that she was nosy, just inquisitive. It went along with her pluck. She heard a noise behind her, and turned. Redmond was standing in the doorway; his left eyebrow was lifting. The other one, the right, remained stationary, but the left eyebrow was definitely lifting,

*appraisingly, lustfully, ruthlessly, causing hot flushes
to sweep over her, while the eye beneath it slid like
a roving oyster over her blushing countenance. Did
Redmond esteem her, or was he filled with a mere
animal lust? She could not tell.*

*Meanwhile Felicia was lying in the shrubbery of
the maze. She knew the maze was dangerous, but this
very fact excited her. Her skirt was hiked to her
waist, so was her petticoat, and her fichu was disar-
ranged. She'd been making love with Otterly, who
lay exhausted beside her, his left hand on her right
breast, his nose against her ear, his ear in her long red
hair. Redmond suspected nothing, which was fatigu-
ing. Felicia wished he would suspect something; then
he would realize how he'd been neglecting her. Although Otterly was ardent and inventive, he was also
a bit of a fool. Felicia sighed and sat up, disengaging
Otterly's hand, nose and ear.*

*Then she uttered a gasp of surprise. There was a
hole in the shrubbery, and watching her through this
hole was an eye. Beneath the eye was a ratlike smile,
broadening into a soundless laugh.*

*"Master'll want to know aboout this, I'm think-
ing," said the voice of Tom the coachman, gloatingly.*

*This had happened before, and Felicia knew it
meant she would have to bribe him. But she no longer
felt like it. She half hoped Redmond would find out;
then at least she would know where things stood.*

*That night she sat in front of her vanity table,
brushing her extravagant red waist-length hair and
looking at her reflection in the mirror. She had dismissed her maid. She was very sad; she suspected
Redmond no longer loved her. If he did, she would
give up her present mode of life and go back to being
a loving, conscientious wife. Charlotte would be dismissed and Felicia would stop having affairs with
the neighboring gentry. "Do you love me?" she asked
him every evening when at last he entered the room,
swaying slightly from the effects of too much port
and brooding over the elusive Charlotte. She rubbed*

up against him like a jaguar. She was wearing only a chemise. She and Redmond had separate rooms, naturally; but Redmond hadn't yet given up his nightly visit to hers, he was not yet that blatant about his wish to be rid of her. Besides, he took a certain delight in tantalizing her.

"Do you love me?" she asked; she usually had to ask twice, because Redmond didn't hear her the first time, or would pretend he didn't. "Of course," he answered with a slightly bored drawl. He was familiar with her chemise, it no longer impressed him the way it used to. She smelled, these days, of wilted hyacinths, a smell of spring decay, not mellow like the decay of autumn but a smell like the edges of swamps. He preferred Charlotte's odor of faintly stale lavender.

"What would I do without you?" Felicia said adoringly.

"You'd inherit a lot of money," Redmond replied with amusement. He was turned toward the window, raising his left eyebrow at himself in the reflection on the pane. An unkind observer might have said he was practicing. He was thinking of Charlotte. He liked making her blush. He'd become tired of the extravagance of Felicia: of her figure that spread like crabgrass, her hair that spread like fire, her mind that spread like cancer or pubic lice. "Contain yourself," he'd said to her, more than once, but she couldn't contain herself, she raged over him like a plague, leaving him withered. But Charlotte now, with her stays and her particular ways, her white flannelette face, her blanched fingers . . . her coolness intrigued him.

Or so Felicia imagined, torturing herself, gnawing on her nether lip, that full, sensuous lip Redmond once loved to caress. Tonight he was later than usual. Felicia snuffled, wiping the tears with the back of her free hand. She was too distraught to bother with the niceties of a handkerchief. Perhaps she could

foresee that life would be arranged for the conve-
nience of Charlotte, after all, and that she herself would
have to be disposed of. A tear rolled down her cheek,
tiny electric sparks jumped from the ends of her
hair. In the mirror there were flames, there was water,
she was gazing up at herself from beneath the surface
of a river. She was afraid of death. All she wanted
was happiness with the man she loved. It was this
one impossible wish that had ruined her life; she
ought to have settled for contentment, for the usual
lies.

I opened my eyes, got up from the typewriter,
and went into the kitchen to make myself a cup of
coffee. It was all wrong.

Sympathy for Felicia was out of the question, it
was against the rules, it would foul up the plot completely. I was experienced enough to know that. If
she'd only been a mistress instead of a wife, her life
could have been spared; as it was, she had to die. In
my books all wives were eventually either mad or
dead, or both. But what had she ever done to deserve
it? How could I sacrifice her for the sake of Charlotte?
I was getting tired of Charlotte, with her intact virtue
and her tidy ways. Wearing her was like wearing a
hair shirt, she made me itchy, I wanted her to fall into
a mud puddle, have menstrual cramps, sweat, burp,
fart. Even her terrors were too pure, her faceless mur-
derers, her corridors, her mazes and forbidden doors.

Perhaps in the new life, I thought, the life to
come, I would be less impressed with capes and more
with holes in stockings, hangnails, body odors and
stomach problems. Maybe I should try to write a real
novel, about someone who worked in an office and
had tawdry, unsatisfying affairs. But that was impossible, it was against my nature. I longed for happy
endings, I needed the feeling of release when everything turned out right and I could scatter joy like rice
all over my characters and dismiss them into bliss.
Redmond would kiss Charlotte so that her eyeballs

rolled right back into her head, and then they could both vanish. When would they be joyful enough, when would my life be my own?

There was no coffee, so I made myself some tea. Then I gathered up my underwear from the places where it was growing, under the table, off the chair-backs, and put it all into the washbasin. I scrubbed it with a bar of stringy green soap in the reddish water, which had a faint odor of iron, an odor too of subterranean gas; the toilet was becoming more slug-gish every day. Bad drains, bad dreams, maybe that was why I hadn't been sleeping well.

I wrung the underwear out; it felt gritty. There were no clothespins, so I draped it over the balcony railing. Then I took a bath, though the water was pink and unpleasantly like warm blood. I dried myself off, put on my last set of underwear, and wrapped myself in towels. I made another cup of tea and went out to the balcony. I sat in the plastic chair, head back, eyes closed behind my dark glasses, and tried to empty my mind. Brainwash. From the valley came a monotonous tinny sound, a boy banging on a metal plate to frighten birds. I grew sodden with light; my skin on the inside glowed a dull red.

Below me, in the foundations of the house, I could hear the clothes I'd buried there growing them-selves a body. It was almost completed; it was digging itself out, like a huge blind mole, slowly and pain-fully shambling up the hill to the balcony . . . a creature composed of all the flesh that used to be mine and which must have gone somewhere. It would have no features, it would be smooth as a potato, pale as starch, it would look like a big thigh, it would have a face like a breast minus the nipple. It was the Fat Lady. She rose into the air and descended on me as I lay stretched out in the chair. For a moment she hovered around me like ectoplasm, like a gelatin shell, my ghost, my angel; then she settled and I was absorbed into her. Within my former body, I gasped for air. Disguised, concealed, white fur choking my nose and mouth. Obliterated.

Chapter Thirty-Two

Redmond was pacing on the terrace. It was night; the wind was sighing through the shrubberies; Redmond was in mourning. He was relaxed, at peace with himself: now that Felicia was dead, drowned in an unfortunate accident when he surprised her fornicating in a punt with his half brother on the River Papple, his life would be quite different. He and Charlotte had secret plans to marry, though because of the possibility of gossip they would not make these public for some time. He gazed fondly up at her lighted window. Once they were married he would renounce his former wild and melancholy ways and settle down. She would play the piano and read the newspaper to him as he reclined beside a cheerful fire, wearing a pair of slippers embroidered by her own hand. They would have children, for now that his brother was dead, struck on the head by the overturning punt, he needed a son and heir to succeed him as the rightful Earl of Otterly. It had all worked out rather well, really. Strange that they never recovered Felicia's body, though he had had the riverbed dragged.

The shrubberies stirred and a figure stepped out from them, blocking his path. It was an enormously fat woman dressed in a sopping-wet blue velvet gown, cut low on the bosom; her breasts rose from the bodice like two full moons. Damp strands of red hair straggled down her bloated face like trickles of blood.

"Redmond, don't you know me?" the woman said in a throaty voice which, he recognized with horror, was Felicia's.

"Well," he said with marked insincerity, "I certainly am glad you didn't drown after all. But where have you been for these last two months?"

323

She evaded this question. "Kiss me," she said, passionately. "You don't know how much I've missed you."

He gave her a perfunctory peck on her white, clammy brow. Her hair smelled of waterweed, of oil and decaying food and dead smelts. He wiped his lips surreptitiously on his shirt sleeve. Hope guttered out in his breast like an expiring candle: what would he do now?

He noted with repugnance that the woman who called herself Felicia was undoing the fastenings of her dress; her fingers fumbled at the hooks. "Remember when we were first married?" she whispered. "And we used to slip out here at night, and embrace by the light of the full moon. . . ." She looked at him with an inviting simper, which turned slowly to an expression of heartbreaking anguish as she read the disgust in his face.

"You don't want me," she said brokenly. She began to cry, her large body shaken by uncontrollable sobs. What could he do? "You didn't want me to come back at all," she wept. "You're happier without me . . . and it was such an effort, Arthur, to get out of that water and come all this way, just to be with you again. . . ."

Redmond drew back, puzzled. "Who is Arthur?" he asked.

The woman began to fade, like mist, like invisible ink, like melting snow. . . .

I could hear footsteps coming down the gravel path, at a great distance, as though through layers of cotton wool. I was still half asleep; I struggled out of the chair and all the towels fell off. I snatched one up, retreating toward the door, but it was too late, Mr. Vitroni was coming around the corner, along the balcony. He had on all his felt pens; under his arm he carried a brown paper parcel.

I backed against the railing, holding the towel in front of me. His eye took in the line of dripping underwear. He gave his little bow.

"I wish I do not disturb?" he said.

"Not at all," I said, smiling.

"Your lightbulbs are shining?"

"Yes," I said, nodding.

"The water is coming out?"

"The house is just fine," I assured him, "I'm having a wonderful time. A wonderful vacation. The peace and quiet is marvelous." I wished very much that he would go away, but it looked as if he was going to sell me another painting. I would be powerless to resist it, I knew.

He looked over his shoulder, almost fearfully, as if he was afraid of being seen. "We will go inside," he said. Seeing me hesitate, he added, "There is something I must tell you."

I didn't want to sit at the table with him in a towel and my underwear; somehow it was more indecent inside than on the balcony. I asked him to wait, went into the bathroom, and put on one of my dresses.

When I came out he was sitting at the table with the paper parcel across his knees.

"You have been to Roma?" he asked. "You like it?"

I began to feel exasperated. Surely he hadn't come here to ask about tourist sites. "It's very nice," I told him.

"Your husband, he likes it as well?"

"Yes, I guess so," I said. "He did like it a lot."

"It is a city one must visit many times to know well, like a woman," Mr. Vitroni said. He took out some tobacco and began to roll himself a cigarette. "He will come soon?"

"I certainly hope so," I said with a hearty laugh.

"I as well wish that he will come soon. It is not good for a woman to be alone. Others will talk of it." He lit his cigarette, brushed the unused shreds of tobacco back into the packet, and replaced it in his pocket. He'd been watching me carefully.

"This is for you," he said. He handed me the package.

I was expecting another black velvet painting, but when I took off the string and unfolded the paper, there were my clothes, the jeans and T-shirt that I'd buried so carefully under the house. They were neatly washed and pressed.

"Where did you get these?" I asked. Maybe I could deny they were mine.

"My father, he has seen them in the earth, down there where are the *carciofi*. He has seen someone was digging. He thinks there is mistake, to bury such clothes, which are not old. He does not speak English, so he ask me to give them to you back. My wife washes them."

"Tell him thank you very much," I said. "Thank your wife also." There was no way I could explain, though he obviously wanted an explanation. He waited; we both looked at my folded clothes.

"People talk of this," he said finally. "They do not understand why you have put your clothes beneath the house. They know of this. They do not know why you have cut off your so beautiful hair, that everyone remembers from the time you are here before, with your husband; you wear always the dark glasses, like a bat, and you have taken another name. These are things nobody understands. They make the sign"— he extended two fingers—"so the evil eye which you have will not make them sick or give them bad luck as well. I myself do not believe this," he said apologetically, "but the older ones. . . ."

So they knew me. Of course they knew me, they remembered everything for five thousand years. What stupidity, to have come back here.

"They ask me to tell you to leave," he went on. "They think your bad luck will come on me, my wife says that."

"I suppose they think I'm a witch," I said, laughing.

But Mr. Vitroni didn't laugh; he was warning me, it wasn't funny.

"It would be better if your husband also would

come," he said gravely. "Also, a man is here this morning. He asks for you. He does not know the name you gave me, but he says, a lady, so tall, with red hair, and I know it is you."

"What?" I said, too quickly. "Who was it?"

He shrugged, studying my face. "I do not think it is your husband. Also he would know where you are living." He could tell I was upset. If he was right and it wasn't Arthur, who was it?

"What did he look like?" I said. "What did you tell him?"

"I think I should tell you first," he said slowly. "I tell him you are in Roma, you will come back after two days. At that time, I tell him, perhaps I can help him. But I say to him perhaps you are not the lady he searches."

"Thank you," I said. "Thank you very much."

After such kindness, I had to tell him something. I leaned toward him and lowered my voice. "Mr. Vitroni," I said. "I'm hiding. That's why I used a different name and cut off my hair. No one is supposed to know where I am. I think someone is trying to kill me."

Mr. Vitroni was not surprised. He nodded, as if he knew such things happened quite frequently. "What have you done?" he said.

"Nothing," I told him. "I haven't done anything at all. It's very complicated, but it has to do with money. I'm quite rich, that's why this person, these people, want to kill me, so they will get the money." He seemed to believe this, so I went on. "This man who came, he may be one of my friends, or perhaps he's an enemy. What did he look like?"

Mr. Vitroni spread his hands. "It is hard for me to say. He had a red car, like yours." He was holding out on me, what did he want? "Perhaps the police should arrest this man," he said.

"That's very good of you," I said, "but I couldn't do that. I'm still not sure who this man is, and besides I have no proof. What did he look like?"

"He was wearing a coat," said Mr. Vitroni helpfully. "A dark coat, American. He was tall, yes, a young man, not old."

"Did he have a beard?" I asked.

"No beard. A moustache, yes."

None of this was any help. It didn't sound like Fraser Buchanan, though. "He says he is a reporter, from a newspaper," Mr. Vitroni said. "I do not think he is a reporter. You are sure you do not wish him arrested? It could be arranged, I could arrange it with them."

Was he asking for a bribe? It occurred to me that his visit was no friendly one. It was a negotiation, and no doubt a similar negotiation had gone on with the man. If I would pay, he would help me. Otherwise he would tell this man how to find me. Unfortunately I didn't have enough money. I decided quickly that I'd have to leave that evening, I'd drive to Rome.

"No, really," I said. "I'll handle it in my own way."

I stood up and held out my hand to Mr. Vitroni. "Thank you very much," I said, "it was very kind of you to tell me all this."

He was puzzled; he must have been expecting me to make a deal with him. "I could help you," he said. "There is a house, farther back, away from the town. You could stay there until this man goes away, we would bring you some food."

"Thank you," I said, "perhaps I'll do that."

As he left, he patted my shoulder.

"Do not worry," he said, "all will be happy."

In the evening I packed my suitcase and carried it up to the car. But when I went to start it, the tank was empty. Stupidity, I thought, remembering it had been low on the trip back from Rome. But then I thought: It's been drained.

Chapter Thirty-Three

I never should have told him I had money. I could see it all now, the plot was clear. They'd always intended it, from the very first. The old man of the artichokes was a spy, he was Mr. Vitroni's father, he'd been sent to watch me, and as soon as he'd seen me without my disguise they'd conspired. If I agreed to hide in the secluded house I would become a prisoner. It would be folly to go to anyone and ask for gasoline. They would know then that I meant to leave. Also, no one in the town sold it, they would have to send out for it, and then Mr. Vitroni would be sure to hear of it. He would come and tell me none could be had. I would beg, and he would say, "Gasoline, that is very expensive."

The soldiers or police were in on it, too, they would help him, and there would be no one to stop them. I'd virtually told him that no one knew where I was; it was an open invitation. When Arthur arrived they would tell him I'd gone away, they had no idea where. Meanwhile I'd be roped and helpless, they'd want me to send away for money, and when none arrived, what would they do then? Would they kill me and bury me in a gravelly grave among the olives? Or would they keep me in a cage and fatten me up as was done among primitive tribes in Africa, but with huge plates of pasta, would they make me wear black satin underwear like the kind advertised at the back of the *fotoromanzi*, would they charge admission to the men of the town, would I become one of those Fellini whores, gigantic and shapeless?

This is serious, I told myself. *Pull yourself together.* Perhaps I was becoming hysterical. I didn't want to spend the rest of my life in a cage, as a fat whore, a captive Earth Mother for whom somebody else col-

lected the admission tickets. I would have to think
of some plan. I had two days though, so I went to bed.
There was no use trying to run away in pitch darkness, I'd only get lost. Or caught: doubtless I was
being watched.

I woke up in the middle of the night. I could hear
footsteps outside my window, on the terrace down
below. Now there was a scraping noise: someone was
climbing the trellis! Had I locked the window or not?
I didn't want to get out of bed to see. I backed against
the wall, staring at the window where the outline of a
head, then the shoulders, was looming into view. . . .
By the light of the moon I could see who it was, and
I relaxed.

It was only my mother. She was dressed in her
trim navy-blue suit with the tight waist and shoulder
pads, and her white hat and gloves. Her face was
made up, she'd drawn a bigger mouth around her
mouth with lipstick, but the shape of her own mouth
showed through. She was crying soundlessly, she
pressed her face against the glass like a child, mascara
ran from her eyes in black tears.

"What do you want?" I said, but she didn't answer. She stretched out her arms to me, she wanted
me to come with her; she wanted us to be together.

I began to walk towards the door. She was smil-
ing at me now, with her smudged face, could she see
I loved her? I loved her but the glass was between us,
I would have to go through it. I longed to console her.
Together we would go down the corridor into the
darkness. I would do what she wanted.

The door was locked. I shook at it and shook
until it came open.

I was standing on the terrace in my torn nightgown, shivering in the wind. It was dark, there was no
moon at all. I was awake now; my teeth were chatter-
ing, with fear as well as with cold. I went back into
the flat and got into bed.

She'd come very close that time, she'd almost done it. She'd never really let go of me because I had never let her go. It had been she standing behind me in the mirror, she was the one who was waiting around each turn, her voice whispered the words. She had been the lady in the boat, the death barge, the tragic lady with flowing hair and stricken eyes, the lady in the tower. She couldn't stand the view from her window, life was her curse. How could I renounce her? She needed her freedom also; she had been my reflection too long. What was the charm, what would set her free?

If someone had to come back from the Other Side to haunt me, I thought, why couldn't it be Aunt Lou? I trusted her, we could have a good talk, she could give me some advice and tell me what to do. But I couldn't imagine Aunt Lou doing this. "You can handle it," she'd say, no matter how much I protested that I couldn't. She would refuse to see my life as the disaster it was.

Whereas my mother. . . . Why did I have to dream about my mother, have nightmares about her, sleepwalk out to meet her? My mother was a vortex, a dark vacuum, I would never be able to make her happy. Or anyone else. Maybe it was time for me to stop trying.

Chapter Thirty-Four

In the morning I had several cups of tea, to give me energy and calm me down. The trick was to be as calm as possible. I would act as though everything was normal, all was well, I would be unhurried; I'd do my shopping and visit the post office as usual, so they'd think I was cooperating. I might even seek out Mr. Vitroni and ask about the house, so they'd think I

was going along with everything. I would wait until
the afternoon, when there were people around.
Then I would simply stroll down the hill, carrying my
handbag but not my suitcase, and hitch a ride to
Rome. I wouldn't be able to take much with me, but
I could get quite a lot into my handbag.

I went through the bureau drawers, deciding
what I would have to leave behind. I packed three
pairs of underpants. Nightgowns were not necessary;
Fraser Buchanan's black notebook was. The typewriter would have to stay, but *Stalked by Love* I
would take with me.

I picked up the manuscript, intending to roll it
into a cylinder for easy packing. Then I sat down and
started leafing through it. I saw now what was wrong,
what I would have to do. Charlotte would have to go
into the maze, there was no way out of it. She'd
wanted to go in ever since reaching Redmond Grange,
and nothing anyone could say, not all the hair-raising
tales of the servants, not all the sneering hints of Felicia had been able to deter her. But her feelings
were ambiguous: did the maze mean certain death, or
did it contain the answer to a riddle, an answer she
must learn in order to live? More important: would
she marry Redmond only if she stayed out of the
maze, or only if she went in? Possibly she would
be able to win his love only by risking her life and
allowing him to rescue her. He would unclench the
hands from around her throat (whose hands would
they be?) and tell her she was a silly little fool, though
brave. She would become Mrs. Redmond, the fourth
one.

Don't go into the maze, Charlotte, you'll be entering at your own risk, I told her. I've always got you
out of it before but now I'm no longer dependable.
She paid no attention to me, she never did; she stood
up, put away her embroidery, and prepared to go outside. Don't say I didn't warn you, I told her. But I
couldn't stop, I had to see it through to the end. I
closed my eyes. . . .

*It was noon when Charlotte entered the maze.
She took the precaution of fastening one end of a ball
of knitting wool, borrowed from Mrs. Ryerson on the
pretext of mending her shawl, at the entrance; she
did not intend to lose her way.*

*The walls of the maze, which were of some prick-
ly evergreen shrub, were indeed sadly overgrown.
Surely no one had been here for many years, Charlotte thought, as she pushed her way through the
straggling branches, which caught on her gown as if
to hold her back. She turned to the left, then to the
right, unwinding her ball of wool as she went.*

*Outside, the sky had been overcast and a cold
February wind had been blowing; but here, sheltered
by the thick walls of leaves and branches, Charlotte
felt quite warm. The sun had come out and the sky
was clearing; nearby, a bird sang. She was losing track
of time; it seemed as if hours had passed while she
walked along the gravel path between the green,
thorny walls. Was it her imagination, or had the maze
become trimmer, better kept . . . and flowers had
begun to appear. Surely it was too early for flowers.
She had an odd sensation, as though unseen eyes
were watching her. She remembered Mrs. Ryerson's
stories about the Little Folk; then she laughed at herself for giving in, even momentarily, to superstition.
It was just an ordinary maze, there was nothing unusual about it. Surely the two previous Lady Red-
monds had met their fate in some other way.*

*She must be getting near the center of the maze.
She turned another corner, and sure enough it was
there before her, an open gravelled oblong with a border of flowers, the daffodils already in bloom. Dis-
appointingly, it was empty. Charlotte peered about
looking for some clue to its evil reputation, but there
was none. She started to walk back the way she
had come. Suddenly it was frightening, she wanted
to get out before it was too late. She didn't want to
know any more, she'd been a fool ever to have come
here. She began to run, but she made the mistake of*

*trying to wind up the ball of knitting wool as she
ran, and her feet became hopelessly entangled. As she
fell, iron fingers closed around her throat . . . she tried
to scream, she struggled, her eyes bulged, she looked
wildly around for Redmond.*

*From behind her came a mocking laugh—Fe-
licia's! "There wasn't room for both of us," she said,
"one of us had to die."*

*Just as Charlotte was sinking into unconscious-
ness, Felicia was flung aside like a bundle of old
clothes, and Charlotte was gazing up into the dark
eyes of Redmond. "My darling," he breathed hoarse-
ly. Strong arms lifted her, his warm lips pressed her
own. . . .*

That was the way it was supposed to go, that was
the way it had always gone before, but somehow it no
longer felt right. I'd taken a wrong turn somewhere;
there was something, some fact or clue, that I had
overlooked. I would have to walk it through, I would
have to find a suitable locale and go through the mo-
tions. I thought of the Cardinal's garden in Tivoli,
with its sphinxes and fountains and its many-breasted
goddess. That would do, it had a lot of paths. I
would go there this afternoon. . . .

But I was forgetting about the man, my car with
its empty tank; I would have to leave the book for
later and concentrate on my escape.

This time I really would disappear, without a
trace. No one at all would know where I was, not
even Sam, not even Arthur. This time I would be free
completely; no shreds of the past would cling to me,
no clutching fingers. I could do anything I wanted, I
could be a hostess in a bar, I could return to Toronto
and give body rubs, maybe that was what I should
have done. Or I could merge into Italy, marry a vegetable man: we'd live in a little stone cottage, I'd have
babies and fatten up, we'd eat steamy food and cover
our bodies with oil, we'd laugh at death and live in
the present, I'd wear my hair in a bun and grow a
moustache, I'd have a bibbed apron, green, with flow-

ers on it. Everything would be ordinary, I'd go to church on Sundays, we'd drink rough red wine, I'd become an aunt, a grandmother, everyone would respect me.

Somehow this was not convincing. Why did every one of my fantasies turn into a trap? In this one I saw myself climbing out a window, in my bibbed apron and bun, oblivious to the cries of the children and grandchildren behind me. I might as well face it, I thought, I was an artist, an escape artist. I'd sometimes talked about love and commitment, but the real romance of my life was that between Houdini and his ropes and locked trunk; entering the embrace of bondage, slithering out again. What else had I ever done?

This thought did not depress me. In fact, although I was frightened, I was feeling curiously lighthearted. Danger, I realized, did this to me.

I washed my hair, humming, as if I were getting ready for a big evening. A lot of the brown came out, but I no longer cared.

I padded out onto the balcony on my wet bare feet to dry my hair. There was a breeze; far below in the valley I could hear gunshots, it must've been someone shooting at a bird. They'd shoot anything that moved here, almost, they ate the songbirds in pies. All that music devoured by mouths. Eyes and ears were also hungry, but not so obviously. From now on, I thought, I would dance for no one but myself. May I have this waltz? I whispered.

I raised myself onto my bare toes and twirled around, tentatively at first. The air filled with spangles. I lifted my arms and swayed them in time to the gentle music, I remembered the music, I remembered every step and gesture. It was a long way down to the ground from here; I was a little dizzy. I closed my eyes. Wings grew from my shoulders, an arm slid around my waist. . . .

Shit. I'd danced right through the broken glass, in my bare feet too. Some butterfly. I limped into the main room, trailing bloody footprints and looking for a towel. I washed my feet in the bathtub; the soles looked as if they'd been minced. The real red shoes, the feet punished for dancing. You could dance, or you could have the love of a good man. But you were afraid to dance, because you had this unnatural fear that if you danced they'd cut your feet off so you wouldn't be able to dance. Finally you overcame your fear and danced, and they cut your feet off. The good man went away too, because you wanted to dance.

But I chose the love, I wanted the good man; why wasn't that the right choice? I was never a dancing girl anyway. A bear in an arena only appears to dance, really it's on its hind legs trying to avoid the arrows. And now I didn't have any Band-aids. I sat on the edge of the bathtub, tears running helplessly from my eyes, blood running helplessly from the tiny cuts in my feet.

I went into the other room and lay down on the bed, feet raised on the pillow so the blood would run the other way. How could I escape now, on my cut feet?

Chapter Thirty-Five

After a couple of hours I got up. My feet weren't as bad as I'd thought, I could still walk. I practiced limping, back and forth across the room. At every step I took, small pains shot through my feet. The Little Mermaid rides again, I thought, the big mermaid rides again.

I would have to walk up to town, hobbling through the gauntlet of old women, who would make horns with their hands, tell the children to throw stones, wish me bad luck. What did they see, the eyes behind those stone-wall windows? A female monster,

larger than life, larger than most life around here anyway, striding down the hill, her hair standing on end
with electrical force, volts of malevolent energy shooting from her fingers, her green eyes behind her dark
tourist's glasses, her dark mafia glasses, lit up and
glowing like a cat's. Look out, old black-stockinged
sausage women, or I'll zap you, in spite of your evil-
eye signs and muttered prayers to the saints. Did they
think I flew around at night like a moth, drinking
blood from their big toes? If I got a black dress and
long black stockings, then would they like me?

Maybe my mother didn't name me after Joan
Crawford after all, I thought; she just told me that to
cover up. She named me after Joan of Arc, didn't she
know what happened to women like that? They were
accused of witchcraft, they were roped to the stake,
they gave a lovely light; a star is a blob of burning
gas. But I was a coward, I'd rather not win and not
burn, I'd rather sit in the grandstand eating my bag of
popcorn and watch along with everyone else. When
you started hearing voices you were in trouble, especially if you believed them. The English cheered as
Joan went up like a volcano, a rocket, like a plum
pudding. They sprinkled the ashes on the river; only
her heart remained.

I walked up the hill, past the black-dressed old
women on the steps, ignoring their hostile eyes,
and along the street that led to the post office. The
policemen or soldiers were in their places; the mas-
sive woman behind the counter was there, too.

She knew who I was by now, I didn't have to ask.
She handed me another of Sam's brown envelopes.
It felt like more newspaper clippings, so I tore it
open.

There were more clippings; but on top of them
was a letter, on crisp law-office stationery:

Dear Miss Delacourt:

My client, Mr. Sam Spinsky, has requested me
to send you the enclosed. He feels there might

be something you could do to help him in his present predicament. He has instructed me not to reveal your whereabouts until further notice.

The signature a scrawl; and underneath the letter,

POETESS FEARED SLAIN IN TERRORIST PURGE!

Forgetting decorum, I sat down on the bench, right beside a policeman. This was terrible. Sam and Marlene had been arrested for murder, they'd been accused of murdering me, they were actually in jail. For a fleeting moment I thought how pleased Marlene would be; but then, she'd be quite cheesed off that I was the cause and not some strike or demonstration. Still, jail was jail. They hadn't told yet, that much was clear.

It was that family on the beach, the one having the picnic. They'd watched me thrashing around in the water, they'd seen me go under. They'd read the account in the paper, the interview with Marlene in which she said they'd thrown me a life preserver. But there was no life preserver, and when the police checked with the boat-rental place they admitted there hadn't even been one on the boat. They found my dress, though, in the bow; that made them suspicious. The family's name was Morgan. Mr. Morgan said he heard a scream (he couldn't have, it was too far away, it was too windy) and looked up in time to see Sam and Marlene leaning over the side of the boat, just after pushing me in. There was a picture of Mr. Morgan, as well as the picture of me, the smiling one taken on the day of my death. Mr. Morgan looked serious and responsible; he was having the time of his life, he was important at last, he was acting out his own fantasy.

Poor Sam. By now he'd had his pockets emptied and his shoelaces taken away, he'd had louse-killer put on him and a finger stuck up his anus. He'd been

grilled by two detectives, one acting kind and offering
him cigarettes and coffee, the other bullying him,
and all because of my stupidity, my cowardice. I
should have stayed where I was and faced reality.
Poor gentle Sam, with his violent theories; he
wouldn't hurt a fly.

I was referred to as a "key figure" in a mysterious
dynamite plot. Marlene's father, apparently, had come
forward with information about some missing dynamite, and Marlene had broken down and admitted to
taking it. But she couldn't produce it. I'd been in
charge of it, she told them; and she told them about
the secondhand car too, but they hadn't been able to
locate it. The police were assuming that what they
referred to as Sam's "cell" had liquidated me because I knew too much and was becoming traitorous.
Arthur had been taken in for questioning, but later
released. It was obvious he was both innocent and
ignorant.

I'd have to go back and rescue them. I couldn't
go back. Maybe I could send the police a token part of
me, just to let them know I was still alive. A finger, an
autograph, a tooth?

I got up off the bench, stuffing the clippings into
my purse. I went outside and headed toward the hill.
Then I saw Mr. Vitroni. He was sitting at an outdoor
café table. There was another man with him. I
couldn't see him clearly, his back was toward me,
but surely this was the man. Come back a day too
soon.

Mr. Vitroni had seen me, he was looking straight
at me. I hurried across the square, I was almost running. I made myself slow down. I looked behind only
once, and Mr. Vitroni was getting up, shaking hands
with the man. . . .

I turned the corner and began to run in earnest.
*I must be calm, I must be collected, I must collect
myself.* My cut feet screamed as they hit the stones.

Chapter Thirty-Six

I finally reached the balcony. The sun was sinking, the balcony was bright with sunlit glass, broken and sharp like fire. In the plate-glass window my reflection ran beside me, the face dark, the hair standing out around my head, a red nimbus.

I unlocked the door and went in. There was no one inside, not yet, I still had time. . . . I hadn't seen him clearly. Perhaps I could elude him. I'd wait until he was walking along the balcony; then I'd slip into the bathroom and bolt the door. While he was trying to get in, I could climb up on the toilet and squeeze through the tiny window.

I went into the bathroom to look at the window. It was too small, I'd get stuck. I didn't want to be either arrested or interviewed halfway out a window. It was too undignified.

Perhaps I could hide among the artichokes. Perhaps I could run down the hill, perhaps I could disappear and never be found. But if I ran I would simply be caught, sooner or later. Instead I was going to defend myself. I refused to go back. I went into the kitchen and got the empty Cinzano bottle out of the garbage can, grasping it by the neck.

I crouched behind the door, out of sight of the window, and waited. Time passed; nothing happened. Perhaps I'd been wrong, perhaps that hadn't been the right man. Or maybe there was no man at all, Mr. Vitroni had made him up in order to frighten me. I began to be restless. It struck me that I'd spent too much of my life crouching behind closed doors, listening to the voices on the other side.

The door itself was ordinary enough. Through the glass pane at the top I could see a small piece of the outside world: blue sky, some grayish-pink clouds.

It was noon when she entered the maze. She was determined to penetrate its secret at last. It had been a hazard for too long. Several times she had requested Redmond to have it torn down, but he would not listen. It had been in his family for generations, he said. It did not seem to matter to him that so many had been lost in it.

She made several turnings without incident. It was necessary to remember the way she had come, and she attempted to do this, memorizing small details, the shape of a bush, the color of a flower. The pathway was freshly graveled; here and there daffodils were in bloom.

Suddenly she found herself in the central plot. A stone bench ran along one side, and on it were seated four women. Two of them looked a lot like her, with red hair and green eyes and small white teeth. The third was middle-aged, dressed in a strange garment that ended halfway up her calves, with a ratty piece of fur around her neck. The last was enormously fat. She was wearing a pair of pink tights and a short pink skirt covered with spangles. From her head sprouted two antennae, like a butterfly's, and a pair of obviously false wings was pinned to her back. Felicia was surprised at the appearance of the woman in pink, but was too well bred to show it.

The women murmured among themselves. "We were expecting you," they said; the first one shifted over, making room for her. "We could tell it was your turn."

"Who are you?" she asked.

"We are Lady Redmond," said the middle-aged woman sadly. "All of us," the fat woman with the wings added.

"There must be some mistake," Felicia protested. "I myself am Lady Redmond."

"Oh, yes, we know," said the first woman. "But

every man has more than one wife. Sometimes all at
once, sometimes one at a time, sometimes ones he
doesn't even know about."

"How did you get here?" Felicia asked. "Why
can't you go back to the outside world?"

"Back?" said the first woman. "We have all tried
to go back. That was our mistake." Felicia looked behind her, and indeed the pathway by which she had
entered was now overgrown with branches; she could
not even tell where it had been. She was trapped
here with these women. . . . And wasn't there something peculiar about them? Wasn't their skin too
white, weren't their eyes too vague . . . ? She noticed
that she could see the dim outline of the bench
through their tenuous bodies.

"The only way out," said the first woman, "is
through that door."

She looked at the door. It was at the other side of
the graveled plot, affixed to a door frame but otherwise
unsupported. She walked all the way around it: it was
the same from both sides. It had a plain surface and a
doorknob; there was a small pane of glass at the top,
through which she could see blue sky and some grayish-pink clouds.

She took hold of the doorknob and turned it. The
door unlocked and swung outward. . . . There, standing on the threshold, waiting for her, was Redmond.
She was about to throw herself into his arms, weeping
with relief, when she noticed an odd expression in
his eyes. Then she knew. Redmond was the killer.
He was a killer in disguise, he wanted to murder her
as he had murdered his other wives. . . . Then she
would always have to stay here with them, at the center of the maze. . . . He wanted to replace her with
the other one, the next one, thin and flawless. . . .

"Don't touch me," she said, taking a step backward. She refused to be doomed. As long as she
stayed on her side of the door she would be safe.
Cunningly, he began his transformations, trying to
lure her into his reach. His face grew a white gauze

*mask, then a pair of mauve-tinted spectacles, then a
red beard and moustache, which faded, giving place
to burning eyes and icicle teeth. Then his cloak vanished and he stood looking at her sadly; he was wearing a turtle-neck sweater. . . .*

"Arthur?" *she said. Could he ever forgive her?*

*Redmond resumed his opera cloak. His mouth
was hard and rapacious, his eyes smoldered. "Let me
take you away," he whispered. "Let me rescue you.
We will dance together forever, always."*

*"Always," she said, almost yielding. "Forever."
Once she had wanted these words, she had waited
all her life for someone to say them. . . . She pictured
herself whirling slowly across a ballroom floor, a
strong arm around her waist. . . .*

"No," she said. "I know who you are."

*The flesh fell away from his face, revealing the
skull behind it; he stepped towards her, reaching for
her throat. . . .*

I opened my eyes. I could hear footsteps coming
down the gravel path. They were real footsteps, they
were on the balcony. They stopped outside the door.
A hand knocked gently, once, twice.

I still had options. I could pretend I wasn't there.
I could wait and do nothing. I could disguise my voice
and say that I was someone else. But if I turned the
handle the door would unlock and swing outward,
and I would have to face the man who stood waiting
for me, for my life.

I opened the door. I knew who it would be.

Chapter Thirty-Seven

I didn't really mean to hit him with the Cinzano bottle. I mean, I meant to hit someone, but it wasn't

personal. I'd never seen him before in my life, he was a complete stranger. I guess I just got carried away: he looked like someone else. . . .

And I certainly didn't think I would knock him out like that; I suppose it's a case of not knowing your own strength. I felt terrible about it, especially when I saw the blood. I couldn't just leave him there, he might have had a concussion or bled to death, so I got Mr. Vitroni to call a doctor. I said I thought this man was trying to break into the house. Luckily he was out cold, so he couldn't contradict me.

It was nice of him not to press charges when he came to. At first I thought it was only because he wanted the story: reporters are like that. I talked too much, of course, but I was feeling nervous. I guess it will make a pretty weird story, once he's written it; and the odd thing is that I didn't tell any lies. Well, not very many. Some of the names and a few other things, but nothing major. I suppose I could still have gotten out of it. I could have said I had amnesia or something. . . . Or I could have escaped; he wouldn't have been able to trace me. I'm surprised I didn't do that, since I've always been terrified of being found out. But somehow I couldn't just run off and leave him all alone in the hospital with no one to talk to; not after I'd almost killed him by mistake.

It must have been a shock for him to wake up in bed with seven stitches, though. I felt quite guilty about that. His coat was a mess, too, but I told him it would come out in the dry cleaning. I offered to pay for it but he wouldn't let me. I took him some flowers instead; I couldn't find any roses so they were yellow things, sort of like sunflowers. They were a little wilted, I said maybe he could get the nurse to put them in water for him. He seemed pleased.

It was good of him to lend me the plane fare. I'll pay it back once I'm organized again. The first thing is to get Sam and Marlene out of jail, I owe it to them. It was Sam's lawyer that gave away the fact that I was still alive; I shouldn't hold it against him, he was just doing his job. And I'll have to see Arthur, though I'm not looking forward to it, all those explanations and his expression of silent outrage. After the story comes out he'll know the truth anyway. He loved me under false pretenses, so I shouldn't feel too rejected when he stops. I don't think he's even gotten my postcard yet, I forgot to send it air mail.

After that, well, I don't have any definite plans. I'll feel like an idiot with all the publicity, but that's nothing new. They'll probably say my disappearance was some kind of stunt, a trick. . . . I won't write any more Costume Gothics, though; I think they were bad for me. But maybe I'll try some science fiction. The future doesn't appeal to me as much as the past, but I'm sure it's better for you. I keep thinking I should learn some lesson from all of this, as my mother would have said.

Right now, though, it's easier just to stay here in Rome—I've found a cheap little *pensione*—and walk to the hospital for visiting hours. He hasn't told anyone where I am yet, he promised he wouldn't for a week. He's a nice man; he doesn't have a very interesting nose, but I have to admit that there is something about a man in a bandage. . . . Also I've begun to feel he's the only person who knows anything about me. Maybe because I've never hit anyone else with a bottle, so they never got to see that part of me. Neither did I, come to think of it.

It did make a mess; but then, I don't think I'll ever be a very tidy person.

ABOUT THE AUTHOR

MARGARET ATWOOD is a writer who, though still in her thirties, has conquered more literary territory than most do in a lifetime. She is the author of seven books of poetry (the first won the Governor-General's Award in 1966) and three novels, *The Edible Woman, Lady Oracle* and *Surfacing,* all of which were widely praised in Canada, the United States and England. *Survival,* a thematic study of Canadian literature, earned her an enduring reputation as a critic of the first order. A new collection, *Dancing Girls and Other Stories* has recently been published. Her fiction and critical articles have appeared in Canadian and American literary magazines. Margaret Atwood has lived and worked in Canada, the United States, England and Italy. She is currently living on a farm near Alliston, Ontario.